THE LOVEC

Edited by S. T. Joshi

Contents

"Just a Colour": Weberian Disenchantment and Paradigm in H. P. Lovecraft's "The Colour out of Space" Isaac Aday	3
Lovecraft: The Big Importance of Small Details Duncan Norris	19
Eating Anarchist Spaghetti with Lovecraft David Haden	48
I May Be the Next: Fear of the Queer in "The Thing on the Doorstep" by H. P. Lovecraft Holly Eva Allen	80
The First Cousins of H. P. Lovecraft Ken Faig, Jr.	96
Was Lovecraft *Psycho*? Shades of the Providence Gentleman in One of Fiction's Most Notorious Killers Harley Carnell	116
Narrative Methods in H. P. Lovecraft's "The Mound" James Goho	139
The Lovecraft Letters Project S. T. Joshi	161
The Colonialism of Cthulhu Edward Guimont	167
Lovecraft Seeks a Comet at Nichols Crossing Horace A. Smith	177
Rick and Morty vs. Cthulhu Duncan Norris	186

How To Read Lovecraft	202
A Column by Steven J. Mariconda	
Reviews	210
Contributors	234
Briefly Noted	47, 138, 160, 176, 201

Abbreviations used in the text and notes:

AT	*The Ancient Track* (Hippocampus Press, 2013)
CE	*Collected Essays* (Hippocampus Press, 2004–06; 5 vols.)
CF	*Collected Fiction* (Hippocampus Press, 2015–17; 4 vols.)
IAP	S. T. Joshi, *I Am Providence: The Life and Times of H. P. Lovecraft* (Hippocampus Press, 2010; 2013 [paper])
LL	*Lovecraft's Library: A Catalogue*, 5th rev. ed. (Hippocampus Press, 2024)
SL	*Selected Letters* (Arkham House, 1965–76; 5 vols.)

Copyright © 2024 by Hippocampus Press
Published by Hippocampus Press, P.O. Box 641, New York, NY 10156
www.hippocampuspress.com

Cover illustration by Allen Koszowski. Hippocampus Press logo designed by Anastasia Damianakos. Cover design by Barbara Briggs Silbert.

Lovecraft material is used by permission of The Estate of H. P. Lovecraft; Lovecraft Holdings, LLC.

Lovecraft Annual is published once a year, in Fall. Articles and letters should be sent to the editor, S. T. Joshi, % Hippocampus Press, and must be accompanied by a self-addressed stamped envelope if return is desired. All reviews are assigned. Literary rights for articles and reviews will reside with *Lovecraft Annual* for one year after publication, whereupon they will revert to their respective authors. Payment is in contributor's copies.

ISSN 1935-6102
ISBN 978-1-61498-452-8

"Just a Colour": Weberian Disenchantment and Paradigm in H. P. Lovecraft's "The Colour out of Space"

Isaac Aday

In "Time, Space, and Natural Law: Science and Pseudo-science in Lovecraft," S. T. Joshi describes the era of Lovecraft's upbringing as

> a time when the findings of nineteenth-century science—notably Darwin's theory of evolution, which was seen by many as destroying the last remaining intellectual support for the notion of an omnipotent deity in its implicit refutation of the "argument from design"—were being synthesized by a wide range of philosophers and scientists who, following Thomas Henry Huxley and Friedrich Nietzsche, were becoming increasingly bold in advancing purely secular theories both of cosmic origins and human motivations. (175)

Sociologist Max Weber (1864–1920) described something similar when he characterized the modern world as "disenchanted"—disenchantment, or *Entzauberung* (literally "de-magicization") involving a period "by which myth and illusion are removed from social life" (Green 52). In the sociological context[1] we might compare the term to concepts such as "secularization" or "rationalization"—an extension of the Enlightenment's preoccupation with human reason (Green 52). As Weber suggests in "Science as a Vocation":

> We are not ruled by mysterious, unpredictable forces, but that,

---

1. To be contrasted with the "philosophical" context that Green clarifies.

> on the contrary, we can in principle control everything by means of calculation. That in turn means the disenchantment of the world. Unlike for the savage for whom such forces existed, we need no longer have recourse to magic in order to control the spirits or pray to them. Instead technology and calculation achieve our ends. This is the primary meaning of the process of intellectualization. (12–13)

In the transition from enchantment to disenchantment, Weber seems to suggest, the "magic" operating within the world—the superstitious attitudes toward the operations of nature, and the belief in influential deities as the explanation for all unexplainable phenomenon—is increasingly jettisoned in favor of empirically testable hypotheses. What was once only explainable by the concept of the supernatural is now explainable by naturalistic means: miracles turn into probability or hallucination; earthquakes requite geological and not theological investigation; crop failure is a result a nitrate imbalance and not an unappeased god; the study of the brain takes precedent over the notion of the soul. In more practical terms, we see in Weber's concept Nietzsche's metaphor of a God who has "bled to death under our knives": with continued probing, human reason pierces the deepest mysteries of the natural world, shining light upon the shadowy visions of magic and devils once held sacred by a darker age (*Gay Science* 181).

Regardless of the extent to which we regard Weber right or wrong, it is not difficult to see the ways in which these processes of enchantment and disenchantment are critical functions of horror fiction. Lovecraft speaks on these connections in his short essay "Supernatural Horror in Literature":

> Man's first instincts and emotions formed his response to the environment in which he found himself. Definite feelings based on pleasure and pain grew up around the phenomena whose causes and effects he understood, whilst around those which he did not understand—and the universe teemed with them in the early days—were naturally woven such personifications, marvelous interpretations, and sensations of awe and fear as would be hit upon by a race having few and simple ideas and limited

experience. The unknown, being likewise the unpredictable, became for our primitive forefathers a terrible and omnipotent source of boons and calamities visited upon mankind for cryptic and wholly extra-terrestrial reasons, and thus clearly belonging to spheres of existence whereof we know nothing and wherein we have no part . . . in general, all the conditions of savage . . . life so strongly conduced toward a feeling of the supernatural, that we need not wonder at the thoroughness with which man's very hereditary essence has become saturated with religion and superstition. (CE 2.83)

"That saturation," he notes further, "must . . . be regarded as virtually permanent so far as the subconscious mind . . . [and] an infinite reservoir of mystery still engulfs most of the outer cosmos, whilst a vast residuum of powerful inherited associations clings around all the objects and processes that were once mysterious, however well they may now be explained" (CE 2.83). Supernatural horror has *not* lost its edge in a "rationalized" world; what struck primitive man as fearsome in an era of the indefinite and unknown retains its most salient emotional features in modern and "learned" man. Innumerable pieces of horror—from Poe to King, *The Exorcist* to *Ringu*—involve what we might refer to as "the willing suspension of disenchantment": that is, the willingness of the reader to *return* to those enchanted worldviews, those supernatural, ostensibly "superstitious" modes of perception, even from within a supposedly "secular" (or at least, more "rationalized") age.[2] The demons, vampires, ghosts, supernatural powers, and clairvoyance featured in such stories fly directly in the face of disenchanted perception. They explicitly demand to be seen through an "enchanted" lens precisely because they are *not* explainable by scientific means. In Stoker's *Dracula*, for instance, garlic, holy images, and the Eucharist are

---

2. It is important to recognize that the "willing suspension of disenchantment" might be applicable not only to secular audiences, but to practically any individual who has come to believe in the material operations of the natural world. We might argue, for instance, that belief in the explanatory power of, say, soil pH for crop success or tectonic plates for earthquakes might qualify as "disenchanted" to a certain degree.

proven effective against an ostensibly "unnatural" scourge—while science appears limited in its ability to appraise, describe, and control vampires. In a reversal of Weberian disenchantment, science gives way to superstition: the explanatory paradigm of the archetypal scientist or professor figure—the character who insists on a naturalistic, disenchanted explanation—is confounded; and the mystic, the religious peasant, madman, or believer successfully appraises, comprehends, and even controls the supernatural reality of each unfolding event.

Fred Botting describes a similar process in the earlier forms of the Gothic as the insistence upon being "overtly but ambiguously, *not rational,* depicting disturbances of sanity and security, from superstitious belief in ghosts and demons" (2; my emphasis). "Gothic styles," he writes further, "disturb the borders of knowing": the items "normally recognized as delusion, apparition, [and] deception" seem to "suggest supernatural possibility, mystery, magic, wonder, and monstrosity" (2). Such texts are, in this sense, antithetical to the concept of the Enlightenment, and to reason itself. Supernatural horrors act as "returns to the past" of darkness, instability, superstition—they are, in essence, a process of *re*-enchantment (Botting 3).

What is unique about several of Lovecraft's stories, however, is the way in which this neat dichotomy between "enchanted" and "disenchanted" meets resistance. Rather than the conversion from one explanatory paradigm to another (disenchantment to enchantment, or disenchantment to *the possibility* of re-enchantment, in more ambiguous stories such as Poe's "Ligeia"), we encounter the *destruction* of paradigms and a refusal to offer new ones. The "gods" of Lovecraft's stories are not quite gods in the religious sense—the powers and qualities they possess are not quite "supernatural" in the sense expected from a ghost or demon—but neither do they seem wholly explainable in naturalistic terms. One cannot easily elevate Cthulhu to the status of a *god* (denoting religion and spirituality) even as a term like *kaiju* (suggesting something purely natural and scientific) is obviously reductive.[3] In a similar way, *At the Mountains of Madness* is not

---

3. Interestingly, in "The Call of Cthulhu," the narrator suggests that, following his

full of explicitly religious or spiritual themes, even as the scientist's discoveries lead only to greater uncertainty, and naturalistic attempts at cohesive explanation leave much unanswered. In Joshi's words, science "peeps out here and there" in Lovecraft's narratives ("Time, Space" 182). The stories "make a gesture toward scientific plausibility" for the sake of added believability, but also remain "overwhelmingly supernatural"—at least in the sense that they are beyond nature as we currently understand it (182).

As opposed to operating within one paradigm or deliberately upending one paradigm for another, these stories thus "transcend" the paradigmatic; they perform what Burleson refers to as an "undoing of categorical thinking"—an "unraveling of any system claiming final mastery" that affects science and naturalism as much as religion, superstition, and mysticism (108). The medium and the religious believer are just as "out of place" as the scientist. Anderson puts it well when he writes that in Lovecraft's universe there "may be no order to the universe after all, that all of our theories may be useless" (82). "The inability of man to know," he continues, "negates all of our beliefs, both scientific and philosophical" (82). The result of such a process is not merely an insistence upon mystery, but, as Anderson notes, unlimited possibility: if a horror is not subject to the laws of nature, then, quite literally, "anything is possible" (81). Borrowing (and perhaps slightly repurposing) sociologist Emile Durkheim's term, we might describe such a condition as "anomic"—representative of an "undetermined state", what some might refer to as a state of *normlessness* (248).

The purpose of this article is not only to illustrate this phenomenon in Lovecraft's short story "The Colour out of Space," but also to call attention to certain formal features of the text that, I believe, deliberately call attention to its operations. In other words, this article will look into the ways in which the structure and language of this piece are involved in the "overturning" of the enchantment/disenchantment dichotomy. In so

---

awareness of Cthulhu, he no longer considers himself a "materialist": "My attitude then was still one of absolute materialism, as *I wish it still were*" (CF 2.43).

doing, I hope to continue the work of defending Lovecraft's prose and form. An underlying assumption of this investigation is that "The Colour out of Space" is a story worthy of a deeper inspection not only in terms of its ability to inculcate feelings of horror, but also in terms of its deliberate formal manipulation and commitment to linguistic aesthetics. As I have written previously, "to reveal the deeper nuances of [Lovecraft's] texts, one must recognize the falsity of the implicit notion that Lovecraft's writing—and perhaps even weird fiction in general—is devoid in some capacity of linguistic merit" (Aday 72). In analyzing the formal aspects of this piece, I believe we will add further evidence to this notion that "Lovecraft's prose and form are not simply weak vessels"—that this idea of Lovecraft as a "pulp hack" is far from a categorical reality.[4]

We might begin this analysis of "The Colour out of Space" by recognizing its obvious involvement in the conversation of religion and science, and its implicit occupation with the enchantment/disenchantment dichotomy. Throughout the tale, considerable attention is given to comparing the perspectives of country "rustics" with the Miskatonic "men of science"—two classes of men that seem to embody the "superstitious" past and "learned," secularized modernity. Both classes experience the same phenomenon—the falling of a strange meteorite and its strange, devastating effects—and try to assess and explain it through their own explanatory paradigms. In his assessment, the rustic Nahum Gardner seems to take a page from the biblical book he was named after: the meteorite's destruction of his farmland "all must be a judgement of sort; though he could not fancy what for, since he had always walked uprightly in the Lord's ways so far as he knew" (CF 2.384). Elsewhere he thanks heaven for sparing a smaller portion of his crops from destruction (CF 2.378). As if a passing reference to the historical processes of secularization, Lovecraft establishes the rustic's enchanted worldview on the classical stage of survival and divine favor: God is worshipped for a successful harvest, and his

---

4. The term "pulp hack" is borrowed from S. T. Joshi's preface to James Arthur Andersen's book (9).

wrath is feared when crops fail. However, there are two salient threats to this paradigm. The first, though weaker, is that this meteorite is something "from some place whar things ain't as they is here" (CF 2.388). As Lovecraft writes in his letters,

> A mere knowledge of the approximate dimensions of the visible universe is enough to destroy forever the notion of a personal god-head whose whole care is extended upon puny mankind . . . Not that science positively refutes religion—it merely makes religion seem monstrously improbable. (quoted in Joshi, "Time, Space" 175)

At least to Lovecraft, the idea that there is indeed a place where things are not as they are here would therefore offer a threat to Nahum's religious explanation. The anthropocentric model of the universe undergoes a Copernican revolution; human insignificance in light of the vastness of the unknown turns the meteorite from an act of God into one of nature's innumerable accidents. Such a notion is compounded by what Joshi refers to as the meteorite's apparent "absence of any sense of willful viciousness, destructiveness, or . . . 'evil'"—or, elsewhere, its nature as "utterly inscrutable" as regards its "goals or purpose" (*Subtler Magick* 137; "Time, Space" 188). It is curiously outside of the ethical; its absence of motive, feeling, and intentionality encourages its perception as something random and meaningless. It is perhaps not a stretch, in this sense, to wonder if the words that precede and follow this passage—"dun't know what it wants"; "one o' them professors said so . . . he was right"—might convey a modicum of disenchantment, a meek willingness to believe that the meteorite may be as naturalistically explainable as the Miskatonic professors believed. The more salient threat to this paradigm, however, is that Nahum is not a sinner. Like the biblical story of Job, the fact that Nahum "had always walked uprightly in the Lord's ways" (CF 2.384) seems incompatible with the idea that he has invoked God's wrath. The enchanted paradigm is therefore challenged here not only by the encroachment of secularized naturalistic theory, but by the question of theodicy brought up in Job: why would something evil befall a good man in a universe governed by a just God?

The Miskatonic men of science offer a different but similarly problematic explanation. In the tradition of supernatural horror, they, as men of reason, take every possible means to avoid attributing legitimacy to the supernatural. Their search is for a naturalistic explanation, devoid of the rustic superstition they so readily condemn. Their attempts fail utterly. Lovecraft's narrator dedicates several pages toward establishing science's total explanatory failure. "The failure was total," he writes; spectrometry, the application of powerful acids, ammonia, caustic soda, alcohol, heating, and a slew of other scientific tests fail to produce any meaningful explanation (CF 2.374). "There was much breathless talk of new elements, bizarre optical properties," the narrator writes before adding, almost in jest, "and other things which puzzled men of science are wont to say when faced by the unknown" (CF 2.372). In a symbolic detail, even efforts to contain the meteor physically fail: its fragments evaporate alongside the hope of a contained and solidified explanation. In this sense, the meteorite poses a distinct threat to the scientific paradigm from which the men of science operate; it is something wholly unknown, something that defies the expectations of a well-ordered laboratory, something that is in fact only barely describable in human language.

Nevertheless, it is evident that they still *believe* in their paradigm: their confounded tests and refuted theories about the meteor do not stop them from labeling Nahum's crop failure as the result of "some mineral element," or from dismissing Nahum's further observations as "mere country talk" (CF 2.377). As the narrator writes, "there was really nothing for serious men to do in cases of wild gossip, for superstitious rustics will say and believe anything"; "they could not believe that anything contrary to natural law had occurred" (CF 2.377, 390). It is important to note that this commitment to the naturalistic paradigm is not made from sheer hubris, ignorance, classism, or an unwillingness to change. This is not a tale, like Stoker's, where the appearance of the supernatural confounds or displaces naturalism; there *is* still reason to believe that a scientific explanation might still be theoretically possible. Lovecraft's narrator may write that the failure of science was total, that the meteorite and color are essentially unnatural; but this is not entirely the case. The scientists' efforts are actually met with limited success. For one, they do certainly establish that the meteor is not something "supernatural" in the sense that ghosts and spirits are supernatural. The meteor has unique physical properties: it "attacks" silicon; it is magnetic; it is a tangible substance, malleable on an anvil. Even if it is not "natural," even if it is "from some place whar things ain't as they is here," it is, in these limited senses, something we might expect from the natural world, and therefore *potentially* explainable (CF 2.391). The question remains, in their conception, epistemological and not ontological: the meteor's uncertainty is not "inherent in nature" but rather related to the "human inability" to explain it adequately (Joshi, "Time, Space" 185). It remains unclear, however, whether such a conception is true. If the meteor were truly inexplicable in an ontological sense—if it were truly supernatural—we could not expect their reactions to be much different. The meteor thus remains suspended in liminal space.

In addition to the adding a sort of renewed believability to this story—as Joshi points out, Lovecraft may have been trying to distance himself from the "standard ghost, goblin, witch, werewolf, or vampire" story, as it was "no longer convincing" to his readers—this concept of something being simultaneously natural and unnatural, theoretically explainable but still inexplicable, clearly has philosophical and epistemological implications ("Time, Space" 182). In this story, the line between the natural and the supernatural, the enchanted and disenchanted, is not *transgressed* in either direction, but rather *confused*. The revelation of the text's "monster" does not necessitate or even encourage the belief in the supernatural as it does in *Dracula*, but neither does it uphold natural law or rational terms. The meteorite is, in a word, *anomalous* to both paradigms. Recalling Joshi's words from above, the combined efforts of explanation only "make a gesture toward scientific plausibility"—as something ostensibly "supernatural," it is not explainable by natural law, but, in its physicality and tangibility, it seems also *somewhat* "natural" and therefore outside of the realm of rustic superstition ("Time, Space" 182). Such a confusion of the supernatural and natural follows "The Colour out of Space" into its apocalyptic revelation: when we finally see the "riot of luminous amorphousness, that alien and undimensioned rainbow of cryptic poison" shoot "vertically up toward the sky" (CF 2.396), explanations continue to remain elusive. Speculation becomes impossible through *any* paradigm; all attempts at explanation, like the color-afflicted Nahum, turn into "dry fragments" (CF 2.387). As Alex Houstoun writes,

> Lovecraft's narrators and characters frequently fail to classify what they experience in comprehensible terms: they are left speechless or babbling senselessly in a state of awe and terror. [If they] attempt a description of what he witnesses, it is often contradictory or utterly beyond human understanding ... [They are] are left in a state of utter despair as they try to grapple with the complete destruction of what was once their concept of reality. It is this absolute lack of recovery or any sort of greater, positive, knowledge that creates the true horror in Lovecraft's stories. (160–61)

The recurring descriptions of ineffability, of inexplicability—Nahum's wife raves exclusively through "verbs and pronouns" (CF 2.380) instead of nouns—in this sense remind us not only of the ineffectual nature of language in describing cosmic horrors, but of the inability to *conceive* of what is being witnessed. The color itself *takes away* paradigms, destroys systems and categorical thinking, but never restores or offers new ones. "Nothin' ... nothin,'" we hear from Nahum, moments from death, "suckin' the life out of everything" (CF 2.387).

At this point we might go on and talk about the philosophical implications of cosmic horror, or the relationship between individual worldview and this recurring theme in Lovecraft of the "ineffable." But such work has already been done, and one other important feature of this story is wholly untouched. It is my estimation that the apparent disregard (or even outright contempt) of Lovecraft's style and prose has caused us to miss one exceptional element in this discussion: that Lovecraft has deliberately manipulated the form of this story in ways that call deeper attention to the "transcendence" of the enchantment/disenchantment dichotomy. The very form of this piece, in other words, presents and mirrors its philosophical problems.

The first instance of this can be seen when we consider "The Colour out of Space" alongside other pieces of Lovecraft's fiction. It is indeed interesting that, alongside the drug-addicted narrator in "Dagon," the mentally disturbed narrator of "The Tomb," and a slew of other narrators who might for various reasons be deemed unreliable, we have in "The Colour out of Space" a surprisingly rational, level-headed, and credible narrator. It is odd further that, unlike *At the Mountains of Madness*, which also features a relatively credible narrator, this narrator seems to play a minor, even negligible role in the action of the story. He is not involved in Nahum's lineage. His interest in the story of the color does not seem as pressing or as intense as that of many other narrators. He is not even an eyewitness: each of the events of the story is in fact related through another character, the rustic Ammi. If we assume Lovecraft was a pulp hack, this of course does not pose a threat to our interpretative paradigm; we can simply look past it. It is evident, however, from one particular passage that this is not only deliberate, but also exceptionally relevant to how we perceive the story: "Often I had to recall the speaker from ramblings, piece out scientific points which he knew only by a fading parrot memory of professors' talk, or bridge over gaps where his sense of logic and continuity broke down. When he was done I did not wonder that his mind had snapped a trifle" (CF 2.3741).

From these lines we can see that the narration of this story is not devoid of some underlying bias. The narrator plainly admits here that he has changed the story, "bridged" these "gaps," to reflect a deeper degree of logic and continuity. He has, in other words, taken the liberty of "making sense" of Ammi's story, putting it into terms that might be relatable and understandable to his readers. Importantly, he does not tell us to what extent he has done so. His influence might have been limited to an explanation of, say, the process of spectrometry—the reader would never believe such a term to emanate from Ammi's lips—or it might have extended well beyond this and included or removed vaster alterations of details, characters, and events. In this passage we also see that the narrator believes Ammi to be slightly—a "trifle"—mad. If we accept this assessment, the narrative is therefore *doubly unreliable:* spoken by a madman and recorded with partiality. The story's integrity must be called into question. Ammi's unreliability as a supposedly "mad" rustic inculcates skepticism. But at the same time, the narrator's confession suggests to us that the horrors as they appear in this text have to *make more* sense than Ammi's original recounting. It is therefore possible that the horrors seen in this story are even more abstract, even more unnatural, and even more fantastic, than what is ultimately revealed. But it is also possible that certain details are exaggerated, forgotten, misrepresented, or even false. We are thrust once more into normlessness.

Another important implication of this passage, however, is that in "bridging over the gaps" where Ammi's "sense of logic and continuity" break down, the narrator exposes himself as *just as caught up in the process of explanation and meaning-making* as the scientists and rustics fifty years earlier. It is evident here that he desires a complete paradigm—a way of explaining what remains mysterious and inscrutable, of solidifying an enchanted or disenchanted perspective. His task in the narrative, in this sense, takes on a new aesthetic role: it realizes, in the story's very narration and structure, the epistemological concepts inherent within the rest of the story. The text itself reflects the fragmentation of paradigms; the narrator's ability to explain the world is just as threatened by these myths, rumors, and stories that emerge from the country as were the paradigms of the first witnesses. (We might assume, in fact, that the very reason he begins this journey is to perform the task that the scientists and rustics failed: to make meaning of a strange, paradigm-threatening event, dwelling in quiet myths and country rumors.) In the final passage of the story, such a notion seems confirmed:

[Ammi] saw so much of the thing—and its influence was so insidious. Why has he never been able to move away? How clearly he recalled those dying words of Nahum—'can't git away . . . draws ye . . . ye know summ'at's comin', but 'tain't no use . . .' . . . I would hate to think of [Ammi] as the grey, twisted, brittle monstrosity which persists more and more in troubling my sleep. (CF 2.399)

The last line is easy to look past. The emphasis of a cursory reading would suggest that the narrator was simply disturbed and haunted by the image of the crumbling Nahum. Troubled sleep would insinuate feelings of horror and disgust. While this may be the case, when we consider again the role of the narrator in this piece, this passage also calls attention to the narrator's inability to escape from the impressions of this event. He, like Ammi, Nahum, and the others, "can't git away." The color's ability to destroy explanatory paradigms, to render senseless any attempt at explanation, has manifested itself within him, and within his very narration: at least metaphorically, he too has been "poisoned" by the color.

With this in mind, some of the narrator's other ostensibly negligible interjections become meaningful. In the last paragraphs of the story, the narrator attempts once more to make sense of Ammi's story. What is most interesting here, however, is that this explanation seems also "fragmented"—the enchantment/disenchantment dichotomy confused once again. While he admits that the story is not fabricated or wholly untrue—the color is "no doubt . . . still down the well"—his explanatory power invokes both rustic superstition and scientific rationalism:

[. . .] one sometimes wonders what insight beyond ours [the rustics'] wild, weird stores of whispered magic have given them . . . I myself am curious about the sensation I derived from my one lone walk before Ammi told me his tale . . . an odd timidity about deep skyey voids above had crept into my soul . . . What it is, God only knows. In terms of matter I suppose the thing . . . would be called a gas, but this gas obeyed laws that are not of our cosmos. This was no fruit of such worlds and suns as shine on the telescopes and photographic plates of our observatories. (CF 2.398–99)

Is it a stretch to see, in such statements, the combined language of two competing paradigms—both utterly failing to make sense of evidence? The narrator attributes a smattering of legitimacy to the rustics' "stores of whispered magic." "God" and the concept of the soul is at least superficially mentioned; curiosity aroused by what we might compare to a "premonition." But yet another attempt is made to provide a naturalistic explanation of the events unfolding: it is a gas, perhaps, but also not quite a gas, and so on. Once more neither paradigm seems to achieve anything close to fullness, and the narrator ends the piece with an admittance of defeat: "it was just a colour out of space"—something totally, utterly unknown, something "from unformed realms ... beyond all Nature as we know it" (CF 2.399). If Lovecraft might be accused of insisting too much upon mystery, upon ineffability, indescribability, it cannot be here. The narrator's "splitness," the slipperiness of the color as it defies both God and man, points once more to the confusion of paradigmatic hegemony.

Fragmentation appears once more as a formal feature in Nahum's dying words. Here we receive a little less than a full page of fragmented discourse, broken up by ellipses: "Nothin' ... Nothin' ... the colour ... it burns ... cold an' wet, but it burns ... it lived in the well ... I seen it ... a kind o' smoke" (CF 2.387). The most obvious difference between this and the rest of the well-ordered text is, of course, that none of these sentences are complete. This might be explainable by the fact that Nahum is clearly dying, but this does not seem to take away from the idea that such "fragmentation" might be symbolically meaningful. What we see here are pieces of a shattered mind:

> "dun't know what it wants ... that round thing them men from the college dug outen the stone ... they smashed it ... it was that same colour ... just the same, like the flowers an' plants ... seeds ... seeds ... they growed ... I seen it the fust time this week ... must a' got strong on Zenas ... jest a colour ... it come from some place whar things ain't as they is here ... one of them professors said so ... he was right ... look out, Ammi, it'll do suthin' more." (CF 2.387)

There is more than meets the eye in such lines. On one hand, this fragmentation clearly mimics the fragmented nature of Nahum's explanatory paradigm. Even as he is dying, he is trying to make sense of the color's origins and effects, drawing connections between events, and trying to decide precisely what happened to his family members. But on the other hand, this passage contains one of Lovecraft's more sinister formal manipulations: in fragmenting Nahum's language, in deliberately obscuring this passage's meaning, Lovecraft prompts the reader to participate in the futile process of explanation and meaning-making. Are the "seeds" referenced here a description of the growth of the color's blight, or are they related to Nahum's mention of flowers and plants? What is the antecedent of "it" in that line, "I seen it the fust time this week"? The seeds? The growth? Do the "seeds" attach themselves to people? Is that what happened to Nahum's wife? Nahum admits here that he isn't thinking straight; to what degree are we to take these lines seriously?

Such uncertainties parallel the story's broader theme of ambiguity: making solidified meaning from this deliberately obscured passage is as futile as each character's attempt to explain the color or meteorite. What Joshi describes in *A Subtler Magick*—that "the source of terror in this tale ... is precisely because we cannot define the nature ... of the entities" (136)—applies to text's *language and structure as well as its content*. The text as a whole is characterized by this process. The double unreliability of the narrator calls for us to sift through the text and piece apart knowable and concrete details; Nahum's disordered speech invites us to investigate semantics and language; the meteorite itself, in its inexplicability, demands a verdict. In each uncertainty we discover an invitation to resist the conclusions of other appraisals—to arrive at some true and genuine explanation of the story, color, or narration that others have missed. But the moment we attempt to investigate the text to try to make sense of any of the text's many questions and ambiguities of form, semantics, or content, we are caught up in the same futile process as the story's characters. We too are "poisoned"; we too are lost in the attempt to make meaning through broken paradigms that will never achieve explanatory fullness. Nahum concludes that it is "jest a colour"; the narrator writes too that "it was just a colour out of space" (CF 2.394). The attempt to suggest otherwise must be made from mere fragments—unreliable narration, questionable facts, sights, and phrases, parts of words, and nounless-adjectives—that uniformly resist and upset paradigms and categories. "Just a colour," in this sense, remains the fate of all speculation.

Works Cited

Aday, Isaac. "Solitary Conversation: A Bakhtinian Exploration of H. P. Lovecraft's "Dagon." *Lovecraft Annual* No. 16 (2022): 62–74.

Anderson, James Arthur. *Out of the Shadows: A Structuralist Approach to Understanding the Fiction of H. P. Lovecraft.* San Bernardino, CA: Borgo Press, 2011.

Botting, Fred. *Gothic.* New York: Routledge, 2014.

Burleson, Donald R. *Lovecraft: Disturbing the Universe.* Lexington: University Press of Kentucky, 1990.

Durkheim, Emile. *Suicide: A Study in Sociology.* Ed. George Simpson, tr. John A. Spaulding and George Simpson. New York: Free Press, 1979.

Green, Jeffrey. "Two Meanings of Disenchantment: Sociological Condition vs. Philosophical Act—Reassessing Max Weber's Thesis of the Disenchantment of the World." *Philosophy and Theology* 17, Nos. 1 & 2 (2005): 51–84.

Houstoun, Alex. "Lovecraft and the Sublime." *Lovecraft Annual* No. 5 (2011): 160–80.

Joshi, S. T. *A Subtler Magick: The Writings and Philosophy of H. P. Lovecraft.* Mercer Island, WA: Starmont House, 1996.

———. "Time, Space, and Natural Law: Science and Pseudoscience in Lovecraft." *Lovecraft Annual* No. 4 (2010): 171–201.

Nietzsche, Fredrich. *The Gay Science.* Tr. Walter Kaufmann. New York: Vintage, 1974.

Weber, Max. *The Vocation Lectures.* Tr. Rodney Livingstone. Indianapolis: Hackett, 2004.

Lovecraft: The Big Importance of Small Details

Duncan Norris

H. P. Lovecraft famously declared that he created his stories "with the care & verisimilitude of an actual *hoax*" (*Dawnward Spire* 244; emphasis in original). Achieving this required a variety of techniques and has had many curious results; not the least of these is an almost surrealistic success in the propagation of ideas that his work is actually in some way true. Some of the methods Lovecraft utilized are more patent than others. As a foundation his research was meticulous. This was not just to add elements of known fact to his creations but, as he recommended to August Derleth, "when inventing the unknown, one must be careful not to contradict the known!" (*ES* 403). That the endless delvings into Lovecraft's sources and usages occasionally uncover errors is unsurprising. The fact that, relatively speaking, they are so few is remarkable. Some are simply errors, while others are errors only apparent to a far later audience. The use of the Piltdown man and piscine associations of Dagon in the eponymous tale are exemplars of the latter. The former was not definitively exposed as a fraud until 1953, long after Lovecraft's death. In a like manner later researchers uncovered a different origin of the meaning of the famous god of the Philistines than the medieval conflation that was made with the Hebrew word for fish.

But importantly, this sense of verisimilitude in Lovecraft's work does not come from a single source, nor from the mere insertion of facts. There is a holistic approach to all this that reaches across a wide spectrum of both tangible concepts—the usage and quoting of genuine if obscure facts and sources being a paradoxically obvious example—and far more intangible ones. Lovecraft talks about following "mankind's natural myth-making tendencies" and writing "in a way consistent with human psychology & illusion as reflected in experience and folklore" (*Letters to C. L. Moore* 268) in creating his own mythopoeia. He also specifies a deliberateness to using cadence in creating antique documents to ensure their own value, noting that "these pseudo-archaic passages depend very largely on their rhythm for effectiveness" (*Letters to E. Hoffmann Price* 296).

Yet there is an overlooked aspect of this subject that adds immeasurably to the sense of reality in Lovecraft's tales. This is the insertion of the small but unnecessary detail. Of course, it could be easily argued that there are no unnecessary details in a well-constructed story, so allow me to clarify. By unnecessary detail I mean one that the removal of which will not significantly impact the plot or take away a moment of importance. The fact of Johansson's hair having turned white after his experiences in "The Call of Cthulhu" is a small element, but unarguably an important one. Removal of it changes, even if only a little, the trajectory of the tale. Likewise the brief description of the amiable, "plump Capt. Norrys" (CF 1.395) is a seemingly trifling detail, but which is essential foreshadowing to his eventual fate as cannibalized victim of the last scion of the house of de la Poer in "The Rats in the Walls." Yet scattered throughout many of Lovecraft's tales are tiny elements whose subtraction will not have such a drastic effect. Their inclusion is, however, one of the many factors that add to the power of Lovecraft's writings and which give them a vibrancy a century out from composition.

Part of this effect is indirect. Intensive description in some areas and vague, indistinct ones in others, when done correctly, unconsciously force readers to fill the gap in information via their imagination. As is long known, that combination creates a very powerful emotional reaction. As an example of such a narrative technique, imagine a scene in which a pathologist gives a detective a rundown of the injuries inflicted on a murder victim, complete with discussion of time taken and instruments used. If the perspective then switches to a detailed scene of the killer claiming the next victim but which cuts away before the assailant commences his assault, it will be far more effective than any lurid description of the assault could be. Yet once again this aspect of technique is not the focus of our examination. Rather it is to highlight in a number of Lovecraft tales his usage of the theoretically superfluous detail to show how such adds an ineffable power to the work.

To switch media momentarily, let us examine another perfect example in the classic horror-comedy film *An American Werewolf in London* (1981). The movie won the inaugural Academy Award for Best Makeup, the first of seven such accolades for the legendary Rick Baker. Unlike the often contentious offerings of such laurels, it is a righteous winner. By common accord the in-full-view and brightly lit transformation of the luckless victim of the lycanthrope's attack into a werewolf himself remains unsurpassed in the decades since. Although this is the acme of the film's showcase of cosmetic and transformational marvels, there are a number of other celebrated and excellently executed effects throughout. This includes the savagely mutilated ghost of the second victim of the werewolf attack who reappears periodically over the course of the film, famously in a more and more decomposed state. This undead visitor is the first extended special makeup effect sequence in the film and is likewise shot in a brightly lit and unobscured manner. The revenant is casually talking to his surviving friend and urging him to commit suicide to end the curse even as he jokes and takes snippets of food from his friend's hospital tray.[1] His face, neck, and left side show the severe damage wrought by the werewolf's vicious attack, and this juxtaposed with his cheery demeanor is part of the fascination and power of the scene. Amidst all the

---

1. This incidentally shows in a different manner how a small element can make a big impression and add verisimilitude: the eating of parts of a patient's meals or snacks in hospital by visitors is certainly one of the grating realties of being confined in such circumstances, but also one to which it is difficult to mount a solid objection without seeming churlish.

cosmetic work there is a very small piece of skin hanging from the prosthetic damage in the center of the left cheek that flaps and jiggles repeatedly as the corpse carries on his conversation with the doomed patient. It is a tiny part of what is a stunningly effective example of the art of special effects makeup. Removing it will still leave an incredible, revolting, yet powerful image on screen. Yet again and again in commentary and remembrance of the film is mentioned that specific part of that amazing makeup appliance. This tiny detail elevates the brilliant to the almost numinous.

To illustrate the concept further inside Lovecraft's own work, consider this line from "The Whisperer in Darkness" wherein Akeley is hastily relating by letter the previous night's assault upon his house. He notes: "Five of the dogs were killed—I'm afraid I hit one by aiming too low, for he was shot in the back" (CF 2.496). Even though a few lines earlier Akeley states that he "raked all around the house with rifle fire aimed just high enough not to hit the dogs" (CF 2.495), the tale has almost the same effect with the removal of the detail that Akeley himself accidentally killed one of his faithful hounds. Yet those sixteen words augment the narrative immeasurably. It adds a sense of pathos and tragedy, and one can feel Akeley's sense of guilt and remorse in that he feels it necessary to confess to his friend this deed even in the midst of the terrors he is undergoing. It also gives an unspoken insight into Akeley's panicked state of mind and the frantic, frenetic nature of the assault, which is deliberately underdescribed.

As a second illustration, and to a similar idea of conveying mental state, consider the thoughts of the protagonist in "The Shadow over Innsmouth" as he sits in fearful brooding in his room in the Gilman House. "This town had some queer people, and there had undoubtedly been several disappearances. Was this one of those inns where travellers were slain for their money? Surely I had no look of excessive prosperity" (CF 3.204–05). The thought processes of someone in this dire situation are likely to go to extravagant possibilities, and it gives an insight into his level of fear. But more importantly, the reader of such a story is probably well aware of the trope of the innkeepers who prey upon their guests. These two lines speak almost directly to the thoughts of the reader and act as a form of misdirection while simultaneously giving a plausible possibility as to what might be occurring. If the line after "disappearances" had simply contained the follow-on sentences "were the townsfolk really so resentful about curious visitors? Had my obvious sightseeing, with its frequent map-consultations, aroused unfavourable notice?" (CF 3.205) the story still holds an idea of brooding menace. The additional lines give the reader a further context to think on, something that that they know may well have happened before. But even more than the first line, the second is key. The protagonist is rationalizing to himself that even if this is a murder hotel he would not be a victim, as he obviously has little of value. Deletion of that second line does not great harm to the narrative. But its inclusion gives the protagonist a sense of genuineness, of verisimilitude, an approach to overwrought and over-thought fears almost all people can relate to. It is much easier to imagine being accidentally targeted in a scheme to rob travelers than to be killed by angry locals for wandering about with a map overmuch.

Such small elements of nuance are present throughout the entirety of Lovecraft's fiction. The intrinsic subjectiveness of it, and the huge volume of potential and actual examples precludes a systemic examination of every instance. Indeed, in examining the work of another author this might be overreaching. Yet Lovecraft was someone who complained about the movement of a comma in his work by editors. His deliberateness in choices is absolute. Thus as a means to re-examine Lovecraft's writing, a selected highlighting of such elements from many of his more important tales is highly illuminating, and a chronological approach seems most apt.

Commencing with "Dagon" (1917), Lovecraft's fictional entry into *Weird Tales*, it is but a single word. The concluding paragraph reads: "I dream of a day when they may rise above the billows to drag down in their reeking talons the remnants of puny, war-exhausted mankind" (CF 1.58). "Puny" serves a powerful adjective here. Removing it still leaves a formidable sentence, especially if slightly rearranged as "I dream of a day when they may rise above the billows to drag down the remnants of war-exhausted mankind in their reeking talons." But the power this single word adds is hugely significant. Something puny is weak, ineffective, petty, minor. To thus characterize the entire human race as such is a nightmarish position to be in, and having such a belief certainly would add to an overwhelming terror leading inexorably to suicide. Compare this to other adjectives in the sentence, and their different natures. "War-exhausted" harkens back to the general setting of the tale. The follies and consequences of war are the driving factors that lead to the narrator's experience. It fits into the wider narrative and was referred to directly three sentences earlier in "my escape from the German man-of-war" (CF 1.58). The phrasing here, rather than "ship," "vessel," "sea-raider," or any number of possible choices, is clearly deliberate. Likewise, "reeking" has antecedents in the tale. The monster seen at the conclusion is never given any olfactory element, yet the stench of dead fish and its coming from sometimes alien creatures from the deep whose forms can be seen in the mud of the risen land are well established in the preceding narrative. Both these descriptors are concluding elements earlier embedded in the narrative. "Puny" stands out all the more for not doing so.

"Beyond the Wall of Sleep" (1919) too has a superfluous yet paradoxically powerful single word in its climatic paragraph. "The climax? What plain tale of science can boast of such a rhetorical effect?" (CF 1.85). In addition to the subtle humor in placing such a rhetorical sentence in such a manner, which in itself highlights the multifaceted approach Lovecraft took to his writing, is the single word "plain." Removing it does not alter the main facts of the statement and what the narrator is attempting to convey, and works almost as well to that effect. But to describe the preceding narrative, concerning alien entities possessing people discovered via a telepathy conductor, as "plain" borders on the ludicrous. Or rather it should. Instead, it emphasizes the scientific nature of the account just given. It is in fact a plain account for it contains no embellishments, no hyperbole. It is a declaration of the truth. Such is the small element that adds much.

The very opening of "The Statement of Randolph Carter" (1919) would seem at first to fit into this mandate. In beginning "I repeat to you, gentlemen, that your inquisition is fruitless" (CF 1.132), there is conveyed the sense of coming into an event already having been going on for some time and which gives an immediate sense of place and time and feeling. But in these lines Lovecraft is setting up the greater picture, and it is both essential to the structure of the story and repeated in variation "again I say," "as I have said," and "once more I say" at the opening of the next three paragraphs. The non-essential small element is the use of "gentlemen." Removing the word doesn't significantly affect the wider narrative. But its inclusion conveys so much detail and implication that I was tempted to exclude it from my analysis as fundamentally essential. The addressing of the interrogators as such implies, without anything overt, a great deal about both them and their subject. From the latter, presented as speech, it takes away the potential he is shouting or ranting. One does not pause to scream "gentlemen" in such a manner in the sentence as given. It also tells us that the subject is himself a gentleman, remaining polite despite the discourtesy of having to repeat himself. A single word sets a template for the entire character of Randolph Carter.

Likewise, a great deal is conveyed with few words in the description—or rather, lack of description—of the African mummy whose opening caused the eponymous figure to burn himself alive in "Facts Concerning the Late Arthur Jermyn and His Family" (1920). "Time and the Congo climate are not kind to mummies" (CF 1.181) is the exact phrase, and its exactness is noteworthy. Lovecraft could have easily written "unkind." The unusual turn of phrase "not kind" enhances the stronger element of anthropomorphism, but adds a deeper layer. Unkindness is a low level of unpleasantry. "Not kind" carries with it vaguer ideas but can cover far more possibilities. A guardian of a child who is described as unkind is not normally seen as abusing them, but the same guardian described as not kind may have. Minor differences, but such make all the difference.

Different in type is the memory of the anthropophagus farmer in "The Picture in the House" (1920), who offers his recollection of buying his infamous book from Captain Holt: "I was up ta his haouse onct, on the hill, tradin' hosses" (CF 1.214). It is a perfectly appropriate reference. It also is perhaps a very subtle joke, exposition of character, foreshadowing, or all three. Such an action as described makes the seemingly harmless old man in truth a rather more notorious character, infamous for his dishonesty and wiliness, in the form of a literal Yankee horse trader. To another point of difference, and highlighting the minutiae of Lovecraft's work, is a tiny element in "The Nameless City" (1921). In the original tale the lost and accused location is truly nameless—the term is not given a capitalization as would be fitting for a proper noun.

Again the value of small choices is apparent in the list of deities to whom the narrator of "The Moon-Bog" (1921) prays after his hideous experience of seeing the fate of Denys Barry and his trespassing workers. "I believe I did ridiculous things such as offering prayers to Artemis, Latona, Demeter, Persephone, and Plouton" (CF 1.263). The last-named god is the key here. This is of course one of the many euphemistic names for the familiar chthonian deity commonly known as Pluto or Hades. Such then might seem merely a stylistic flourish. Yet Lovecraft was well acquainted with the Greek classics of Homer, wherein the god of the underworld is noted as the most hateful toward human beings. Moreover, the name Plouton has a meaning often translated as "giver of wealth/the wealthy one" and refers to the value of gems and precious metals that lie buried in the earth, Pluto's natural domain. This euphemistic naming convention—as noted by no less an authority than Plato—reflected Greek fears of the notoriously disproportionate wrath of the gods generally, and Pluto specifically. The gods frequently killed mortals, but Pluto had the power to punish them horrifically eternally. Such naming conventions was a propitiatory act—the Furies were referred to as the Kindly Ones for the same reasons—and this is exactly what the narrator is seeking to accomplish with his uncustomed pagan importunings.

The conclusion of "The Outsider" (1921) carries in a single word a deep pathos and sense of searing loss in the line "yet in my new wildness and freedom I almost welcome the bitterness of alienage" (*CF* 1.272). Removal of "almost" still leaves a powerful sentence. Its inclusion carries with it a terrible burden of being resigned to a horrid fate but holding deep within the sorrows and longing for things lost and beyond obtainment.

"The Music of Erich Zann" (1921) has a most curious minor inclusion in its opening paragraph where the narrator tells of his hunt for, and lack of success in finding, the Rue d'Auseil. He notes that "despite all I have done it remains an humiliating fact that I cannot find the house, the street, or even the locality" (*CF* 1.280). Humiliation is a very specific feeling, and in many ways out of alignment with the unearthly horror of the tale. This small element points to pathos, frustration, and a need to be proven right, to be believed rather than be an object of derision, or pity, or tinged with madness. Removing it causes no such excessive harm, but its inclusion carries a weight disproportionate to its size.

"Herbert West—Reanimator" (1921–22) is notoriously overwritten, which might make it seemingly a poor choice for this examination. The alert reader will have noticed a lack of those stories by Lovecraft which are commonly classified as Dreamlands tales in the examination thus far. This is not coincidental. They are filled with a baroque excessiveness and a surfeit of manufactured elements that means that single words and lines of such nature are part of the overall feel of these tales, making them, if not in every case strictly essential according to the chosen definition, part of a holistic approach to the tale. Thus they are not a small element but rather part of a much larger one. "Herbert West—Reanimator" could be seen in a similar light, with its excessive use of synonyms, descriptors, and, well, excess. Yet even in this hyperbolic state Lovecraft includes little flourishes that show their value and his skill. Consider the ending of the third section, where the anthropophagus monster comes back to West like a demoniac hound and appears "covered with bits of mould, leaves, and vines, foul with caked blood, and having between its glistening teeth a snow-white, cylindrical object terminating in a tiny hand" (CF 1.308). A worthy conclusion, conveying the full horror of this reanimate nightmare having killed and devoured an innocent child in a third of a line. Yet the original of course actually reads "covered with bits of mould, leaves, and vines, foul with caked blood, and having between its glistening teeth a snow-white, terrible, cylindrical object terminating in a tiny hand." That single additional word "terrible" elevates the sentence in an inexplicable manner as impossible to define as it is to deny.

Another more florid tale is "The Lurking Fear" (1922), which was likewise a commission, albeit at a very poor remittance. Its concluding paragraph about the fate of "the terrible and thunder-crazed house of Martense" (CF 1.373) has the interesting section describing its fate as "the frightful outcome of isolated spawning, multiplication, and cannibal nutrition above and below the ground" (CF 1.373). It would be plainer simply to say cannibalism, and the idea would be conveyed quite well. The idea of "cannibal nutrition" creates a far more powerful juxtaposition. Nutrition carries with it associations of healthfulness and has a patent base similarity with its word origin in nurture, and a connection with the young. Placing it thus with the eating of human flesh is very deliberate and adds an extra measure of revulsion. This is an absolutely deliberate contrast and connection. The word "nutrition" never appears again in the body of Lovecraft's fiction.

A curious element of "The Rats in the Walls" (1923) is the inclusion of a very personal element from Lovecraft in his description of the vaults under Exham Priory as "not the debased Romanesque of the bungling Saxons" (CF 1.386). It is hardly necessary to refer to the Saxons thus as bunglers, and it does not accord with the general perspective of the narrator. Yet Lovecraft and his noted distaste for the ages between the fall of Rome and the enlightenment of the eighteenth century almost cannot help but slip in a barb. But more significant to the text proper is the line "Ultimate horror often paralyses memory in a merciful way" (CF 1.388). "Often" plays a very precise role here. Remove it and the sentence still works, and it is repeatedly foreshadowed throughout the story. The absence of knowledge, of memory, is what damns the narrator. Included, the word conveys the idea that this is something that the narrator has experienced multiple times, or that others have also experienced. It adds to the sense of the personal, of authority, and adds credibility to the idea that what the narrator has experienced is an ultimate horror. After all, he has temporality lost memory in connection with events.

"The Festival" (1923) holds a different set of small elements that are individually barely noticed and which could be removed or altered, but whose totality adds immeasurably to the tale. "It was the Yuletide, that men call Christmas though they know in their hearts it is older than Bethlehem and Babylon, older than Memphis and mankind" (CF 1.406) is a powerful line on any number of levels. Lovecraft consistently refers to the celebration in the tale as "the Yuletide," which is grammatically correct but gives it a differentiation from the more commonplace Christmas. Calling it "the Yuletide" also gives an altered air that is difficult to define but has a sense of personification, of greater importance. But such is not the most formidable aspect to the sentence. Rather it is the rhythm Lovecraft creates recurrently in the lines with the alliterative repetition of various distinct moments. The initial one, "that men call Christmas," has a certain staccato quality emphasizing the intrusive nature of Christmas on a far older Yuletide celebration. "Older than Bethlehem and Babylon, older than Memphis and mankind" is an extension of this use of alliteration, and it creates a rolling cadence that gives the sentence such a power disproportionate to its size. It is all very deliberate. Bethlehem and Babylon both have three syllables, Memphis and mankind two, which further adds the syllabically shorter words as the conclusion to the sentence. In conjunction with the repetition of "older than" this has decidedly poetic, almost musical, quality. This sonic quality makes it seem almost an incantation, foreshadowed and heightened by the use of "the spell of the eastern sea was upon me" in the opening sentence of the story.

In general this examination excludes Lovecraft's revisions

and ghost-writings, but "Under the Pyramids" (1924) had only the most minor suggestions as a framework given by Harry Houdini, the putative author, and thus is more useful to our purposes. The line near the conclusion, "The Great Sphinx! God!—that *idle question* I asked myself on that sun-blest morning before" (CF 1.450) has the curious inclusion of the term "sun-blest," which Lovecraft will not use again in another story.[2] As in many of Lovecraft's revisions, there is often a sense of overwriting, as if Lovecraft perhaps feels the need to venture into thesauric excess to give his client the full value of his extremely extensive vocabulary. "Sun-blest" seems at first glance to be part of this tendency. Yet there are deeper implications that probably pass by the reader at first glance. Probably easily understood is the value of light in the nighted undervaults of the undead monstrosities as implied by the sun. Less consciously, however, the term "sun-blest" invokes the very Egyptian ideas of the benevolent solar deities who were worshipped in the land of the Nile for millennia. In a place where the literal truth of chthonic Egyptian gods is on patent display, such a term as "sun-blest" is filled with subtle implications that alternatives such as "sunny" or "sunlit" do not convey.

"The Shunned House" (1924) has an interesting small inclusive element holding a metatextual aspect that is probably lost on the modern readership, although it would have been far more noticeable to the contemporary reader. Twice mentioned is "a large and specially fitted Crookes tube" (CF 1.470) used in the investigation of the paranormal in the eponymous location. This is a genuine piece of scientific equipment, a partial vacuum electric discharge tube that led to the discovery of both electrons and X-rays. Superseded now, it is very much the prototypical device of ghost-hunting or movie laboratory equipment, with glass and electric components and an eerie glow associated with its function. Yet these ideas too are largely later impositions. Far more important is its English inventor, William Crookes (1832–1919). Crookes, who held a number of prestigious positions and

---

2. It does appear in the poem "The Poe-et's Nightmare," but in a poem a poetical term is obviously rather more commonplace.

academic medals, is highly esteemed for his contributions to science, including a number of further crucial inventions. He was in fact nominated for Nobel prizes in both physics and chemistry and was eventually knighted for his services to both. Yet to the contemporary audience he would have been as much familiar for his belief in spiritualism and psychical phenomena. Crookes was the co-author of works such as *Remarkable Spirit Manifestations* (1874) and a president of the Society for Psychical Research and Ghost Club, Council member of the Theosophical Society, and an initiate into the Hermetic Order of the Golden Dawn. He was (and is) held up endlessly as the poster boy for the serious scientific achiever who placed validity in such ideas, and this enmeshed with his popularization of science placed his name foremost in the public perception with supernatural investigations. Such a connection, in the context of a tale about psychical investigations blended with science, is absolutely deliberate on Lovecraft's part yet acts largely on a subconscious level, which the hand of time has accidentally largely erased.

Another such element appealing subconsciously to verisimilitude appears in "The Horror at Red Hook" (1925). This tale was written by Lovecraft with a deliberate eye toward a specific but unfamiliar market. At the time of its composition he had previously suffered the first of his soon-to-be many rejections by *Weird Tales* editor Farnsworth Wright, and he was angling "The Horror at Red Hook" to be picked up by *Detective Tales*, which was run by former *Weird Tales* editor Edwin Baird. There was much crossover between writers in both magazines, and Baird was far more receptive to Lovecraft's work, having accepted everything thus far offered during his tenure at *Weird Tales*. Lovecraft obviously hoped this would translate to the new magazine if the tale could be "cast it a sufficiently 'detectivish' mould" (*Letters to Family and Family Friends* 324). This plan was ultimately a failure—ironically, Wright would eventually pick up the tale after Baird rejected it—but Lovecraft strove to make it as palatable to the detective market as possible without sacrificing his integrity. This results in many interesting aspects not present in Lovecraft's other work, and shows well how Lovecraft could turn a cliché—the Irish policeman—into a fascinating character via a single line.

Thus he notes of protagonist Thomas Malone that "he had the Celt's far vision of weird and hidden things, but the logician's quick eye for the outwardly unconvincing; an amalgam which had led him far afield in the forty-two years of his life, and set him in strange places for a Dublin University man born in a Georgian villa near Phoenix Park" (CF 1.482); shortly after building upon this, Lovecraft says of Malone that "in youth he had felt the hidden beauty and ecstasy of things, and had been a poet; but poverty and sorrow and exile had turned his gaze in darker directions, and he had thrilled at the imputations of evil in the world around" (CF 1.483). But such is the craft of storytelling and character development. More significant to our survey is a later observation in which it is lamented that "What Malone would have unearthed could he have worked continuously on the case, we shall never know. As it was, a stupid conflict between city and Federal authority suspended the investigations for several months, during which the detective was busy with other assignments" (CF 1.491). Two separate small factors combine here to add power to the tale. The obvious one is that, as the rest of the tale constantly hints at and allows occasional glimpses of, there is so much more that could have been unearthed. Such is almost the prototypical Lovecraftian literary device. The unusual and extractable aspect is the "stupid conflict between city and Federal authority." The modern reader is so habituated to this trope that it probably passes unnoticed. But given the frequent vicissitudes of intergovernmental departments and the sometimes notorious rivalry between police agencies, this underplayed aspect subtly adds to the feeling of actual events that hang over the tale.

In "He" (1925) Lovecraft uses the examples of "the marvels of Carcassonne and Samarcand and El Dorado and all glorious and half-fabulous cities" (CF 1.506) to highlight his ideas about the protagonist's initial favorable and mystically tinted image of New York. This is in accord with other of his usages. Carcassonne is a prominently beautiful southern French city noted for its medieval architecture. To Lovecraft specifically it is noteworthy as the title of a tale by Lord Dunsany from *A Dreamer's Tales* (1910) in which a warrior king is fated to a futile quest to never come to Carcassonne, and which casts the locale into a far more fantastic and unobtainable light. Samarcand is now more commonly spelt Samarkand, and even in Lovecraft's day this usage was becoming antiquated. Whether this reflects Lovecraft's passion for older usages, the alliterative quality of the repetition of the *c*, or both, remains unclear. In any case, Samarcand is likewise celebrated for its beauty, and with a history stretching back into deep antiquity, having been famously conquered by Alexander the Great, but is a more exotic and lesser-known locale, especially to the Western audience of Lovecraft's day. El Dorado is the mythical city of gold long sought in the Americas by explorers and dreamers, and whose fabulousness can be extrapolated as far as the reader's imagination, given that it is itself fabulous.

In such a treatment Lovecraft is following a convention he offers in many variants throughout his work, often mixing in the better known, the rare, and the entirely fictional. Equally he acknowledges the nature of the citing with the telling phrase "half-fabulous." This applies poetically to Samarcand: its legendary Bibi-Kanyum Mosque has lost none of its splendor for being so oft told of, and it was a ruin in Lovecraft's day, which allows its reconstruction as the viewer saw fit. That Samarcand was the site of Alexander's infamous drunken killing of his general Cleitus, which led the scene to be depicted numerous times in European art, with almost no regard to the reality of the setting, reinforces this hazy idea of the truth of the fabled locale. El Dorado is of course entire fictional. Yet the phrasing of "half-fabulous" is juxtaposed with the extant marvels of that sought-after but never attained offering of the Dunsany tale of Carcassonne, and the ruinous glory of Samarcand holds a subtle implication that perhaps there is some lost truth to the magnificence of El Dorado too. All this is not foregrounded or repeated. Rather it is subtle and subconscious, designed to evoke such ideas but without drawing the attention of the reader to them. A few lines earlier Lovecraft seeds his description with "the Cyclopean modern towers and pinnacles that rise blackly Babylonian under waning moons" (CF 1.506), foreshadowing the "hellish black city of giant stone terraces with impious pyramids flung savagely to the moon" (CF 1.514) the narrator sees in his vision of a future New York.

Yet the small element in all this is Carcassonne. Dunsany was inspired to compose his tale after a reader sent him the poetical line "but he, he never came to Carcassonne." Although Dunsany himself didn't know it, the verse is from the poem "Carcassonne" by the nineteenth-century French *chansonnier* Gustave Naduad, and is of a peasant's failed journey to see the great beauty of the magnificent locale. The fame of the city derives from its fortifications, which were heavily expanded upon after its capture during the Albigensian Crusade. Carcassonne was a center of the Cathar heresy so brutally suppressed in the early thirteenth century, and the population was infamously expelled as a result in 1209. The beauty of Carcassonne is decidedly grim and certainly tainted, and its population, like New York, comes from an immigrant heritage divorced from its founders. There are no shortage of beautiful cities in Europe; in fact, there were far more in Lovecraft's lifetime before the apocalypse that was the Second World War. In "Pickman's Model" (1926), written the year after, "gargoyles and chimaeras on Notre Dame and Mont Saint-Michel" (CF 2.58) are used as examples of Old World beauty and grotesquery. In a story of wherein "this city of stone and stridor is not a sentient perpetuation of Old New York as London is of Old London and Paris of Old Paris, but that it is in fact quite dead, its sprawling body imperfectly embalmed and infested with queer animate things which have nothing to do with it as it was in life" (CF 1.507), the choice of Carcassonne is both deliberate and yet passes the reader by almost unnoticed.

"In the Vault" (1925) contains a curious choice of phrasing in that the undertaker George Birch, trapped in the titular locale and looking to reach the transom window, "toiled in the twilight, heaving the unresponsive remnants of mortality with little ceremony as his miniature Tower of Babel rose course by course" (CF 1.524). The usage at first glance seems an odd one, although fitting in with the New England Protestant aesthetic that suffuses the tale. The biblical tale in Genesis explains the reason why humanity speaks so many different languages, a deliberate confusion sowed by God as a reaction to the building of "a city and a tower, whose top may reach unto heaven; and let us make us a name, lest we be scattered abroad upon the face of the whole earth" (Gen. 11:4). Yet the common morality of the lesson is that humanity was punished for hubris.[3] The use of the Tower of Babel thus subtly foreshadows that Birch will be punished for his actions, as the implication of the name replicates an action previously having led to a ruinous but not fatal occurrence.

By now the reader will probably see immediately the significant phrasing in the line "including a once celebrated French physician now generally thought dead" (CF 2.18) from "Cool Air" (1926). Death is a final process and, for all its mysteries, is fairly obvious even to the layman. The expression "now generally" could be removed and the foreshadowing of the line retains its effect. But the enigma as to why a famous person might be "now generally" thought dead opens the door of possibilities and thoughts in a manner that "including a once celebrated French physician thought dead" fails to stimulate.

The observant reader will also probably have noticed how often these small elements have been taken from the introduction or conclusion of Lovecraft's tales. This is not accidental. It is in these key sections a small addition makes the biggest impact. The opening lines of "The Call of Cthulhu" (1926) is the prototypical exemplar:

> The most merciful thing in the world, I think, is the inability of the human mind to correlate all its contents. We live on a placid island of ignorance in the midst of black seas of infinity, and it was not meant that we should voyage far. The sciences, each straining in its own direction, have hitherto harmed us little;

---

[3]. Modern scholars often see it as more in terms of aetiology for linguistic differences, but this was definitely the prevalent perspective in HPL's day.

but some day the piecing together of dissociated knowledge will open up such terrifying vistas of reality, and of our frightful position therein, that we shall either go mad from the revelation or flee from the deadly light into the peace and safety of a new dark age.

    Theosophists have guessed at the awesome grandeur of the cosmic cycle wherein our world and human race form transient incidents. They have hinted at strange survivals in terms which would freeze the blood if not masked by a bland optimism. But it is not from them that there came the single glimpse of forbidden aeons which chills me when I think of it and maddens me when I dream of it. That glimpse, like all dread glimpses of truth, flashed out from an accidental piecing together of separated things—in this case an old newspaper item and the notes of a dead professor. I hope that no one else will accomplish this piecing out; certainly, if I live, I shall never knowingly supply a link in so hideous a chain. I think that the professor, too, intended to keep silent regarding the part he knew, and that he would have destroyed his notes had not sudden death seized him. (CF 2.21–22)

The first one and a half paragraphs of Lovecraft's most famous tale are justly famous, highly praised, and oft-imitated. They capture not only the entirety of the basis for the story but foundationally create the template for what is cosmic horror. But this is well known, and there is little need to re-examine these much-studied lines in totality, although for ease of reference the entirety is included.

The crucial small element is brought in by the tiny, slightly paused addition of "I think" in the initial line. Stylistically it adds by breaking up the opening sentence, important to the cadence of a duo of paragraphs that are filled with long sentences, as was done in "The Statement of Randolph Carter." It finds a repetition in "certainly, if I live," and "the professor, too," with the breaks in the sentences caused by the pauses adding to their effect. Each of these, too, deal with personal opinion rather than facts as presented elsewhere. It gives a sense of immediacy, as if the narrator "the late Francis Wayland Thurston" is talking to us directly. Not merely as a written narrative but as if the dead man himself is specifically addressing us, as per a conversation.

Yet even more than this is the lack of surety that "I think" conveys. "The most merciful thing in the world is the inability of the human mind to correlate all its contents" is still a great opening. But the idea of doubt, of uncertainty, of humanity this expresses makes the horror to come—and it is under a heading of "The Horror in Clay"—more visceral for a sense of the personal, all the more so for the lack of any actual horror seen or experienced by Thurston himself. The inclusion actually makes the tale more powerful upon repeated readings. Thurston concludes by offering that "even the skies of spring and the flowers of summer must ever afterward be poison to me" (CF 2.55) because of what he now thinks.

Pickman's distraught guest in "Pickman's Model" tries to explain his trauma upon seeing the technique in the creature depicted in canvas: "The monster was there—it glared and gnawed and gnawed and glared" (CF 2.69). Such a direct repetition is not a common Lovecraftian technique and it works especially well here, feeding into the frantic and slightly confused rushing narrative as given by the fearful and increasingly drunk protagonist. Saying of the creature "it glared and gnawed" would be effective, but the readjusting of the phrasing in repeating it gives a feeling of kinetic energy, of the creature actually and actively gnawing in a manner that "glared and gnawed and glared and gnawed" doesn't quite convey to the same level of effectiveness. In the following sentences Lovecraft doubles down by using this echoing of wording "like heavy wood falling on stone or brick—wood on brick," "a vibration as if the wood had fallen farther," and "more wood and brick grating" (CF 2.70), deliberately adding this element to continue this dynamic aspect of the tale, breathlessly told by someone who has thought the events over and over.

Another subtle allusion that time has unconsciously paved over is to be found in a reference in "The Silver Key" (1926) to the fact Randolph Carter, "as early as 1897 that he turned pale when some traveller mentioned the French town of Belloy-en-Santerre, and friends remembered it when he was almost mortally wounded there in 1916, while serving with the Foreign Legion in the Great War" (CF 2.85). As it stands, this is merely an interesting means by which the author lets the reader know the changes in the flow of time and sequence that are happening with Carter. The contemporary reader would understand a lot more by the mention. The Battle of Belloy-en-Santerre took place as part of the wider Battle of the Somme on the first Tuesday of July 1916. Like so many of the individual battles of the Somme, it was a bloodbath and saw the Foreign Legion Regimental Combat Team (RMLE)—by 1919 the most decorated unit of the French army—devastated, with the loss of almost all officers and NCOs and some 800 of 2000 troops.[4] Yet in the meat-grinder of men that was World War I combat such numbers were, tragically in itself, almost unremarkable.

What was notable to the contemporary reader was the death of American poet Alan Seeger there in French uniform as a member of the RMLE. This was much reported on in both France and America, and the already notable Seeger became a truly famous figure, an American martyr for France. This was reflected in the famous propaganda moment concerning the repayment of the debt owed to America Revolutionary War hero the Marquis de Lafayette. General Pershing, leader of the American Expeditionary Force in World War I, and staff arriving in Paris in 1917 paid a call on that most significant of date of 4th of July to the grave of Lafayette as the conclusion of a moral-building march of their rather limited number of landed troops. His aide, Col. Charles E. Stanton, was fluent in French and addressed the assembled crowd, saluted, and concluded his speech proclaiming "Lafayette, we are here." Like most Americans of the time, Lovecraft—who referenced all this in his poem "To Alan Seeger" (AT 413)—would have believed Pershing had said it, censorship not allowing Stanton's name to be published at the time. Seeger's acclaim was such that he was known as the American Rupert Brooke, with his own most famous poem "I

---

4. For whatever one thinks of the cost, the RMLE won its objective, taking the village and ultimately capturing 750 German prisoners, more than its own effective combat force.

Have a Rendezvous with Death," like Brooke's "The Soldier," having an immortal resonance in connection with the tragedy of losses in World War I even as their authors died in the conflict. The eventual 1923 Memorial to the American Volunteers in the Place des États-Unis in Paris has an image of Seeger as its surmounting statue. Lovecraft was certainly aware of Seeger and his sacrifice having, as just noted, written a memorial poem to him in 1918.

I have previous discussed the clever implications and power of Lovecraft's use of heresy in "The Strange High House in the Mist" (1926) in the line "but cannot prove their heresy to any real Kingsporter" (*CF* 2.89), so instead let us consider Lovecraft's also much-discussed use of Nodens in the tale. A genuine deity but drawn in to Lovecraft's work by way of Machen—Lord of the Great Abyss is a title not attested to Nodens in historic sources but was manufactured by Lovecraft's great Welsh idol—what is noticeable is the two separate descriptors affixed to his name in the tale. He is "primal Nodens" and "hoary Nodens." With these two adjectives Lovecraft manages to convey almost all the information about him necessary to the reader, part of the sentences "the grey and awful form of primal Nodens, Lord of the Great Abyss" (*CF* 2.94) and "hoary Nodens reached forth a wizened hand" (*CF* 2.94). Nodens is impossibly ancient and seems it, while simultaneously being filled with terrible power. Lovecraft has set up his title earlier, noting only two paragraphs previously that "there are strange objects in the great abyss, and the seeker of dreams must take care not to stir up or meet the wrong ones" (*CF* 2.93). The underdescription makes the image all the more powerful, and it is a conceit Lovecraft will continue.

Nodens' further six mentions in *The Dream-Quest of Unknown Kadath* (1926–27) all are prefaced by a similar descriptor, of the repeated "hoary," "immemorial," or "archaic." The latter tale, which never underwent true final revision and thus shows some odd elements, is filled with the small touches that add such vibrancy to Lovecraft's work. There are numerous small details whose excisions have a limited effect on the tale but which add the unimportant details that paradoxically are so important to Lovecraft's authorial power. An example is a small section that I cannot recall being spoken of or much mentioned in the many exegeses of Lovecraft's work. After Carter is captured by the moon-beasts and during the journey to their lunar city, the narration observes:

> The close aspect of the moon as the galley drew near proved very disturbing to Carter, and he did not like the size and shape of the ruins which crumbled here and there. The dead temples on the mountains were so placed that they could have glorified no wholesome or suitable gods, and in the symmetries of the broken columns there seemed to lurk some dark and inner meaning which did not invite solution. And what the structure and proportions of the olden worshippers could have been, Carter steadily refused to conjecture. (CF 2.114)

This is never built upon or referred back to again in any manner, and is probably forgotten amongst the many other wonders presented in the tale. But it crafts another strange element of this very strange world, background that helps give a depth to the horrors and wonders that are encountered, but which is itself largely forgotten.

It is tempting to see the use of "alienist" in *The Case of Charles Dexter Ward* (1927) as a clever piece of double meaning, given the very alien intrusion into Ward by Curwen. This may also have been part of Lovecraft's intent, but equally reflects his overall usage—the ubiquitously familiar modern term "psychiatrist" never appears in his work.[5] "Alienist" strikes the modern reader as strange and archaic, the term "alien" having almost been exclusively colonized in the popular consciousness by "extraterrestrial," but this again is an artefact of time rather than intent. Likewise, the interrogation auricularly witnessed by Ezra Weeden—"an alternately raging and sullen figure was questioned in French about the Black Prince's massacre at Limoges

---

5. Perhaps he is in accord with Philippe Chaslin (1857–1923), a French alienist critical of the tendency in psychiatry to a lack of precision in language and an excessive use of neologisms, including the very term psychiatry, whose use he deliberately avoided.

in 1370, as if there were some hidden reason which he ought to know. Curwen asked the prisoner—if prisoner it were—whether the order to slay was given because of the Sign of the Goat found on the altar in the ancient Roman crypt beneath the Cathedral, or whether the Dark Man of the Haute Vienne Coven had spoken the Three Words" (CF 2.244)—is a small element in the tale, but carries with it linkages and essential building blocks to the narrative, in addition to Lovecraft's habitual admixture of history, fiction, and delicate adaptation of particulars. More in tune with our wider examination is what was found in the fields a week after Curwen's death: "this body, so far as could be seen in its burnt and twisted condition, was neither thoroughly human nor wholly allied to any animal which Pawtuxet folk had ever seen or read about" (CF 2.261). The final qualifier "or read about" could be removed and the sentence conveys its message perfectly well. The inclusion transmits that which was found from mysterious to something seemingly completely unknown. As ever small differences are the difference.

"The Colour out of Space" (1927) was one of Lovecraft's own favorite tales, and even more than his regular wont it exudes the aura of the unknown. There are many small flourishes that make it so effective. The doomed Nahum trying to comprehend the unknowable via his own country theology—"It must all be a judgment of some sort; though he could not fancy what for, since he had always walked uprightly in the Lord's ways so far as he knew" (CF 2.384)—adds a human poignancy to the work added to by the mockery he had suffered publicly after the "mistake of Nahum's to tell a stolid city man about the way the great, overgrown mourning-cloak butterflies behaved in connexion with these saxifrages" (CF 2.378). Such ties in well with "the roses and zinneas and hollyhocks in the front yard were such blasphemous-looking things that Nahum's oldest boy Zenas cut them down" (CF 2.381) and as such forms an essential part of the narrative.

Less obvious is the description of the fright of the McGregor boys who had shot "a very peculiar specimen" (CF 2.376) of woodchuck. Also commonly known as a groundhog, this member of the squirrel family is not a creature much noted in connection with horror. Rather to the opposite, they are often given a friendly association, being easily anthropomorphized and frequently seen as cute. That the boys—given an impression of hardiness in being hunters—"were genuinely frightened" enough to throw away their kill "at once" (CF 2.376) speaks deeply to the reaction. This usage of "genuinely" elevates the verisimilitude, taking away any quantity of playfulness or childish exaggeration. Genuine fear is an entirely different and elevated experience than mere fear, and the reader responds to this subtle difference.

"The Dunwich Horror" (1928) contains an interesting detail in the wake of Wilbur's death in the sixth section of the story. "They filed a ponderous report at the court-house in Aylesbury, and litigations concerning heirship are said to be still in progress amongst the innumerable Whateleys, decayed and undecayed, of the upper Miskatonic valley" (CF 2.441). The ultimate fate of the Whateley estate is in no way germane to the plot, but it is such a prosaic element of legalities in the wake of an unexpected death as might be expected. Such ordinary events are rarely referenced unnecessarily in horror tales. In part Lovecraft uses it to again bring in the idea of the "decayed and undecayed" familial lines, which will emerge again toward the end of the tale. Yet in the main it is a slice of the interaction of the mundane juxtaposed against the ultramundane that makes up the bulk of the tale, and thus quietly adds to the acceptance of the latter.

Having already examined "The Whisperer in Darkness" (1930), we can add a coda to a possible foreshadowing when Wilmarth receives a picture of the Black Stone: "Akeley had photographed it on what was evidently his study table, for I could see rows of books and a bust of Milton in the background" (CF 2.482). Milton is one of many natural choices for a bust in the home of a literary man, and as such is seemingly unremarkable. Yet when Lovecraft earlier describes Akeley's scholastic achievements he cites him as "a notable student of mathematics, astronomy, biology, anthropology, and folklore" (CF 2.474). None of these cry out "Milton!" But Milton is commonly said to have died of gout, and Noyes makes the explanation of his host's incapacity that "his feet and ankles swelled, too, so that he had to bandage them like a gouty old beef-eater" (CF 2.515). Possibly this is coincidence, but given the care with which Lovecraft made his fictional choices such deliberateness cannot be discounted entirely: his own copy of *Paradise Lost* and *The Poetical works of Milton, Young, Gray, Beattie, and Collins* both note in their biographical sections that Milton is said to have died of gout.

At the Mountains of Madness (1931), being more a true novel rather than an extended short story or novella, naturally allows for much extraneous detail that would be omitted in a smaller work. But like the Nodens example cited earlier, it is a descriptor that makes the small addition to the power of the story. The unfortunate Gedney is, like most characters in a Lovecraft tale, vastly underdescribed. Yet he is mentioned by name nineteen times and plays a crucial role, for all that he is a dead body for most of the story's events. The only descriptor of him as a person—outside of portrayals of sympathy ("poor," repeated thrice after his body is found), location ("missing"), and possible state ("mad")—is "young." This too is repeated only thrice, once at the discovery of the cave filled with specimens, repeated in the line "Eleven known dead, young Gedney missing" (CF 3.53), and with the discovery of "the bodies of young Gedney and the missing dog" (CF 3.130). The first sets up the information, the second adds pathos to the horror and mystery, the third highlights the tragedy. After this he is only ever referred to as "poor Gedney." It is a subtle injection of humanity into a tale striving for cosmic horror, and this counterpoint almost subconsciously adds to the effect of the work. The overarching narrative is of the almost inconceivable horrors of the past uncovered by Lake and Danforth, juxtaposed and highlighted by the very comprehensible loss of a young man delving into that and suffering the penalty for it.

A second distinct yet small element in "The Shadow over Innsmouth" (1931) occurs after Zadok Allen frantically runs off after giving his drunken narration. Despite a swift pursuit—and bear in mind this is a young man chasing an intoxicated ninety-six-year-old—the narrator reports that "there was no remaining trace of Zadok Allen" (CF 3.201). Such ends the third section on a powerful note of ominousness and foreboding. It is only on later reflection that a reader might note the narrator recalling that "The government men never found poor Zadok" (CF 3.221) and tie it specifically back to this incident. It is possible that Allen was taken to his unknown but assuredly vile fate for revealing the cult's secrets at this very moment, although this is deliberately ambiguous. But Allen ultimately disappearing without trace is thus constructed in the reader's mind without recourse to the clichéd use of the actual phrase.

"The Dreams in the Witch House" (1932) is layered with horrors, with hundreds of years of child murder being deliberately covered up by the citizenry of Arkham. Yet echoing this at the micro level are the behaviors of the implied lover of Anastasia Wolejko, whose child is kidnapped as the last sacrifice made by Keziah Mason and Brown Jenkin:

> The mother, it appeared, had feared the event for some time; but the reasons she assigned for her fear were so grotesque that no one took them seriously. She had, she said, seen Brown Jenkin about the place now and then ever since early in March, and knew from its grimaces and titterings that little Ladislas must be marked for sacrifice at the awful Sabbat on Walpurgis-Night. She had asked her neighbour Mary Czanek to sleep in the room and try to protect the child, but Mary had not dared. She could not tell the police, for they never believed such things. Children had been taken that way every year ever since she could remember. (CF 3.263)

The paragraph resonates with dread and is complete in itself. Yet it is the final sentence that adds the additional element that elevates Lovecraft far above his pulp competitors: "And her friend Pete Stowacki would not help because he wanted the child out of the way anyhow" (CF 3.263). A very human selfishness pervades the actions of Pete, who is never mentioned again and is inessential to the plot. But the callow horror of the implications of this line compete with any bloody tunnelings by Brown Jenkin for the greatest nastiness in the tale.

In "The Thing on the Doorstep" (1933) Lovecraft is able to create a purposeful element merely by a distinct usage of pluralities. After Derby has killed Asenath and is trying to explain his fears and predicament to the narrator, he observes that "there are certain groups of searchers—certain cults, you know" (CF 3.348) involved in the background of the matter and which clearly have malign intentions. That Asenath—or rather, Ephraim—was a member of a coven was earlier established, and the line could easily have been "there are a certain group of searchers—the cult, you know." But the idea of cults and groups of searchers conveys a far deeper menace, all the more so for the implications they exude and the vagueness implied.

"The Shadow out of Time" (1934–35) contains a very Lovecraftian artefact in that when the narrator is taken to the past civilization of the Yithians he does not come to the fullest flowering of their development. Rather he notes: "The sciences were carried to an unbelievable height of development, and art was a vital part of life, though at the period of my dreams it had passed its crest and meridian" (CF 3.404). This second part of the sentence is not necessary to the plot. It does highlight Lovecraft's fixation on the decline of civilizations, present in all his works; but more importantly it adds an unconscious aspect of reality. Unlike realistic fiction, it necessarily deals with the biggest, best, and brightest elements the narrator or reader will encounter. The admission that the narrator was in the unimaginably vast past but not at the height of its civilization is reflective of the experience of reality, where the archaeologist far less commonly comes upon the perfect moment or absolute zenith of perfection.

It would be remiss of a serious look at the work of Lovecraft and his use of small elements to create big effects not to mention the forbidden books that so heavily populate memory of his work and which are an almost inevitable aspect of later pastiches. "The Haunter of the Dark" (1935) contains a particular germane roll call of such works:

> a Latin version of the abhorred "Necronomicon", the sinister "Liber Ivonis", the infamous "Cultes des Goules" of Comte d'Erlette, the "Unaussprechlichen Kulten" of von Junzt, and old

> Ludvig Prinn's hellish "De Vermis Mysteriis". But there were others he had known merely by reputation or not at all—the Pnakotic Manuscripts, the "Book of Dzyan", and a crumbling volume in wholly unidentifiable characters yet with certain symbols and diagrams shudderingly recognisable to the occult student. (CF 3.460)

It is fitting that these titles are respectively created by Lovecraft, Clark Ashton Smith (Lovecraft supplied the Latin for Smith's original *Book of Eibon*), Robert Bloch (with the author being a play on August Derleth), Robert E. Howard (with the translation from *Nameless Cults* supplied by Derleth at Lovecraft's request), Bloch again (with the real Ludvig Prinn being given an additional item in his catalogue—the Latin for *Mysteries of the Worm* being again supplied by Lovecraft), and the Pnakotic Manuscripts being Lovecraft's first-named invented tome way back in "Polaris" (1918). The *Book of Dzyan* is the outlier and unnecessary element here. It too is an invention, but unlike the others is claimed as a genuine work, written in the equally imaginary language of Senzar. The person who claimed the work as authentic is famed fabulist and occultist Helena P. Blavatsky, who placed alleged translations of it into her own works. The juxtaposition of a fake volume claimed as real and published as if a genuinely ancient work with his own actual imaginary volumes that even by his stage in Lovecraft's career many believed to be genuine adds once more that subtle element which has gone on to elevate Lovecraft to literary immortality.

While issues of essentiality will always cloud such discussions of the minutiae in Lovecraft's writing, it is beyond question that his deliberateness of creation and addition of perfectly placed details play a key part in the ineffable and seemingly unrecreatable process that have elevated Lovecraft's work into a permanent place in both the literary and pop-cultural canon.

Works Cited

Lovecraft, H. P. *Letters to C. L. Moore and Others*. Ed. David E. Schultz and S. T. Joshi. New York: Hippocampus Press, 2017.

———. *Letters to E. Hoffmann Price and Richard F. Searight*. Ed. David E. Schultz and S. T. Joshi. New York: Hippocampus Press, 2021.

———. *Letters to Family and Family Friends*. Ed. S. T. Joshi and David E. Schultz. New York: Hippocampus Press, 2020. 2 vols.

———. *Letters to Robert Bloch and Others*. Ed. David E. Schultz and S. T. Joshi. New York: Hippocampus Press, 2015.

———, and August Derleth. *Essential Solitude: The Letters of H. P. Lovecraft and August Derleth*. Ed. David E. Schultz and S. T. Joshi. New York: Hippocampus Press, 2008. 2 vols.

———, and Clark Ashton Smith. *Dawnward Spire, Lonely Hill: The Letters of H. P. Lovecraft and Clark Ashton Smith*. Ed. David E. Schultz and S. T. Joshi. New York: Hippocampus Press, 2017.

Briefly Noted

The French scholar Gilles Menegaldo has assisted in the making of a splendid new documentary on Lovecraft. The documentary was prepared by Marc Charley under the title *Le Monde de Lovecraft*. Menegaldo writes: "The documentary (two one-hour parts) was screened in several French festivals and public reception has been quite positive. We also had two screenings in Paris so far and attendance has been good too." Charley and Menegaldo are in the process of preparing a version with English subtitles, to be titled *The World of H. P. Lovecraft*.

This summer the long-awaited hardcover edition of Lovecraft's *Collected Fiction: A Variorum Edition—Revisions and Collaborations* (Volume 4) was published. It may be ordered from Hippocampus Press.

Eating Anarchist Spaghetti with Lovecraft

David Haden

During his time living in Brooklyn, H. P. Lovecraft favored a number of eateries. He at first warmed to the interior of the large Tiffany cafe, finding its neo-colonial wood-panelled interior much to his taste.[1] The place even included "mirror panels arranged like arched Georgian windows." But after some months he discovered its clients could not be ignored in favor of the décor: "the clientele was past enduring [...] young toughs and gangsters [...] I got all my stomach could stand after three or four months and thereafter switched to Bickford's—near Borough Hall" (*Letters to Wilfred B. Talman* 103–04).

Lovecraft's letter appears to make a distinction between young teen gangs and adult mobsters of the sort who then ran

---

1. Also known as the "Tiffany Cafeteria." HPL states that plain-clothes police would sometimes raid the place and make the "young noisy bums" turn out their pockets, seeking guns. A few of his other important haunts were the upmarket Taormina, "Peter's" in Joralemon Street, the Scotch Bakery on the corner of Court Street and Schermerhorn, and the bohemian coffee bar known as the "Double R" or "Double-R Coffee House." His friend George Kirk stated, in a letter to his fiancée (in Hart and Joshi, *Lovecraft's New York Circle* 45), that the "Double R" was well known for its discreetly gay clientele. Samuel Loveman much later recalled of the Scotch Bakery: "The toughs (and I mean *toughs*) from Red Hook used to congregate there nightly. We listened to them recounting their marauding and robberies in the choicest and vulgarist Brooklynese slang" (22), which he recalls HPL was soon able to mimic due to his talent with dialect. Of course, HPL also supped coffee and petted the cats in many lesser New York City cafés and small family restaurants, these being too numerous to document here.

the local rackets, handled pilfered goods from the cargo-ships, and supplied the illegal liquor trade during the era of Prohibition. Official city reports confirm this clear distinction between the two forms of gangs, albeit with the most hardened local youngsters "graduating" into the older gangs.[2] Other letters and

---

2. The blandly New York Crime Commission report titled *A Study of Delinquency in a District of Kings County* (1927) is online and offers a thorough official study of those dealt with by the juvenile courts in that part of Brooklyn, aged 16 or under. The report's authors undertook a major fieldwork study in the winter of 1926–27 and were also able to draw on local court records, on an earlier summer study by another city body, and on the accounts of local priests and even a long-serving policeman who had made Red Hook his 20-year beat. Reading between the lines, it appears the researchers were not able to penetrate the close-knit and insular Christian Syrian community in Red Hook, and little is heard of the small Norwegian and German populations that were recorded in the 1920 census. The resulting report found more than seventy local gangs and claimed on good evidence "that Red Hook's juvenile population was the third-most delinquent in the world." Apart from confirming HPL's outline of the area's demographics, the report illuminates the settings in "The Horror at Red Hook" by stating that basements were often the choice of gang rendezvous and headquarters: "It is almost impossible for children to make the roofs their rendezvous as is done on the East Side and in Harlem. Therefore, they utilize basements, or the street itself [. . .] There is very little attention paid [by adults] to the basements in these sections, since there are no [basement] furnaces and one caretaker will usually manage several houses. [Lack of roof access] eliminates pigeon-flying, a source of gambling and stealing in some sections of the city [such as his good friend Everett McNeil's Hell's Kitchen district; see HPL's "The Pigeon Flyers"], and it eliminates the roof as gang headquarters." HPL later learned of the report via press reports and further press cuttings sent to him via Dwyer. He was pleased that his story had been shown to have been accurate in its use of local detail. For the benefit of future researchers examining the demographics of HPL's "Red Hook" I should add that the report has a usefully thorough demographic breakdown of the area, with a rough map of "who lived where," albeit with its numbers based on the 1920 census and thus out-of-date in terms of the growing Syrian influence and dwindling of other groups. The Syrians of Red Hook were eastern Christians of various types and sects, fleeing the long persecution and massacres of Christians and Jews that has left the Middle East the impoverished monoculture it is today. They were almost entirely from the then-forested uplands of Mount Lebanon, and thus could also be called "Lebanese Christians." Around 10,000 were living in Brooklyn by 1930. The 1920 census shows no Spanish speakers,

reminiscences have Lovecraft rubbing shoulders with hardened criminals in Brooklyn cafés. His's long Brooklyn story "The Horror at Red Hook" (1925) would later find a vivid fictional use for these "young toughs and gangsters."

Bickford's

Lovecraft thus made an early switch from the Tiffany, confirmed by his 1925 diary, to patronize "Bickford's" (CE 5.150). This was a growing cafeteria chain, and there was more than one branch. The *Chain Store Age* trade magazine of the period usefully reveals that a Bickford's branch wasn't located at 425 Fulton Street until 1927. Thus Lovecraft's haunt must have been the 58 Court Street branch. This is indeed very "near Borough Hall," being just a few steps away down Court Street. Lovecraft described his chosen branch of Bickford's as a "one-arm," meaning that it was both cheap and that it had "side-arm" tables just wide enough to hold one's plate of food.

This is not to say that it was cheap-looking from the outside. Bickford's branches all had the same architect and designer, one F. Russell Stuckert. Thus the Court Street branch's exterior would probably not be too different from the nearby 425 Fulton Street branch established in 1927. This later branch can be seen on archive photos, where it sports a classy frontage, pleasingly designed and with a sweeping sign-writer's logo on the window-glass and use of surrounding leaded stained-glass. A certain level of elegance may thus have been part of what enticed Lovecraft

---

and the bulk of Red Hook's large Spanish-speaking population arrived later in time. HPL's "Red Hook" has an opening description that mentions some Spanish in passing, so possibly a few were starting to arrive as early as 1925. HPL was correct on the local demographics in almost all instances, but the central figure of the police detective Malone is made Irish rather than Italian. The Irish nationality and Dublin origin were probably chosen to give him a plausible interest in mystical and occult things, though the 1920 Red Hook census did record a small Irish population, which may still have been there in 1926. Note also that Malone was raised and remained a Catholic, since HPL states he had been published in the Catholic *Dublin Review*.

to choose Bickford's, although he disliked its utilitarian white-tiled interior.

Interestingly, the Bickford's café chain later became an enduring and much-loved feature of Brooklyn's richly layered cultural landscape. David W. Dunlap wrote about the enduring cultural aura of Bickford's in Brooklyn in 2000, for the *New York Times*. For instance, he noted that in the 1950s Allen Ginsberg's generation of beat writers and poets "sank all night in submarine light of Bickford's" (a line from Ginsberg's famous poem *Howl*), and that the early genius of Woody Allen found solace there: "I got no money. I'll go sit in Bickford's" (from *Getting Even*, 1971). Other lesser twentieth-century New York artists, writers, and musicians also mention it as a meeting place. But Dunlap did not pick up on the fact that a certain Mr. Lovecraft had, as with so many other things, done it first.

John's

From May 1925 Lovecraft came to favor a certain "John's" for his beloved Italian cuisine, and in one letter he even calls this establishment his spaghetti "headquarters." The exact address and nature of this spaghetti house has, so far as I know, until now been a small mystery to Lovecraftians. It was at No. 7 Willoughby Street, and before it was "John's" it was "Fritz's." when—as can be seen in the following archive pictures—it was then Hungarian.[3] This 25-cent restaurant would thus have made a natural and easy transition to an Italian eatery, most likely with newer signs done in slightly more mid-1920s sign-writing, and probably decked in the usual Italian colors of red, green and white.

---

3. Online city court records show that "on or about the 24th day of March, 1902, the defendant conducted and now conducts a restaurant at No. 7 Willoughby street, Borough of Brooklyn." In 1901 the place was named "7 Willoughby Street, known as Fritz's restaurant."

The future "John's," when a Hungarian restaurant, invited customers up a flight of steps to No. 7 Willoughby. We are looking toward the distant and busy Fulton Street and its rattling "elevated" railway. This is a 1916 "record picture," made prior to subway work beneath. The *Brooklyn Citizen* newspaper building is hidden behind the rounded metalwork canopy that extends from the corner bar at No. 1 Willoughby. With thanks to the City Transit Museum, Subway Construction Photograph Collection, 1900–1950. The Museum has museum-quality archival prints of its collections available for sale, on demand.

The photograph above shows same frontage from a different angle. This excellent picture above shows No. 7 in 1916, nine years before John opened as an Italian place in May 1925. Again, it is one of a set of high-resolution glass plate photographs made to forestall any legal actions that might arise due to the planned subway works beneath the street. Bristol's restaurant has not yet expanded into what is here the "Lady Barbers" seen on the left hand side of the picture. With thanks to the City Transit Museum, Subway Construction Photograph Collection, 1900–1950.

This "John's" then became a habitual as well as a special eating place on Sundays for Lovecraft. For instance, see this letter from May 1925: "at twilight, I wended my homeward way, pausing at John's Spaghetti place for my usual [30-cent] Sunday dinner of meat balls and spaghetti, vanilla ice cream, and coffee" (*LFF* 289).

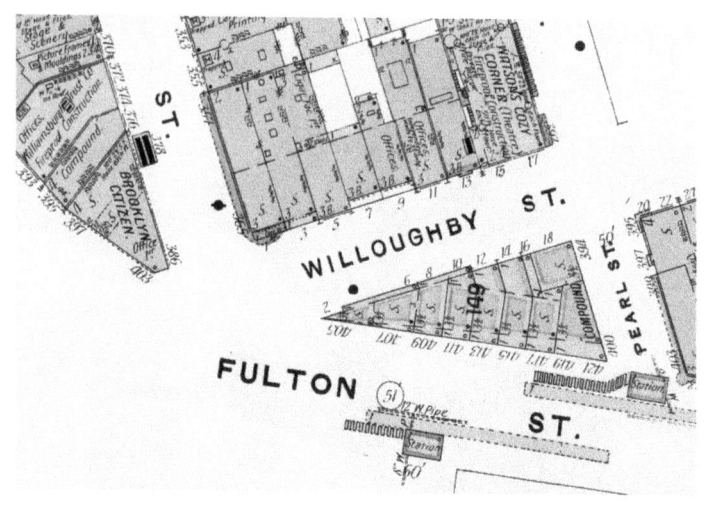

Part of a 1904 set of city map plates, showing the layout and numbering at Fulton and Willoughby. "John's" at No. 7. From Sanborn's 1904 *Brooklyn Atlas*.

A Suit-able View?

As we can see from the above pictures, "John's" was not ideal at the front, in terms of the customer's chance of obtaining a table with a street view. This raises a small problem in relation to the letters. How did Lovecraft sit and look out at the *Brooklyn Citizen* building? It is likely that he did so, because that was where and how he tells us he acquired his cheap suit from Monroe Clothes, seen across the street in an upper window. In *Letters to Family* he tells of how he found a suit that he then vitally needed. He was eating an Italian meal at his regular "John's" and recalled that, being with Sonia, he had been given a window table. Casually surveying the scene across the street, "up one flight," he thereby spied a bargain suit advert from the "Monroe Clothes" outfitters (*LFF* 305). Monroe was a big national chain and in large cities had special "Upstairs Monroe Clothes Shops" with regular bargains. "A short flight to economy" served as their slogan.[4] But how could Lovecraft have seen the upper floors of the *Citizen* building when eating at John's at No. 7? I can only assume, from the maps, that No. 7 may have had some kind of extended rental of the upper roof-spaces of No. ½ (a bar) through 5, in order to have a large upper banquet area and perhaps also more "tables with a view." At the far end of such an arrangement, the view would indeed have taken in one side of the *Citizen* newspaper building—and thus their floor that hosted Monroe Clothes. The alternative possibility is that Monroe had an overflow of stock at that time and had opened a temporary annex or show-window a stone's throw away, more or less opposite the "John's" frontage.

Summer Belt-Tightening

Lovecraft's habits then seem to have shifted a little as the summer waned. In the fine autumn/fall weather (his friend Kirk's diary says that New York enjoyed an especially fine "Indian Summer" [Hart and Joshi 31]),[5] his friends Samuel Loveman and Arthur Leeds tipped him off to two places where the diner could still obtain a 25-cent spaghetti dinner. His interest in such savings was perhaps aided by "John's" upping the price of a dinner from 30 to 35 cents. Even a coffee at "John's" was 10 cents,

---

4. I have found the address. A 1922 copy of the *New York Times* has the Monroe Clothes chain's main Brooklyn branch at 413 Fulton Street, a.k.a. the *Citizen* newspaper building. The company then failed in December 1925–June 1926 after being "dragged into bankruptcy" by a vexatious creditor. When the official receiver was appointed for the Monroe Clothes bankruptcy on 15 June 1926, it was usefully listed at "409–21 Fulton Street." This then is further confirmation that the store was indeed at 413 Fulton Street by 1922, having earlier been further down at Fulton and Hoyt. 413 Fulton was probably its main ground-floor entrance, and then it had sales and stock rooms above that stretched across Nos. 409–21 and was probably above the newspaper offices. This tallies with HPL's description of "up one flight," and various maps and photos of the locations.

5. A remark by HPL also indicates that the Indian Summer's terminus was in mid-November (*LFF* 491) when the fine weather finally broke.

he records. A ten-cent saving on a meal may not seem a lot today, but such things were starting to matter to Lovecraft as the summer faded. The city was at the start of a long nationwide coal strike, and it sounds from his letters as if everyone was putting up prices in anticipation of an expensive 1925–26 winter. His landlady even raised the price of his underheated and rodent-ridden corner room. Note also that January 1925 had seen New York's worst snowstorm in living memory, only a day or so after Lovecraft had moved into his room on the seedy edge of Red Hook. Thus many, including Lovecraft, were now expecting more of the same: another freezing winter, on top of a severe coal (and thus heating-oil) shortage due to the strike. They would have been partly right about the likely weather, since February 1926 saw not one but two snowstorms hit the city. Both were of similar severity to the great storm of January 1925. Lovecraft also states that the coal strike caused the city to lift the outright ban on burning bituminous (i.e., very smoky) coal. Thus the autumnal and winter atmosphere, in which he was exploring colonial sections of the city at night, would have been especially atmospheric. The sunsets he loved may also have had richer atmospheres and coloring.

All these price rises meant that Lovecraft was having to economize even further than usual, in the face of even higher price inflation in future. Toward the end of the year he tried to restrict his spaghetti meals to Sundays only, if he had not already done so, since he anticipated having to find the cost of running his room's oil heater during the winter. As the really cold weather set in, a 35-cent Sunday meal and a 10-cent coffee at "John's" would have seemed a warming feast by comparison. Lovecraft also ventured into Red Hook dockside area itself and sampled the cheap cafés there, since in one letter he talks of sampling "Red Hook's modestly priced bean-bureaus," and in another letter he states: "I took several walks of exploration around the [Red Hook] waterfront rookeries, and acquired a very fair pictorial and oral image of the whole blight even in its extremist phases" (*Letters to Maurice W. Moe* 437).

John Sloan, "Snowstorm in the Village," 2–3 January 1925. This is the same "worst in living memory" snowstorm that almost immediately greeted HPL on his arrival in Red Hook: on 31 December 1924 he was then "half moved" to 169 Clinton St., and on 1 January 1925 he "moved final load." He awoke in his new room to find the snowstorm engulfing the city. Here we see an "on the spot" recording of the elevated railway and the snow falling in Greenwich Village. With thanks to the Smithsonian American Art Museum, which now has 4.5 million pictures freely available online.

All these price rises meant that Lovecraft was having to economize even further than usual, in the face of even higher price inflation in future. Toward the end of the year he tried to restrict his spaghetti meals to Sundays only, if he had not already done so, since he anticipated having to find the cost of running his room's oil heater during the winter. As the really cold weather set in, a 35-cent Sunday meal and a 10-cent coffee at "John's" would have seemed a warming feast by comparison. Lovecraft also ventured into Red Hook dockside area itself and sampled the cheap cafés there, since in one letter he talks of sampling "Red Hook's modestly priced bean-bureaus," and in another letter he states: "I took several walks of exploration around the [Red Hook] waterfront rookeries, and acquired a very fair pictorial and oral image of the whole blight even in its extremist phases" (*Letters to Maurice W. Moe* 437).

Given all this, we can then surmise that his attempt at the start of August to speed-write "The Horror at Red Hook" was designed to produce a saleable story that would pay for the winter's heating oil by the time the colder weather was setting in. True, it was in part an attempt to pick up an idle café challenge from a member of "the gang." But now, thanks to the new *Letters to Family* volumes, we also know that this tale was plotted and written at great speed over a solid "clear the decks" period of about 36 hours (*LFF* 331). The friend's challenge then seems to have been the spur to something of a speed-writing experiment for Lovecraft: how quickly could he turn out a long saleable pulp "shocker" story that addressed his own concerns and his lived local experience, and also the wider politics of the nation (e.g., the apparent failure of the Immigration Act of 1924, on which so many hopes had been pinned, since by 1925 this had only reduced legal immigration by just over 50%)? It was a story that had all that, and yet remained only somewhat outside the "formula" expected by his new target market of *Detective Tales*. The very act of writing and mailing the story further shows that, at least in part, Lovecraft was still seeking a way to earn money at that point. Given the speed of the plotting, writing, and the competing commercial and aesthetic demands, it is natural that the result fails to satisfy many modern critics.[6] But "Red Hook" is still very entertaining and even intriguing, at least to myself,[7] especially since it also has a biographical side that provides useful—if rather pungent—glimpses into Lovecraft's psychological state at the start of August 1925, as his pressure-cooker mind began to boil over on the edge of an odorous and noisy New York City slum.

Anarchist and Bootlegger

Of course, Lovecraft found some oases of calm in the "pest-zone," his favored "John's" being one of them. But was "John's" all that it seemed? Just another Brooklyn spaghetti house? Well, it was . . . and it wasn't. John Pucciatti (1885–1967), the immigrant entrepreneur who ran John Pucciatti's Spaghetti House, was quite a character in 1910s and '20s New York. He is still remembered to this day in the local restaurateur lore. It turns out he was an early Italian anarchist. At that time such heartfelt utopian beliefs were not as rare in New York City as one might think. Doctrinaire 1930s communism, for instance, had not yet shouted down, driven into labor camps, or outright murdered many of the world's anarchists. Indeed, Lovecraft knew a few anarchists. In July 1929 he wrote:

> There's nothing about 'anarchists' to be afraid of! [. . .] they are very harmless folk. [. . .] Despite their bold talk they are timid

---

6. I should, however, note that it quickly had commercial success. It found a home in the Selwyn & Blount anthology *You'll Need a Night Light*, a major British mass-market anthology for 1927 and that this gave HPL his first hardcover publication. It had thus passed the "sniff test" under scrutiny by two people, the London agent for *Weird Tales*, Charles Lavell, and then Selwyn & Blount's house anthologist Christine Campbell Thomson, who made the final choice and arrangement of Lavell's picks.

7. My personal theory is that the attentive reader is eventually intended to realize that Suydam can be understood as having risked all, including passing through death, to foil the cult's raising of Lilith by toppling her vital occult pedestal back into the watery abyss at the key moment. In my interpretation, he is not seeking the pedestal for himself, but rather seeks a way to put it beyond the reach of Lilith. Suydam can thus be seen as the real hero, of a sort, in "Red Hook."

> & ineffectual creatures, most of whom would not hurt a fly if they could. I know many of them . . . [i.e., his friend James F. Morton, and probably also Loveman in a rather closeted way].[8] [They are to be distinguished from the Greenwich Village 'radicals' who adopt] a slovenly insincerity & cheap posing habit, which merely uses the guise of radicalism as an easy way of attracting attention. (*Letters to Elizabeth Toldridge* 82)

Yet Pucciatti was probably of a somewhat different order from Morton or the posers whom Lovecraft and his circle sometimes encountered at the Double-R café or at New York parties such as those given by the poet Hart Crane. I suggest John was probably more of an anarcho-syndicalist, meaning an anarchist far more interested in industrial trades unions and "black flag" wildcat strikes than the other more romantic varieties of anarchism exemplified by Lovecraft's good friend Morton. My armchair surmise would of course depend on how much experience John had of the sudden and jarring industrialization of Italian cities before he left for America. Yet I have made a discovery that means we can at least be sure that he advertised in worker-oriented leftist publications, though we still can't be quite sure of his exact ideas, since he doesn't appear to have left us any writings. On Pucciatti the book *Radical Gotham: Anarchism in New York City* can only state that his restaurant was one of

> a multitude of Italian cafes and restaurants offered cheap meals and distraction, serving as important social and political centers. Founded in 1908 by John Pucciatti, an immigrant from Umbria, John's on East 12th Street[9] was legendarily known as "the favorite meeting place of free thinkers of all nationalities." (Bencivenni, "Fired by the Ideal" 59)

Other popular anarchist hangouts named included Albasi's gro-

---

8. Morton's anarchism is well known and is now relatively well documented. HPL said of Loveman's political beliefs: "According to my social and political theories he ought to be shot or in gaol" (*Letters to Maurice W. Moe* 443). For an overview of the evidence for the various political opinions of HPL's circle during the Great Depression, see my essay "Reds in New York."
9. A.k.a. "John's of 12th Street," Brooklyn.

cery on East 106th Street and the Vesuvio restaurant on 3rd Avenue near 116th Street in East Harlem, places where for a reputed one dollar[10] radicals could enjoy a cheap banquet while debating the coming revolution. Another book, *Making Italian America,* has the same information but adds a little more due to a recent in-depth biography of the labor organizer and editor Carlo Tresca:

> In the United States, the *sovversivi's* [subversives'] most popular hangout was John's Spaghetti House on East Twelfth Street in New York City (now simply John's), which was commonly advertised in Italian radical newspapers as "the favorite meeting place of free thinkers of all nationalities." Established in 1908 by John Pucciatti, an immigrant from Umbria, its menu offered an appetizer, main dish, dessert, and cup of coffee for under a dollar. Carlo Tresca, Arturo Giovannitti, and other famous *sovversivi* regularly ate there, often holding special radical banquets at John's private apartment upstairs. (Bencivenni, "Culture and Leisure" 127)

Various sources state that Pucciatti had at least one local artist "fresco" the walls, paid for in free meals. A later copyrighted photo I found shows John looking more like a well-groomed patrician ancient Roman nobleman than the swivel-eyed bomb-throwing type of anarchist.[11] His place had a classy look which

---

10. That was three times the amount HPL paid for his Sunday meal, so one imagines that intoxicating "extras" were perhaps also served.

11. There were different types of anarchist, many pacifist. But I would be remiss if I did not add that violent anarchism was not a myth and thus HPL's political fairy tale "The Street" (1919) would not have been read as hyperbolic or misleading at the time. There were intense provocations in the U.S. during the 1918–25 period: the forceful spreading of violent political doctrines that glorified terrorism, huge mob-handed riots and dangerous industrial disruption, many increasingly supported by a new revolution-exporting totalitarian state in Russia; a national U.S. terrorist movement simultaneously able to explode seven bombs in public places, including bombs that demolished a church, in cities that included Boston and Cleveland; a series of sophisticated and deadly mail bombs each specially designed to blow the hands off those who opened them; and a horse-drawn tram, packed with 100 pounds of dynamite and sawn-up

matched his own appearance, being a formal white-tablecloth Italian restaurant with apron-wearing waiters and what appears to be ancient Roman frescos on the walls. Again, one can see why "Lovecraft the Roman" might have been attracted to such an ambience. Anarchist spaghetti it may have been, but it was classy anarchist spaghetti served with a hint of Rome.

Yet I have also found that, by the early 1920s, John had slipped over from idealistic tub-thumping 1910s Italian anarchism to illegal tub-brewed booze. His place thus became a key part of the first wave of U.S. gangsterism. The slide became quite evident from 1922, according to one authority on the early history of the Italian mob. Indeed, such things were increasingly hard for the public to miss—for instance, in August 1922 a hail of bullets suddenly riddled the gangster boss Umberto Valenti during a supposed peace meeting held at "John's" (Donati 25). A gangster lieutenant, one "Lucky" Luciano, is said to have fired the fatal shot as the gangster boss staggered outside and tried to hail a cab. Shortly after this, the main "John's" became the most popular watering hole for Luciano and other proto-Mafia gangsters, as the old-time rackets were taken over and the Mafia was born. At this time "John's" "also operated as a well-known speakeasy [i.e., illegal liquor purveyor] during prohibition. The ground floor continued as a restaurant, while wine and whiskey were made in the basement and served in espresso cups on the second floor" (Levine).[12]

Entrance to the upstairs was via a hidden staircase. Head hootch-brewer "Mama John" had a candle lit in the window when the fresh—and probably rather hair-curling—liquor was ready to be served. Any sign of the police in the area, and the candle was snuffed out as a warning. This main "John's" was thus ground-zero for the subsequent growth of the Italian Mafia in

---

iron curtain-weights as deadly shrapnel being exploded in the middle of New York City. Thankfully, in some cases the police were able to deploy the first audio bugging devices to gather hard conclusive evidence.

12. One historian says the brewing was done in backyard sheds. The U.S. TV series *The Sopranos* apparently attempted to recreate the main "John's" for the screen.

the U.S. Such activities may explain his low profile as a business during Prohibition, keeping the new branch out of any directories and not advertising it except in radical journals likely to bring the "right" type of clientele, and by invitation cards such as the one kept by Lovecraft and inscribed by him "my favourite restaurant."

Lovecraft at John's

Was Lovecraft, who in his youth and young man had always taken a staunch and outspoken anti-liquor stance, aware of such things? It is difficult to say. There is a later anecdote from one of his friends, who recalled that on New York night-walks Lovecraft would insouciantly stroll down any darkened alley in pursuit of yet another shapely Georgian door-knocker or an especially winsome stray kitten. In doing so he would have to be rescued if he inadvertently discovered the door to a speakeasy. But on the other hand, he was no one's fool in terms of knowing what was going on in a place, as the wealth of accurate and personally observed local topography and demography in "The Horror at Red Hook" shows.[13] He may also have overheard snatches of radical conversation at other restaurant tables while twizzling up his spaghetti and cheese. He was certainly politically astute enough to have been able to extrapolate an ideology after hearing a few words of radical jargon, and probably knew a lot about

---

13. Several of his New York friends were also no fools in terms of knowing "how things were" underneath the surface. Arthur Leeds of the gangster-ridden Chicago and the seamy side of Coney Island, for instance, often ran with and worked closely with the theatrical, freak-show and circus crowd. In July 1931 Leeds was running a Coney Island bookshop (*LFF* 935), revealed a page later to be The Half Moon on Surf Avenue, the main drag. HPL purchased there a 10-cent copy of *Beowulf* in "a good school translation." (He presumably later read it and thus encountered the monstrous Grendel's Mother depicted "on the doorstep" of the Anglo-Saxon hall, only a year or so before imagining the female Asenath's putrefying corpse arriving on the doorstep in his own tale "The Thing on the Doorstep" [1933]). It seems quite likely from contemporary sources that Leeds's bookshop was in the lobby of The Half Moon Hotel (opened 1927) on Coney Island, a well-known haunt of 1930s New York City gangsters.

anarchism via his long talks with Morton and possibly with Loveman. Admittedly, Lovecraft did not speak Italian, but words such as *rivoluzione* and *anarchismo* are not difficult to understand.

Until now nothing has passed into New York restaurateur lore about Pucciatti's 1925-30(?) Brooklyn branch, which is partly why it has eluded Lovecraftian researchers. But the existence of this branch can now be confirmed through new primary sources, along with some exact dates. I have found evidence for a 24-month block of advertisements that John took out in *Worker's Monthly*, now freely available as scans at Archive.org. In March and April 1925 his first advertisements appeared, but the new Brooklyn branch was not then being advertised.

> *The favorite Restaurant of Radicals and their Friends*
> ## "JOHN'S"
> *Italian Dishes a Specialty*
> 302 EAST 12th STREET,   BROOKLYN BRANCH
> NEW YORK CITY   7 Willoughby St.
>
> Popular for its good food, reasonable prices and interesting companionship
> Private Dining Room for Parties
> John Pucciatti, Prop.   Phone Stuyvesant 3816

"The favorite Restaurant of *Radicals* and their Friends," advertised in *Worker's Monthly* (my emphasis).

Then in May 1925 the Brooklyn branch appeared on the ad, and these ads (now including the Brooklyn branch) continued through February 1927, when they ceased. I assume a discounted 24-month block-booking was by then over. Thus the Brooklyn branch opened in spring 1925 and was still in existence in early 1927. "John's" first appears in Lovecraft's 1925 diary on 4 May, which both fits with and helps to confirm the opening date. Quite possibly there was a grand Friday, 1 May ("May Day") opening day, something that would be most suitable for an anarchist. Indeed, the *Brooklyn Citizen* carried a small public opening notice on Monday, 4 May 1925. The 1925 diary shows that Lovecraft returned to "John's" to eat on the 6 and 7 May, and frequently thereafter. It became, as he wrote on one of John's cards, "my favorite restaurant."[14] That summer his diet became "prodigiously Italianised," as he put it, but he reassured his aunt in the same letter that this was quite healthy eating, since it gave "an almost ideal balance of active nutritive elements, considering the wheaten base of spaghetti, the abundant vitamines in tomato sauce, the assorted vegetables in minestrone, & the profusion of powdered cheese common to both" (*LFF* 396).

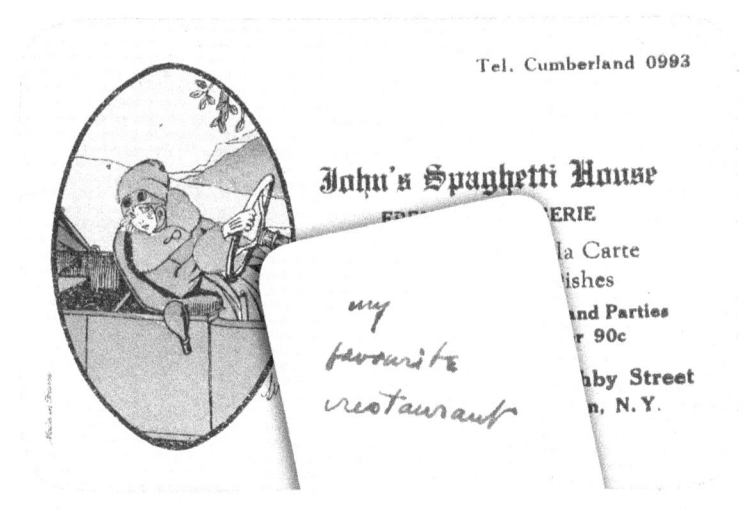

HPL has written "my favourite restaurant" on the back of one of John's invitational cards for parties. The fancy colour invitation card appears to have been aimed at the more upmarket customer and reveals that a private-party "chicken banquet" could be had for a relatively modest 90 cents a head.

Other, cheaper places may have been tried, but John's remained Lovecraft's favorite spaghetti "headquarters," as he later phrased it, when he could afford it. And for good reason. He was undoubtedly getting the best that 1920s Brooklyn could offer, made to recipes perfected in little hill-villages in the south of

---

14. Late in writing the article I found this Brown Digital Repository item: "John's Spaghetti House" at repository.library.brown.edu/studio/item/ bdr:926654/

"the old country." Most likely they were also made with imported Italian tomatoes and cheeses, fresh from the gangster-pilfered dockside. This must have been quite some spaghetti and served in fine surroundings, as I have already established. Lovecraft would afterwards find it difficult to obtain a comparable "New York flavored" spaghetti meal in Providence, though the new tranche of Frank Belknap Long letters reveal that he at least once enjoyed a meal at an authentic spaghetti house in the Italian-dominated Federal Hill district of Providence.[15] He considered the wholly Italian atmosphere there to be *almost* like being back in New York City, as he piled on the Parmesan cheese which he adored: "[I] like Italian cooking very much—especially spaghetti with meat and tomato sauce, utterly engulfed in a snowbank of grated Parmesan cheese" (*A Means to Freedom* 464–65).

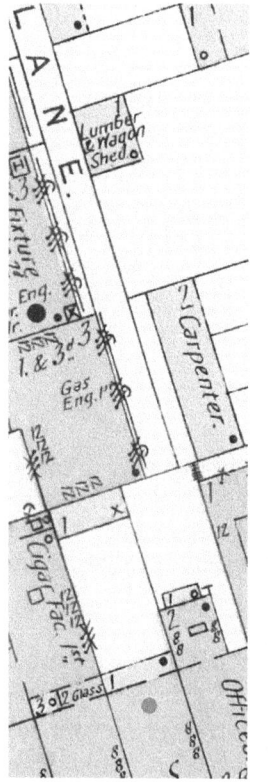

Home Brew?

I also went snooping around the rear of "John's." In Sanborn's 1904 *Brooklyn Atlas.* showing 7 Willoughby Street ("John's") in plan and context, the place had a large isolated yard and sheds out back. The lower large dot shown here marks the rear of "John's." This is possibly of relevance, in terms of its being a suitable site for Prohibition liquor-brewing in the backyard, something which we know went on regularly at the main branch of "John's." I note adjacent sheds and back-alley buildings involved in cigar making, carpet cleaning, and gas engineering. Alcohol fumes from any il-

---

15. This particular letter has been read aloud, in advance of publication, on the *Voluminous* podcast. See the episode "Curious Wonders and Spaghetti," dated 7 March 2022.

legal stills might have been cloaked by such neighboring odors. It seems from the map that there was also a back entrance to the yard, through two gates, for small trucks using the long and undoubtedly insalubrious Union Lane. Admittedly this is just my informed surmise, but it looks to me like a perfect site for Prohibition-era "backyard brewers."

The U.S. prohibition on liquor ended in December 1933, but Lovecraft's "John's" had closed before summer 1931. He states it was "defunct" by July 1931, and it was presumably a victim of the Great Depression: "All three now set out for dinner—at the old Bristol Dining Room in Willoughby Street near Fulton, next door[16] to the now defunct John's, which was my Brooklyn headquarters for spaghetti in the old days" (*LFF* 937).

Did HPL Know John?

Was John Pucciatti—the anarchist who looked like an ancient Roman nobleman but who was actually from the "little medieval village of Bevagna, between Spoleto and Assisi" (Maher)[17]— known to Lovecraft? I don't have all the books of letters, but so far as I know no letter mentions his meeting or conversing with John. Was John ever on the premises? One would expect so, and possibly on a Sunday, when Lovecraft was most likely to be there, as anarchists are not likely to be devout Catholic churchgoers on Sundays. Consider also that I have shown that Lovecraft was in at the opening and was then a frequent patron thereafter. It seems unlikely that John would simply leave the place to look after itself in this vital May–July start-up period. He would probably be around to help the place and the staff to become established. Perhaps the new branch was also a welcome escape from the big-name gangsters who frequented his main

---

16. Why does HPL say in a letter that John's was "next door" to Bristol's, at No. 7, when Bristol's was No. 3? The New York City plot map and a 1914 ad reveals its office address was indeed No. 3. But the dining rooms were classed as Nos. 3–5. HPL was evidently aware of this double-frontage numbering when he later referred to John's as being "next door."

17. Maher interviews Nick Sitnycky, then owner of the still existing John's of 12th Street, Brooklyn. Mr. Sitnycky has researched John's history and family.

place. But unless any Lovecraft letters can show otherwise, we have no evidence that John was sitting down at the table to chat with Lovecraft about political philosophy and utopian dreams of a self-organizing future without governments, nor that Lovecraft engaged in chat with other "radical" or "interesting" customers at "the favorite meeting place of free thinkers of all nationalities."

Could There Have Been an Influence on the Fiction?

What of the fiction? Well, one can suggest a general parallel with the New York story "He" (written August 1925). Readers will recall the line "I'm afeared the squire must have sarved them monstrous bad rum" and "ye swilled yourselves sick [with rum]" (CF 1.515), relating to the spirits of the native Indians of New York who come to take horrible revenge on the central character. 1920s rot-gut Prohibition liquor was not famed for its health-giving properties. In "The Horror at Red Hook" (also written August 1925) there is of course a general furtiveness and evasion of the law behind "the green blinds of secretive windows," even a "primitive chemical laboratory in the attic" and "betraying odours deadened by the sudden kindling of pungent incense" (CF 1.497). Youths sit in "stupefied dozes" in Borough Hall cafés, and Detective Malone makes "well-timed offers of hip-pocket liquor" (CF 1.489) to entice information from his Red Hook street informants. Later in the tale, men's clothes are recalled as having "bulged damnably" (CF 1.496) with many concealed bottles full of horrible liquid (in this case, drained human blood rather than liquor). Young children in Red Hook suffer vile brutality (off camera and implied, I should add) just as the children of many alcoholics do. I suggest there is definitely something in "Red Hook" and "He," albeit ably transformed and sublimated into a deeper horror, of Brooklyn's clandestine "liquor culture" in the Prohibition era.

By that time Prohibition had also enhanced the idea of "the swamp" in the popular mind. Such places were then partly drained but still vast and trackless, prior to the extensive heavy-logging and draining of the mid-1930s work programs. Swamps had become key criminal conduits for running higher-grade liquor and narcotic drugs into the U.S., and it appears that some swamp dwellers had added baby-farming to the list of crimes. All this fed into the imaginative popular culture of the 1920s, as seen in prominent movies such as the major Mary Pickford vehicle and successful "swamp-horror" movie titled *Sparrows* (May 1926).[18] Thus the background of Prohibition is implicit in the vivid swamp "Bacchanal"[19] scene of the cultists in "The Call of Cthulhu," and some of the sharper pulp readers of the period would have recognized this. "Cthulhu" was of course conceived while Lovecraft was in New York City, though not written and polished until later.

The Wider Willoughby Street "Oasis"

My investigation of "John's" has also uncovered more about the general environs. There is a sub-store seen in the 1916 photographs, located below the restaurant frontage. What was in this? Well, by mid-1922 Harry E. Spilbor, Sign Writer, was listed as at No. 7 Willoughby, and one has to assume he had taken the sub-shop that was photographed tatty and empty in 1916. By the mid-1930s the *New York State Manufacturers* directory puts him next door at No. 9. My guess is that he started in the sub-shop at No. 7 at the beginning of the 1920s and then later moved next door when No. 7's original frontage was ripped out and "boxed" in (as seen on some 1930s photos). Spilbor also evidently wrote sign cards for show-windows in stores, something that put him in the same line of business as Lovecraft's New York

---

18. The horror in *Sparrows* is baby-farming and child-slavery in a remote swamp in New Orleans, with a lavish three-acre sound-stage set serving as the stylized Gothic swamp. The Library of Congress's restored version of *Sparrows* is now available on DVD. The timing of its initial release suggests it as a possible inspiration for the swamp scenes in "The Call of Cthulhu."

19. HPL chose the word with care for his all-male "orgy," in the knowledge of what the ancient Roman Bacchanal had usually involved: nocturnal rites, a foreign priest-magician performing "miracles" and tricks and urging debauchery and promiscuity, abandoning of social class and other boundaries, mixing of the old with the very young . . . and plenty of strong wine. For more on this comparison see Quinn.

friend Ernest Dench. Next door to "John's" in 1923 at No. 9 was Mike's Radio Shop (the Kranz Brothers), in either the upstairs section or the sub-shop. It is known that they were still in business in 1925 because they made a payment to the city, though no address is stated alongside the bookkeeper's entry. Barbers do not tend to go out of business unless the owner dies, and my guess would be that the 1916 barber's was still there in 1925 and had Mike's Radio in the sub-shop below. Across the street was a cigar store, possibly a corner sandwich counter, and other stores that the various photographs leave uncertain—perhaps a while-you-wait tailor. At the end of the street the tall *Brooklyn Gazette* building fronted onto and somewhat screened Fulton Street, where there was an adjacent elevated railway station used by Lovecraft and his circle. The station must have been very convenient, just a few steps away in Fulton Street and with one platform serving the "up" and the other the "down" tracks.

Interior of the 1933 art-deco Automat next door to the former "John's." We see the steps up to thpe Fulton St. elevated railway line, through its huge plate-glass windows. Enlarged detail from New York Public Library Collections photo No. 58263927.

All the above fills in a little more mid-1920s detail on the immediate surroundings for one of Lovecraft's favorite Italian eateries. The nearby *Brooklyn Gazette* newspapermen had only to walk the few yards back into Willoughby to enter its large and rather magnificently fronted corner bar at numbers 1–2. Then came the long-standing and highly regarded Bristol's Dining Rooms at 3–5. I have discovered that Lovecraft's New York friend and colleague La Touche Hancock, the professional light versifier and fellow British Empire loyalist, worked from an office above Bristol's. Below we see Hancock advertising at this address in *Student Writer*, which ran his ads from 1922 through 1924.

THE STUDENT WRITER 25

're to be made in this ma-
consider it to be a good
urchase which would in-
es made by your company
hat much more secure?
this slant on the publish-
gan to sell material fre-
e me to throw up a good
ance writer.
ot this slant was by being
eting a lot of editors.
New York, I roomed on
itor of a leading publica-
a young girl who then
uch in writing but whose
rly in *The Saturday Eve-*
ld so on. The most strik-
itor was the fact that he
ad a clear, common-sense,

**STRENGTHEN YOUR WORK
AND INCREASE YOUR SALES**
By Having Me Criticise Your Manuscripts
Fee—Fifty Cents per Thousand Words
Circulars on Request
G. GLENWOOD CLARK
2225 W. Grace Street   Richmond, Virginia

LA TOUCHE HANCOCK
Author and Critic
Thirty years' experience. Revises Mss.
and gives advice as to their disposal. Send
stamp for circular.
5 Willoughby St., Brooklyn.

Mss. Typewritten and Marketed
Manuscripts carefully revised and typed double

His ads also ran in at least one movie magazine of the period. This adds a little to our knowledge of Hancock. We now know that, like Lovecraft, he was also a jobbing revisionist of long standing.[20] It seems to me quite likely that he introduced Lovecraft to Willoughby Street. Sadly, as Lovecraft observed in his letters, Hancock was an alcoholic in his final years and he died in 1926.

---

20. He was also, like HPL, the first to give a robust survey of a popular art form. Hancock was personally familiar with many cartoonists and comic-strip artists of the 1890–1922 period, and his long survey article "The American Comic and Caricature Art," in the *Bookman* for November 1902, proved to be the seminal article on the craft and its craftsmen.

Then came "John's" at No. 7, with Mr. Spilbor the signwriter below in the sub-shop. Next door, No. 9 was probably still a barber shop (as seen in the 1916 photographs shown earlier), with Mike's Radios in the sub-shop below. Beyond that, the new Edison Electric block (Brooklyn Edison Co.) at a single "No. 15." This had subsumed numbers 11–13–15 in 1923/24 and swept away the large vaudeville/cinema called the Royal Theater, formerly Watson's Cozy Corner Theatre (which had been at 11–16 Willoughby and the corner of Pearl).[21]

The overall picture that emerges for the mid-1920s is of a very male environment, even a somewhat writer-friendly "oasis," albeit one that had become a little seedy since its 1900s heyday. This "oasis" additionally benefited from several nearby still-extant theatres, and even one large burlesque dancing-girls venue as seen in a 1928 record picture. All are set sufficiently back from the much busier and noisier Fulton Street and its rattling elevated train line. Apart from the dancing-girls, the corner newspapermen's bar, and the occasional "lady barber," this manly place would have felt comfortable to a writer like Lovecraft.

No. 7 in Later Years

In later years Bristol's Dining Rooms briefly became the "American Book Exchange" (late 1931), but was soon gutted and remodeled as a slick 1930s art-deco Automat. Very good pictures of the interior and exterior survive, and it is just possible that they also show an Automat once patronized by Lovecraft and his circle in the early to mid-1930s. Next door, "John's" had by then become a wine and liquor store. In 1954 the Automat was gutted and remodeled again, and a photo of this process reveals that No. 7 was still standing alongside. Appropriately enough for a place frequented by Lovecraft, the final fate of the former "John's" can be seen in a giant illustrated sign declaring it to be

---

21. Today the bottom of Willoughby Street starts with a cursory and cluttered new "plaza" containing only No. 15, the large former building of the Brooklyn Edison Co. electricity company. The rest, along with the *Citizen* newspaper building and "John's," has been scoured away by a huge multi-lane ground-level highway.

a "Pen Clinic" for the repair and adjustment of ink fountain-pens. Readers will of course recall Lovecraft's fastidious attention to his pens, both in their purchase and in the fine adjustments of their ink feeds and nibs.

In another curious link with Lovecraft, from circa 1961 there was a Binkin's Book Center bookshop a little way along at 54 Willoughby Street. This was the home and store of the eccentric used bookseller Isei ("Irving") Binkin, who purchased, and thus saved for posterity, the significant Jack Grill collection of Lovecraft material. On seeing photos of the distinctive Mr. Lovecraft, Binkin recalled him browsing in his old bookstore, which had been just around the corner at 252 Fulton Street (est. 1932). That would have been after the "John's" period, but it is not impossible that Lovecraft returned to this small area in the early 1930s; in fact, we know he did because his letters tell us he dined at Bristol's in July 1931. His friend Frank Belknap Long was also fond of browsing the used book and curiosity shops of the Brooklyn side of Fulton Street, giving another reason for Lovecraft to return there circa 1932–35. Binkin by all accounts feared book thieves, and thus interrogated and kept a close eye on his clientele. All this suggests that he may not have been mistaken in his faint memory of Lovecraft.

Lovecraft and the Bootleggers

Lovecraft appears to have read deeply in anti-liquor tracts in his youth and early manhood.[22] He certainly knew about the battles that Poe, his idol, had with liquor. In New York he witnessed first-hand the pitiful liquor debauches of the then-emerging poet Hart Crane. He later learned much about the ways of the bootleggers and gangsters over the years, and partly did so from his correspondents. Some of these, such as Andrew Lockhart and the proto-communist Woodburn Harris, were firebrand anti-liquor campaigners of the most ardent sort. Robert E. Howard also had much experience among the hard-drinking men of the Texas oil towns, and interestingly in a 1932 letter to Howard,

---

22. For a substantial survey of his probable early influences, see Pedersen.

Lovecraft links liquor and biological devolution: "the more drink sodden they get, the worse their biological stock becomes" (*A Means to Freedom* 365).[23] Some key correspondents such as E. Hoffmann Price were no strangers to alcohol. But even as early as his "Old Bugs" (written c. July 1919) Lovecraft implied he had knowledge of the trade's ethnically Irish aspect in Chicago in 1950 (the future setting of the tale), presumably gleaned from a correspondent (since he never read the "police reports" sec-

---

23. The possibility of human devolution—remember that this was prior to the scientific understanding of genetics and the laws of inheritance—was then common on both the political left and right, and it had been widely used in science fiction classics ranging from Wells's *The Time Machine* (1895) to Stapledon's *Last and First Men* (1930). However, these fictional uses were over vast time scales, and thus they differ from HPL's uses of the idea. HPL, by then strongly under the then-respectable influence of the ethnographer and historian Margaret Murray regarding the "witch-cult," appears to have believed that family degeneration and alcoholism—and consequent feeble-mindedness—was one of the prerequisites for the development of forms of superstitious "Devil-worship" in an isolated region. In the wider context many in America believed "three generations is enough," a common point made about degenerate families, positing the outright danger of failing to prevent the "fourth generation" of devolution. The believed sequence ran: nervous temperament and moral laxness in the first generation; then their children with severe neurotic behavior leading to addictions such as alcoholism; leading in the third generation to insanity and suicide; then a fourth generation with outright cretinism, also often sterile or with malformed bodies and heads. HPL's "The Lurking Fear" goes beyond the then-existing research in that he portrays constant violent weather in an isolated landscape as the key trigger that starts the degeneration of a lone family. But note that the process of the lightning-and-thunder-provoked degeneration of this family thus took exactly 140 years (1670–1810). The Bible states that 140 years is the requisite time for four generations: "lived Job an hundred and forty years, and saw his sons, and his sons' sons, even four generations" (Job 42:16, KJV). HPL thus seems to be implicitly nodding to the "fourth generation" framework, which was often promoted as part of a philanthropic Christian worldview. Of course, in later tales such as "The Shadow over Innsmouth" HPL adds cross-breeding with fish-monsters to geographical isolation, a plot mechanism that ensures a horrific ongoing (and even world-threateningly fecund) fertility of the degenerate and cross-bred stock, who would otherwise become infertile within the real-world "fourth generation" framework.

tion in the newspapers). In "Old Bugs" he stated that "Sheehan's is the acknowledged centre to Chicago's subterranean traffic in liquor and narcotics" (CF 1.88).

Liquor often finds its way into his fiction in small ways. In "Beyond the Wall of Sleep," a "whiskey debauch" (CF 1.73) is the trigger for an alien entity to try to possess the body of the degenerate Joe Slater. Several revision tales also mention whiskey debauches. In *The Case of Charles Dexter Ward* we learn of the hijacking of clandestine "liquor shipments" (CF 2.303–04). In "The Shadow over Innsmouth" the narrator procures some under-the-counter bootleg liquor to lubricate the tongue of old Zadock Allen. Alcohol is featured in "The Quest of Iranon," with the pivotal tragedy being how "Romnod who had been a small boy in granite Teloth grew coarser and redder with wine" (CF 1.253). In *The Dream-Quest of Unknown Kadath* some of the exotic wines of the Dreamlands appear unimaginably potent for a visitor, as when our hero Carter takes "only the least sip [of wine, and], he felt the dizziness of space and the fever of unimagined jungles" (CF 2.111). In "The Dunwich Horror," the final monster is deemed a product of backwoods whiskey by snide journalists, evidenced by "a facetious little item from the Associated Press, telling what a record-breaking monster the bootleg whiskey of Dunwich had raised up" (CF 2.453).

As he grew older Lovecraft learned about bootlegging gangsters closer to home. Shortly after he returned from New York he explored more of the Italian quarter on Federal Hill (*Letters to Wilfred B. Talman* 31) and thus he apparently knew where it might be possible to obtain "hootch" in his own city of Providence. He once joked that he might acquire a local case of bootleg whiskey to ship to *Weird Tales* editor Farnsworth Wright (to help steady the famous editor's physical jitters, induced by his Parkinson's disease): "I feel tempted to unearth a local bootlegger [and know where, since] Providence's Italian quarter is a miniature Chicago of hootch, gang wars, and rackets!" (*Essential Solitude* 158).

This was indeed the state of affairs in Federal Hill under the Morelli gang, which had been allowed to become established there from 1917 (see Luconi).[24] Prohibition was said to be very unpopular in Providence, and it seems likely some blind eyes were turned. That was one of the problems of Prohibition: it tended to bring the interest of gangsters and politicians into an uneasy alignment, and the gangsters then had the cash and blackmail scams with which to entrap the politicians.

Lovecraft had not always been so light-hearted about the matter. After a Providence night-walk in an insalubrious section in October 1916, having there encountered an evening open-air speech given from an open car by a member of the anti-liquor Prohibition Party, HPL wrote of liquor:

> And even in the open air the stench of whiskey was appalling. To this fiendish poison, I am certain, the greater part of the squalor I saw is due. [. . .] I counted at least five American countenances in which a certain vanished decency half showed through the red whiskey bloating. [. . .] It is the deadliest enemy with which humanity is faced. Not all the European wars could produce a tenth of the havock occasioned among men by the wretched fluid which responsible governments allow to be sold openly. [. . .] I am perhaps an extremist on the subject of prohibition, but I can see no justification whatsoever for the tolerance of such a degrading demon as drink. (*Miscellaneous Letters* 26–27)

"Demon" was then a commonplace Christian motif to describe intoxicating drink. But even in the earliest issues of Lovecraft's *Conservative*, one finds a "monstering" of liquor that goes further and almost seems to foreshadow his later fiction. He talks of "the Hydra-monster Rum" (CE 1.51) and of the "unspeakable evil" and "horrors [that] are utterly beyond the realisation of the sheltered [ladies of Boston]" (CE 5.20). His poem "The Power of Wine" (1915) imagines the latter stages of a drinking party and the "nameless things that fill thy shadow'd room" at that

---

24. Morelli was a New York gangster who moved to Providence to establish his own gang and rackets among the Italian immigrants. At least two early attempts at novels featuring an imaginary HPL have him entangled with the Morelli gang on Federal Hill.

point, which turn out to be ghouls with "black wings" (AT 213). His slightly later poem "Monody on the Late King Alcohol" (1919) imagines alcohol as a dead god-king being mourned by misguided or evil acolytes.

Yet by 1928, after he had recovered from trying to live in New York City, Lovecraft was more sanguine about the practicalities of legal prohibition:

> to a cynical soul [there comes] the question of whether or not the law is worth the trouble of enforcing. [. . .] This I am beginning to doubt. In 1919 I was a whole-hearted prohibitionist, but in 1928 I am more or less of a neutral [on the question of] legalised liquor versus futile and troublesome prohibition [. . .] It is an aesthetic matter with me. I think drink is ugly, and therefore I have nothing to do with it. [. . .] my own aesthetic theory cannot help carrying it onward to the ideal of total extinction. Let the graces of wine live in literature. (*Letters to Woodburn Harris* 357–58)

By 1930, writing to Morton, Lovecraft even seems to admit that literature can for some be a viable alternative to liquor. He states that "hootch" is one of three "refuges" for a man who finds life to be a "losing game" of pain and loss:

> there's so goddam much **more** pain than pleasure in any average human life, that it's a losing game unless a guy can pep it up with pure moonshine—either the literal 95-proof pink-snake-evoker [i.e., hard liquor, liable to evoke monstrous visions in the *delirium tremens* stage], or the churchly hootch of belief in immortality and a benign old gentleman with long whiskers [i.e., God] . . . or else the Dunsanian conjuration of an illusion of *fantastick & indefinite possibility* [. . .] (*Letters to James F. Morton* 226)

He goes on to call the first option "highly unaesthetic in practice and degrading in symbolism." Yet his strong reaction to it surely means that something of the *horror* of hard liquor lives on—albeit sublimated within Lovecraft's unique horrors—in his own strongly symbolic literature. Does his love of spaghetti live on in the same way? Perhaps. I, for one, will never look at the dangling mouth-tentacles of Cthulhu in quite the same way again.

Works Cited

Bencivenni, Marcella. "Culture and Leisure among the Early Twentieth-century American Left." In Simone Cinotto, ed. *Making Italian America: Consumer Culture and the Production of Ethnic Identities*. New York: Fordham University Press, 2014.

———. "Fired by the Ideal: Italian Anarchists in New York City, 1880s–1920s." In *Radical Gotham: Anarchism in New York City*. Urbana: University of Illinois Press, 2017.

Diamond, Bob. *The World's Oldest Subway: The Atlantic Avenue Tunnel*. N.p.: Lulu.com, 2015.

Donati, William. *Lucky Luciano: The Rise and Fall of a Mob Boss*. Jefferson, NC: McFarland, 2020.

Dunlap, David W. "Old York" (newspaper column). *New York Times* (10 December 2000).

H. P. Lovecraft Historical Society. *Voluminous* audio podcast, "Curious Wonders and Spaghetti." Episode dated 7 March 2022.

Haden, David. "Reds in New York: An Aspect of Lovecraft's New York Circle in the 1930s." In Haden's *Lovecraft in Historical Context: A Fifth collection*. N.p.: Lulu.com, 2014.

Hart, Mara Kirk, and S. T. Joshi, ed. *Lovecraft's New York Circle: The Kalem Club, 1924–1927*. New York: Hippocampus Press, 2007.

Lovecraft, H. P. *Essential Solitude: The Letters of H. P. Lovecraft and August Derleth*. Ed. David E. Schultz and S. T. Joshi. New York: Hippocampus Press, 2008. 2 vols.

———. Inscription on "John's Spaghetti House" promotional card. Online at the Brown University Repository at repository.library.brown.edu/studio/item/bdr:926654/

———. *Letters to Elizabeth Toldridge and Anne Tillery Renshaw*. Ed. David E. Schultz and S. T. Joshi. New York: Hippocampus Press, 2014.

———. *Letters to Family and Family Friends*. Ed. S. T. Joshi and David E. Schultz. New York: Hippocampus Press, 2020. 2 vols. [Abbreviated in the text as *LFF*.]

———. *Letters to James F. Morton*. Ed. David E. Schultz and S. T. Joshi. New York: Hippocampus Press, 2011.

———. *Letters to Maurice W. Moe and Others*. Ed. David E. Schultz and S. T. Joshi. New York: Hippocampus Press, 2018.

———. *Letters to Wilfred B. Talman and Helen V. and Genevieve Sully*. Ed. David E. Schultz and S. T. Joshi. New York: Hippocampus Press, 2019.

———. *Letters to Woodburn Harris and Others*. Ed. S. T. Joshi and David E. Schultz. New York: Hippocampus Press, 2022.

———. *A Means to Freedom: The Letters of H. P. Lovecraft and Robert E. Howard*. Ed. S. T. Joshi, David E. Schultz, and Rusty Burke. New York: Hippocampus Press, 2009. 2 vols.

———. *Miscellaneous Letters*. Ed. David E. Schultz and S. T. Joshi. New York: Hippocampus Press, 2022.

Levine, Lucie. "Travel Back to the Roaring Twenties." *6Sqft* blog, 27th January 2020.

Library of Congress and the Mary Pickford Foundation. *Sparrows: 4k Restoration*. Washington, DC: Library of Congress, 2021. 2-disc Blu-Ray/DVD set.

Loveman, Samuel. "Of Gold & Sawdust." In Anthony Raven, ed. *The Occult Lovecraft*. Saddle River, NJ: Gerry de la Ree, 1975.

Luconi, Stefano. *The Italian-American Vote in Providence, Rhode Island, 1916–1948*. Rutherford, NJ: Fairleigh Dickinson University Press, 2004.

Maher, James. "Out and about in the East Village" (magazine column). *East Village Grieve* (18 December 2013).

New York City Transit Museum. Subway Construction Photograph Collection, 1900–1950.

New York Crime Commission. *A Study of Delinquency in a District of Kings County by the Sub-Commission on Causes and Effects of Crime*. New York: J. B. Co., 1927.

Pedersen, Jan. "'Now Will You Be Good?': Lovecraft, Teetotalism, and Philosophy." *Lovecraft Annual* No. 13 (2019): 119–44.

Quinn, Dennis. "Endless Bacchanal: Rome, Livy, and Lovecraft's Cthulhu Cult." *Lovecraft Annual* No. 5 (2011): 189–215.

Sanborn, Daniel Alfred. *Sanborn's Brooklyn Atlas*. New York: Sanborn Map Co., 1904.

I May Be the Next: Fear of the Queer in "The Thing on the Doorstep" by H. P. Lovecraft

Holly Eva Allen

At the very opening of H. P. Lovecraft's "The Thing on the Doorstep," the reader is presented with a narrator whose journey has already ended, whose self-appointed harrowing and task, the banishment of evil, has already concluded. Our character, Daniel Upton, claims that he has "purged the earth of a horror whose survival might have loosed untold terrors on all mankind" (CF 3.325). While death and destruction are some of the immediate terrors that might come to mind for the curious reader, Lovecraft continues with threatening ambiguities as Daniel assures us that "there are black zones of shadow close to our daily paths, and now and then some evil soul breaks a passage through. When that happens, the man who knows must strike before reckoning the consequences" (CF 3.325). Just what abominable horror requires immediate action with no cause for careful consideration? What threat is so unnamable that our narrator feels the need to stall the narrative with amorphous remonstrations? While the neophytic reader might attribute this to the indescribable quality of eldritch beings often depicted in such cosmic horror pieces, the indescribable aspect here is not so apparent. In fact, the so-called horror of this piece is best unpacked by applying queer theory. What is supposedly indescribable here is that which does not clearly abide by the gender binary.

Queer analysis of H. P. Lovecraft's work is not an endeavor that sparks enthusiasm in the majority of Lovecraft scholars. In fact, many of the academics who write on Lovecraft with some degree of regularity have railed against such practices ad nauseam. For many of these scholars, sex, gender, and associated topics are simply nonexistent in Lovecraft's original text and the discussion of such topics is, therefore, little more than a chimeric endeavor. In *H. P. Lovecraft: Against the World, Against Life*, for example, Michel Houellebecq writes that "certain critics have concluded that his entire body of work is in fact full of particularly smoldering sex symbols. Other individuals of a similar intellectual caliber have proffered the diagnosis of "latent homosexuality. Which is supported by nothing in either his correspondence or his life. Yet another useless hypothesis" (57–58). This unyielding philosophy of biographical criticism allows Houellebecq to reject the application of any theory or episteme that is not directly referenced by the author, essentially putting good literary analysis and close reading of the original stories to waste. Perhaps more appalling still is the fact that Houellebecq is demonstrating that he knows nothing of queer theory.

This lack of comprehension is unsurprising. The more nuanced definition of queerness as proposed in many iterations of queer theory is not commonly understood nor employed by theorists of other specialties. In the heterosexual, cisgendered vernacular, the term queer is almost exclusively applied to sexuality. More exactly, it is applied to those sexualities thought to be abnormal as they deviate from the strict heterosexual norms enforced by dominant patriarchal systems. Such an employment of this narrowly defined queerness is undoubtedly one of the reasons that certain writers, such as Houellebecq, find a queer analysis of Lovecraft's work wholly untenable. Instead, one ought to use the broader application of "queerness" that includes all iterations of sexuality and gender expression that go against societal ideals. While queer theory scholars have interchangeably employed terms such as gay, inverted, homosexual, gender nonconforming, and more, "queer" is perhaps the most flexible of these and is, after all, applied to the field of queer theory as a whole. As Karl Whittington notes in his article "Queer," a piece that covers the term in detail, "queer's ambiguity is built into its dictionary definition" (157). Proper application of this particular denotation of queerness and use of adequately nuanced queer theory unearths a new kind of horror present in "The Thing on the Doorstep": the fear of the queer.

Briefly, it should be mentioned that the fear of the queer written into the "The Thing on the Doorstep" does not contradict biographical information nor first-hand material put down by Lovecraft, such as his oft-cited letters. Part of the aforementioned aversion to an application of queer theory in Lovecraft's work, as demonstrated by the previously proffered Houellebecq quotation, is due not only to a misunderstanding of queer theory but also to an assumption about the aim of such theoretical employments. As Dylan Henderson notes in his recent article, "The Disgusting Thing on the Doorstep," "a number of scholars" suspect and have suspected "that Lovecraft either repressed or hid his homosexuality" (16). As Henderson's article further details and as other scholars such as S. T. Joshi have previously noted, it might be more appropriate to say that Lovecraft's aversion to eroticism and his dislike for overly romantic behavior and aesthetics might place him somewhere under the umbrella of asexuality.

While asexuality is and has been placed squarely in the greater queer community for decades, the aim of this article is not to muddy the water by sorting through Lovecraft's letters and connecting material therein with the story at hand in an attempt to make a biographical statement about his sexuality. Rather, our aim is to apply queer theory and associated literary concepts to "The Thing on the Doorstep" in order to demonstrate that the fear of queerness and confused gender roles are certainly at work in the text. It is worth noting that although the aim of this article is not biographical in nature, the fear of queerness that will be evinced in the following pages is not incongruous with the disgust Lovecraft held for all things sexual—a subject I would direct readers search for in the aforementioned article by Dylan Henderson, as it is both astute and comprehensive in that regard.

Now that the biographical issue has been addressed, it may be beneficial to break down the aforementioned ineffectual definition of queerness as it identifies binaries and conceptions that will play a major contextual role when covering our story. The common Western taxonomy of queerness-as-sexual-abnormality applies two opposing theories of sexual orientation and ways of being. One of these theories, commonly referred to as the theory of inversion, posits that a homosexual man is merely the body of a man piloted by the soul of a heterosexual woman. Similarly, this same concept posits that a lesbian woman is only a woman physically and that the female body in question is inhabited by the soul of a heterosexual man. Celebrated queer theorist Eve Kosofsky Sedgwick further elaborates on the theory of inversion by noting that "while these attributions of 'true' 'inner' heterogender may be made to stick, in a haphazard way, so long as dyads of people are all that are in question, the broadening of view to include any larger circuit of desire must necessarily reduce the inversion or liminality trope to a choreography of breathless farce" (87). In other words, if observably homosexual men and lesbian women were the only queer orientations to address, then such a concept might be passable. However, the theory of inversion does nothing to address or explain cases of bisexuality, asexuality, and other non-monosexual identifiers short of dismissing them entirely. This is, of course, to say nothing of the particularly reductive way this theory lumps homosexual and transgender individuals into a singular, imprecise group. One might also question the implied import of the human soul present at the omphalos of this theory without accompanying epistemological justification.

Despite the fact that this first theory is littered with logical fallacies, it is likely to sound appealing to Lovecraft scholars hoping to analyze "The Thing on the Doorstep." After all, the story itself, on a surface level, seems to follow a man, Edward Derby, whose wife, Asenath, had her mind forced out of her body by her father, Ephraim Waite. In the simplest of terms, this seems to be the body of a woman possessed by the spirit or mind of a man. However, this interpretation is far too simple to function in practice. The fact that Asenath is married to a man complicates the matter, as the reader is never told whether or not Asenath and Edward consummate their marriage. In other words, the reader cannot be assured that the theory of inversion is applicable in "The Thing on the Doorstep," as Ephraim's sexuality is unknown and the only indication that the reader has is the fact that he fathered Asenath. That is to say that we know that Ephraim has had sex with a woman in the past in order to procreate, but we have no indication that Asenath's body, while possessed by Ephraim, did not have intercourse with Edward at some point in time.

It is worth mentioning that the reader's lack of knowledge as to the sexual goings-on of Asenath/Ephraim and Edward Derby shows a lack of what Foucault identifies as the confession. For Foucault, confessing one's sexual activity or desire is of utmost importance in cultures with a focus on the Christian theme of penance. Such sexual confessions connect the confessor to the ideal of truth and, by extension, forgiveness (Foucault 61). The absence of this ritual confession in the original text further queers the characters from normative sexual and sexually adjacent practices.

What's more, even if the reader assumes that this lack of confession implies that Asenath/Ephraim managed to lead Edward along without consummating their marriage, the reality of the situation is not as simple as Ephraim-possessing-Asenath. In his book *H. P. Lovecraft's Dark Arcadia*, Gavin Callaghan notes the myriad identities represented by Asenath/Ephraim. He writes: "after his honeymoon . . . Derby looks 'slightly changed,' wearing what Lovecraft calls 'a look of almost genuine sadness,' presumably due to the revelation of Asenath's true identity as wife, father, and mother, all in one" (74). In other words, Asenath/Ephraim might represent multiple gendered aspects or ways of being simultaneously. Asenath/Ephraim's female body ensures their social experience is a subjugated, feminine-coded one excluding those moments when Edward Derby is possessed by the mind of Ephraim. During such scenes, one must recognize that our characters are still subverting assigned social roles and gender norms as Ephraim's possession of Derby places a dominant father-in-law in the body of the submissive son-in-law, creating an uncomfortable allusion to abuse-of-power dynamics and probable rape. At the same time, such a mind-swap, if this term may be used, places Derby in the body of Asenath, in which case the reader still finds that the mind or consciousness of a man has now inhabited a body coded as female.

So the theory of inversion is one rife with assumption, both in overall premise and especially in application to the text at hand. The second of these two theories, that of pure gender separatism, is just as problematic. This theory relies on an absolute interpretation of the gender binary in both biology and cultural experience, presenting the idea that both lesbians and homosexual men are drawn together by commonalities. As Sedgwick explains, "Under this latter view, far from its being of the most essence of desire to cross boundaries of gender, it is instead the most natural thing in the world that people of the same gender . . . should bond together also on the axis of sexual desire" (87). It does not take a particularly astute reader to notice that this theory seems to shirk the responsibility of explaining how heterosexual partners are attracted to one another as their experiences are, by the very logic of the theory itself, very dissimilar and, therefore, not likely to encourage romantic partnering. Furthermore, the theory is not necessarily applicable to intersex individuals, nor does it readily adapt to explain possible queer relationships between same-gendered individuals of different social classes. Aside from the fact that this theory also oversimplifies the many iterations of both sexuality and gender, it also has no discernible application in analyzing our text. As the reader cannot claim that the sexual orientation of any of the characters is known with certainty, such a theory would not reliably expose the latent queerness present in "The Thing on the Doorstep." Rather, we must turn to the more intricate and all-encompassing concept of queerness regularly used by queer theory scholars.

Perhaps one of the earliest and most celebrated texts to present a useful view of queerness is *Homosexual Desire* by Guy Hocquenghem. In it, the author contends that queerness, even represented simply as "homosexuality," is more varied than most people understand, as it "expresses something—some aspect of desire—which appears nowhere else, and that something is not merely the accomplishment of the sexual act with a person of the same sex" (50). In support of this powerfully varied applicability of homosexuality or queerness, one might consider that homosexuality is not the only abnormal expression of desire, longing, or ways of being of which cis-hetero society is wary. As Hocquenghem implies in the previously provided quotation, homosexuality is often an umbrella idea, under which paranoid members of heterosexual hegemonic structures might place homoeroticism, homosocial interactions, and traits or mannerisms that might be deemed overly androgynous or suspicious for going against the expectations associated with the gender one was assigned at birth.

The overeager paranoia concerning the appearance of such queer ways of being is examined at length by Hocquenghem. In queer theory as he presents it, "neurosis consists first of all in the impossibility of knowing . . . whether one is male or female, parent or child. And hysteria, too, is the impossibility of knowing whether one is male or female" (101). Here we find three puissant applications to "The Thing on the Doorstep." First is the fear of the unknown. Such fear is one of the most frequently covered in the entire body of Lovecraft's work. The terror of that which is beyond human comprehension is central to cosmic horror as an entire genre, astronomical themes and eldritch or extraterrestrial beings functioning as embodiments of the incomprehensible itself.

With regard to "The Thing on the Doorstep," one finds that the idea of how Ephraim managed to possess his daughter is incomprehensible. From a moral and psychological standpoint, one might claim that it is "incomprehensible" that a father might do such a thing to his own daughter. However, there is also the literal interpretation. Edward Derby is not intimately familiar with the magic used by Asenath/Ephraim to possess others. Edward is not able to perform this magic despite all his familiarity with the occult, as his magical ability is apparently limited to minor defensive rituals that merely deter Asenath/Ephraim for a short time. In this way, Asenath/Ephraim is incomprehensible in the sense that the magic or practice of possession Ephraim has mastered and used on his daughter is, for most of our characters, unlearnable. Concurrently, the presence and telepathic ability of Asenath is unknowable, as the regularity with which Ephraim possesses his daughter is not discernible. Although the reader is told that Asenath's schoolmates of her youth feared her due to her power of possession, it is not necessarily clear if this was because young Asenath employed a skill she inherited from her father or if such occurrences were early appearances of Asenath/Ephraim. This indicates that Asenath/Ephraim is not only a symbol for the horror of the incomprehensible, he/she/it is a manifestation of blurred lines between father and daughter, woman and man, as they cannot always be distinctly defined as one or the other.

So the fear of the unknown, the "impossibility of knowing," as Hocquenghem writes (101), that Lovecraft plays upon in "The Thing on the Doorstep" leads us into the second application of the previously proffered piece of queer theory. This second application involves the aforementioned blurred lines between Asenath and Ephraim or "the impossibility of knowing whether one is male or female" (Hocquenghem 101). In a patriarchal culture that values the supposed strength, wisdom, and ability of men while simultaneously emphasizing the fragility of women, delineation between women and men is necessary. Asenath/Ephraim clearly defies such obvious demarcation.

Some Lovecraft scholars overlook the blurring of these lines entirely, believing that issues of gender and queerness are not covered in the text due to the focus on telepathy. In his annotations on "The Thing on the Doorstep," Peter Cannon dismissively writes that "Lovecraft leaves unexplored the whole issue of gender-switching implicit in the mind-exchange premise" (*More Annotated Lovecraft* 249). Despite these oversimplifications, allusions to blurred gender are made throughout the text. For example, the queering of gender and identity spreads from Asenath/Ephraim to Edward just as cis-hetero patriarchal structures might posit in their paranoid treatment of the queer as contagion. One particularly notable example of such blurring is mentioned in regard to gender performativity and the perception of the spectator or listener: "But the oddest rumors were about the sobbing in the old Crowninshield house. The voice seemed to be a woman's, and some of the younger people thought it sounded like Asenath's ... And then someone complicated matters by whispering that the sobs had once or twice been in a man's voice" (CF 3.344). The fact that a man, in this case Edward, who is supposed to be emotionally resilient might sob as a woman does raises questions concerning Edward's character. Is possessing the body of his wife feminizing him? Or is his innately submissive and shy nature easily identified as feminine with a meager shift in tone of voice? In the previous case, the confines of a feminine form affecting the mind or soul of an individual alert the reader to the possibility of the nonbinary or gender-fluid mind—that is, that the consciousness of the individual is genderless and therefore performing to meet the social perceptions and expectations that put pressure on them based on the perceived gender of the body that they inhabit. The latter option presents us with the fact that Lovecraft has constructed Edward as a character who is not traditionally masculine from the start of the text.

While the blurring of man and woman, husband and wife, and, one might even say, father-in-law and son-in-law, is certainly a notable example of such blurred lines, the case of obfuscation that demands the greatest attention is that which results in what has up to this point been referenced as Asenath/Ephraim. While some readers of Lovecraft might refer to the blurred character in question as Ephraim, equating individual and identity to the mind alone, retaining the Asenath aspect in naming Asenath/Ephraim is of the utmost importance. First, as previously noted, one explanation of Edward's hopeless sobbing when forced into the body of Asenath is that the body itself is feminizing his character. Such an explanation indicates Lovecraft is presenting the argument that a body is inherently gendered, taking on certain mannerisms due to an unseen natural force imposed by the physical form itself. If that is the case, then Ephraim's consciousness or mind may be undergoing a process of feminization merely by inhabiting his daughter's body.

Even if the reader does not subscribe to this interpretation of the text, favoring instead the idea that Edward has been at least moderately feminine from the onset of the story, an active feminine presence in the text can be confirmed by observing the language Lovecraft employs. Throughout "The Thing on the Doorstep," even after the narrative has revealed that Asenath is actually Asenath/Ephraim, Lovecraft uses the feminine pronouns, she/her. Take, for example, the following excerpt of the text: "The worst thing was that she was holding on to him longer and longer at a time. She wanted to be a man—to be fully human—that was why she got hold of him. She had sensed the mixture of fine-wrought brain and weak will in him" (CF 3.339). A reader might be tempted to think of this entity as Ephraim alone, considering that the association with humanity and manhood and, therefore, the dehumanization of the feminine form is something that might be attributed to his character. So one might assume that Ephraim is looking to return to a body assigned the gender that he himself associated with throughout the course of his own life. However, this does not explain why the narration continues to employ feminine pronouns despite the revelation of Ephraim's involvement having already passed. The use of feminine pronouns, along with the urgency and desperation with which Ephraim seeks to take control of Edward's body in the previously provided lines, indicate that Ephraim may fear that Asenath's body is somehow affecting him, that some feminine aspect still remains just as the use of the feminine pronoun remains. The story itself is indicating that a body coded as female has some invasive feminizing effect on the consciousness possessing it.

This idea that a body, particularly one coded as female, might have some villainous hold on Ephraim indicates a subtle and continuous queering of Ephraim's consciousness. It also impresses on the reader a moral commentary regarding Ephraim's method of supposed immortality. Consider the fact that "There are Christian and Cartesian precedents . . . which . . . understand 'the body' as so much inert matter, signifying nothing or, more specifically, signifying a profane void, the fallen state: deception, sin, the premonitional metaphorics of hell the eternal feminine" (Butler 176). As Judith Butler succinctly puts it, the restrictive tie to Earth, to the material plane, that the physical form places on the human soul is often coded as feminine. Ephraim desires to be free from the social constraints and feminizing force of his daughter's body by possessing Edward. In this way, Asenath's body itself might be seen as a prison, a kind of punishment that calls back to such discussions of the material and the body versus the spiritual and the soul. The fatal flaw in Ephraim's plan, particularly from the perspective of a Western mind surrounded by Christian influences, is that his interpretation of immortality ties him to the material world. He is, therefore, denying the Christian God, the messiah, and other spiritual forces that are almost exclusively coded as masculine and ascribing importance on life in the material world.

The inherent queerness of Asenath/Ephraim can be explored with the assistance of writers within the discipline of queer theory, as we have now seen with Butler, and even by those whose work is frequently criticized by these queer scholars. One might, for example, look to the work of Jacques Lacan. Lacan's *Feminine Sexuality* discusses gendered interactions between men and women at great length and specifically breaks down the function of the feminine role in heterosexual interactions by emphasizing that "in order to be the phallus . . . woman will reject an essential part of her femininity . . . But she finds the signifier of her own desire in the body of the one to whom she addresses her demand for love" (84). By applying Lacan's theory of woman performing the phallus to embody this signifier of desire, we find that Ephraim is not only possessing the body of a woman, he is quite literally embodying the function of the feminine. Ephraim has taken over the body of his daughter and yet he desperately yearns to possess the body of a man, Asenath/Ephraim's husband. He is thereby functioning as a literal interpretation of Lacan's feminine desire to both be and possess the phallus.

Yet applying Irigaray's critique of Lacan's *Feminine Sexuality* functions just as smoothly in exploring how Ephraim, by way of becoming a part of Asenath/Ephraim, has queered himself. Irigaray remarks that "we might suspect the phallus (Phallus) of being the contemporary figure of a god jealous of his prerogatives . . . the signifier and/or the ultimate signified of all desire, in addition to continuing, as emblem and agent of the patriarchal system, to shore up the name of the father (Father)" (67). Such a description certainly seems to suit Ephraim at first glance due to his obsession with moving on to a male-coded body and his dismissal of the capabilities of Asenath's body. Both of these indicate that Ephraim is phallus-obsessed and self-obsessed, two qualities depicted in Irigaray's previous quotation. Yet one ought to note that Irigaray's play on the word father, indicating both the patriarch and the Christian God, demonstrates the two things that Ephraim is not. Ephraim's search for immortality and zealous use of the arcane indicate a desire for godhood. Additionally, at the very start of the text he is introduced as the father of note in the narrative. Yet Ephraim's desire to live forever is thwarted by the end of our story. Furthermore, Ephraim's possession of Asenath's body resulted in her death. One might assume that a father who once had a child, a father whose daughter is dead, is still a father by some definition. Even in such a case, the fact that Ephraim's mind now inhabits a female-coded body conjures a plethora of questions concerning the validity of such a claim. Would one still refer to Ephraim as a father despite possessing the body of a woman? Has the aforementioned feminine materiality of being tied to the mortal plane feminized Ephraim to the point where he might no longer be seen as a father or god? The self-perpetuating hypocrisy of Ephraim's desires and actions, with Irigaray's theoretical analysis of Lacan in mind, indicates that Asenath/Ephraim cannot possibly embody the narcissistic, patriarchal conception of the phallus despite every indication that he might perfectly fit such an ideal. In looking to become a man with godlike ability, Ephraim has become Asenath/Ephraim and therefore irrevocably distanced and queered himself from both manhood and godhood.

While a plethora of varied theories might be applied to the text to demonstrate how Ephraim, in being Asenath/Ephraim, has queered himself, there are perhaps a few meager lines that the doubtful scholar might turn to in an attempt to argue feebly against the validity of such readings. One might, for example, search the text for all pronoun usage. The narrative certainly plays on this hypocrisy by primarily employing feminine pronouns in reference to Asenath/Ephraim, as previously covered. However, a scholar averse to queer analysis of Lovecraft's work might point out that there are, in fact, a few moments in the text when Lovecraft employs other pronouns in reference to Asenath/Ephraim. Perhaps the most notable of these is found late in the text in a portion of Edward Derby's dialogue that reads: "My body'd have been hers for good . . . She'd have been a man, and fully human, just as she wanted to be . . . I suppose she'd have put me out of the way—killed her own ex-body with me in it, damn her, *just as she did before*—just as she, he, or it did before" (CF 3.347). Scholars who are loath to agree that a queerness is present in "The Thing on the Doorstep" may draw attention to the use of the masculine pronoun here, completely ignoring the use of the objectifying and dehumanizing pronoun "it." By employing all three pronouns and ending with that which removes obvious gendering altogether, the text acknowledges that applying a single gendered identifier to Asenath/Ephraim is not appropriate. Instead, Edward's eventual use of the pronoun "it" likens the queer body to an inexplicable thing or object. Referring to Asenath/Ephraim as a thing is a striking sign of homophobic sociolinguistic practices to those queer theorists who recognize the cis-heteronormative dehumanizing practice of referring to androgynous or atypically gendered individuals in terms like "thing" or "it." The very use of a pronoun typically attributed to non-human objects does more than call the reader's attention to the uncertainty of gender, however. It calls attention to the uncertainty of two additional qualities—identity and perception.

Identity has already been discussed at length as Ephraim is now Asenath/Ephraim, but it must be addressed more directly, as it is the third of the three aforementioned applications of Hocquenghem's description of homophobia, of "neurosis," which "consists first of all in the impossibility of knowing . . . whether one is . . . parent or child" (101). Hocquenghem further explains that such paranoia "is linked the fear of loss of identity," since "the direct manifestation of homosexual desire stands in contrast to the relations of identity, the necessary roles imposed by the Oedipus complex in order to ensure the reproduction of society . . . family heterosexuality guarantees not only the production of children but also (and chiefly) Oedipal reproduction, with its differentiation between parents and children" (106). Thus, Lovecraft is playing on the homophobic fear of the loss of identity and even the loss of the heteronormative construction of Oedipal reproduction through the inversion of the Oedipus myth itself. While Oedipus had intercourse with his mother, Ephraim, the father, has entered is daughter in a manner that reduces the two individuals to a single entity. Ephraim has queered heterosexual roles to the extreme—where reproduction multiplies, Ephraim's equation simplifies.

In calling attention to perception and thinghood, Lovecraft is referencing back to the very title of the story at hand. "The Thing on the Doorstep" is a tale in which our narrator is visited by what was once his friend, but is now only a shambling, inarticulate corpse, a "thing." This forces the reader to consider metaphysical questions when contemplating the text and the commentary on identity within, as Burleson writes: "Here the Thing of philosophical inquiry struggles for its very existence, standing as a strangely hybrid presence upon the doorstep (the threshold, the border), perhaps to be allowed to pass through, perhaps not—alternatively, perhaps to pass into metaphysical acceptability, perhaps to pass beyond it" (196–97). The concept of thinghood and indeterminateness permeate the tale, pushing us to wonder what Asenath/Ephraim really is. If Edward Derby, a man the narrator so loved that he named his own son after him, might easily be reduced to a vile "thing" by inhabiting the body of another, what is Asenath/Ephraim?

The very concept of the perception or understanding might be broken down with Kantian logic, as Kant explains that "If we withdraw our subjective constitution, the represented object . . . is nowhere to be found, and cannot possibly be found . . . We then believe that we know things in themselves, though in the world of sense, however far we may carry our investigation of its objects, we never deal with anything but appearances" (77). Applying this chain of reasoning to "The Thing on the Doorstep" provides a similar conclusion to those critical theories previously proffered, from Hocquenghem to Irigaray. An observer, such as our narrator, can only determine the quality of an object based on the representation of the object according to their senses. If Asenath/Ephraim appears to be Asenath and sounds like Asenath, then one will assume she/he/it is, in fact, Asenath. Allowing some slight intrusion of Lacanian reasoning, if one observes that Asenath/Ephraim marries Edward Derby, wants to possess Edward Derby, and prioritizes the value of the phallus, then Asenath/Ephraim is rejecting femininity in order to become the phallus itself.

In summary, the senses of the aforementioned individual would lead them to conclude that Ephraim is not merely functioning according to the feminine aspect due to his role as part of what might be called Asenath/Ephraim, she/he/it is functioning as an observable woman. In this way the story has come full circle in queering the characters therein. At the opening of the story Ephraim wants to possess his daughter in order to continue living, and by the close of our tale Asenath/Ephraim desperately wants to be free of his daughter's body and desires the phallus of Edward—the husband. The inversion of the Oedipal complex has led to the mind of a man who desires the body of another man and the queered blurring of identity beyond the point of humanity. When Daniel, our narrator, warns that "there are black zones of shadow close to our daily paths" (CF 3.325), he is warning the reader about the queerness lurking nearby or even within.

Works Cited

Burleson, Donald R. "The Thing: On the Doorstep." In Burleson's *Lovecraft: An American Allegory: Selected Essays on H. P. Lovecraft*. New York: Hippocampus Press, 2015. 195–202.

Butler, Judith. *Gender Trouble*. New York: Routledge, 1990.

Callaghan, Gavin. *H. P. Lovecraft's Dark Arcadia: The Satire, Symbology and Contradiction.* Jefferson, NC: McFarland, 2013.

Foucault, Michel. *The History of Sexuality.* New York: Vintage, 1990.

Henderson, Dylan. "The Disgusting Thing on the Doorstep." *Lovecraft Annual* No. 17 (2023): 15–35.

Hocquenghem, Guy. *Homosexual Desire.* Durham, NC: Duke University Press, 1993.

Houellebecq, Michel. *H. P. Lovecraft: Against the World, Against Life.* Tr. Dorna Khazeni. San Francisco: Believer, 2005.

Irigaray, Luce. *This Sex Which Is Not One.* Ithaca, NY: Cornell University Press, 1985.

Kant, Immanuel. *Critique of Pure Reason.* Tr. Marcus Weigelt. New York: Penguin, 2007.

Lacan, Jacques. *Feminine Sexuality.* Tr. Jacqueline Rose. New York: W. W. Norton, 1985.

Lovecraft, H. P. *More Annotated H. P. Lovecraft.* Ed. S. T. Joshi and Peter Cannon. New York: Dell, 1999.

Sedgwick, Eve Kosofsky. *Epistemology of the Closet.* Berkeley: University of California Press, 1990.

Whittington, Karl. "QUEER." *Studies in Iconography, Volume 33.* Trustees of Princeton University, Medieval Institute Publications, Board of Trustees of Western Michigan University through its Medieval Institute Publications, 2012. 157–68, www.jstor.org/stable/23924280.

The First Cousins of H. P. Lovecraft

Ken Faig, Jr.

MATERNAL	PATERNAL
Phillips Gamwell (1898–1916)	Ida Emma (Hill) Lyon
Marion Rhoby Gamwell	(1874–1951)
(1900–1900)	

Phillips Gamwell and Marion Rhoby Gamwell

Phillips Gamwell at age 4½.
Credit: findagrave.com.

My cousin was a great kid—a Belknap[1] and Alfredus[2] rolled into one. They remind me of him—he was my best and earliest grandson! I can still see myself training him when he was three & I was eleven!—H. P. Lovecraft to James F. Morton, 24 June 1923. (JFM 49)

Lovecraft did not have many first cousins. The family of his maternal grandparents Whipple V. Phillips (1833–1904) and Robie Alzada (Place) Phillips (1827–1896) consisted of five children: Lillian Delora Phillips (1856–1932) (m. 1902 Franklin Chase Clark), Sarah Susan Phillips (1857–1921) (m. 1889 Winfield Scott Lovecraft), Emeline Estella Phillips (1859–1865), Edwin Everett Phillips (1864–1918) (m. 1894 and 1903 Martha H. Mathews) and Annie Emeline Phillips (1866–1941) (m. 1897 Edward Francis Gamwell). Of these children, Emeline Estella Phillips died as a child. Of those who married, Lillian Delora Phillips and Edwin Everett Phillips had no children. Lovecraft himself was the only child of Sarah Susan Phillips and her husband Winfield Scott Lovecraft. Annie Emeline Phillips and her husband Edward Francis Gamwell had two children: a son Phillips Gamwell (b. 23 April 1898 Cambridge, Massachusetts, d. 31 December 1916 Roswell, Colorado), and a daughter Marion Rhoby Gamwell (b. 9 February 1900 Cambridge, Massachusetts, d. 14 February 1900 Cambridge, Massachusetts).

Edward Francis Gamwell (b. 22 May 1869, d. 10 May 1936),[3] the father of Phillips, had met Annie Emeline Phillips while he was a student at Brown University in Providence (A.B., 1894). Edward remained as an English and rhetoric instructor at Brown in 1894–95. Annie and Edward married on 3 June 1897 at the home of the bride's father at 454 Angell Street in Providence. Annie's nephew H. P. Lovecraft acted an usher at the ceremony.

1.. Frank Belknap Long. In a similar vein, HPL wrote to his aunt Annie Emeline (Phillips) Gamwell on 24 September 1922 that Long reminded him of her son Phillips (*LFF* 74).

2. Alfred Galpin.

3. Edward was the son of Franklin Bert Gamwell (1829–1904) and Victoria Clarissa Maxwell (1843–1920).

Edward's editorial positions were: managing editor, Providence *Atlantic Medical Weekly*, 1894–96; city editor, Cambridge *Chronicle*, 1896–1901; editor and proprietor, Cambridge *Tribune*, 1901–12; associate editor, *Budget* and *American Cultivator*, 1913–15. From 1915 onward he worked as an advertising agent. On 2 December 1896, Edward worked at

> **GAMWELL—PHILLIPS.**
>
> **Cambridge Newspaper Man Weds a Prominent Providence Society Girl.**
>
> PROVIDENCE, June 3—Miss Annie Emeline Phillips and Edward Francis Gamwell, Brown 94, were married today at the residence of the bride's parents, 454 Angell st, by Rev Henry M. King, pastor of the First Baptist church.
>
> The bride wore white silk and mousseline de soie and carried bride roses. Miss Edna W. Lewis of Providence, maid of honor, wore organdie with daffodil ribbons. Irving H. Gamwell, principal of the Bristol high school, brother of the groom, was best man.
>
> Mr and Mrs Gamwell will reside in Cambridge, Mass, the home of the groom. He is city editor of the Cambridge Chronicle. Mrs Gamwell is the daughter of Whipple V. Phillips, president of the Providence trust company. She is prominent in Providence society.

573 Massachusetts Avenue and resided at 371 Harvard Street (Faig 25). In 1898, Edward worked at 573 Massachusetts Avenue and made his home at 65 Ellery (Cambridge Directory 1898). Annie's and Edward's son Phillips was born in Cambridge on 23 April 1898. By 14 November 1898, Edward resided at 538 Broadway (Faig 25). On 1 June 1900 (enumeration date of the 1900 U.S. census), Edward and his family resided at 538 Broadway, where Edward remained at least through the 1916 Cambridge Directory. Half of a large double house, 538 Broadway was near the Latin School and Harvard Yard.

The stage seemed to be set for Phillips to matriculate at the Latin School[4] (where he was graduated in 1915 or 1916) and progress on to Harvard University (unless he elected to attend his father's alma mater, Brown University).

---

4. Amateur journalist Albert A. Sandusky (d. 13 February 1934 West Roxbury, Massachusetts) had known Phillips slightly while both were at the Cambridge Latin School (q.v., HPL to Edward H. Cole, February 1934 [AG 72–73]).

436–438 Broadway, Cambridge, Massachusetts. Credit: Google Maps. (438 Broadway is right-hand side.)

Vicinity of 438 Broadway (dark dot). Credit: Google Maps. (Note Cambridge Rindge & Latin School and Harvard Yard.)

Cambridge Latin School (1910). Credit: Library of Congress.

Circumstances prevented the realization of a university education for Phillips. He was stricken with tuberculosis. In October 1916, his mother accompanied him to Colorado in the quest for a cure, or at least an abatement, of his condition. Lovecraft wrote to Walter J. Coates on 4 January 1927: "He was taken by his mother to Colorado Springs as soon as the presence of consumption was discovered, but died on the last day of 1916" (*WH* 109). According to his death certificate, Phillips had resided in Colorado since 7 October 1916. After Christmas, Phillips suffered a sudden turn for the worse and died in Roswell, Colorado, at 1:45 A.M. on the last day of 1916. His body was shipped back to Providence for burial in Whipple V. Phillips's lot at Swan Point Cemetery, where he is buried next to his mother Annie and his sister Marion Rhoby. Lovecraft's poem "An Elegy on Phillips Gamwell, Esq." (*AT* 427–28) appeared in (1) the Providence *Evening News* (5 January 1917), (2) the Cambridge *Chronicle* (6 January 1917), and (3) the Cambridge *Tribune* (13 January 1917). Lovecraft's friend Eugene B. Kuntz published his own tribute to Gamwell, "He Walked with Life," in the amateur magazine *Little*

Budget in 1917 (see HPL to Lillian D. Clark, 30 July 1925 [*LFF* 315] and 7 September 1925 [*LFF* 336]).

Perhaps the illness and death of Phillips was the final blow for the marriage of his parents. While they never divorced, Annie and Edward lived separately from 1917 onward (and perhaps earlier). When Phillips died, Edward was residing at 65 Hancock Street in Boston. Annie returned to Providence to live with her brother Edwin E. Phillips at 874 Chalkstone Avenue. Annie's sister-in-law Martha H. (Mathews) Phillips had died on 9 February 1916 and when Annie returned to Providence she kept house for her widowed brother Edwin Everett Phillips. Edwin himself died on 14 November 1918, and by 1 January 1920 Annie was working as a schoolteacher and keeping house for her nephew Lovecraft in the 598 Angell Street home of her sister Sarah Susan (Phillips) Lovecraft, who had since March 1919 been a patient at Butler Hospital. Lillian Delora (Phillips) Clark and Annie—one or both of them—continued to keep house for Lovecraft at 598 Angell Street until he eloped to Brooklyn to marry Sonia H. Greene on 3 March 1924.

Phillips Gamwell (1909). Credit: *Nyctalops*, April 1973.

The downfall of Edward F. Gamwell was alcohol. He lost the Cambridge *Tribune* position in 1912. By the time of his son's death, Edward was living at 65 Hancock Street in Boston. By 1920, he was selling advertising and residing at 54 South Russell Street in Boston. In 1924, he was still working as a salesman but had removed to 48 South Russell Street, where he still resided in the 1935 Boston directory. He died in Boston in 1936 and was buried in Arms Cemetery, Shelburne Falls, Massachusetts.

Boston was only an hour's train ride from Providence, and Cambridge perhaps only a half hour's additional travel, so Annie and her husband kept in close communication with Whipple V. Phillips and his family after her move to Cambridge in 1897. Sister Sarah Susan (Phillips) Lovecraft had lived with her parents ever since her husband was committed to Butler Hospital in 1893. Winfield Scott Lovecraft died there on 19 July 1898 and was buried in Whipple Phillips's lot at Swan Point Cemetery. Sister Lillian Delora Phillips did not marry Dr. Franklin Chase Clark (1847–1915) until 1902. Whipple Phillips had been a widower since 1896, so there was plenty of spare room at 454 Angell Street for Annie, her husband Edward, and her son Phillips to visit.

Phillips Gamwell ca. 1915. Credit: dimeweb.blogspot.com.

But day to day the Gamwell family resided in Cambridge, so Lovecraft soon resorted to correspondence to stay in touch with his cousin Phillips Gamwell. He wrote to Maurice W. Moe on 5 April 1931:

> Not until I was twenty years old did I write any letters worthy of the name—and my beginning then was due to the fact that my well-beloved little cousin Phillips Gamwell (died 1916) had reached the age of twelve and blossomed out as a piquant letter-writer eager to discuss the various literary and scientific topics breached during our occasional personal conversations. Four or five years of Johnsonese periods loosed upon this youthful and encouraging audience form'd the preparation for the verbal deluges which you sampled in the 1914–15 season. (*MWM* 303)

We know for a fact that Annie and Phillips were both living with Edward F. Gamwell at 438 Broadway in Cambridge when the census was enumerated on 15 April 1910. If in fact Phillips graduated from Cambridge Latin School in 1915 or 1916, he and his mother probably continued to reside with Edward F. Gamwell at 438 Broadway until then. The fact that Lovecraft wrote that he began to correspond with his cousin Phillips Gamwell about 1910 also points toward Phillips's continued residence in Cambridge. Writing to Rheinhart Kleiner on 9 November 1919, Lovecraft stated that he had not been in Boston since January 1916 nor in Cambridge since 1910 (*RK* 147). However, Lovecraft wrote to Kleiner on June 29, 1915: "I frequently go thither to visit my young cousin in Cambridge" (*RK* 36). As the more contemporary, Lovecraft's 1915 statement is probably to be preferred over his 1919 statement.

As early as 1 January 1915, Lovecraft wrote to his friend Maurice W. Moe: "It is almost with envy that I view the steady and regular progress of a healthy and vigorous youth like my cousin Phillips Gamwell. He will ere many years surpass me" (*MWM* 47). Writing to Kleiner on 16 November 1916, Lovecraft described Phillips Gamwell as "a very scholarly youth of 18" (*RK* 72). From Lovecraft's correspondence we do have a few bits of knowledge regarding Phillips's intellectual interests. In his letter to Kleiner of 16 November 1916, Lovecraft described Phillips as "rather an authority on the French language and literature" (*RK* 72). Lovecraft's own mother Sarah Susan (Phillips) Lovecraft had studied French at the Wheaton Seminary, and this may have formed a link between Phillips and his aunt. Phillips also admired the essay collection *From a College Window* (1906) by Arthur Christopher Benson (1862–1925) (see HPL to Maurice W. Moe, 1 September 1929 [*MWM* 303]). Lovecraft would later become familiar with the brothers Benson (A. C., E. F., and R. H.) as writers of ghost stories. Like Lovecraft, Phillips enjoyed viewing motion pictures during the early silent era. He was an especial admirer of the work of Japanese actor Sessue Hayakawa (1886–1973) (see Lovecraft to Gallomo, 30 September 1919 [*ML* 65]). Like Lovecraft, Phillips also enjoyed the popular music of the day. Lovecraft remembered Phillips's singing "Bedelia" at the age of six in 1904 (see Lovecraft to J. Vernon Shea, 4 February 1934 [JVS 230]). Phillips and Lovecraft also shared an interest in stamp-collecting. Lovecraft wrote that he gave his own stamp collection to Phillips in 1916 in the attempt to foster his cousin's interest (see Lovecraft to James F. Morton, 24 June 1923 [JFM 49]). Annie was so attached to her son's memory that Lovecraft was reluctant to ask for the collection back so that Morton could have it.

We even have a few bits of information on excursions Phillips and Lovecraft shared. In 1906, Lovecraft accompanied Phillips and his mother Annie on a visit to Smithfield, Rhode Island, home of the seminary that Lovecraft's maternal grandmother Robie Alzada (Place) Phillips had attended in the 1840s (Lovecraft to Lillian D. Clark, 29 September 1924 [LFF 159]). Lovecraft inherited a few of his grandmother's astronomy textbooks from her time at the Smithfield Seminary (later the Lapham Institute). In 1916, Lovecraft accompanied Phillips and Annie on a final visit to Newport, Rhode Island (see Lovecraft to Lillian D. Clark, 26–27 October 1925 [LFF 473]). Perhaps Phillips and Annie were on a visit to Providence before departing for Colorado in the quest for relief for Phillips's tuberculosis.

A clipping of Lovecraft's "Elegy on Phillips Gamwell" from the Cambridge *Tribune* (with a penciled correction in the author's hand) survives in the Lovecraft Collection at Brown University (BDR 425738). However, there is no correspondence between Lovecraft and Phillips in the Lovecraft Collection. Perhaps Annie's affection for her late son was such that she kept all such surviving items.[5] Whether any remain in the hands of Phillips family members is not known to me. Of course, Lovecraft also treasured the memory of his cousin. Writing to Lillian D. Clark on 30 March 1924 (*LFF* 128) regarding items he desired to be sent to him in New York, Lovecraft included the photographs of his cousin Phillips over his clothespress door.

---

5. Beverly Bryer (Downing) Schroeder, granddaughter of Edward Francis Gamwell's brother Irving Henry Gamwell (1871–1963), still had in 1990 a knife and fork that had belonged to Phillips Gamwell, which Annie Emeline (Phillips) Gamwell had given to her mother (Faig 30).

[Mary J.][6] Ida Emma (Hill) Lyon (b. 15 April 1874 Mount Vernon, New York, d. 22 April 1951 Pelham, New York)

The family of Lovecraft's paternal grandparents George Lovecraft (1815–1895) and Helen (Allgood) Lovecraft (1821–1881) consisted of three children: Emma Jane Lovecraft (1849–1925) (m. 1872 Isaac C. Hill), Winfield Scott Lovecraft (1853–1898) (m. 1889 Sarah Susan Phillips), and Mary Louise Lovecraft (1854–1916) (m. 1893/94 Paul Mellon). Emma Jane (Lovecraft) Hill and her husband had a daughter Ida Emma Hill who married 1898/99 or 1900/01 David Lyon (b. 10 February 1874 New York, d. 20 April 1945 Pelham, New York). R. Alain Everts indicates that the Lyons had a son who died in childhood. The marriage of Mary Louise Lovecraft and Paul Mellon (1863–1910) was apparently childless.[7]

Ida was the daughter of Isaac Carpenter Hill[8] (b. December

---

6. Ida was recorded as Mary J. Lyon in the 1900 U.S. census (see below), but the author has preferred Ida Emma as her given names. Some genealogists make Mary J. (——) Lyon a first wife of David Lyon (married 1898/99) and Ida Emma (Lovecraft) Lyon a second wife (married 1900/01). However, I believe that the identity of birth month and year between Mary J. and Ida makes it likely they were the same woman.

7. The 1900 U.S. census enumerated the following household at 66 South Fifth Avenue, Mount Vernon, New York: Sarah Allgood (head), age 69, single, born July 1830 New York of English-born parents; George E. Taylor (nephew), age 22, single, born October 1877 New York of English-born parents; Mary L. Mellon (niece), age 45, married for 6 years, born October 1854 New York of English-born parents. Mary L. Mellon continued to be listed at this address in Mount Vernon directories through 1916. Starting in 1912, she was listed as the widow of Paul Mellon. Sarah Allgood (b. 8 July 1830 New York, d. 23 January 1908 Mount Vernon, New York) was the sister of Helen (Allgood) Lovecraft (1821–1881), wife of George Lovecraft (1814–1895), who had been the householder at 66 South Fifth Avenue in 1892 and 1885 (Mount Vernon Directories). HPL borrowed family genealogical records from her for copying in 1905. When she died in 1908, Sarah Allgood left a $50 bequest to HPL. When she died in 1916, her niece Mary Louise (Lovecraft) Mellon left a $2,000 bequest to HPL.

8. Isaac was probably the son of John J. Hill (1812 or 1815–1880) and his wife Mary Jane (——) Hill (1814–1880). The family was enumerated in White

1848 New York City, d. 5 January 1932 Stamford, Connecticut) and Emma Jane Lovecraft (b. 1849, d. 6 September 1925 North Pelham, New York). Her parents married in Mount Vernon on 13 November 1872. At the time of their wedding, Isaac was teaching school in White Plains and Emma in Mount Vernon. Their only daughter Ida Emma Hill was born in Mount Vernon on 15 April 1874. The 1880 U.S. census enumerated the family in Pelhamville, Westchester County, New York: I. C. Hill (head), age 31, born New York of New York-born parents, teacher; Emma J. Hill (wife), age 30, born New York of English-born parents; Ida E. Hill (daughter), age 6, born New York of New York–born parents.

Lovecraft was apparently unaware of the existence of his cousin Ida Emma (Hill) Lyon. He wrote to Maurice W. Moe on 5 April 1931: "George [Lovecraft] also had daughters, whose childless next generation complete [sic] the dead-ending" (*MWM* 294). In 1921, he transferred his remaining interest in George Lovecraft's lot at Woodlawn Cemetery to his aunt Emma Jane (Lovecraft) Hill. He had no later interaction with his paternal relatives, and did not attempt to look them up during his own residency in Brooklyn in 1924–26. His aunt Emma Jane (Lovecraft) Hill died in Pelham on 6 September 1925.

The 1900 U.S. census enumerated Ida's parents in North Pelham, New York: Isaac Hill (head), age 46, born December 1853 New York of New York-born parents, teacher, married 27 years; Emma J. Hill (wife), age 47, born March 1853 New York of English-born father and Welsh-born mother, married 27 years, 1 child borne, 1 child living.

The 1910 U.S. census enumerated Ida's parents at 107 Third Avenue,[9] Pelham, New York: Isaac C. Hill (head), age 60, in

---

Plains, Westchester County, New York in the 1870 U.S. census: John J. Hill, age 58, provision dealer, born New York; Mary Jane Hill, age 56, housekeeper, born New York; James Hill, age 23, at home, born New York; Isaac Hill, age 20, at home, born New York; Charles Hill, age 17, at home, born New York; William Hill, age 15, at home, born New York; Mary Hill, age 10, at home, born New York; Alfred Taylor, age 22, butcher, born England; Julia Hiland, age 23, servant, born Ireland.

9. Zillow dates the current double house at 105–107 Third Avenue to 1920.

first marriage for 37 years, born New York of New York-born parents, public school teacher; Emma J. Hill (wife), age 61, in first marriage for 37 years, born New York of English-born father and Welsh-born mother, 1 child borne, 1 child living; Anne M. Felt (servant), age 56, single, born New York of New York-born parents, private family nurse.

MR. AND MRS. ISAAC C. HILL.

Pelham couple who celebrated the fiftieth anniversary of their wedding at their Third avenue home last Monday. They were married in the Village of Mount Vernon in 1872.

Emma Jane (Lovecraft) Hill and Isaac C. Hill, 1922. Credit: Blake-2.

There are handsome Victorian houses at 102 and 103 Third Avenue (corner of Second Street). Zillow dates these two houses to 1850 and 1900, respectively.

Ida Hill and David Lyon[10] married in 1898 or 1899. The 1900 U.S. census enumerated the following household in North Pelham, Westchester County, New York: David Lyon (head), age 26, born February 1874 New York of New York-born father and English-born mother, married 1 year, tin smith; Mary J. [sic] Lyon (wife), age 26, born April 1874 New York of New York-born parents, married 1 year, 0 children borne, 0 children living.

Isaac Carpenter Hill, Principal Hutchinson Grammar School.. Credit: Blake-3

In the 1910 U.S. census, Ida and her husband David Lyon were enumerated in Pelham, Westchester County, New York: David Lyon (head), age 36, in first marriage for 9 years, born New York of New York-born parents, sheet metal (building); Ida E. Lyon (wife), age 35, in first marriage for 9 years, born New York of New York-born parents, 0 children borne, 0 children living. Everts gives 1899 as the marriage year for the Lyons. He states they had a son, but the author has found no son in their home in any of the relevant censuses.

---

10. David was the son of David Lyon (1839–1899) and Eleanora Braidwood (1844–1909), who married on 4 August 4, 1864 in Mamaroneck, New York. The 1880 U.S. census enumerated the following household in Pelham, New York: David Lyon (head), age 40, foreman on farm, born New York of New York-born parents; Eleanora Lyon (wife), age 35, housekeeper, born England of Scottish-born father and English-born mother; Alice Lyon (daughter), age 15, at school; Ralph H. Lyon (son), age 13, at school; Frank M. Lyon (son), age 11, at school; Eugene Lyon (son), age 8, at school; David Lyon (son), age 6, at school; William Lyon (son), age 3; Joseph Lyon (son), age 1. All the children were born in New York of a New York–born father and an English-born mother.

The 1920 U.S. census enumerated the following household at 132 Third Avenue, Pelham, Westchester County, New York: David Lyon (head), age 45, born New York of New York-born father and English-born mother, heating (plumber shop); Ida Lyon (wife), age 45, born New York of New York-born parents, no occupation; Isaac C. Hill (father-in-law), age 70, born New York of Nova Scotia-born father and New York-born mother, no occupation; Emma J. Hill (mother-in-law), age 70, born New York of English-born parents, no occupation.

The 1930 U.S. census enumerated the following household at 128 Third Avenue, North Pelham, Westchester County, New York: David Lyon (head), age 56, married at age 22, born New York of New York-born father and English-born mother, retired; Ida E. Lyon (wife), age 55, married at age 22, born New York of New York-born parents; Isaac C. Hill (father-in-law), age 80, widower, born New York of New York-born parents, retired.

Isaac C. Hill died on 5 January 1932 in the hospital at Stamford, Connecticut. His residence at the time of his death was 128 Third Avenue, North Pelham, New York. His obituary appeared in the White Plains (NY) *Daily Argus* for 6 January 1932. His age at death was stated as 83.

The 1930 New Rochelle, New York Directory listed David Lyon (wife Ida), supervisor, Town of Pelham, house 128 Third Avenue (North Pelham).[11] The 1938 Pelham Directory listed David Lyon (wife Ida), house 128 Third Avenue, North Pelham.

The 1940 U.S. census enumerated the following household at 128 Third Avenue, Pelham, Westchester County, New York: David Lyon (head), age 66, 8th grade education, born New York, same residence on 1 April 1935; Ida Lyon (wife), age 66, four years of college,[12] born New York, same residence on 1 April 1935.

David Lyon, age 71, died in Pelham, New York on 20 April 1945. His obituary appeared in the White Plains (NY) *Daily Argus* for 20 April 1945. He was survived by his wife Ida and his siblings Ralph, Eugene, William and Joseph.

---

11. David Lyon held this office as early as 1921 (see *Yonkers* [NY] *Herald-Statesman*, 13 December 1921).

12. A woman named Ida E. Hill was graduated from Boston University in 1901.

The 1950 U.S. census enumerated the following household at 128 Third Avenue, Pelham, New York: Ida E. Lyon (head), age 75, widow, born New York.

Ida Emma (Hill) Lyon, age 77, died in Pelham, New York on 22 April 1951. Her obituary appeared in the New Rochelle (NY) *Standard-Star* for 23 April 1951. She had been born 15 April 1874 in Mount Vernon, New York, and resided at 128 Third Avenue in Pelham at the time of her death.[13]

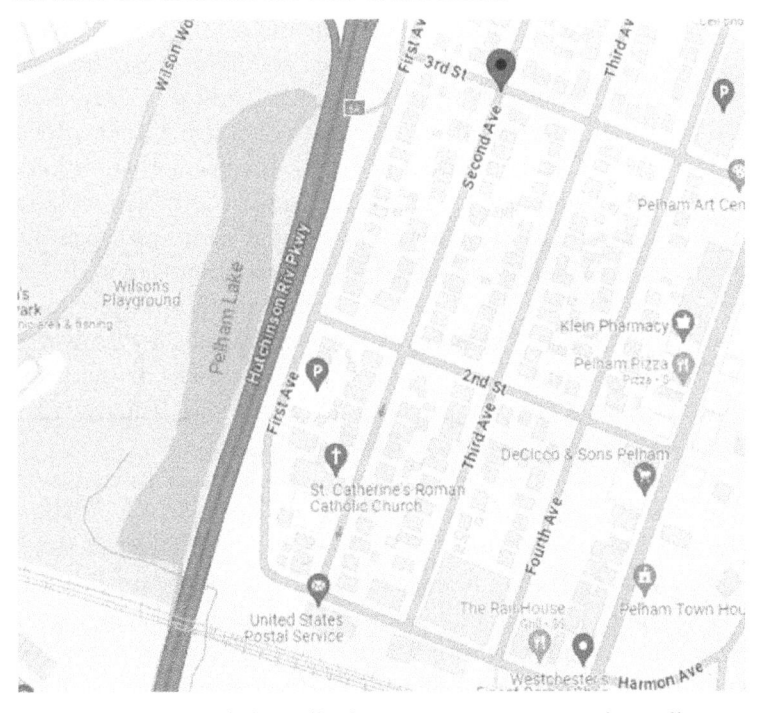

When he witnessed the will of Mary Louise (Lovecraft) Mellon on 14 February 1903, Isaac C. Hill resided on Second Avenue at the corner of Third Street (dark dot in above map). Alas, Zillow indicates the oldest surviving house at the intersection (151 Second Avenue) was built in 1929.

---

13. Ida Lyon had been recorded at 128 Third Avenue in Pelham, New York, in the 1930, 1940, and 1950 U.S. censuses. She was recorded at 132 Third Avenue in the 1920 U.S. census.

Hill–Lovecraft–Lyon lot marker, Woodlawn Cemetery, Bronx, New York. Credit: Bobby Derie.

128 Third Avenue, Pelham, New York (built 1928 according to Zillow). Home of Ida Emma (Hill) Lyon was located here from 1920 to 1951.[14]

---

[14]. One must, however, always allow for the possibility of changes in street numbering.

South Fourth Avenue business district, Mount Vernon, New York, ca. 1903. Credit: Library of Congress.

67 South Fifth Avenue, Mount Vernon, New York (left).[15] To the right can be seen the former Sacred Heart School and (across Second Street) the former Sacred Heart Church (1878) (now Sharon Seventh Day Adventist Church).

(The former Lovecraft–Allgood home at 66 South Fifth Avenue stood across the street, on a site now occupied by a parking lot.)

---

15. The structure, which was the former Sacred Heart parish convent, was damaged by a fire in 2018.

Acknowledgment

The author thanks David E. Schultz for identifying references to Phillips Gamwell in H. P. Lovecraft's correspondence.

Bibliography

Bell, Blake A. "Excerpts of January 8, 1889 Remarks Dedicating a New School Building in Pelhamville." 11 August 2014, historicpelham.blogspot.com/2014/08/excerpts-of-january-8-1889-remarks.html [Blake-1]

———. "An Historic Fiftieth Anniversary in Pelham During 1922." 5 March 2018. historicpelham.blogspot.com/2018/03/an-historic-fiftieth-anniversary-in.html?m=0. Original source: *Pelham Sun* (17 November 1922): 1, 4 (with portrait of Mr. and Mrs. Hill). [Blake-2]

———. "Isaac C. Hill, Involved with Public Education for Forty-Five Years, Retired in 1922," 12 January 2015. historicpelham.blogspot.com/2015/01/isaac-c-hill-involved-with-pelham.html. Original source: *Pelham Sun* (5 September 1922): 7 (with portrait of Hill). [Blake-3]

———. "More Reminiscences of Isaac C. Hill of Early Public Schools in Pelham," 28 March 2006. historicpelham.blogspot.com/2006/03/more-reminiscences-of-isaac-c-hill-of.html [Blake-4]

———. "I. C. Hill's Reminiscences of Early Public Schools in Pelham." 27 September 2005. historicpelham.blogspot.com/2005/09/i-c-hills-reminiscences-of-early.html [Blake-5]

Derie, Bobby. "Her Letters to Lovecraft: H. P. Lovecraft's Other Aunts." *Deep Cuts in a Lovecraftian Vein* [blog], 3 November 2021. deepcuts.blog/2021/11/03/her-letters-to-lovecraft-h-p-lovecrafts-other-aunts/ (Derie reproduces [1] wills for Eliza Allgood, Sarah Allgood and Mary Louise (Lovecraft) Mellon and [2] Hill–Lovecraft–Lyon lot marker at Woodlawn Cemetery, Bronx, New York.)

Everts, R. Alain. "The Lovecraft Family in America." *Xenophile* 2, No. 6 (October 1975): 7, 16.

Faig, Kenneth W., Jr. *Edward Francis Gamwell and His Family.* Glenview IL: [Published by the author], 1991

Lovecraft, H. P. *Letters to Alfred Galpin and Others.* Ed. S. T. Joshi and David E. Schultz. New York: Hippocampus Press, 2020. [AG]

———. *Letters to Family and Family Friends.* Ed. S. T. Joshi and David E. Schultz. New York: Hippocampus Press, 2020. [LFF]

———. *Letters to J. Vernon Shea, Carl F. Strauch, and Lee McBride White.* Ed. S. T. Joshi and David E. Schultz. New York: Hippocampus Press, 2016. [JVS]

———. *Letters to James F. Morton.* Ed. David E. Schultz and S. T. Joshi. New York: Hippocampus Press, 2011. [JFM]

———. *Letters to Maurice W. Moe and Others.* Ed. David E. Schultz and S. T. Joshi New York: Hippocampus Press, 2018. [MWM]

———. *Letters to Rheinhart Kleiner and Others.* Ed. S. T. Joshi and David E. Schultz. New York: Hippocampus Press, 2020. [RK]

———. *Letters to Woodburn Harris and Others.* Ed. S. T. Joshi and David E. Schultz. New York: Hippocampus Press, 2022. [WH]

———. *Miscellaneous Letters.* Ed. David E. Schultz and S. T. Joshi. New York: Hippocampus Press, 2022. [ML]

Squires, Richard D. *Stern Fathers 'neath the Mould: The Lovecraft Family in Rochester.* West Warwick, RI: Necronomicon Press, 1995.

Note

Only descendants of Whipple V. Phillips and Robie Alzada (Place) Phillips are admitted as maternal cousins of H. P. Lovecraft. Only descendants of George Lovecraft and Helen (Allgood) Lovecraft are admitted as paternal cousins of H. P. Lovecraft. Exclusive of Sonia H. Lovecraft (1883–1972), Lovecraft's surviving next of kin would have been his aunt Annie E. (Phillips) Gamwell (1937–41), his first cousin Ida Emma (Hill) Lyon (1941–51), and then his second cousins descending from his great-grandparents. See: en.wikipedia.org/wiki/Next_of_kin.

Was Lovecraft *Psycho?*
Shades of the Providence Gentleman in One of Fiction's Most Notorious Killers

Harley Carnell

The assertion that H. P. Lovecraft wrote as many as 100,000 letters in his life (as propounded, for example, by the H. P. Lovecraft Historical Society), has been disputed by Joshi and Schultz (in Lovecraft, *Lord of a Visible World* 8). But, as they point out, even if this number was reduced to 75,000, this would still render Lovecraft "among the most exhaustively self-documented individuals in human history."

As illuminating as Lovecraft's letters can be,[1] a reader of his fiction can perhaps somewhat selfishly lament—in the way that John Sutherland does with regard to Seamus Heaney's teaching requirements—that his epistolary endeavors diverted him from his fictional output. Or, as Robert Bloch puts it: "The problem [with extensive correspondence] is if you are not selective, you'll never get your *own* work done" (Schow; Bloch's emphasis).

Perhaps Bloch had Lovecraft in mind when making this statement, as Bloch was one of Lovecraft's many correspondents.[2] Bloch first wrote to Lovecraft as a starstruck, doe-eyed sixteen-year-old having been "enamored" with Lovecraft's stories in *Weird Tales* (cited in Winter 24). Lovecraft, unfailingly kind even to this unknown teenage correspondent,[3] not only re-

---

1. Indeed, Joshi has argued that HPL's letters "may ultimately be his greatest accomplishment" (*Weird Tale* 170).
2. By the end of his life, HPL admitted to having as many as 97 separate correspondents (see *RB* 7).
3. Another of his teenage correspondents, Willis Conover, claimed that his

sponded to Bloch's letter but offered him extensive feedback on two stories he submitted to him (see *IAP* 866–67). Their relationship would endure until Lovecraft's death in 1937. It is no wonder that Bloch, when later asked if he "owed [his] career" to Lovecraft, unequivocally replied: "I most certainly do!" (cited in Lofficier and Lofficier).

Although they never met, Bloch and Lovecraft had an intimate friendship. This, along with the many facets of his most celebrated novel, *Psycho* (1959), that I will go on to discuss, have made me wonder whether the character of Norman Bates may be in some sense based on Lovecraft.

At first, this might seem a ridiculous proposition, not only because there is a sharp distinction between an unassuming, scholarly, self-professed eighteenth-century gentleman and a maniacal killer, but also because there are worlds of difference between the kinds of fiction that Bloch and Lovecraft wrote.

The ultimate realization of Lovecraft's vision of cosmic horror was an eschewing of the anthropocentric view of the universe. For Lovecraft, true horror came in the recognition of humanity's insignificance, as exemplified by Henry Akeley in "The Whisperer in Darkness": "They could easily conquer the Earth, but have not tried so far because they have not needed to. They would rather leave things as they are to save bother" (*CF* 2.477). Lovecraft had no interest in exploring people, or the trivial mundanities of their lives, in his fiction. As Thomas Ligotti[4] has pointed out, in Lovecraft "one does not care about the characters—they are only a perspective from which to view

---

"jaw was hanging open" after a simple unsolicited question to HPL about the *Necronomicon* elicited a lengthy response from the author (cited in *RB* 7).

4. Ligotti goes even further than Bloch in his adoration for HPL. Ligotti, who has frequently spoken of his mental health struggles, identifies deeply with HPL. On first reading him, he "immediately knew that [he] wanted to write horror stories." He also felt a resonance on a more personal level with HPL and went as far as to say: "I don't know what would have become of me if I hadn't discovered Lovecraft" (cited in Wilbanks). Matt Cardin has argued that Ligotti's "response to Lovecraft, and in particular his sense of identification with Lovecraft's worldview, has been so intense that it has led him to impute too much of himself to his idol" (49).

the horror of the plot" (203). Joshi has noted how "for the type of cosmic fiction [Lovecraft] was writing, strong or distinctive human characters might militate against the effects he sought" (*Unutterable Horror* 510). Lovecraft himself stated to Edwin Baird that "[o]ne can't write a weird story of real power without perfect psychological detachment from the human scene" (*Lord of a Visible World* 167); and in his treatise "Supernatural Horror in Literature" he outlined his belief that the focus of cosmic/weird fiction should move away from "the literature of *mere* physical fear and the mundanely gruesome' (*CE* 2.84; my emphasis).

In Algernon Blackwood's "The Willows" (which Lovecraft famously declared the greatest weird tale ever written [see Ashley 109]), there is the following remarks: "There are forces close here that could kill a herd of elephants in a second as easily as you or I could squash a fly. Our only chance is to keep perfectly still. Our insignificance perhaps may save us" (Blackwood 360). Although not from a Lovecraft story, I believe this quotation to be a remarkable encapsulation of the "cosmic indifferentism," to deploy Lovecraft's neologism, that comprised much of the worldview he was attempting to impute into his fiction. I would add that it is Lovecraft's eschewing of characters and backgrounding of people that makes his work so distinctive. People's almost fetishistic adherence to the idea of characters being of chief, if not sole, importance to any given story largely persists,[5] but Lovecraft was at the vanguard of the attempt to relinquish this focus.

Psycho, then, seems to pertain to nothing Lovecraft or Lovecraftian.

I will offer a very brief plot, as it is probably entirely familiar to readers, if only through its 1960 Alfred Hitchcock adaptation. Norman Bates runs a small motel with his abusive and domineering mother, who, in one of horror fiction's great twists, turns out to have been dead the whole time. Dressing up as his mother (while blacked-out through drink), Bates kills an attractive young woman, Mary Crane, who has come to stay at the motel after stealing money from her boss. He also murders a pri-

---

5. For a refreshing contrast, see Adam Nevill's collection *Wyrd and Other Derelictions* (2020), which has literally no characters in any of the stories.

vate detective hired by Mary's company to investigate the missing money. The book culminates with Bates's arrest and subsequent institutionalization. At this point, it seems that Bates has been entirely subsumed by his mother's personality.

To reiterate, this plot is hardly resonant with anything Lovecraft wrote. Yet interestingly, the work of both authors was their respective response to the conditions in the world at the time, particularly in the wake of the two world wars. This environment was encapsulated perfectly by Virginia Woolf: "that the Earth is 3,000,000,000 [sic] years; that human life lasts but a second [...]; that science and religion have between them destroyed belief; that all bounds of union seem broken; it is in this atmosphere of doubt and conflict that writers now have to exist" (*Selected Essays* 75).[6]

At the time, there were scientific innovations with regard to the age of the universe, as well as Einstein's theory of relativity and the subsequent discoveries in quantum mechanics that would challenge humanity's ability to describe the laws of physics in all conditions. Geological discoveries propounded the sheer antiquity of the Earth.[7] The ongoing aftershocks from Darwinian natural selection inexorably linked *Homo sapiens* to their nonhuman ancestors.[8] Freud, and the revisions of his work led by protégé Jung, brought psychology, sexuality, and the unconscious to public consciousness. Movements such as Cubism and Futurism were reshaping art. The movement that would later become Modernism was usurping and upending literature. And, finally, the mechanistic slaughter in both world wars, as well as the ultimate culmination of *homo homini lupus* as evinced by the Holocaust, the Rape of Nanking, the dropping of the atomic bomb on Hiroshima and Nagasaki, and other early- to

---

6. Woolf addresses this problem in her novel *To the Lighthouse* (1927). In the celebrated "Time Passes" interlude, the death of a main character is described almost flippantly: "A shell exploded. Twenty *or* thirty young men were blown up in France, among them Andrew Ramsay, whose death, mercifully, was instantaneous" (145; my emphasis).
7. As explored by HPL in *At the Mountains of Madness* (1931).
8. As explored by HPL in "The Rats in the Walls" (1923).

mid-twentieth-century horrors, reshaped the way all fiction, including weird fiction, was written. As Bloch explains:

> By the mid-1940s, I had pretty well mined the vein of ordinary supernatural themes until it had become varicose. I realized, as a result of what went on during World War Two and of reading the more widely disseminated work in psychology, that the real horror is not in the shadows, but in that little twisted world inside our own skulls. (Winter 27)

The specific inspiration for *Psycho* was, famously, the crimes of the Wisconsin killer Ed Gein—or, rather, the discoveries subsequent to the crimes. The lurid scenes encountered by police when searching Gein's house included bones, body parts, and various furnishings covered with human skin. Gein had also fashioned himself a female skin-suit. Notably inspiring *Psycho*, *The Texas Chainsaw Massacre*, and *The Silence of the Lambs*, Gein's gruesome crimes cast a long shadow over American culture and psyche. In *Psycho*, these are alluded to obliquely: "Some of the write-ups compared it to the Gein affair up north, a few years back" (143).

Bloch attempted to distance himself from the Gein portrayal, saying that he "did not use Ed Gein as a basis for Norman Bates at all," and he alluded to his irritation at the persistent questioning about Gein (cited in Schow). This is something I can certainly sympathize with. In the same way that Lovecraft might have been horrified at the extent to which the so-called "Cthulhu Mythos" has come to dominate discussions of his work, I can appreciate why Bloch would be annoyed that the large corpus of his work is reduced to this single novel, and that novel is seen as merely a fictionalization of a real crime. However, unfortunately for Bloch, such comparisons are inevitable. Even if Gein was not explicitly mentioned in the book, the fact that Bates is both dominated by his religious mother and dresses up as her inevitably leads to comparisons with Gein. It is also clear that Bloch had more than a passing interest in Gein, later writing a story on him called "The Shambles of Ed Gein."

But I will concede that Gein cannot be said to be the only influence on Bates. Potentially, he is not even the *main* influence on Bates. For, as I will argue, the main influence may in fact be Lovecraft.

The first thing to note is that Bloch and Lovecraft had portrayed each other before. In 1935, Bloch wrote a story called "The Shambler from the Stars," in which a first-person narrator modeled on Lovecraft is killed off. Bloch actually wrote to Lovecraft to ask his permission to do this. Lovecraft was so amused by the idea that he responded to Bloch with a fake legal document, signed by himself and attested by Abdul Alhazred and some of his other fictional creations, giving Bloch permission to "portray, murder, annihilate, disintegrate, transfigure, metamorphose, or otherwise manhandle" his fictional Lovecraft (see *RB* 142). Lovecraft responded to Bloch's story with one of his own: "The Haunter in the Dark." In the story, Bloch—thinly disguised as Robert Blake—is a "writer and painter wholly devoted to the field of myth, dream, terror, and superstition, and avid in his quest for scenes and effects of a bizarre spectral sort" (*CF* 3.452).

"Painter" refers to the fact that, in addition to his celebrated career as an author, Bloch had a keen interest in art, with Lovecraft offering enthusiastic feedback for sketches and illustrations he would send him. He said that Bloch showed a "marked aptitude for weird portraiture" (*RB* 59) and was "replete with genuine talent" (*RB* 65). He also showed them to his friend Clark Ashton Smith, the author and artist, who described them as "'powerful'" and "'startling'" (*RB* 72). Lovecraft would state his belief that Bloch would make a "prize-winning mural painter" (*RB* 123). Bloch would even draw a picture of Lovecraft himself, eliciting this enthusiastic response: "Bless my soul, but you certainly have caught the authentic expression of Grandpa's[9] diabolic & sombrely brooding countenance!" (*RB* 78).

Blake, like Bloch, is from Milwaukee and lives at a house that is representative of Lovecraft's own residence at 66 College

---

9. HPL would often refer to himself as Grandpa (or Grandpa Theobald) to his correspondents, playfully referring both to his status as a self-professed 18th-century gentleman and alluding to the fact that many of his correspondents were significantly younger than him.

Street in Providence.[10] The story culminates with Blake's death.

So, if Bloch already portrayed Lovecraft before, was he portraying him again in *Psycho*? Let us first look at Bates's physical appearance: "The light shone down on his plump face, reflected from his rimless glasses, bathed the pinkness of his scalp beneath the thinning sandy hair" (2). Throughout his life, Lovecraft did not enjoy a particularly healthy diet, partly because of a predilection for sweet treats and ice cream, but mostly due to poverty. Indeed, Lovecraft's later reliance on low-quality food, and often out-of-date canned products, has been speculated to be at least partially causal to his early death from stomach cancer (see *IAP* 1004–5). There were certain occasions where he did put on weight, as can be seen in the following letter to Maurice Moe: "You knew how fat I was in 1923, and how bitterly I resented the circumstance. In 1924 I grew even worse, till finally I had to adopt a 16" collar" (*Lord of a Visible World* 190). He also told Robert Bloch, with his typical self-effacement, that he was at one point worried about becoming "too much like a brother of the hippopotamus" (*RB* 46). However, descriptions of Bates as actively overweight are *passim* in *Psycho*. While Lovecraft may have gained some weight, I don't think that this sobriquet would be applicable to him. Also, his dark brown hair could not be described as "sandy," and he did not habitually wear glasses as Bates does.

So, physically speaking, there is little to connect Lovecraft to Bates. But I believe that the lack of similarities ends there. First, we can look at Bates's troubled relationship with his domineering mother.[11] Throughout the book she insults him: "You're a

---

10. HPL was enamored of the house, telling Bloch that "I can hardly believe that I am actually *living* here" (*RB* 31; HPL's emphasis). Scheffler has noted that Bloch would subsequently visit this house in 1975, when he was in Providence to collect the inaugural Lifetime Achievement Award at the World Fantasy Awards (36).

11. All "conversations" between Bates and his mother are in fact imaginary monologues, as she has been long dead by the time of the novel. However, for expediency's sake, I will relate all interactions between them as if they are real conversations happening in real time; not least because the conversations are almost certainly meant to be exemplary of actual conversations that did take place between the two when she was alive.

Mamma's boy. That's what they [his childhood bullies] called you, and that's what you were. Were, are, and always will be. A big, fat, overgrown Mamma's boy!" (7). As unpleasant as this is to read, Lovecraft's own mother (Susie) was equally as capable of being cruel to him. She is on record as having referred to her son as "hideous" (see *IAP* 131). Yet conversely, Susie was also very protective of Lovecraft, as the following anecdote from a friend of the Lovecrafts demonstrates:

> Mrs Lovecraft refused to eat her dinner in the dining room, not to leave her sleeping son alone for an hour one floor above. When a diminutive teacher friend, Miss Ella Sweeney, took the rather rangy youngster to walk, holding his hand, she was enjoined by Howard's mother to stoop a little lest she pull the boy's arm from his socket. (Cited in *IAP* 93)

One cannot imagine what this admixture of admonishment and cossetting must have been like for a child. As Lovecraft's wife Sonia aptly put it, Susie can be argued to have "lavished both her love and her hate on her only child" (*IAP* 131). Darrell Schweitzer does not hold back in his assessment of her, saying that Susie was the "epitome of the unworldly, inhibited Victorian matron, with more than a generous measure of neuroses sprinkled in," and that she was a "cross between a domineering monster and smothering protectress" who "gave [Lovecraft] lasting psychological scars" (3). Or, as Bates puts it: "Mothers are sometimes overly possessive" (5).

However, as Susie is a real person unlike Mrs. Bates, it is worth offering a defense of her. She had to deal with the institutionalization of her husband, a descent into relative financial hardship, and the raising of a young boy whose own mental breakdowns and difficulties adjusting to the world could not have made him the easiest child to deal with. There is also her own mental health to consider. Susie, like her husband, would end her life in a mental health facility. While there has been much speculation on the precise nature of Susie's illness, at least two of DSM-5's diagnostic criteria of borderline personality disorder[12] seem applicable to her:

---

12. Borderline personality disorder is currently classified by the ICD as "emo-

Frantic efforts to avoid real or imagined abandonment.

A pattern of unstable and intense interpersonal relationships characterised by alternating between extremes of idealization[13] and devaluation. (*DSM-5* 663)

As for Bates's father, he "went away when I was still a baby. Mother took care of me all alone. There was enough money on her side of the family to keep me going, I guess, until I grew up. Then she mortgaged the house, sold the farm land,[14] and built the motel" (24).

All this seems eerily similar to Lovecraft's own life. His father also left at a young age; however, in his case, it was due to having been admitted to a sanitorium for what scholars now believe was syphilis. Joshi has noted how Lovecraft's recounting of his father's condition to his friends is patently false, and thus Lovecraft was probably shielded from the true nature of his father's illness by his mother (*IAP* 25).

Unlike Lovecraft's, Bates's father seems to have abandoned the family, although there is no clue as to what precisely occurred. I believe that a simple explanation may be that the father left his wife for another woman, probably a young woman. This would explain the rampant misogyny that Mrs. Bates demonstrates throughout the novel, particularly toward attractive young women.

Like Bates, the Lovecrafts also survived mostly on money that was in the family rather than a steady income. Although forced to move out of his beloved childhood home—which Lovecraft told J. Vernon Shea left him feeling suicidal (*Lord of a Visible World* 58)—they were able to live mostly on money from

---

tionally unstable personality disorder." As the DSM sources its classifications from the ICD, it is possible that they will adopt this nomenclature when the pending DSM-6 is released.

13. For example, Susie referred to her son as a "poet of the highest order" (cited in *IAP* 305). While this would certainly be attributable to HPL if his career is taken *in toto*, at the time it was made in the late 1910s it would hardly have been accurate and instead constitutes a mother speaking positively about her child to an unrealistic extent.

14. That Bates grew up on a farm is another link to Gein.

the family. Bates, forty at the time of the novel, is able to live his dream of living in his childhood home forever: "There was something quite pleasant and reassuring about being surrounded by familiar things. Here, everything was orderly and ordained; it was only there, outside, that the changes took place" (1).

Mary thinks to herself that the house is "straight out of the Gay Nineties" (23); the 1890s being, of course, when Lovecraft was born and growing up. The house's state of stasis is reiterated by Lila, Mary's sister:

> Lila wasn't quite prepared to step bodily into another era. And yet she found herself there, back in the world as it had been long before she was born.
>
> For the décor of this room had been outmoded many years before Bates's mother died. (137)

That the room outdates even Bates's mother is significant. Lovecraft was famous for his love of the past. While his fiction is incredibly formative and forward-looking, embracing as it does contemporary scientific developments, he himself was avowedly backward-looking. While he loved many different eras, stretching as far back as Roman and Egyptian times, he spoke most often of his love of the eighteenth century (his "persistent eighteenth-centuryism," as he called it [*Lord of a Visible World* 46]).

Another similarity between Bates and Lovecraft is with regard to their shared lack of sex. However, there is a stark difference in how this is realized in the two.

It is clear that Bates is interested in sex and women. When Mary arrives at the motel, coming in from the rain, Bates visibly blushes after making the innocuous remark that she will want to get out of her wet clothes (22). During supper, Bates admits that he has never even sat down at a table with a woman (25). Bates's interest in sex manifests itself in a warped way, as he later watches Mary undress through a small hole he has installed in the bathroom wall to spy on women (36). The absurdity of Norman's misogyny is comically portrayed here, as he covertly watches Mary undressing in the bathroom yet castigates her for tempting him:

> Now she was going to take them off, she was *taking* them off, and he could see, she was standing before the mirror and actually *gesturing!*
>
> *Did she know?* Had she known all along, known about the hole in the wall, known that he was watching? Did she want him to watch, was she doing this on purpose, the bitch? (36; Bloch's emphasis)

That Norman Bates has never had the sex life he desires is due to his mother, as the following passage illustrates:

> "Never had the gumption to leave home [...] or even find yourself a girl—"
>
> "You wouldn't let me!"
>
> "That's right, Norman. I wouldn't let you. But if you were half a man, you would have gone your own way." (4)

Lovecraft was similarly inexperienced in sex. Before meeting his eventual wife Sonia Greene, he was almost certainly a virgin, and Greene was the one to initiate sex between the two. Gina Wisker (in Simmons) has pointed out that in many ways Sonia "offered an alternative, more modern and independent" type of woman than what Lovecraft was used to from his mother and aunts (34). That Sonia took the lead in this aspect of their relationship is representative of this. Unlike Bates, however, Lovecraft simply seemed uninterested in sex. He also considered it a somewhat bestial, primitive instinct unbefitting to a gentleman. I am reminded somewhat of Celaphus's recounting of Socrates in Plato's *Republic,* when he talks about his declining amorous interests in his old age: "It is my greatest delight to get away from all that, like a slave from the raving of a savage monster" (5, 329c).

Bates's mother, like Lovecraft's, is virulently anti-alcohol, forcing Bates to hide his liquor from her. One of the most delicious ironies of the book is that it is actually through the drinking of alcohol, and the blackouts it leads to, that Bates transforms into his mother and commits his crimes. However, unlike Bates, Lovecraft shared his mother's opposition to alcohol, going as far as to actively support Prohibition (see *IAP* 225). Lovecraft also wrote a humorous story, called "Old Bugs," after learning of his young friend Alfred Galpin's desire to have a drink before the implementation of Prohibition. In it, the titular character becomes incensed when learning that young Alfred Trever (Galpin's fictional equivalent) is planning on drinking, smashing a bar up and causing a number of "men, or things which had been men" to lap up the spilled contents from the floor (CF 1.94), and repeatedly shouting, "He shall not drink!" (CF 1.94). This story, with its use of absurdist exaggeration, is a brilliant satire. It also displays Lovecraft's humor at its best, such as Trever's belonging to a fraternity called Tappa Tappa Keg (CF 1.90).

Bates, like Lovecraft, is an avid reader. Early in the novel he defends his reading to his mother, saying that it improves his mind, which elicits this response: "Call *that* improvement? You don't fool me, boy, not for a minute. Never have. It isn't as if you were reading the Bible, or even trying to get an education. I know the sort of thing *you* read. Trash! And worse than trash" (6; Bloch's emphasis). If the reference to education implies that Bates did not finish school, then this would also mirror Lovecraft. It was a source of long-standing shame to Lovecraft that he did not get a college degree. However, while Lovecraft may not have been formally educated, he was a noted autodidact, with a particular interest in astronomy and other sciences. As a youth, he wrote frequent articles on astronomy for local papers. He also incorporated much of this learning into his fiction. Take, for example, the avalanche of knowledge deployed in a tale such as *At the Mountains of Madness*. Reading this, or many of Lovecraft's science-infused stories, readers unacquainted with him would perhaps be even more impressed with his perspicacity if they were to learn that he lacked a college, or even high school, qualification.

I would now like to discuss the various books that are cited in *Psycho*. It is my belief that some of these books are attributable to Bates and his character. Others, I believe, are more readily applicable to Lovecraft. I have designated these books Bates Books (BB) and Lovecraft Books (LB) respectively:

The Realm of the Incas, Victor W. Von Hagen, 1957 [BB]
A New Model of the Universe, Pytor Ouspenskii, 1931 [LB]
The Witch-Cult in Western Europe, Margaret Murray, 1921 [LB]
The Extension of Consciousness, Charles Wolfran Oliver, 1932 [BB]
Dimension and Being [LB]
Là-Bas, Joris-Karl Huysmans,[15] 1891 [BB]
Justine, Marquis de Sade, 1791 [BB]
Hamlet, William Shakespeare, 1623[16] [BB]
Macbeth, William Shakespeare, 1623 [BB]

In addition to the books listed, there are references to a few unnamed books. Bates's mother talks of a "filthy" book about the South Seas (6). Lila picks up a book at random from Bates's shelf which contains images which are "almost pathologically pornographic" (136).

All the named books are real, with the exception of *Dimension and Being*, which I suspect is a nod to Martin Heidegger's *Being and Time* (1921).

Let us start with the Bates Books.

Justine is a novel by the Marquis de Sade, famously the etymological origin of the term sadism. It, along with the unnamed book Lila discovers, seems to pertain to Bates's partiality to violent sexual imagery. While Mrs. Bates's misogyny and antiquated opinion of society would probably result in her having a low bar for designating something "filthy," I think that in this case she may be accurate—if only from a descriptive rather than a value-judgment perspective. That is, I think the implication here is that the book about the South Seas probably had some inserts that featured nude images of natives. *Là-Bas*, by Huysmans, is about Satanism. While Lovecraft was interested in the occult, I have designated this a BB because I think that the book

---

15. Although I have denoted this a Bates book, for reasons I will explain, HPL did own a copy of another Huysmans book, *À Rebours* (1884), or *Against the Grain*, in the translation of John Howard.

16. The publication history of *Hamlet*, particularly with regards to its differing quarto versions, is complex and beyond the scope of this essay. For expediency, the date given is its publication date in the First Folio.

is meant to serve as a signifier for Bates's interest in disturbing phenomena. *The Extension of Consciousness* is a book that pertains to metapsychology. Freud outlined his theory of metapsychology in his 1915 article "The Unconscious": "It will only be right to give a special name to the way of regarding things which is the final result of psychoanalytic research. I propose that, when we succeed in describing a mental process in all its aspects, dynamic, topographic and economic, we shall call this a *metapsychological* presentation" (130; Freud's emphasis). This book thus pertains to Bates's interest in psychology, which he speaks about throughout the book. Freud's most celebrated theory is, of course, the Oedipus Complex. It is worth taking a quick digression here to discuss this briefly as it relates to both Bates and Lovecraft.

Psychological, particularly psychosexual, imputations of characters/books drawn by literary theorists can at times be indicative of academical excess, as satirized brilliantly by academic/author David Lodge in his novel *Changing Places:*

> Readers of Jane Austen, he [Morris Zapp[17]] emphasised, gesturing freely with his cigar, should not be misled by the absence of overt references to physical sexuality in her fiction into supposing that she was indifferent or hostile to it [...] Morris demonstrated that Mr Elton was obviously implied to be impotent because there was no lead in the pencil that Harriet Smith took from him. (195)[18]

However, in *Psycho,* the Oedipal connections between Bates and his mother are blatant within the text itself, requiring no need for amateur psychologizing or theorizing. (This, incidentally, is a recurrent theme throughout the novel, where Bloch is at

---

17. A parody of the academic Stanley Fish, most noted for his book *Is There a Text in This Class?* (1980). This, the most egregious of Fish's own brand of theoretical tripe, argues for his idea of "interpretative communities." Essentially, the idea is that there is no such thing as objectivity in a given text, or an objective interpretation to be had from it. Rather, readers bring their own equally valid understanding to texts, which are all indisputably true.
18. The reference is to Austen's *Emma* (1815).

pains to ensure his readers do not miss any of the allusions he is trying to make.) Virtually at the novel's beginning, we are introduced to the Oedipal nature of their relationship, as Mrs. Bates castigates Norman for mentioning the "filthy" theory to her, to which Norman responds: "But I was only trying to explain something. It's what they call the Oedipus situation, and I thought if both of us could just look at the problem reasonably and try to understand it, maybe things would change for the better" (6).

This theme is repeated throughout the novel. As Mary's corpse is sinking into the swamp, Norman has the following interior monologue: "Now it was up over her breasts, he didn't like to think about such things, he never thought about Mother's breasts, he mustn't" (49). His mother's partner after his father is "Uncle"[19] Joe Considine. Norman is clearly jealous of Joe and hates him, at one point thinking: "Uncle Joe could wrap her around his little finger. He could do anything he wanted with Mother. It would be nice to be like that, and to look the way Uncle Joe Considine did" (76).

Lovecraft's relationship with his mother was, as we have seen, hardly healthy either. This is not to say that it can in any way be compared to that of Norman and Mrs. Bates. However, Winfield Townley Scott consulted the medical records of Susie before they were destroyed in a fire, noting that her psychologist made reference to an Oedipal complex between her and her son (see *IAP* 305). Whether we could go as far as to agree with this, I am not sure. However, I do think the psychiatrist was accurate in encapsulating just how unhealthily close and cloistered their relationship was.

To return to the books, there is the one about the Incas. A small passage from it is quoted in *Psycho:* "The drumbeat for this was usually performed on what had been the body of an enemy: the skin had been flayed and the belly stretched to form a drum, and the whole body acted as a sound box while throbbings came out of the open mouth—grotesque, but effective" (2). Now this could simply be taken as another book that indicates Bates's fascination with the morbid and macabre. However, whether Bloch

---

19. I will return to the significance of this soubriquet later.

likes it or not, I think it is another item that is more resonant with Gein than Bates. Gein was notable for having used human skin to decorate a number of his home furnishings, as well as the female skin-suit he wore. While Bates is a killer, he does not display any interest in desecration in the way Gein did, nor do I think it can just be meant to relate to Bates's interest in taxidermy. It reads almost verbatim like the sort of instructional text a person like Gein may have used to assist his crimes.

Finally, I would like to address the two Shakespeare plays. I am not designating these BB to suggest that they could not pertain to Lovecraft. As an incredibly well-read autodidact, Lovecraft did own several complete editions of Shakespeare (see *LL* 140–41), as well as seeing a number of his plays as a child, telling J. Vernon Shea that they were, along with those of Richard Brinsley Sheridan (1751–1816), his favorites (*Lord of a Visible World* 45). However, there is a clear application for Shakespeare, and these two specific plays, in the events of *Psycho*.

First of all, they more generally relate to Bates's interest in psychology. Bates notes how "Shakespeare had known a lot about psychology" (78). This is an understatement. Shakespeare's astounding psychological acuity is one of the many reasons his plays persist in popularity today, just over four hundred years since the publication of the First Folio (1623). The realistic psychological makeup of Shakespeare's characters has led some scholars to claim that this accounts for both the longevity and the universality of his plays, and constitutes the primary reason for their resonance with so many people. This theory is perhaps best, and most extravagantly, evinced by Harold Bloom in his controversial *Shakespeare: The Invention of the Human* (1998). Or, finally, as Lovecraft puts it: "Other books feed different parts of the mind—Shakespeare feeds the entire brain" (*CE* 2.187).

Macbeth is referenced fairly transparently in a scene where Bates is washing his hands and thinking himself a "regular Lady Macbeth" (78). This of course alludes to the celebrated scene in *Macbeth* where a guilt-ridden Lady Macbeth washes imaginary blood from her hands: "Here's the smell of blood still. All the perfumes of Arabia will not sweeten this little hand. Oh, oh, oh!"

(5.1.44–55). However, if Bloch is trying to make some connection between Bates and Lady Macbeth, I do not think the comparison is realized in the novel. Lady Macbeth's guilt-induced psychological unraveling does not seem to be paralleled in Bates. For the most part, Bates does not seem to express much guilt for his crimes, unless one can argue that his depersonalization and subsequent subsumation by his mother's personality are evidence of this guilt. In any case, guilt and its consequences are not as evident in Bates as in Lady Macbeth. Indeed, at one point Sam, Mary's boyfriend, does not believe he has committed the crime, as "[Bates] didn't seem like a man who had anything on his conscience" (127). Perhaps we could make recourse to King Duncan's assertion that "There's no art / To find the mind's construction in the face" (1.4.12–13). But in Bates we see nothing like the mental deterioration of Lady Macbeth or, say, Raskolnikov in *Crime and Punishment* (1866),[20] following his crimes.

Instead, I think the more accurate link to *Psycho* in *Macbeth* is in the relationship between Bates and his mother, and how it compares to the two Macbeths. When chiding Macbeth, who has second thoughts about killing Duncan—a move that will make him king—Lady Macbeth says:

> What beast was't, then,
> That made you break this enterprise to me?
> When you durst do it, then you were a man
> (1.7.48–50)

This taunt is echoed later, when Macbeth is unable to hide his terror at seeing Banquo's ghost, with Lady Macbeth asking him "are you a man?" (3.4.59).[21] The parallel between Lady Macbeth and Mrs Bates is plain here.

---

20. Which, for good measure, also has its own imagined blood scene. After committing his murders, Raskolnikov thoroughly inspects his clothes and sees that they are clean (75). But then "a strange idea entered his head: perhaps all his clothes were soaked and stained with blood and he could not see it because his mental powers were failing and crumbling away" (76–77).

21. Lady Macbeth even utilizes this tactic on herself, asking the "spirits" to "unsex" [her] (1.5.39) and telling them to "[c]ome to [her] woman's breasts /

The connection with *Hamlet* is fairly obvious at first glance. If it wasn't, Bloch has again spelled it out to us, explicitly mentioning Hamlet's father's ghost. The appearance of the ghost is one of the greatest and most impactful supernatural depictions in all literature, particularly where he tells his son of his banishment to Limbo (1.5.10–23). In one of Shakespeare's most celebrated lines, he demands that Hamlet avenge his "murder most foul" (28) at the hands of Hamlet's uncle Claudius, and it is from this injunction that the rest of the play evolves. I will not dwell further on this point, as it is beyond our purposes. But the connection to Bates is clear. Unlike in *Hamlet,* Joe is not Bates's literal uncle ("he wished mother wouldn't insist on calling him 'Uncle Joe.' Because he wasn't any real relation at all—just a friend[22] who came round to see Mother" [76]). Nor did Joe kill Bates's father as Claudius did. And, crucially, it was Bates's father's abandonment that led to the relationship in the first place. But Bates clearly sees Joe as representative of Claudius and thus a threat to his and his mother's relationship, and so he poisons them both with strychnine.

Now for the Lovecraft Books. At least in my consultation of S. T. Joshi and David E. Schultz's extensive catalogue *Lovecraft's Library,* I cannot find evidence of Lovecraft owning any of the books I have designated LB. However, Lovecraft *had* read Margaret Murray's 1921 book *The Witch-Cult in Western Europe,* mentioning it in both "The Horror at Red Hook" (CF 1.485) and "The Call of Cthulhu" (CF 2.24). Lovecraft also cited it as an influence for his story "The Festival" (see IAP 463), and he recommended it in his "Suggestions for a Reading Guide" as a "thrilling and shuddersome background of a sinister belief" (CE 2.193).

As for the others, while I have no direct evidence that Lovecraft read them specifically, they all pertain in one way or another to his general spheres of interest, and he certainly owned

---

And take [her] milk for gall" (45–46) when trying to psych herself up to order Duncan's death.

22. The use of "friend" here is interesting, denoting as it does both Bates's delusion and inability to accept the obviously romantic/sexual relationship between the two.

books like them. *A New Model of the Universe* was by the Russian esoteric P. D. Ouspensky, utilizing contemporaneous scientific and philosophical developments to ponder outré and bizarre claims. While as a pragmatic materialist Lovecraft probably wouldn't have paid any heed to the arguments made in this book, he certainly would have had an interest in it. (Indeed, see Joshi's discussion regarding Murray's book, and how its bizarre origin-theory of witchcraft was somewhat subscribed to by Lovecraft [*IAP* 463–64].) I have no evidence that Lovecraft read Martin Heidegger's highly influential philosophical work *Being in Time*, if I am correct in my surmise that this is what *Dimension and Being* is based on. However, whether the book is meant to be Heidegger's or an entirely invented work, the title alone can be seen as a nod to Lovecraft. In particular, its use of "dimension" seems to me to be an allusion to Lovecraft's fascination with other dimensions of time and space that are encompassed in our current scientific understanding, which recurs throughout his fiction, in particular in "The Dreams in the Witch House":

> Perhaps [Walter] Gilman ought not to have studied so hard. Non-Euclidean calculus and quantum physics are enough to stretch any brain, and when one mixes them with folklore, and tries to trace a strange background of multi-dimensional reality behind the ghoulish hints of the Gothic tales and the wild whispers of the chimney-corner, one can hardly expect to be wholly free from mental tension. (*CF* 3.232)

Bates displays no interest whatsoever in cosmology, astrology etc., and there is nothing about his character—at least as evinced in the book—that would suggest he would be interested in them. There is also this description about Bates, who thinks of himself as a "man who studied the secrets of time and space and mastered the secrets of dimension and being" (76). Again, given that throughout the book Bates is much more interested in psychology, this seems far more applicable to Lovecraft than Bates.

Finally, Bates, like Lovecraft, was rejected by the army (145). When the US joined the First World War, Lovecraft attempted to enlist, if you can imagine such a thing. I do not think that

Tom Collins is being unduly harsh when he declares Lovecraft "hopelessly unqualified" for such an endeavour (3). Lovecraft's mother was at least partly responsible for his rejection by the Army, enlisting the help of the family doctor to declare him physically unfit, in one of the rare instances of her helicopter parenting being of some benefit. However, Lovecraft retained a sense of shame that he was not able to join. Although he was more of an Anglophile than a patriotic American, he still wished to represent his country. Perhaps the following lines from his poem "The Volunteer," which valorizes such people, are representative:

> For the man of faint heart, who needed a start [. . .]
> The hero we raise above all common praise—
> The valorous volunteer! (*AT* 408)

Lovecraft also disdained pacifists, as demonstrated in his poem "Pacifist War Song—1917," whose final stanza should suffice:

> Our fathers were both rude and bold,
> And would not live like brothers;
> But we are of a finer mould—
> We're much more like our mothers! (*AT* 401)

If Robert Bloch was disconcerted at the suggestions that Norman Bates was based on Ed Gein, then I can only imagine what he would have thought about the argument I have put forward. However, in the spirit of *Psycho* itself, in which unconscious motivations drive the main character's actions, even if Bloch did not openly base Bates on Lovecraft, perhaps he did without being aware of it. All authors base characters on people they know, as well as themselves, whether this is in large or small scope. I hope I have demonstrated that the resemblances between Lovecraft and Bates are striking and potentially beyond recourse to coincidence.

But what would Lovecraft himself think? Even a cursory glance at his life would disavow one of the anachronistic depictions of him as a curmudgeonly, reclusive loner. As well as having a number of friends whom he met both in person or corresponded with, Lovecraft was universally regarded by all these individuals as generous, kind, and good-humored. Potentially he would think my argument mere tosh and not worth his bother. But I would like to think that he would simply find it amusing and take it all in good spirit.

Works Cited

American Psychiatric Association. *DSM-5*. Washington and London: American Psychiatric Publishing, 2013.

Ashley, Mike. *Starlight Man: The Extraordinary Life of Algernon Blackwood*. London: Constable, 2001.

Blackwood, Algernon. *The Willows and Others: Collected Short Fiction—Volume 1: 1889–1907*. Ed. S. T. Joshi. New York: Hippocampus Press, 2023.

Bloch, Robert. *Psycho*. 1959. London: Bloomsbury, 1997.

Cardin, Matt. *What the Daemon Said: Essays on Horror Fiction, Film and Philosophy*. New York: Hippocampus Press, 2022.

Collins, Tom. "Introduction." In H. P. Lovecraft, *A Winter Wish*. Chapel Hill, NC: Whispers Press, 1977. 1–11.

Dostoevsky, Fyodor. *Crime and Punishment*. Tr. Jessie Coulson. New York: W. W. Norton, 1989.

Freud, Sigmund. *General Psychological Theory: Papers on Metapsychology*. Ed. Philip Rieff. Tr. Cecil M. Baines. New York: Macmillan, 1963.

Joshi, S. T. *Unutterable Horror: A History of Supernatural Fiction*. Hornsea, UK: PS Publishing, 2012. 2 vols.

———. *The Weird Tale*. Austin: University of Texas Press, 1990.

Ligotti, Thomas. *The Conspiracy against the Human Race*. New York: Hippocampus Press, 2010.

Lodge, David. *Changing Places*. 1975. London: Vintage, 1991.

Lofficier, Randy, and Jean-Marc Lofficier. "What Robert Bloch Owes to H. P. Lovecraft." *Readers Almanac: The Official Blog of the Library of America*. blog.loa.org/2010/09/what-robert-bloch-owes-to-h-p-lovecraft.html#:~:text=Weird%20Tales%20 required%20Bloch%20to,In%20November%201935%20 Lovecraft%20responded.

Lovecraft, H. P. *Lord of a Visible World: An Autobiography in Letters*. Ed. S. T. Joshi and David E. Schultz. 2000. New York: Hippocampus Press, 2019.

———. *Letters to Robert Bloch and Others*. Ed. S. T. Joshi and David E. Schultz. New York: Hippocampus Press, 2015. [Abbreviated in the text as *RB*.]

Nevill, Adam. *Wyrd and Other Derelictions*. Devon, England: Ritual Limited, 2020.

Plato. *The Republic*. Tr. Christopher Rowe. London: Penguin, 2012.

Shreffler, Philip A. *The H. P. Lovecraft Companion*. Westport, CT: Greenwood Press, 1977.

Schweitzer, Darrell. *The Dream Quest of H. P. Lovecraft*. San Bernardino, CA: Borgo Press, 1978.

Schow, David J. "Conversation with Robert Bloch." *Robert Bloch Official Website*. robertbloch.net/a-conversation-with-robert-bloch.html. Accessed 23 February 2024.

Simmons, David. "The Outsider No More?" In David Simmons, ed. *New Critical Essays on H. P. Lovecraft*. London: Palgrave Macmillan, 2013. 1–12.

Shakespeare, William. *Hamlet*. In *The Norton Shakespeare*. Ed. Stephen Greenblatt et al. 3rd ed. New York: W. W. Norton, 2016.

———. *Macbeth*. In *The Norton Shakespeare*. Ed. Stephen Greenblatt et al. 3rd ed. New York: W. W. Norton, 2016.

Sutherland, John. "Seamus Heaney Deserves a Lot More than £40,000." *The Guardian* (March 2009) theguardian.com/books/booksblog/2009/mar/19/seamus-heaney-david-cohen-prize Accessed 21 February 2024.

Wilbanks, David. "10 Questions for Thomas Ligotti." *Thomas Ligotti Online* (May 2007), ligotti.net/showthread.php?t=1248. Accessed 24 February 2024.

Winter, Douglas E. *Faces of Fear: Encounters with the Creators of Modern Horror*. London: Pan, 1990.

Wisker, Gina. "'Spawn of the Pit': Lavinia, Marceline, Medusa, and All Things Foul: H. P. Lovecraft's Liminal Women." In

David Simmons, ed. *New Critical Essays on H. P. Lovecraft.* London: Palgrave Macmillan, 2013. 31–54.

Woolf, Virginia. *Selected Essays.* Ed. David Bradshaw. Oxford: Oxford University Press, 2009.

———. *To the Lighthouse.* London: Penguin, 2000.

Briefly Noted

The great Lovecraft scholar Robert H. Waugh died on 13 April 2024. Beginning in the late 1980s, Waugh hosted an annual H. P. Lovecraft Forum at the State University of New York at New Paltz, where he was a professor of English. Many leading Lovecraft scholars on the East Coast attended this event over the more than two decades during which it was held. Waugh's first volume of critical essays on Lovecraft, *The Monster in the Mirror,* appeared from Hippocampus Press in 2006. Two further volumes subsequently appeared: *A Monster of Voices* (2011) and *A Monster for Many* (2021). Waugh also edited the notable critical anthology *Lovecraft and Influence* (Scarecrow Press, 2013). Other notable figures who have died lately are the Lovecraftian authors David A. Drake (d. 10 December 2023), Brian Lumley (d. 2 January 2024), and Fred Chappell (d. 4 January 2024), and the filmmaker Roger Corman (d. 9 May 2024), who directed the Lovecraftian film *The Haunted Palace* (1963).

Narrative Methods in H. P. Lovecraft's "The Mound"

James Goho

This essay explores H. P. Lovecraft's narrative methods in "The Mound" (1929–30). In this ghostwritten (for Zealia Brown Reed Bishop [1897–1968]) yet original story, Lovecraft experimented with shifting narrative vectors such as voice, history, and genre.[1] In this article I will focus on the status of the novelette as a narrative, or rather as a set of narratives; that is, I am examining its methods of telling (the voices), the histories and sequences of the narrative, and the genres, especially the Gothic, embedded in the novelette.

Lovecraft enriched the central narrative with layers of tales as he explored the nature of storytelling. Early in the first chapter he hints at this when the townspeople of Binger, Oklahoma, use binoculars to watch people who explore the mysterious mound in the story as if they are an audience and the mound is a place for spectacle. Lovecraft wrote this story not merely to tell it but also to showcase the manner of telling it. He deployed several characters in the narrative communication, some of whom retell or quote others' stories. In this process, a voice may reveal a teller's social status. In addition, Lovecraft layered the novelette in eras of history and experimented with varying sequences of time. The narrative also features various genres, as Lovecraft infused it with conventions from Gothic, science fiction, and adventure tales.

---

1. The inspiration for taking this approach to HPL's novelette arises from my reading of *Joseph Conrad: Voice, Sequence, History, Genre* (2008) edited by Jakob Lothe, Jeremy Hawthorn, and James Phelan.

The core of the novelette concerns the mystery of that mound near Binger patrolled by two ghostly figures[2] whom for two generations many people have sought. Some of the searchers returned bored and unscathed. Others returned to tell stories of their horrific experience at or in the mound and warned people not to go there. Their physical and mental injuries limited their lives or drove them to commit suicide. Some adventurers never returned from the mound. The primary narrative arc of the work is the discovery of a lost world. But this conception does not do justice to the richness and depth of "The Mound."

The novelette starts with the unnamed ethnologist narrator reflecting on his experience in Oklahoma in 1928. It is separated into seven chapters. The first features the ethnologist documenting the many tales about the mysterious mound. In the second chapter he conducts a field study of the mound, where he discovers a metallic cylinder containing an old manuscript penned "in wretched and ill-punctuated script" (CF 4.225–26) by Pánfilo de Zamacona y Nuñez. The following four chapters trace Zamacona's hazardous trek underground and his harrowing experiences in the underground society of Xinaián (phonetically: K'n-yan).[3] In the last chapter, after reading Pánfilo's lengthy manuscript, the ethnologist travels again to the mound with the manuscript. He descends deep into the underground world, where he makes a

---

2. One of the ghosts is a headless Indigenous woman (the text contains a derogatory term for "woman"). The man "was certainly *not a savage*. He was the product of a *civilisation*," which suggests that the narrator or HPL did not believe the Indigenous people had a civilization (CF 4.219). S. T. Joshi points this out (DW 128). This negative attitude toward Native Americans appears frequently in the novelette. Readers must wait to know the origin of these two figures until later in the story. This technique is sometimes referred to as "delayed decoding" (Watt 175), which means that an author portrays scenes or characters whose meaning is not revealed until later in the story.

3. The narrator explains this word by arguing that Zamacona's explanations suggested that this would be the best representation that he (the narrator) could provide for "Anglo-Saxon ears" (CF 4.249). This suggests that Zamacona attempted to convey the thought-transfer method of the people of K'n-yan into vocal expression in his manuscript for Spanish readers and that the narrator altered this for English readers.

horrific discovery. It causes him to flee precipitously, dropping the manuscript and dashing Zamacona's final hope. Peter Cannon sees Zamacona "composing his narrative" (100) as a means to secure his greatness. While planning his final escape attempt from K'n-yan, Zamacona yearned that his manuscript would "reach the outer world at all hazards" (CF 4.279).

The novelette is long for Lovecraft, at about 25,000 words. The longest part of the novelette consists of Zamacona's manuscript, but it is not told directly by him. The unnamed ethnologist narrator translates, edits, and comments on the manuscript. Zamacona's voice does emerge through this method. "The Mound" has varying narrative frames, shifting temporal orders, and historic ambiguities and distortions. It is a compelling analysis of a society's decline, tempered by an intense historical longing for its fabled past and despair at its inevitable decay.

The work is Lovecraft's and not that of Zealia Brown Reed Bishop, whose name has appeared as the author of the novelette. S. T. Joshi definitively established Lovecraft's authorship in his "Who Wrote the Mound?" In their introduction to Lovecraft's *Letters to Woodburn Harris and Others,* Joshi and David E. Schultz write that "it is safe to say that both the conception and composition of the tale are entirely Lovecraft's" (20). Moreover, Lovecraft wrote to Elizabeth Toldridge outlining the plot of the story and noted that it "amounts to original composition" (*ET* 114).

Francesco Borri remarks that many of Lovecraft's letters to Bishop read like a creative writing course. Lovecraft encouraged Bishop to practice writing (providing notes on style and expression), to read (including book suggestions), and to understand different markets (including notes on various publications). His letters are always courteous, informative, and encouraging. "The Mound" is mentioned in a few of his letters to her, but he does not go into any discussion of the content of the novelette with Bishop.

"The Mound" does exhibit some minor differences from Lovecraft's general patterns. It is set in Oklahoma, which is unusual. And there is a female character who plays a slight but important role in the story that is not common in Lovecraft's work. But it is Lovecraft's novelette and is a fine work worthy of his canon.

Voices in "The Mound"

Lovecraft layered the novelette within multiple narrative frames and built it with several forms of storytelling such as the sketch, the tall tale, survivor testimony, and the found manuscript. The unifying voice is that of the ethnologist narrator, which sounds throughout much of the tale. He is a homodiegetic narrator, that is, he is a teller and commentator on tales, but also an active character in the novelette. In this way, the ethnologist is continuously engaged with the reader. The novelette starts as an after-the-fact reflection of the narrator's experiences in 1928. But soon other voices will be heard. These personal accounts enliven the drama of the legend, so a reader may encounter the phenomena of the mound directly.

The narrator's voice resounds with authority. He is educated and a Virginian who traces his heritage back to a landowning family in England. This is a voice that Lovecraft established as one that could be trusted to record the truth. But when we think about what we know about him, it is not much, not even his name. In a sense, he comes to life through the story he is telling, especially how he narrates the central mystery—the nature of the mound in the Oklahoma countryside near Binger—through many other voices.

In the first chapter of the novelette, the narrator says he had gone into Oklahoma to document and record ghost tales "woven around the vast, lonely artificial-looking mounds" of Western Oklahoma (CF 4.205). He retells a "yarn" of 1892 about "great armies of invisible spectres" battling in the sky, originally attributed to John Willis but widely told (CF 4.205).[4] He gathers more tales from Mr. Compton ("a man of high intelligence and local responsibility") and his mother, known as "Grandma Compton," who is presented as one of the first pioneers in Oklahoma (CF 4.208).[5] They tell the history of the many mound

---

4. HPL decodes this later in the novelette. Zamacona relates a tale of how some people of K'n-yan when they sleep make "half-material visits to a realm of mounds and valleys," which may be the outer world "to live over the old, glorious battles of their forefathers" (CF 4.252).

5. This means she was one of first non-Indigenous people who occupied a por-

explorations to the ethnologist. In some of the tales the voices of those who went to the mound and returned are heard directly. Heaton is one of those characters. Villagers watched him disappeared under the mound in 1891 (soon after the Oklahoma Land Run of 1889). He returned in a state of panic and exclaimed:

> "great God, they are older than the earth, and came here from somewhere else—they know what you think, and make you know what they think—they're half-man, half-ghost—crossed the line—melt and take shape again—getting more and more so, yet we're all descended from them in the beginning— children of Tulu[6]—everything made of gold—monstrous animals, half-human—dead slaves— madness—Iä! Shub-Niggurath!— *that white man—oh, my God, what they did to him! . . .*"[7] (CF 4.210)

The voice attributed to Heaton displays his hysterical state of mind as he speaks in quick, broken sentences. The narrator comments that the Comptons said that Heaton became the "village idiot for about eight years, after which he died in an epileptic fit" (CF 4.210). Another of the Comptons' stories told to the narrator describes three men dragged down by dim forms spied by a watcher from the village. This tale is retold by the narrator, who hears it from the Comptons, who repeat a story from an unnamed witness. This mode of telling holds for two archaeologists who in 1915 traveled to Binger to dig at the mound but never returned. The tales are reported matter-of-factly with no mention of how the people of the village felt about the disappearances, derangements, suicides, and apparent deaths related to the mound, except their fear. They often observe with binoc-

---

tion of the Oklahoma Unassigned Lands of the former Indian Territory, which had earlier been assigned to the Creek and Seminole peoples. The Dawes Act of 1888 opened these lands. The Land Run occurred in 1889 when white settlers raced to occupy lands.

6. Throughout the novelette, HPL introduces entities that are in his other stories.

7. This yet another example of delayed decoding. The identity of this "white man" is revealed late in the story.

ulars but do not seem to rush out to help. Fear seems to rule them. The binoculars give them a view, but no one takes photographs neither of the ghostly figures nor any of the searches while in progress.

There are other tales of those who explore the mound. This includes Captain Lawton, who searched the mound in 1916. He disappeared while twenty people watched with binoculars. More than a week later, "the object," which may have been Lawton, returned to Binger and "muttered":

> "always down there, before there were any living things—older than the dinosaurs—always the same, only weaker—never death—brooding and brooding and brooding—*the same people, half-man and half-gas*—the dead that walk and work—oh, those beasts, those half-human unicorns—houses and cities of gold—old, old, old, older than time—came down from the stars—Great Tulu—Azathoth —Nyarlathotep—waiting, waiting. . . ." (CF 4.212)

The object that was Captain Lawton speaks in sentence fragments akin to Heaton, but his speech seems less articulate. Soon after that incident, Joe Norton and Rance Wheelock searched at the mound while Clyde Compton watched through binoculars. They disappeared and were never seen again. These disappearances incite fear and panic among the populace of Binger, but no one seems to mourn. Their emotion appears to be awe in the face of something seemingly out of the unknown. Grandma Compton, the Indigenous people, and a few others suspect "unholy vistas and deep cosmic menace" from the mound (CF 4.216).

Another tale told to the narrator by the Comptons involves two Clay brothers, who after World War I hunted the mound for gold. One never returned, but Ed Clay did, only to shoot himself. He did pen the following note (in abbreviated form here):

> "For gods sake never go nere that mound [. . .]—they what live forever young as they like and you cant tell if they are really men or just gostes—and what they do cant be spoke about and

this is only 1 entrance—you cant tell how big the whole thing is—after what we seen I dont want to live aney more France was nothing besides this—and see that people always keep away o god they wood if they see poor walker like he was in the end." (CF 4.215)

Ed Clay's note has spelling errors, lacks capitalization, misuses pronouns, and has little punctuation. The voice (from a written note) of this character exhibits his lower status than either the Comptons or the narrator. Generally, the testimony of characters who ventured down into the underground world depicts their hysterical state through their use of the fractured language caused by their experience.

Another voice heard early in the novelette is Grey Eagle. After the incident of Captain Lawton, he offered the following counsel and advice (in abbreviated form here):

> "You let um 'lone, white man. No good—those people. All under here, all under there, them old ones. Yig, big father of snakes, he there. Yig is Yig. [. . .] Nobody come out, let nobody in. Get in, no get out. You let um 'lone, you have no bad medicine. Red man know, he no get catch. White man meddle, he no come back. Keep 'way little hills. No good. Grey Eagle say this.[8] (CF 4.212)

Grey Eagle's voice is presented in this manner at other times in the novelette. His voice varies significantly from the white people's voices. The language attributed to Grey Eagle adheres to a long tradition in American writing that stages Native Americans as linguistically incompetent, and, hence, less intelligent than white characters. Barbra A. Meek suggests that it is a form of linguistic segregation. She shows how linguistic features of Native American articulations in stories are depicted in "dysfluent speech forms" (93)—a style she finds in movies, on television, and in literature. In "The Mound" the voice of Grey Eagle is a "composite of grammatical "abnormalities" (Meek 95). A few of

---

8. This style of speech is also used earlier in the novelette to depict the Indigenous people speaking about the incident originating with John Willis.

the abnormalities in Grey Eagle's voice, which he is said "to grunt,"[9] are "lack of tense, deletion (of various grammatical elements), and substitution" (Meek 99). And the use of "um" is also characteristic of this exaggerated form of speech.

I will note just a few examples of dysfluent sentences (followed with a fluent version) from Grey Eagle's depiction. "You let um 'lone, white man." (You *leave them alone*, white_man.) "All under here, all under there." (*They are* all under here; *they are* all under there.) "Red man know, he no get catch." (*The* Red man knows; he *does not* get *caught*.) "Grey Eagle say this." (Grey Eagle *says* this.)

Although Grey Eagle is depicted as speaking in this dysfluent manner, he appears to be the wisest in his counsel and most generous in his help to the ethologist. For example, Grey Eagle unaccountably lends a family heirloom, a talisman made of an unknown metal, to the narrator.[10] It is essential to the narrator's discovery at the mound of a metallic cylinder containing an old manuscript written in Spanish.

With these contrasting voices, Lovecraft tells readers tales of the dangerous world under the mound near Binger. The stories vary slightly, and the voices are different, as Lovecraft gives each speaker a unique character expressed through their words.

Pánfilo de Zamacona y Nuñez is another prominent voice in the novelette. He wrote the manuscript found by the narrator. It unfolds over four chapters. Lovecraft's interlacing of these two voices is a central triumph of the novelette, as it stages the ancient Spanish manuscript so that a reader directly experiences Zamacona's expedition to and experience within the civilization of Xinaián, yet maintains a literary distance through the commentary of the narrator. Zamacona is described as a member of the campaign of Francisco Vázquez de Coronado (1510–1554) in the southwest of the United States in 1540–42. He speaks several languages and the underground people treat him with

---

9. In her research, Meek found that "grunting" is commonly used to characterize the speech of Indigenous people (94).

10. The narrator does return the talisman to Grey Eagle. Hence, he will flee from Binger with no evidence of his discovery.

respect and hospitality not shown to any of the others who had the misfortune to discover them. In fact, he is said to be a "higher grade man" than anyone else who had ventured into the mound (CF 4.250).

In his manuscript, Zamacona writes about the voice of a Native American, Charging Buffalo. Zamacona says Charging Buffalo informed him about the underground world of gold and led him to a portal that would lead down to that world—a journey Charging Buffalo had undertaken. Lovecraft has Charging Buffalo give Zamacona an abbreviated sketch of the underworld, including the arduousness of the trek underground, the people's horrific and repulsive practices, their mutilated slave classes, and their amazing and fearsome powers. The narrative frames here include the narrator translating Zamacona's manuscript, where he retells the sketch of the underworld told to him by Charging Buffalo. Charging Buffalo is not quoted directly. His speech patterns are fluent, as related by Zamacona and translated by the narrator.

In the underground land of *Xinaián*, Zamacona experiences what Charging Buffalo had told him. The people communicate telepathically. In the novelette, Zamacona describes the method as concentrating on someone's eyes to receive a message and to reply by "summoning up a mental image of what he wished to say, and throwing the substance of this into his glance" (CF 4.248). An underground inhabitant, Gll'-Hthaa-Ynn, tells the history of the underground world through this method and introduces Zamacona to the pleasures and horrors of the underworld. His thoughts are expressed in the voice of Zamacona through the narrator, yet there is always an element of menace in his telepathy that seems to seep into Zamacona's voice, who was told that he must remain below and is a prisoner.

The four chapters of Zamacona's manuscript display a composite voice. There is Zamacona, of course, but there is always the narrator, who is more than the translator. He sometimes slips into the background as Zamacona's thoughts, anxieties, and increasing desperation and fear are prominent. But the narrator often emerges to explain, to censor, or to comment on the

Spanish text. At times they seem to merge into a single voice, with one from the far past and the other from the present (of the novelette). The narrator often combines his view of the manuscript with Zamacona's actions and thoughts. For example, Zamacona's first contact with the people of Xinaián occurs when he is awakened in a gold temple he had rested in after his long journey. He hears a voice:

> "calling out, in a not unmusical voice, a formula which the manuscript tries to represent as *'oxi, oxi, giathcán ycá relex.'* Feeling sure that his visitors were men and not daemons, and arguing that they could have no reason for considering him an enemy, Zamacona decided to face them openly and at once." (CF 4.246)

This type of discourse illustrates Lovecraft's ability to reveal Zamacona's inner thoughts and feelings through his narrator's voice while remaining at an observational distance.

While in the world of Xinaián, Zamacona hears many tales and legends about the underworld spanning eons.[11] He heard of their space journey (with no explanation of how) and their peopling of the Earth. He listened to stories of their early surface civilizations and the eventual sequestering of the land of Xinaián from the surface world. Indeed, the manuscript is loaded with tales about the underworld not just the "blue-litten" one of the people of K'n-yan. There is a "red-litten region called Yoth" (CF 4.252) and a "forbidding black realm of N'kai" (CF 4.262) that is patrolled by black slime.

As the narrator allows full expression to Zamacona's thoughts and feelings, the Spaniard's revulsion becomes more explicit as his exposure to the depraved society increases. And a reader may also sense a growing revulsion from the narrator as he edits and censors some of the manuscript. This may engender a phenomenological experience as the reader directly encounters the depravity of the underground civilization.

Zamacona's revulsion leads to escape attempts. At this point

---

11. In contrast, the time span of the experiences at the mound on the surface amounted to only two generations.

in the manuscript, another character or voice emerges. Zamacona enlists a female of the land of *Xinaián* to help him escape. She does not have a direct voice, but she tells of a secret portal through which they both can escape.[12] It fails because Zamacona tries to carry off gold. For the attempted escape, T'la-yub is tortured and mutilated in an amphitheater of sadistic pain and suffering. She leaves as a headless thing that is set as a sentinel on the mound near Binger.[13] The manuscript ends with Zamacona's last desperate attempt to escape. But his final screams seem palpable in the hysteria of the narrator when he discovers Zamacona's disfigured body below the mound at the end of the novelette.

"The Mound" is a series of tales within tales (layered narrative frames) with multiple agents in the narrative transmission culminating in the manuscript of Pánfilo de Zamacona y Nuñez as told by the unnamed narrator. But readers hear many stories in the novelette. All the narratives (whether a tale, a sketch, or the lengthy, tragic manuscript) seem anxious to discover the mystery of the mound. Early in the novelette, the repetitious tales are told to establish a sense of observational truth about the mystery that the manuscript proves in astonishingly intricate, imaginative detail. Lovecraft's narrative methods in the four chapters revealing the manuscript show the inner workings of his characters. It reveals their inner emotions and thoughts while remaining at an objective distance. Lovecraft's voices tell this novelette through narrative frame techniques that display his command of storytelling. He was a master of deploying multiple voices, various perspectives, and narrative frames within his literary work.

History in "The Mound"

Lovecraft spanned the novelette across years of history and millennia of imaginative antiquity. The overall time sequence of "The Mound" is short while the narrator is in the Binger area

---

12. It is not entirely clear why she would betray her people to assist Zamacona.
13. Thus solving the mystery of one sentinel on the mound.

but is immeasurable in its imaginative scope. The early tales tell of the mound over two generations, but the telling occurs in a day. The narrator translates Zamacona's 1545 manuscript during a long night, but that manuscript tells of eons. Time expands in the novelette through the imbedded tales that the narrator hears or reads.

Although set in 1928 (for the present time of the novelette), the novelette ranges over the ages. Indeed, a theme is deep time. The novelette starts with the narrator reflecting on the depth of time in the Americas, especially his experience of the "stupefying—almost horrible—ancientness" he found in Oklahoma (CF 4.204). But the present-day aspect of the novelette is brief—only a few days—as the narrator is recollecting it from an unknown date after the events in Binger. Lovecraft also links the fictional events in the tales to historical events such as the Oklahoma Land Rush, World War I, and Coronado's campaign in the southwest of the United States in 1540–42.

After the narrator discovers the manuscript, the novelette regresses imaginatively. Dazzled by his discovery of the manuscript in the present time (of the novelette), the narrator is "thrown back nearly four centuries" and the time of the Spanish in the southwest of America (CF 4.229). At that time, Zamacona leaves Coronado's force and strikes out for gold, wealth, and fame. In the underground, he marvels at the tales of the people of *Xinaián* who came from outer space to Earth when "its crust was fit to live on" (CF 4.249). The first life forms (microbes) appeared on Earth about 3.7 billion years ago. Thus, the people of K'n-yan are "almost infinitely ancient" (CF 4.249). While he learns of that long history, Zamacona lives out his four years underground with an ever-increasing sense of revulsion at the violent, depraved, and sickening practices, games, and liaisons of the people. Zamacona's final escape attempt happens offstage. Then we return to the present in 1928 for the last chapter. The novelette is a time-spanning marvel.

During his translation (or retelling) of Zamacona's manuscript, the narrator identifies with him. Zamacona had boasted of his exploits and his future expectations arising from his discovery of *Xinaián*. Thinking of his own discovery, the narrator imagines the two of them standing together with renowned ancients on the shore of infinity. He writes that "before that gulf Pánfilo de Zamacona and I stood side by side; just as Aristotle and I, or Cheops and I, might have stood" (CF 4.229). They meet deep time together.

At the close of the second chapter, the narrator feels an "abysmal timelessness" and the "dizzying gulfs" of primal mysteries (CF 4.229). Peter Cannon writes that Lovecraft imagined the "sweep of time on a geological scale" in "The Mound" (99). This feeling of deep time is a geological matter, represented by the underground world where, as Francesco Borri writes, human beings are marginal. Lovecraft's novelette articulates the awe and terror at the concept of deep time that started in the Victorian Era, continued into the twentieth century, and may still be felt today. James Hutton (1726–1797) initiated the discovery. It was extended by Charles Lyell (1797–1875) in his geological work and confirmed by Charles Darwin (1809–1882) in his revolutionary work on evolution. During an era when biblical time was the belief, the notion of hundreds of millions of years (not to speak of billions) seemed unfathomable. Browser and Croxall claim that Lyell's work "staggered the Victorian imagination" (4). And Stephen Jay Gould writes that it is still "difficult to comprehend, so outside our ordinary experience" (2). The invisible depths of time become visible in "The Mound" where the people of K'n-yan represent incomprehensible antiquity. K'n-yan seems timeless, or to have existed for eons beyond the comprehension of someone akin to Zamacona, who would have conceived of Earth as only thousands of years old. The trajectory of "The Mound" rebels against the alleged linearity of historical progression and its fundamental teleology of continuing advancement and improvement not only for the beings of *Xinaián* but also for human beings.[14]

An actual historical part of the narrative is Coronado's campaign from 1540 to 1542 across the American Southwest. The

---

14. They are beings who may have been the originators of humans, which suggests that humans may have devolved. S. T. Joshi suggests this (*DW* 139–40).

narrator glorifies only one history of that campaign while others are ignored or silenced. The narrator says that the early section of Zamacona's manuscript differed in "no essential way from the account known to history" (CF 4.227). But the question is: whose account, the Spanish or the Indigenous peoples'? The narrator idolizes the Spanish, commenting on the "intrepid fire of those Renaissance Spaniards who conquered half the unknown world" (CF 4.260). So I assume the account would not have told the truth about the effects of Coronado's campaign on the Indigenous people whom he and his army met on their search for fabled gold.

The campaign devastated Indigenous people, especially women. The Spanish routinely exploited, raped, and killed Indigenous peoples. Some Spaniards recognized this soon after Coronado and his force returned to Mexico City. Its treatment of the native population was "denounced to Spanish king Carlos I" (Flint 233). There was an investigation, of sorts, led by Lorenzo de Tejada, but Coronado escaped any penalty. The Spanish were brutal in their campaign. Richard Flint says that "hundreds died, hundreds more were injured, thousands were impoverished and deprived of their homes and livelihoods" (252). Coronado's campaign was a campaign of terror consistent with "sixteenth-century Spanish expeditionary/settlement behavior throughout the New World," which included stealing food and clothing, the seizure of women, and the use of terror tactics (Flint 245). Indigenous captives were frequently tortured in an attempt to extract information about gold. It was not uncommon for the Spanish to cut off the hands and noses of Indigenous people to spread horror (Flint 244; Todorov 148). The narrator of the novelette remarks that "[h]istory knows the story of that expedition," writing that the Spanish heard of gold at Cicuyé, also called Cicuique, which is located south of Santa Fe, New Mexico (CF 4.230). In fact, the Spanish took Cicuique leaders as prisoners. They were tortured by members of the expedition in an attempt to locate the fabled gold (Flint 238). They set dogs on the leaders (Flint 244), and wives and daughters were taken by force from Cicuique (Flint 254). The narrator of this story is not omniscient. Zamacona, if an actual member of Coronado's campaign, would have at least known and probably participated in these brutal acts against the Indigenous peoples. Hence his shock and dismay at the acts of the people of K'n-yan suggest that they were especially unspeakably shocking and horrendous.

The mound in Lovecraft's story is imaginative. It was a key part of the brief idea sent to Lovecraft by Bishop: "There is an Indian mound near here, which is haunted by a headless ghost. Sometimes it is a woman" (*IAP* 745). In the story, Charging Buffalo leads Zamacona to the "region of great mounds" (*CF* 4.232). These mounds are portrayed as entrances to an underground world. Mounds are real features of the Oklahoma landscape. Binger is in Caddo County, where there are mounds. Some of the names of the mounds evoke a sense of mystery, for example Ghost Mound, Dead Woman Mound, and Lone Mound. However, as A. C. Shead documents, these mounds are buttes and not unnatural formations.

There are more interesting mounds in eastern Oklahoma, for example the Spiro Mounds. Kenneth Gordon Orr and Juliet E. Morrow provide details of the site and its history. It is an 80-acre Indigenous archaeological site. Between 850 and 1450 C.E., the Caddoan-speaking Indigenous people built twelve mounds, ceremonial areas, and a city. Craig Mound, the site's only burial mound, contained some of the most exceptional pre-Columbian artifacts ever discovered. Unfortunately, the site was looted the site and many artifacts were dispersed widely. David La Vere and Jeffrey P. Brain document the looting of the site. This has also happened to many of the earthenwork land features constructed by Adena, Hopewell, and Mississippian Indigenous cultures across America. George R. Milner provides a comprehensive overview of these Indigenous cultures.[15]

But the mound in the novelette is an imaginative mound created by Lovecraft as a mysterious portal to an underground

---

15. The cause of the collapse of these Native American cultures has been attributed to the spread of new infectious diseases brought from the Old World, such as smallpox and influenza, which decimated most of the Native Americans from the last mound-builder civilization.

society in a state of degeneration, retrogressing from ethical, scientific, and cultural ideals. Kelly Hurley might characterize it "as sliding into decline, into senility, dementia, and death" (77). The population of quasi-human people at one time was a progressive, inquisitive, and learning society. But the society spiraled into degeneration despite its amazing powers. There is no "kindness" (CF 4.272) in the "tall city of Tsath," where all the people of K'n-yan had sequestered (CF 4.252), as if they had forsaken their history, as if time had worn them to a parody of their former selves. S. T. Joshi views the story, in part, to be Lovecraft's metaphor for the possible collapse of Western civilization (*IAP* 746–47). Steven J. Mariconda also sees the novelette as a "metaphor for dystopic Western civilization" (227).

"The Mound" encompasses eons of time that are layered with real and fictitious history. Lovecraft constructed this complex story with several frames of time and history. First there is the sequencing of time on the surface of the story, which is short. But the imaginative mound disrupts the sense of regular time as it creates a sense of deep time, an immense antiquity. Joel Lane suggests that "The Mound" could "stand alongside Wells' *The Time Machine* as an allegory of the human future" (152). Traveling into the mound, for Zamacona, is akin to time travel. And he cannot escape back to his original time.

Genre in "The Mound"

Lovecraft drew from genre literature in his construction of "The Mound." There are elements of the adventure story, the lost world story, science fiction, and Gothic horror. Zamacona's journey is an adventure into a lost civilization that has existed on Earth for millennia. I will focus on the Gothic horror aspects of the work, especially the extreme, morbid physicality of the underground civilization. In "Supernatural Horror in Literature" (1927), Lovecraft suggested that supernatural literature arises from and appeals to our "inmost biological heritage" (26). Jack Morgan argues that physiological fear is at the root of much Gothic and horror writing, film, and art. He suggests that biological horror arises from the dread of defilement, decay, degeneration, and death. The underground civilization is a center of biological deformations, mutations, and obscenities. Steven J. Mariconda comments that the "sadism and violence in this story is like nothing else in Lovecraft" (227). K'n-yan is a state of biological perversity.

The ruling people of K'n-yan, who consider themselves to be the highest level of beings in the underworld, bred "an extensive array of inferior and semi-human industrial organisms" (CF 4.253). They constructed this slave class from "conquered enemies, outer stragglers of the world, dead bodies, and naturally inferior members of the ruling class" (CF 4.253). They also fabricated a second dead-alive slave class, called y'm-bhi, who were "reanimated corpses" (CF 4.234). These creatures have horrible bodily mutilations. For example, some are headless and others had suffered singular and "seemingly capricious subtractions, distortions, transpositions, and graftings in various places" (CF 4.265). Many of these creatures were horribly deformed while being tortured for the amusement of the ruling people. In their amphitheaters, they conduct sadistic mutilations, amputations, and deformations on their fellows.

The land of *Xinaián* is a center of biological horror. Other Gothic bodies include the *gyaa-yothn*, which Captain Lawton called "those beasts, those half-human unicorns" (CF 4.212). These Gothic bodies are "admixed, nauseating, abominable" (Hurley 9). In his manuscript, Zamacona expresses his disgust at seeing these manufactured creatures, whose facial features are egregiously described in the novelette.[16]

The K'n-yan world is a society with "no values and principles" where "art and intellect" had become "listless and decadent" and science was "falling into decay" (CF 4.255–56). It is a slave society that routinely creates creatures of deformed biology for the amusement and comfort of the ruling class. A society focused on inflicting pain and enjoying the spectacle of agony and mutilation in their amphitheaters. The people of *Xinaián* have a kind of immortality, yet there is a declining population, which

---

16. They has "flat-nosed, bulging-lipped faces" (CF 4.259).

suggests the collapse of the culture, as some choose to die out of ennui. Lovecraft created a sick world of mental, physical, and moral decay.

Morgan argues that the Gothic empathizes assaults upon the flesh and the body's decay and disintegration. He sees horror literature confronting readers with our "elemental biological reality" (99). In the underground world, biological engineering transforms bodies into Gothic atrocities. Kelly Hurley might refer to these grotesque creations as "abhuman," a term she borrowed from William Hope Hodgson (1877–1918). Hurley claims that this is an essential feature of much Gothic writing. The "abhuman" is typified by "morphic variability" and is "in danger of becoming not-itself, becoming other" (3–4). The term signifies a "Gothic body," or something only vestigially human or in the process of becoming something monstrous (5). The underground creations by the people of Xinaián are blasphemous monstrosities. Moreover, this extreme corruption of bodies is symbolic of the corruption and decay of the underworld culture and society, which is what Lovecraft set out to exhibit in "The Mound."

In the city of Tsath, there is no fellow feeling.[17] The only feeling arises from inflicting torture and pain. There is a collapse of any ethical standards. In this abhuman paradise, all "values and principles" are abolished (CF 4.254). As Kelly Hurley might suggest, the ruination of that society is "violent, absolute and [. . .] repulsive" (3). Zamacona notes in his manuscript that the "omnipresent moral and intellectual disintegration was a tremendously deep-seated and ominously accelerating movement" (CF 4.272). The culture has sealed itself off and hides from any real contact with the outside world. It has closed its borders to the new, the different, and the diverse. Its isolation has culminated in decay, dissolution, and immolation. Lovecraft created a society mired in a pathology of ritualistic, performative, and violent dehumanization of each other. It is a pathology of cosmic dimensions.

Chris Baldick argues that the Gothic tells of "a fearful sense

---

17. "Fellow-feeling" is considered to be the foundation of morality by many philosophers, for example, Peter Glassen (47).

of inheritance in a time with a claustrophobic sense of enclosure in space," which results in a "sickening descent into disintegration" (xix). The people of *Xinaián* are bound by space and time. They are enclosed underground and their nearly infinite heritage is a disease causing an appalling descent into disintegration, degradation, and dissolution. The narrator at one point muses on "kindness" as an essential feature of civilization (CF 4.272). There is no fellow feeling in the land of K'n-yan. And Zamacona exhibits little kindness. He thinks he might have the woman, T'la-yub, who tried to help him escape "sojourn amongst the plains Indians" (CF 4.274). After she is mutilated, Zamacona shows little remorse or mourning for her. But in the end he becomes a Gothic body, one of the *y'm-bhi*, similar to her.

The images of the Gothic world of the people of K'n-yan that Lovecraft created are not frightening. They are disturbing, disquieting, which describes much of Lovecraft's weird fiction. K'n-yan demonstrates human entropy. The underground world enclosed itself and declined into a grotesque obsession with spectacles of cruelty and pain and the loss of any sense of fellow-felling. In "The Mound," Lovecraft created an ominous portrait of a society descending toward disorder and death.

In Conclusion

In "The Mound," H. P. Lovecraft created a complex, compelling story worthy of his sophisticated narrative structure. The novelette's intricate textuality enriches the story, as the central narrative is told from many perspectives. His variations in presentation styles enhance the overall main-story line. By doing so, Lovecraft highlighted the status of the novelette as a narrative, or rather, as a set of narratives. He experimented with methods of delivery, sites of the telling, voices of delivery, and the history of the telling. He used various narrative frames, including a first-person unnamed narrator, personal written statements, first-person accounts, tales told by observers, a found manuscript that includes tales stretching over millennia, and an overall form of free indirect discourse through four chapters that is the narrator's version of Pánfilo de Zamacona y Nuñez's manuscript. In addition, Lovecraft told the story through varying time sequences and layered the story with fictional and historical periods, blending the real with the uncanny. The narrative also pays tribute to various genres, as Lovecraft shaped the novelette with icons from adventure tales, science fiction, and the Gothic. However, the biological Gothic is especially dominant in his revelation of the state of the underground world. In this novelette, Lovecraft proved his virtuosity in storytelling.

Works Cited

Baldick, Chris. "Introduction." In Chris Baldick, ed. *The Oxford Book of Gothic Stories*. Oxford: Oxford University Press, 1992. xi–xxiii.

Borri, Francesco. "The Year of the Red Moon: 'Out of the Æons,' Revisions, and Deep History." *Lovecraft Annual* No. 17 (2023): 87–114.

Brain, Jeffrey P. "The Great Mound Robbery." *Archaeology* 41, No. 3 (1988): 18–25.

Bowser, Rachel A., and Brian Croxall. "Introduction: Industrial Evolution." *Neo-Victorian Studies* 3, No. 1 (2010): 1–45.

Cannon, Peter. *H. P. Lovecraft*. Boston: Twayne, 1989.

Flint, Richard. "Results and Repercussions of the Coronado Expedition to Tierra Nueva from Documentary and Archaeological Sources." *New Mexico Historical Review* 77, No. 3 (2002): 233–59.

Glassen, Peter. "Are There Unresolvable Moral Disputes?" *Dialogue: Canadian Philosophical Review / Revue canadienne de philosophie* 1, No. 1 (1962): 36–50.

Gould, Stephen Jay. *Time's Arrow—Time's Cycle: Myth and Metaphor in the Discovery of Geological Time*. Cambridge, MA: Harvard University Press, 1987.

Hurley, Kelly. *The Gothic Body: Sexuality, Materialism and Degeneration at the Fin de Siècle*. Cambridge: Cambridge University Press, 2004.

Joshi, S. T. *H. P. Lovecraft: The Decline of the West*. Mercer Island, WA: Starmont House, 1990. [Abbreviated in the text as *DW*.]

———. "Who Wrote the 'The Mound'?" In Joshi's *Lovecraft and a World in Transition*. New York: Hippocampus Press, 2014. 343–46.

———, and David Schultz. "Introduction." In *Letters to Woodburn Harris and Others*. Ed. S. T. Joshi and David E. Schultz. New York: Hippocampus Press, 2022. 7–25.

Kristeva, Julia. *Powers of Horror: An Essay on Abjection*. Tr. Leon S. Roudiez. New York: Columbia University Press, 1982.

La Vere, David. *Looting Spiro Mounds: An American King Tut's Tomb*. Norman: University of Oklahoma Press, 2007.

Lane, Joel. *This Spectacular Darkness*. Ed. Mark Valentine and John Howard. Leyburn, UK: Tartarus Press, 2016.

Lothe, Jakob; Hawthorn, Jeremy; and Phelan, James, ed. *Joseph Conrad: Voice, Sequence, History, Genre*. Columbus: Ohio State University Press: 2008.

Lovecraft, H. P. *The Annotated Supernatural Horror in Literature*. Ed. S. T. Joshi. New York: Hippocampus Press, 2nd ed. 2012.

———. *Letters to Elizabeth Toldridge and Anne Tillery Renshaw*. Ed. David E. Schultz and S. T. Joshi. New York: Hippocampus Press, 2014. [Abbreviated in the text as *ET*.]

———. *Letters to Woodburn Harris and Others*. Ed. S. T. Joshi and David E. Schultz. New York: Hippocampus Press, 2022.

Meek, B. A. "And the Injun Goes 'How!': Representations of American Indian English in White Public Space." *Language in Society* 35, No.1 (2006): 93–128.

Milner, George R. *The Moundbuilders: Ancient People of Eastern North America*. London: Thames & Hudson, 2004.

Morgan, Jack. *The Biology of Horror: Gothic Literature and Film*. Carbondale: Southern Illinois University Press, 2002.

Morrow, Juliet E. "The Sacred Spiro Landscape, Cahokia Connections, and Flat Top Mounds." *Central States Archaeological Journal* 51, No. 2 (2004): 112–14.

Orr, Kenneth Gordon. "The Archaeological Situation at Spiro, Oklahoma: A Preliminary Report." *American Antiquity* 11, No. 4 (1946): 228–56.

Shead, A. C. "Some Natural Landmarks of Western Oklahoma." *Proceedings of the Oklahoma Academy of Science for 1966* Vol. 47 (1967): 173–95.

Todorov, Tzvetan. *The Conquest of America.* Tr. Richard Howard. New York: Harper Collins, 1985.

Watt, Ian. *Conrad in the Nineteenth Century.* Berkeley: University of California Press, 1980.

Briefly Noted

Katherine Kerestman has made an interesting observation regarding the Hammer film *Horror Hotel* (1960; titled *The City of the Dead* in the UK). She believes it to be an uncredited adaptation of Lovecraft's "The Festival." Consider the overall plot, as Kerestman has recounted it: "The woman [Venetia Stevenson, playing the character Nan Barlow] is studying history and she tells her professor (Christopher Lee) that she wants to do her senior paper on the Massachusetts witch trials, goes to a small town there, which is not on the maps and is covered in mists (of course), which is made up of 17th-century buildings, and which is full of Satanic witches who have gathered for the Feast Day. She finds the witches (occasioning her demise as a Candlemas Feast sacrifice) by lifting a trap door in her room at the inn and descending into a subterranean tunnel. Before she makes the descent, she is reading an antient volume on Satanism in New England, which she has borrowed from the bookstore owner."

The Lovecraft Letters Project

S. T. Joshi

With the imminent publication of the joint correspondence of H. P. Lovecraft and Frank Belknap Long, the issuance of Lovecraft's complete extant letters by Hippocampus Press will be complete. The project began with *Essential Solitude* (2008), containing the letters of Lovecraft and August Derleth. One volume in the series, *O Fortunate Floridian: H. P. Lovecraft's Letters to R. H. Barlow* (2007), was published by University of Tampa Press. As such, the Arkham House edition of Lovecraft's *Selected Letters* (1965–76; 5 vols.), is now obsolete.

For the assistance of scholars, I advise the use of the following abbreviations when citing the Hippocampus editions of these letters:

AG   *Letters to Alfred Galpin and Others* (2020)
CLM *Letters to C. L. Moore and Others* (2017)
DS   *Dawnward Spire, Lonely Hill: The Letters of H. P. Lovecraft and Clark Ashton Smith* (2017)
DW *Letters with Donald and Howard Wandrei and to Emil Petaja* (2019)
EHP *Letters to E. Hoffmann Price and Richard F. Searight* (2021)
ES   *Essential Solitude: The Letters of H. P. Lovecraft and August Derleth* (2008)
ET   *Letters to Elizabeth Toldridge and Anne Tillery Renshaw* (2014)
FLB *Letters to F. Lee Baldwin, Duane W. Rimel, and Nils Frome* (2016)
HB   *Letters to Hyman Bradofsky and Others* (2023)
JFM *Letters to James F. Morton* (2011)

JVS	*Letters to J. Vernon Shea, Carl F. Strauch, and Lee McBride White* (2016)
LFF	*Letters to Family and Family Friends* (2020)
MF	*A Means to Freedom: The Letters of H. P. Lovecraft and Robert E. Howard* (2009)
ML	*Miscellaneous Letters* (2022)
MWM	*Letters to Maurice W. Moe and Others* (2018)
OFF	*O Fortunate Floridian: H. P. Lovecraft's Letters to R. H. Barlow* (2007)
RB	*Letters to Robert Bloch and Others* (2015)
RK	*Letters to Rheinhart Kleiner and Others* (2020)
SP	*A Sense of Proportion: The Letters of H. P. Lovecraft and Frank Belknap Long* (2024)
WBT	*Letters to Wilfred B. Talman and Helen V. and Genevieve Sully* (2019)
WH	*Letters to Woodburn Harris and Others* (2022)

Note that several editions initially published in two volumes (e.g., *ES*, *MF*, and *LFF*) are numbered consecutively through both volumes, so that there is no need to cite a volume number when referring to these editions. This applies also to *DS*, which initially appeared in a one-volume hardcover edition and subsequently as a two-volume paperback edition.

As it is not always obvious in which volume the letters to a given correspondent appear, the following index of correspondents is provided. This index includes both the individual correspondents in *ML* as well as the recipients (either individuals or periodicals) in the "Published Letters" section of that volume.

Abramson, Ben	ML
Ackerman, Forrest J	ML
Anger, William F.	RB
Babcock, Ralph W.	HB
Bacon, Victor E.	ML
Baird, Edwin	WH
Baldwin, F. Lee	FLB
Barlow, R. H.	OFF
Bautz, W. G.	ML

Bishop, Zealia Brown Reed	*WH*
Birss, John H.	*ML*
Blish, James	*ML*
Bloch, Robert	*RB*
Board of Executive Judges, NAPA	*ML*
Bonner, Marian F.	*LFF*
Bradofsky, Hyman	*HB*
Braithwaite, William Stanley	*ML*
Bryant, William	*ML*
Bullen, John Ravenor	*ML*
Bureau of Critics	*ML*
Campbell, Paul J.	*RK*
Clark, Lillian D.	*LFF*
Coates, Walter John	*WH*
Cole, Edward H. & E. Sherman	*AG*
Conover, Willis, Jr.	*RB*
Convention of the NAPA	*ML*
Coryciani	*ML*
Davis, Edgar J.	*ML*
de Castro, Adolphe	*AG*
Derleth, August	*ES*
Dragnet	*ML*
Dunn, John T.	*AG*
Dwyer, Bernard Austin	*MWM*
Eddy, C. M and Muriel	*ML*
Edkins, Ernest A.	*ML*
Eshbach, Lloyd Arthur	*ML*
Exeter [NH] *News-Letter*	*ML*
Farnese, Harold S.	*ML*
Finlay, Virgil	*HB*
Frome, Nils	*FLB*
Gallomo	*ML*
Galpin, Alfred	*AG*
Gamwell, Annie E. P.	*LFF*
Gothamite	*ML*
Greene, Sonia H.	*ML*
Haggerty, Vincent B.	*ML*

Haldeman-Julius Weekly	ML
Harris, Arthur	RK
Harris, Woodburn	WH
Hartmann, J. F.	ML
Heins, John Milton	ML
Henneberger, J. C.	WH
Hoag, Jonathan E.	ML
Homeland Company	ML
Hornig, Charles D.	ML
Houdini, Harry	ML
Howard, Robert E.	MF
Hughes, Mrs. H. H.	ML
Hyde, Edna	ML
Jackson, Winifred V.	RK
Jacobi, Carl	ML
Kelley, Earl C.	ML
Kirk, George W.	ML
Kleicomolo	ML
Kleiner, Rheinhart	RK
Kuttner, Henry	CLM
Leeds, Arthur	RK
Leach, Orville L.	ML
[Letter Seeking Employment]	ML
Leiber, Fritz & Jonquil	CLM
Little, Myrta Alice	ML
Long, Frank Belknap	SP
Lovecraft, Sarah Susan	LFF
Loveman, Samuel	MWM
Lowndes, Robert A. W.	ML
Lumley, William	WH
Macauley, George W.	ML
McColl, Gavin T.	ML
Mashburn, Kirk	ML
Members of the NAPA	ML
Michael, Robert Hartley	ML
Miller, William, Jr.	ML
Moe, Maurice W.	MWM

Moe, Robert E.	MWM
Moore, C. L.	CLM
Morse, Richard Ely	HB
Morton, James F.	JFM
Munn, H. Warner	ML
Munsey Magazines	ML
Nelson, Robert (& Mrs. Elmer)	RB
New-York Tribune	ML
Ohio Amateur Journalists' Club	ML
Omaha World-Herald/Daily Bee	ML
Pabody, Frederic Jay	CLM
Pearson, James Larkin	RK
Peirce, Earl, Jr.	ML
Perry, Alvin Earl	ML
Petaja, Emil	DW
Plaisier, Jennie K.	HB
Price, E. Hoffmann	EHP
Providence Sunday Journal	ML
Pryor, Anthony	ML
Quinn, Seabury	ML
Rausch, Bertha	LFF
Renshaw, Anne Tillery	ET
Rimel, Duane W.	FLB
Rogers, Nelson	LFF
Schwartz, Julius	ML
Scientific American	ML
Searight, Richard F.	EHP
Shea, J. Vernon	JVS
Shepherd, Wilson	RB
"Sideshow, The"	ML
Smith, Charles W.	ML
Smith, Clark Ashton	DS
Smith, Edwin Hadley	ML
Spink, Helm C.	HB
Starrett, Vincent	MWM
Sterling, Kenneth	RB
Stone, Lee Alexander	ML

Strauch, Carl F.	JVS
Sully, Genevieve	WBT
Sully, Helen V.	WBT
Sutton, Mayte	LFF
Swanson, Carl	ML
Sylvester, Margaret	HB
Talman, Wilfred B.	WBT
Tilden, Leonard E.	ML
Toldridge, Elizabeth	ET
Ullman, Allan G.	ML
Utpatel, Frank	HB
Wandrei, Donald	DW
Wandrei, Howard	DW
Weir, John J.	HB
Weiss, Henry George	ML
White, Lee McBride	JVS
Widner, Arthur	ML
Wollheim, Donald A.	RB
Wooley, Natalie H.	RB
Worthington, W. Chesley	ML
Wright, Farnsworth	WH
Ziegfeld, Henriette	ML

Barring the emergence of additional caches of Lovecraft's correspondence, the Hippocampus edition should be regarded as definitive. At a later stage, the letters may become available in an electronic edition that will allow for easier searching of individual elements (names, book titles, subjects, etc.) in the letters.

The Colonialism of Cthulhu

Edward Guimont

H. P. Lovecraft's life spanned an important period in European colonization, termed the New Imperialism, when the Industrial Revolution and the political force of nationalism drove the rapid expansion of colonial holdings. Lovecraft was born five years after the Berlin Conference, when the major European powers divided nearly the entire African continent between themselves, inaugurating the Scramble for Africa that would last until World War I. His March 1937 death was less than a month after Italian forces completed the occupation of the last independent African state, Ethiopia—a war Lovecraft supported—which served as the height of European domination of Africa. Lovecraft even claimed that the question, "What of unknown Africa?," helped persuade himself to reject suicide in 1904 (*IAP* 98).

Explicit depictions of European imperialism in Africa are rare in Lovecraft's work, most apparent through the role of Madagascar in "The Mysterious Ship"; the Congo in "The Picture in the House" and "Facts concerning the Late Arthur Jermyn and His Family"; Egypt in "Under the Pyramids"; Zimbabwe in "The Outpost," "Medusa's Coil," and "Beyond Zimbabwe"; and several British colonies in "Winged Death." But while outright depictions of the European colonial system are rare in Lovecraft's works, its influence is not absent. Indeed, the core justifications used by Europeans in Africa (Morgan 133–70) can be found across Lovecraft's work via the colonization of Earth by alien entities seeking resources (Mi-Go), refuge (the Great Race), religious converts (Cthulhu—to frame it loosely), and settler territory (Elder Things). In contrast, the theme of native defense of land from settler occupation (the man-lizards of Venus) can also be found, perhaps tellingly at the end of Lovecraft's output.

The way in which Lovecraft's aliens influenced the neocolonialist ancient alien trope has been well documented (Colavito 127–39), and likewise Lovecraft was far from the only speculative fiction author, then or since, whose fiction implicitly adopted colonial narratives (Rieder 44–45). But there are subtler ways in which Lovecraft's worldview, expressed both in his fiction and his letters, was influenced by European colonization of Africa. There is the influence of settler colonial mythologies of African history on Lovecraft's extraterrestrial mythologies. Another is the influence of racial categorizations developed by the European colonial project not only on Lovecraft's notions of miscegenation, but on his views on the relative habitability of different planets for their respective denizens. More narrowly focused on his fictional output is how the trope of exploration, particularly with its scientific justification, resulted in Miskatonic University symbolizing an imperial metropole and its faculty—with expeditions to Antarctica, Australia, or western Massachusetts—as metaphors for colonialists engaged in civilizing missions and territorial conquests. These tropes can be explored through two broad themes of Lovecraft's fictional and nonfictional writing: the lost race genre and the role of anti-colonial resistance.

The lost race genre can broadly be defined as the belief that ruins encountered by Europeans outside of Europe were the not products of indigenous peoples. Instead, their provenance was attributed to waves of hypothetical European explorers or settlers who either built the structures themselves or educated the natives in how to do so. This was applied by Europeans across the world, but particularly to Africa. As far back as the Greek historian Strabo, in his first century B.C.E. work *Geography*, Europeans attributed the ruins of cities along the African coast to ancient travelers from Europe or the Near East (Strabo 159–61). But the pinnacle of this trope was the city of Great Zimbabwe, in the Central African country now named after it. The largest pre-colonial settlement in sub-Saharan Africa, it was built by the Shona people and served as their capital from approximately the eleventh through the fifteenth century. After its abandonment, probably due to environmental changes, Arab traders from the Swahili Coast claimed it to be Ophir, the biblical gold mine of King Solomon built with his control over djinn.

Portuguese explorers later adopted the legend and transmitted it to later waves of settlers. In 1871, Europeans rediscovered the ruins, and they were eventually taken into the British Empire in 1890 by Cecil Rhodes, who incorporated them into the colony of Rhodesia he named after himself. Rhodes was not alone in believing that Great Zimbabwe had been built by an ancient white race of gold miners, possibly Israelites or Phoenicians, and that their attempts to create civilization had been destroyed by their ungrateful African subjects, who had risen up and overthrown their foreign rulers (Guimont 17–58).

Lovecraft was interested in theories of Great Zimbabwe. As early as 1920, his story "The Cats of Ulthar" seemingly references Zimbabwe through its implicit placement of Ophir in Africa (CF 1.151). In 1925, Lovecraft heard about Zimbabwe firsthand when his friend, the amateur journalist and Edward Lloyd Sechrist, described his visit to the ruins (Haden 207–8). There had not been a professional archaeological survey of the ruins since 1905, and while that expedition firmly established the city's provenance as medieval African, popular sentiment—as well as the official policy of the Rhodesian settler government until it collapsed in 1979—was that it was the product of an ancient white race (Garlake 209–10n6). The Rhodesian government banned study of the ruins and exiled the University of Rhodesia's leading archaeology professor, Peter Garlake, for his work on the city's provenance (Garlake 203–4). One can draw a parallel to the dangers of studying forbidden ancient cities encountered by Miskatonic professors.

The version of Zimbabwe told by Sechrist Lovecraft in 1925 was the popular version originating with Arab traders: that Zimbabwe was an enormous stone monument built in ancient times with a Near Eastern king who was aided by celestial beings, and that the city's civilization was ultimately destroyed by an uprising of dark-skinned slave workers (Haden 208). Ironically, the fact that the lost race trope involved the white civilization being defeated by the natives, meant that during the 1964–79 Zimbabwean War of Liberation the trope served as a unifying ideal for not only the white Rhodesian settlers, but also African nationalists for whom Great Zimbabwe was a center of religious ritual providing spiritual support for their war (Guimont 234–45; Fontein 787–89). Connections might be drawn to the political disturbances in various colonies linked to Cthulhu's awakening in "The Call of Cthulhu" (CF 2.29) or Marceline's occult abilities, used to destroy the Riverside plantation, being linked to both Zimbabwe and R'lyeh in "Medusa's Coil" (CF 4.269).

In line with this irony, David Haden has noted that in the entry for Zimbabwe in the 1911 *Encyclopædia Britannica*, one of Lovecraft's chief sources for research, solidly endorses a medieval African construction for the city (Haden 210; *Britannica* 980–81). Lovecraft's commitment to the idea of ancient white rulers reflects not only the romantic strength of the lost race trope, but also the strong racist attitudes—not only by Lovecraft—that shored up that appeal. Lovecraft first used Great Zimbabwe in his 1929 poem "The Outpost," where he associated it with an interior African domain of the alien Fishers from Outside (AT 77–79). In the process, "The Outpost" demonstrated how closely the later ancient alien concept draws from the earlier lost white race trope, with ancient aliens replacing ancient white races. Notably, "The Outpost" also includes references to domes in Zimbabwe, which do not exist in the real city and reflect Lovecraft's imagined connection with more classical European architecture. In his letters to James F. Morton about the poem, Lovecraft specifically identifies the unnamed king in the poem as K'nath-Hothar, "of pure Phoenician stock" (*Morton* 202). Lovecraft would also use Zimbabwe in his 1934 poem "Beyond Zimbabwe" (AT 95) and his 1930 short story revision for Zealia Bishop, "Medusa's Coil," which also locates Atlantis in the Hoggar Mountains of Algeria (CF 4.254).[1]

However, the most prominent use of Great Zimbabwe in Lovecraft's fiction is *At the Mountains of Madness*. While Zimba-

---

1. A placement probably inspired by Pierre Benoit's 1919 novel *Atlantida*, which HPL had read by 1927 (*Dawnward Spire* 145).

bwe is not featured in the story itself, Lovecraft does mention it in his notes as inspiration for the Elder Things' city along with the Babylonian city of Ur (*CE* 5.247), and the novella is a natural continuation of what might be called the ancient alienification of the white race trope of Zimbabwe that began with "The Outpost." As with the Zimbabwe of "The Outpost," the Elder city also contains domes (*CF* 3.73). Of note as well the work by historian Daniella McCahey, illustrating that exploration of Antarctica in the past two centuries, especially by Britain, was intricately tied to the expansion and maintenance of what might be termed the traditional empires (McCahey 302–24).

Outside of Sechrist and the *Encyclopedia Britannica,* there is one work that probably influenced Lovecraft's use of Zimbabwe. In August 1927, the astronomer and part-time science fiction author William Henry Christie, writing under the pseudonym Cecil B. White, published his story "The Retreat to Mars" in *Amazing Stories*. Notably, this was the issue prior to the one containing "The Colour out of Space," so Lovecraft almost certainly read it (Guimont and Smith 257). In the story, the narrator is an astronomer specializing in Mars. The astronomer is approached by a Smithsonian Institution archaeologist, whose focus is on proving that humanity evolved in Central Africa rather than Central Asia, as was the dominant hypothesis into the 1950s. While on a six-year expedition to Central Africa, the archaeologist excavates a mound that is revealed to have been built over an ancient structure with writings inside. Translating the records, the archaeologist discovers that it was built by ancient Martians, and that human beings are the degenerate descendants of Martian colonists artificially adapted for survival on Earth, before losing their alien civilization. Shown images of the past glories of Mars, the archaeologist notes that it resembles Babylonian architecture. Ultimately, the archaeologist discovers that the Martians left two other such libraries: one on what seems to be Atlantis and one in Australia, which "may yet be found" (White 467). A number of details from "The Retreat to Mars" appear in later Lovecraft works. Obviously, the creation of human beings from aliens, and the decline of alien culture in their Earth colony, are central concepts of *At the Mountains of Madness*, while an ancient alien library in Australia describes the city of the Great Race from "The Shadow out of Time." Christie's association of a lost city with Babylonian traits in Central Africa seems to indicate inspiration from contemporary ideas of Great Zimbabwe.

In "The Outpost," Lovecraft specifies that the Fishers from Outside were located deep inland from Zimbabwe (AT 77). In "Winged Death," his 1932 revision story for Hazel Heald, this is apparently established as being in Uganda, where "a trace of Cyclopean ruins" is all that remains of the Fishers' abode (CF 4.348).[2] In reality, in 1909 Europeans discovered the remains of enormous earthworks dating from approximately the same time as Great Zimbabwe, called Bigo Bya Mugenyi, or "Strangers' Forts" (Gray 226–33). Like the area around Zimbabwe, Uganda had been visited by Arab traders long before the European arrival, and from the Arab Muslims the local Buganda had learned about the Book of Genesis and the so-called Curse of Ham. In this belief, originating in Europe and adopted by Arabs, Noah's son Ham, whose offspring were cursed to servitude after finding his father naked, was the progenitor of Black Africans. Lovecraft himself was aware of this concept (*Means to Freedom* 2.889).

When British explorers first reached Uganda in 1862, they were surprised to find the local rulers not only familiar with Ham but claiming descent from him, showing the British the location of his supposed tomb. The Buganda rulers had synthesized Genesis with the local Ganda creation myth, identifying Ham with the Ganda folk hero Kintu, traditional founder of the Buganda state. As such, the story of Ham was not a curse to the Buganda rulers, but something that allowed them to claim legitimacy by making them a direct descendent of one of the religious figures revered by the new colonial powers, Arab and British alike (Robinson 95–107). In other words, members of the Buganda ruling circle embraced the idea that they were of hybrid descent from a foreign god to gain favors from alien powers, and whose ancient tomb was located deep in Uganda—which

---

2. Although in "The Outpost," the Fishers' residence is implicitly to the west from Zimbabwe, while Uganda is north.

would all be familiar to readers of Lovecraft. These are also not idle connections. In "Winged Death," Lovecraft specifies that the expedition to the Fishers' ruins are not native Ugandans, terrified of the site, but rather "Gallas" (*CF* 4.348). "Galla" was a colonial-era pejorative for the Oromo people of Ethiopia, who early European ethnologists also believed were descended from ancient white settlers (Robinson 92, 105). Moreover, even the local hero Kintu was claimed to be of Oromo descent as well (Robinson 102). Knowingly or not, Lovecraft's use of "Gallas" to explore an ancient ruin in Uganda resonated with actual local mythologies.

In line with "Winged Death," there is another of Lovecraft's lesser-known works involving settlers discovering ancient ruins and natives defending them which has much subtext to unpack. This is his one complete work of space opera, his collaboration with Kenneth Sterling, "In the Walls of Eryx." The story is set in a future where human employees of a terrestrial power company steal energy crystals from the man-lizard natives of the jungle-like Venus who worship them. The titular walls of Eryx are an invisible maze within which the narrator becomes trapped, and is convinced that some unknown elder race, rather than the primitive man-lizards, must have built the labyrinth. Before perishing as his air supply runs out, the narrator comes to the realization that the human treatment of the man-lizards is cruel, and that Venus belongs to its natives, not to the humans settling the world to strip mine it and steal the natives' religious objects (*CF* 4.578–80).

The ending of "Eryx" has been seen as a critique of empire (Guimont and Smith 191–96). This is in contrast to Lovecraft's lament 29 May 1936 lament to Wilson Shepherd, that the "average interplanetary tale is just a camouflaged 'western' with the pioneers & soldiers called 'space-explorers', & the Indians called 'Martians' or 'lunarians'" (*Bloch* 350). But from statements he made in letters to Natalie Wooley (*Bloch* 194–95) and Nils Frome (*Baldwin* 348–50), it is clear that, despite the plethora of cosmic entities in his fiction, Lovecraft believed the solar system, if not the entire universe, to be potentially barren. More interestingly, it indicates that Lovecraft's pessimism over the likelihood of interplanetary colonization stemmed from the same xenophobic views on habitability that colored his anti-immigration sentiment. To Lovecraft, just as ethnic groups should not attempt to emigrate to the nation-state of another ethnicity, whose institutions and environment alike were foreign to them—a sentiment he sometimes used to selectively critique terrestrial empires and colonization—there was no point for a species perfectly evolved for the environment of one world to migrate to a world for which it was manifestly unsuited (*Bloch* 157–58; *CE* 5.13–14). The Mi-Go, after all, come to Earth merely to find metal, preferring to remain in both metaphorical and literal dark, not even eating food from Earth (*CF* 2.471–72). Even their Yuggoth base is a regional headquarters, merely "populous outpost" rather than homeworld (*CF* 2.489). The aliens who did settle on Earth, the Elder Things and Great Race, were ultimately doomed to degeneracy and extinction in their adopted home. As Lovecraft argued in his 5 March 1935 letter to Helen V. Sully, even if extraterrestrial life forms existed, the distances separating planets—let alone solar systems—would make alien interaction, let alone invasion and colonization, impossible (*Talman* 404).

However, despite the insignificance of sentient life of all forms when viewed from a cosmic perspective, when viewed from a human perspective, minute differences could still engender base prejudices. "Eryx" was written in the middle of the Italian subjugation of Ethiopia. Lovecraft's co-author Sterling was Jewish, and American Jewish sympathies were firmly with the Ethiopians, as Lovecraft himself noted; Lovecraft's, however, were emphatically not (Leman and Branney). While Venusian lizards might have Lovecraft's anti-colonial sympathies, Black Africans were seemingly still a world apart.

Works Cited

Colavito, Jason. *The Cult of Alien Gods: H. P. Lovecraft and Extraterrestrial Pop Culture*. Ahmerst, NY: Prometheus Books, 2005.

Encyclopedia Britannica. Eleventh Edition, Vol. 28. New York: Cambridge University Press, 1911.

Fontein, Joost. "Silence, Destruction and Closure at Great Zimbabwe: Local Narratives of Desecration and Alienation." *Journal of Southern African Studies* 32 (December 2006): 771–94.

Garlake, Peter S. *Great Zimbabwe*. New York: Stein & Day, 1973.

Gray, John M. "The Riddle of Biggo." *Uganda Journal* 2 (January 1935): 226–33.

Guimont, Edward. "From King Solomon to Ian Smith: Rhodesian Alternate Histories of Zimbabwe." PhD dissertation. Storrs, CT: University of Connecticut, 2019.

Guimont, Edward, and Horace A. Smith. *When the Stars Are Right: H. P. Lovecraft and Astronomy*. New York: Hippocampus Press, 2023.

Haden, David. *Lovecraft in Historical Context: The Fifth Collection*. Morrisville, NC: Lulu Press, 2014.

Leman, Andrew, and Sean Branney. "Enemies of Civilization." *Voluminous* 71 (3 April 2022), www.hplhs.org/voluminous71.php

Lovecraft, H. P. *Dawnward Spire, Lonely Hill: The Letters of H. P. Lovecraft and Clark Ashton Smith*. Ed. David E. Schultz and S. T. Joshi. New York: Hippocampus Press, 2017.

———. *Letters to F. Lee Baldwin, Duane W. Rimel, and Nils H. Frome*. Ed. David E. Schultz and S. T. Joshi. New York: Hippocampus Press, 2016.

———. *Letters to James F. Morton*. Ed. David E. Schultz and S. T. Joshi. New York: Hippocampus Press, 2011.

———. *Letters to Robert Bloch and Others*. Ed. David E. Schultz and S. T. Joshi. New York: Hippocampus Press, 2015.

———. *Letters to Wilfred B. Talman and Helen V. and Genevieve Sully*. Ed. David E. Schultz and S. T. Joshi. New York: Hippocampus Press, 2019.

———. *A Means to Freedom: The Letters of H. P. Lovecraft and Robert E. Howard*. Ed. S. T. Joshi, David E. Schultz, and Rusty Burke. New York: Hippocampus Press, 2009. 2 vols.

McCahey, Daniella. "Britain's Polar Empire, 1769–1982." In Adrian Howkins and Peder Roberts, ed. *The Cambridge History of the Polar Regions*. Cambridge: Cambridge University Press, 2023. 302–24.

Morgan, Cecilia. *Building Better Britains? Settler Societies Within the British Empire, 1783–1920.* Toronto: University of Toronto Press, 2017.

Rieder, John. *Colonialism and the Emergence of Science Fiction.* Middletown, CT: Wesleyan University Press, 2008.

Robinson, Michael F. *The Lost White Tribe: Explorers, Scientists, and the Theory That Changed a Continent.* Oxford: Oxford University Press, 2016.

Strabo. *The Geography of Strabo, Volume VIII.* Tr. and ed. Horace Leonard Jones London: William Heinemann, 1932.

Briefly Noted

David E. Schultz has radically revised his 1987 annotated edition of Lovecraft's *Commonplace Book*, expanding it to include a facsimile of the handwritten manuscript, an exhaustive commentary, and a number of supplemental texts by Lovecraft, including "Weird Story Plots," "Notes on Writing Weird Fiction," and several other pieces. It is one of the finest annotated editions of any work by Lovecraft ever prepared—rivalled only by Schultz's own annotated edition of *Fungi from Yuggoth* (2017). The book should appear from Hippocampus Press in 2025.

Lovecraft Seeks a Comet at Nichols Crossing

Horace A. Smith

As spring arrived in the year 1910, Halley's Comet closed upon the inner solar system for the first time since 1835. As the comet brightened, life was not very bright for nineteen-year-old Howard Phillips Lovecraft. Two years before, his dreams of college and a career in astronomy had collapsed. He suffered the breakdown that S. T. Joshi called the most serious of his life (*IAP* 126–28), from which he had not yet emerged. Astronomy did not escape the curtailments that came with Lovecraft's incapacity. His newspaper columns on astronomy, begun in 1906, ended in 1908. His self-published astronomy magazines likewise ceased. However, although Lovecraft's engagement with astronomy waned, his interest in the subject had not departed (Guimont and Smith 48–50).

Beginning in 1909, Lovecraft sporadically maintained a personal notebook of astronomical observations.[1] Entries were sparse, with only one recorded for the entire year 1910. That entry, however, describing his observation of Halley's comet on the evening of 26 May, is the highlight of the notebook. In his detailed account, Lovecraft recorded and sketched the appearance and apparent position of the comet. He also informed the reader that he saw the comet not from his Providence home, but from a spot miles away in rural Massachusetts. In this paper I clarify Lovecraft's observing location and describe how to find it today. I also explore why Lovecraft might have selected that location

---

1. HPL's *Astronomical Notebook* is online courtesy of Vilanova's Digital Library. digital.library.villanova.edu/Item/vudl:593162#?xywh=-1784%2C344%2C5471%2C1666

rather than Providence for his sole documented observation of Halley's famous comet.

The year 1910 had begun with another bright comet, a new discovery that was in some ways more spectacular than Comet Halley. Lovecraft did not see this Great January Comet, an omission he blamed on illness: "I missed the bright one earlier in that year by being flat in bed with a hellish case of measles" (letter to R. H. Barlow, 23 July 1936; *O Fortunate Floridian* 356). As the year progressed, Lovecraft recovered from the hellish measles, but he added no entries on Comet Halley, or anything else, to his *Astronomical Notebook*.

Meanwhile, Comet Halley continued its increase in brightness as winter turned to spring. By early May, observers without optical aid could easily see the comet in the predawn sky. Anyone who read the newspapers of the day would have been apprised of its approach. The Providence *Evening Bulletin*'s front page on 14 May 1910 highlighted observations of the comet by a local astronomer, Frank Seagrave, who maintained a private observatory behind his home at 119 Benefit Street. Winslow Upton, the director of Brown University's Ladd Observatory who in 1903 opened the facility to Lovecraft, gave the comet top billing in his 1 May 1910 newspaper column.[2] Still, although he was doubtless well aware of when and where to look for it, and owned binoculars and a three-inch telescope to supplement observations with the naked eye, Lovecraft recorded no comet observation as the comet loomed in the morning sky.[3]

On 18 May, Halley's comet passed in front of the sun as seen from the earth. Some were alarmed by spurious newspaper reports that life on earth might then be snuffed out by poison in the comet's tail. However, life continued as the comet swung from the morning to the evening sky. Those who had not risen before the sun to catch the comet now had an opportunity to look for it at a more convenient hour. Immediately after the

---

2. Upton's monthly columns appeared in the *Providence Journal* and a few other newspapers.

3. HPL listed his optical equipment in his *Astronomical Notebook*. His instruments are also discussed in Guimont and Smith.

18th, the glare of the sun hid the comet, but it soon moved away from the sun's position in the sky. As it became better placed for evening observation, it also began gradually to fade in brightness. At first the inhabitants of Providence were not lucky, and clouds disappointed those who hoped to witness the comet. However, lingering clouds eventually broke and forecasts for Thursday, 26 May, looked promising (Figure 1). Lovecraft would have his chance to see Comet Halley, if he chose to take it. It is hard to imagine that the Lovecraft of 1903 to 1907, who filled his handwritten and hectographed *Rhode Island Journal of Astronomy* with his own observations, would not have managed to see the famous comet long before the evening of 26 May. The Lovecraft of 1910, two years after the 1908 breakdown, was apparently a very different fellow. Nevertheless, in the end he did not miss the once-in-a-lifetime celestial visitor.

WEATHER MAY PERMIT VIEW OF COMET TO-NIGHT

While Conditions in Previous Evenings Have Been Against Observations, Forecaster Emery Says Skies May Clear, Allowing Sight of Fiery Traveller.

Figure 1. A front-page headline in the Providence *Evening Bulletin* for 26 May 1910 touted the possibility of good observing conditions for seeing Halley's comet.

The comet with its long tail would become visible in the west as soon as evening twilight faded sufficiently. As the evening hours progressed, the comet would slowly sink toward the horizon, setting at about 11 P.M., some four hours after sunset. On the 26th, a waning gibbous moon would rise in the southeast at about 10 P.M., too late to interfere seriously with comet observations. If the weather forecast held, Lovecraft should have no difficulty finding the comet, but as noted, he would not attempt to do so from his Angell Street home. In his *Astronomical Notebook* he wrote that he observed from the "Providence–Taunton Pike at a point just N.E. from Nichol's Crossing looking westward" (Figure 2). Where, exactly, was that, and why did he go there?

The Providence–Taunton turnpike, completed in 1829, ran from Providence, Rhode Island, to Taunton, Massachusetts, passing through the towns of Seekonk and Rehoboth, Massachusetts, along the way. It generally followed the path of the present Massachusetts Route 44. In the late nineteenth century the road connecting Providence and Taunton (by then no longer a toll road) was joined by an interurban trolley line, which in 1910 belonged to the Old Colony Streetcar Company. According to a guide to historical sites Street Railway crossed Bay State

Figure 2. Sketch of Halley's comet from Lovecraft's *Astronomical Notebook* with his description of his observing location. H. P. Lovecraft Collection. Digital Library@Villanova University.

Road, with the Nichols house serving as a company depot: "Taunton–Providence Street Railway's trolley tracks came out of the woods here and crossed Bay State Road."[4] A sign on Bay State Road today marks the approximate location of Nichols Crossing (Figure 3). The trolley tracks departed from the path of the old turnpike to go into the village of Rehoboth before turning northward near Nichols Crossing to rejoin the turnpike route, as shown in Figure 4.

Figure 3. The historical marker on Bay State Road (at this point also Massachusetts Route 118) recalling Nichols Crossing. Photograph courtesy of Donovan Loucks.

---

4. *Rehoboth, Massachusetts: A Guide to Historic Sites*, revised edition, (2017). Online at www.town.rehoboth.ma.us/sites/g/files/vyhlif4911/f/uploads/Rehoboth_historic_sites_booklet.pdf

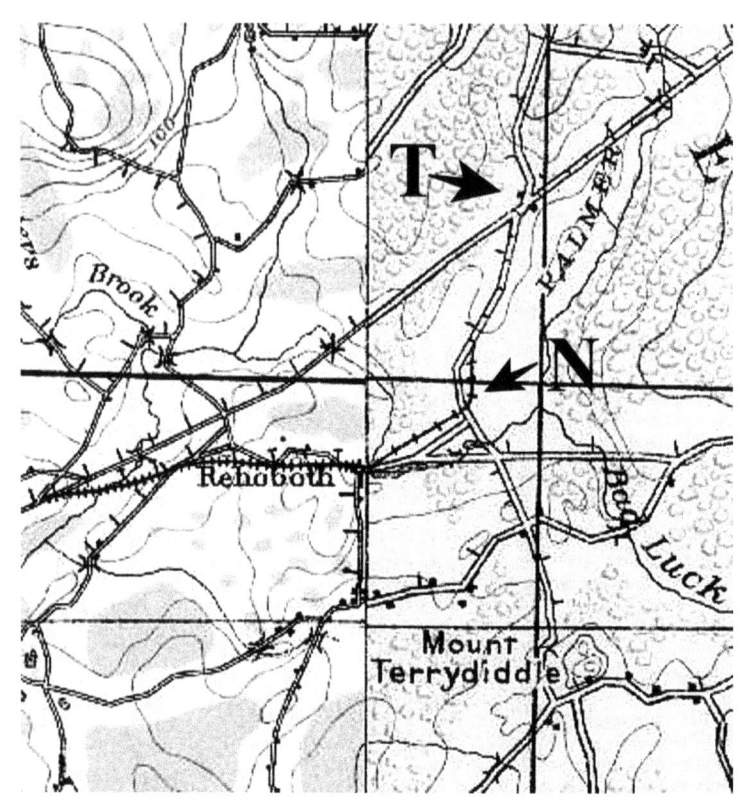

Figure 4. A combination of United States Geological Survey 1:62500 maps from 1921 (left side) and 1918 (right side). N marks the location of Nichols Crossing. T marks Lovecraft's observing location on the Providence–Taunton turnpike. The streetcar tracks are indicated, turning northward at Nichols Crossing. Lovecraft observed from the intersection of today's Massachusetts Routes 118 and 44. Merged maps courtesy of Donovan Loucks.

If Lovecraft alighted from the trolley at Nichols Crossing, he would have had a walk of little more than a half-mile northeast on Bay State Road to reach that road's intersection with the Providence–Taunton turnpike, no distance at all for a Lovecraft used to long walks. It was near that intersection that Lovecraft looked westward to see Halley's Comet between 8:45 and 9:30 P.M. In 1910, the Anawan House, a tavern, occupied the north-west corner of the intersection, near the place where a gas station now sits, although I don't know what refreshments it might have offered to the astronomically minded visitor.

Why did Lovecraft leave Providence and travel to Rehoboth to see the comet? Tempting though it is to picture a despondent Lovecraft traveling to the crossroads to conclude some eldritch pact beneath the comet's glow, Lovecraft's actual motivation was likely less exotic. We know that he would have been able to see the comet from locations closer to his Angell Street home. The *Norwich* (CT) *Bulletin* for 27 May 1910 reported that on the 26th, "Brown students gathered on College Hill tonight and cheered Halley and his comet. The parks throughout the city were thronged by thousands of comet gazers." On the same day, the Providence *Evening Bulletin* stated that on the previous evening "All Providence took to the streets most of the evening to see the heavenly visitor." According to the *Evening Bulletin*, Frank Seagrave was very pleased with his view from the city, although some of the public were disappointed that the comet was not brighter.

Light pollution, which obscures dim celestial objects, was in 1910 generally much less than in today's cities, but it was not entirely absent. As early as 1909, Frank Seagrave had some screens erected to block the glow of streetlights at his Benefit Street observatory.[5] In 1914, he would give up on Providence observing and move his observatory to North Scituate.[6] Seagrave wrote that the new location would escape the "smoke, dust, haze, and electric lights of a big city" (Seagrave 462). Lovecraft, a skilled amateur astronomer, would have been aware of the deterioration in city observing and might have suspected that a better view would be obtained away from the smoke and lights of his home town. Four years later Lovecraft would complain that his view of Comet Delavan was "hampered by electric street lights" when he saw it from the grounds of his residence (*Astronomical Notebook*, 16 September 1914). A view to the west from his Angell Street home would place the comet over the

---

5. *Providence Sunday Journal* (10 October 1909).
6. Providence *Evening Bulletin* (11 March 1914).

worst of the city's glow and haze. Thus, Lovecraft had a very practical reason to seek a more rural observing location from which to view the comet. But why a spot near Rehoboth?

The trolley enabled a convenient trip to Rehoboth, but Lovecraft was already familiar with the Rehoboth area. S. T. Joshi wrote that around 1906 Lovecraft and his friends would bicycle along the Taunton Pike to rural Rehoboth, where they built an addition to a small wooden shack to use as a clubhouse, named the Great Meadow Country Clubhouse (*IAP* 108). The clubhouse was north of the Providence–Taunton turnpike, but not far from Lovecraft's chosen observing location.

Lovecraft does not state how he got to his observing spot on May 26. A trip by trolley seems likely. It would have been easier than bicycling and would avoid the perils of bicycling home in the dark.[7] Arrival by trolley would also explain the specific reference to Nichols Crossing, a trolley stop. The *Trolley Wayfarer* guide for 1908 indicates that the eight-mile trip from Providence to Rehoboth took about 35–40 minutes and cost about a dime. Lovecraft certainly took advantage of trolleys and would celebrate his twenty-first birthday the following year with a day-long trolley excursion.

I think it likely, then, that Lovecraft took the streetcar to Nichols Crossing, but, if he did so, he may have narrowly missed some excitement. The Providence *Evening Bulletin* and the Fall River *Evening Herald* editions of 27 May 1910 reported that on the 26th a trolley express car bound from Providence to Taunton caught fire and burned just before it reached Nichols Crossing at about 4:30 P.M. If Lovecraft made his way to Rehoboth by trolley, service along the streetcar line must not have been long interrupted, although Lovecraft could have arrived early and spent part of the day in the area. I have not found a detailed trolley schedule for the time in question.

What can we conclude from what was, after all, a minor episode in Lovecraft's life? First, Lovecraft's detailed description and depiction of Halley's Comet serve to confirm his abilities as

---

7. HPL wrote that, after 1901, he did not spend a night away from home until 1920 (*Letters to Woodburn Harris* 50).

an experienced amateur astronomer rather than a casual observer. No surprises there, as he had watched the skies and studied astronomy since at least 1903. Lovecraft's familiarity with the Rehoboth area meant that he knew what to expect there, and that it would provide the dark skies he required. Lovecraft's trip also shows that, once he decided to see Halley's Comet, he would take some efforts to see it well.

I am not certain that Lovecraft was alone when he traveled to Rehoboth on the 26th, but I suspect that such was the case. Lovecraft's account mentions no other observers, and a solitary excursion would be consistent with what we know of his reclusiveness in the years following the 1908 breakdown. Nonetheless, we might speculate that Lovecraft's choice of an observing spot may not have been purely practical. It might also have reflected a fondness for lost days when he and a few friends enjoyed companionship at the Great Meadow Country Clubhouse.

I thank Donovan K. Loucks for helpful comments on and corrections to a draft of this paper, as well as for supplying photographs and maps used in Figures 3 and 4.

Works Cited

Guimont, Edward, and Smith, Horace A. *When the Stars Are Right: H. P. Lovecraft and Astronomy*. New York: Hippocampus Press, 2023.

Lovecraft, H. P. *Letters to Woodburn Harris and Others*. Ed. S. T. Joshi and David E. Schultz. New York: Hippocampus Press, 2022.

———. *O Fortunate Floridian: H. P. Lovecraft's Letters to R. H. Barlow*. Ed. S. T. Joshi and David E. Schultz. Tampa: University of Tampa Press, 2007.

Seagrave, F. E. "A New Observatory." *Popular Astronomy* 22 (August–September 1914): 462.

Rick and Morty vs. Cthulhu

Duncan Norris

In my previous discussion of the intersection of the popular adult sci-fi cartoon program *Rick and Morty* and the works and ideas of H. P. Lovecraft, which clearly demonstrated the tendrils of both, the most patent proof was in the opening credits. The final vignette, which as of the seventh season remains consistent, is of Cthulhu pursuing Rick's spacecraft through the ruins of R'lyeh. Aboard are the amoral genius scientist Rick and his grandchildren Morty and Summer Smith, all clearly terrified, while the reason for the pursuit can be inferred by the infant Cthulhoid monster Summer is holding. As previously noted, we then literally go down Cthulhu's gullet to start the show, a rather unsubtle metaphor that simultaneously seems to pass the casual observer by. As is the standard for any successful contemporary television show, in addition to the more obvious merchandising material ubiquitous to the modern marketing landscape, there are a variety of spun-off stories appearing in other media. This includes video games, anime, and particularly large sets of comic book offerings. The latter includes a main continuity, a *Rick and Morty Presents* line that features various characters from the show having their own adventures, and assorted limited series. As is commonly the case, the canonicity of such materials, especially as it is largely done without substantial input from the primary creators, is questionable. Such minutiae become even more esoteric when considering that the Rick and Morty Universe is unambiguously a multiverse, with some of the comics explicitly set in alternative dimensions, while occasional references are made in the show to events in the comics and both occasionally break the fourth wall to address the audience directly. All this leads to the four-issue limited series *Rick and Morty vs. Cthulhu* (2022–23).

It is not the point of this essay to be an extended review of this work. Rather it is to examine *Rick and Morty vs. Cthulhu* from a more critical perspective to see what we can discern of the influence of Lovecraft's work, the perceptions of his tropes and of the man himself inside popular culture. Thus it is best to begin with a summary of the comics, which despite publication in four separate issues shall be treated as a collective unit as per the trade paperback. The plot is relatively straightforward— relatively being a particular relative qualifier given the medium and universe, both being noted for often outré and obtuse stories.

After a typical scam-gone-bad scenario Rick performs a scan of the Smith house and finds it filled with Mythos molecules, indicating an infestation caused by Cthulhu. The entire Smith family—father Jerry and mother Beth as well as the children— decide to go with Rick to deal with the problem on a quest into the Lovecraft Dimension. As the name implies, the characters, places, and events of Lovecraft's fiction are real, although Rick specifically speaks of them as fictional. The initial access point takes the family to the events of "The Colour out of Space," wherein Rick catches it and grinds it into "Cthulian [sic] Corpse Dust." Next they go to Miskatonic University during Wilbur Whateley's abortive burglary from "The Dunwich Horror," and Summer kills Wilbur as (broadly) per the tale, although Rick's personal forcefield failed to work when Wilbur attacks him.

Jerry becomes filled with esoteric dread after receiving Wilbur's touch and is sent back with Beth. The dust previously collected is to be spread in a circle about their house as protection, but it is clear that Jerry has already been infected and is spreading such. The remaining trio of Rick, Morty, and Summer kill the Dunwich Horror, but afterward Rick's portal gun fails to function, another effect of the realm. They attempt to infiltrate Innsmouth in period disguise but were expected and Rick is immediately killed, ending the original comic, which is herein chapter one.

Following on, Summer and Morty are placed in prison, where

Summer meets a mystical Zadok Allen who teaches her how to meditate into the Dreamlands, although he is killed shortly thereafter and she runs for her life. Summer is saved by a clowder of cats, whose master is Nyarlathotep. Morty's cellmate is a suspiciously wholesome girl of his own age named Cathy, who convinces him to have sex so as to ruin the ritual he is being kept for, which requires a virgin. The sacrifice goes ahead, but Dagon instead chooses to keep Morty as his new son.

Chapter 3 begins with Rick, who it transpired had his mind taken by the Yithians at the exact moment of his death. He has a series of misadventures there with his captors before ultimately escaping via displacing his mind into a vat clone he has prepared in the future, the present day of the tale. He arrives to find Beth is now totally possessed by Lovecraftian forces. The final chapter begins with Morty narrating a letter about how much he loves his new life as Dagon's son, but Nyarlathotep arrives with his acolyte Summer and the siblings fight on behalf of their respective masters. Rick is battling a possessed Beth, and Jerry is killed as he and Rick try to escape. The latter eventually portals back to the Lovecraft Dimension to the discovery of R'lyeh in "The Call of Cthulhu" and attacks the awakened Cthulhu with anti-Cthulhu weaponry. Summer and Morty kill each other, and Rick vanquishes Cthulhu.

After this Azathoth arrives and crushes Rick with the metanarrative that he is "the fever dream of two insignificant fools who like causing s**t and making money"[1] while going on to say, "I am the original existential terror pulled from mankind's deepest subconscious. I am the truth that *nothing* we do matters and *all* we create will vanish and be *forgotten*." Rick accepts this and asks only that no sequel be made, and Azathoth puts things back to the way they were. Epilogue one shows Morty seeing Cathy in the bathroom mirror, where she reveals her full name as Cythlla, Daughter of Cthulhu, and that Morty is pregnant with her star seed to allow "future crossover adventures." Epilogue two, four weeks later, shows a panel version of

---

1. It is not the editor being censorious here: this is how the text appears in the comic.

the opening credits of the show with Cthulhu chasing them offering "can't we all just get along?!" The bottom panel, as they go into Cthulhu's maw, states "to be conthulhued?"

Perhaps the most interesting aspect of *Rick and Morty vs. Cthulhu* to examine first is the depth of direct adaptation and reference on display. Many works utilizing Lovecraft either make shallow references, place a gloss of Cthulhu over existing works and ideas, are simple pastiche, or tend toward very thematic adaptations, wherein the Lovecraftian elements are there by feel and association rather than direct mention. While all these are in *Rick and Morty vs. Cthulhu* and will be addressed in turn, the direct connections with Lovecraft's work on display are legion. As such it is less than surprising that the trade paperback contains eight pages of "Eldritch Endpapers," containing short summaries of the key stories referenced in the comic, excerpts from the same as well as early concept illustrations.

Discussing every Lovecraftian detail in *Rick and Morty vs. Cthulhu* would be tedious, so a shortened selection of some examples will suffice to give the overall impression. In "The Colour out of Space" section, in addition to the obvious—the meteorite, well, and spreading color in the now almost mandatory violet-pink-mauve as per numerous adaptions—a specific date is mentioned, 15 March 1883, along with the names of Nahum and Thaddeus, the woodchuck the McGregors found in the woods that gave them such a fright, and the professors from Miskatonic University. 1883 is when the culminating events take place at the Gardner residence, although the date is not specifically mentioned in the tale itself; 15 March is Lovecraft's date of death. "The Dunwich Horror" has the confrontation with Wilbur in the Miskatonic Library, which includes Wilbur's dying words, the blowing of a pre-prepared substance to make the monster visible, its killing of cows, and resting in a glen.

Innsmouth is typically portrayed, which is to say everybody is a very overt fish-monster, but Zadok Allen is broadly true to the character in "The Shadow over Innsmouth," talking of the Oath of Dagon, fish bloods, and Cap'n Obed, and when they travel to the Dreamlands he seeks out Zoogs for their moon-wine, in line with his alcoholic nature and the connection with liquor and the doom that finds him in the original tale. He is also killed by moon-beasts, who are represented as described in Lovecraft's tale, and the cats who save Summer remark that "few mortals find themselves this close to Ulthar."

Nyarlathotep appears in his Egyptian guise and Dagon as an aquatic monster, while the Yithians are again accurately portrayed as per the account in "The Shadow out of Time." Likewise the overall feel of their city seems to sit within Lovecraft's broader descriptions, including the guards over the portals to where the hidden horrors lurk, which are eventually set free by Rick to facilitate his escape. Dagon utters the variation line on the stars are right in "under the proper constellations," while Rick gripes about the transition to an epistolary approach to narrative when he arrives on the *Alert* to storm R'lyeh. The final confrontation with Cthulhu itself has Rick ramming his ship into the monstrous being as per the tale, and the nihilistic end with the deaths of all the Smith family and Rick accepting the meaninglessness of existence is very much in line with Lovecraftian tropes.

Of course, a Lovecraft adaptation is expected to adapt Lovecraft. At least one would think. Yet many such works instead draw more from secondary material, such as the "posthumous collaborations" and dogmatic good-vs.-evil duality introduced by August Derleth, the numerous pastiches that began to proliferate even before Lovecraft's death in 1937, and most especially the codification that became a strong part of many people's entry to the Cthulhu Mythos in the wake of the hugely successful roleplaying game (RPG) *The Call of Cthulhu*.[2] Perhaps most notable is that, to a large degree, *Rick and Morty vs. Cthulhu* eschews many of these common adaptational accretions. A deliberate reference in Jerry being eaten by the Hounds of Tindalos is a liminal example, the titular story being Frank Belknap Long's but his creation being added into the Mythos by Lovecraft himself. Hints of others are also present. The title Sleeper

---

2. In a wonderful, and as shall be seen curiously relevant, quotation, Paul St. John Mackintosh stated that "*Call of Cthulhu* is now the Pepsi of RPG franchises, alongside *D&D*'s Coke."

of R'lyeh is present in the background of one panel. The term is very much in line with Lovecraftian usage but is one of a number of such coming from divers hands.

The most notable inclusions from the, for want of a better term, secondary canon are the city of the Yithians being named as Pnakotus and the Daughter of Cthulhu, Cthylla. The former term is a retcon deriving from Lovecraft's Pnakotic manuscripts, first mentioned in Lin Carter's 1976 novella *The Horror in the Gallery* (a.k.a. *Zoth-Ommog*), and incorporated as lore in the aforementioned *Call of Cthulhu* RPG. Unlike many later arrogations of Lovecraft's work and ideas, this sits fairly well inside the Mythos as Lovecraft ever so loosely conceived of it, and I suspect many Lovecraft fans are unaware it is even a later addition. Cthylla is less canonically consistent, coming out of Brian Lumley's second Titus Crow book, *The Transition of Titus Crow* (1975). But this time the dilution of the Mythos by familiarity, the intrusion of Derleth's ideas, and the desire to create new tales resulted in the inexplicable and utterly unhuman gods of Lovecraft's conceptions becoming codified—as Lumley terms them, the Cthulhu Cycle Deities—and given more understandable motivations and actions. This is not to attack such on its own merits or to decry such things being done to posthumously as destroying the legacy of Lovecraft. The Old Gent himself wrote humorous family trees of his deities and even as he was dying read Henry Hasse's "The Guardian of the Book" (*Weird Tales*, March 1937), a seemingly completely straight Mythos pastiche that featured Cthulhu as a university student. Lovecraft cited the tale as one of three that "seem to carry off the honours" (*Letters to C. L. Moore* 263) in its issue. The inclusion of Cythylla is thematically necessary to the comic, and how much one can complain about canon in a story that features Dagon playing football with his adopted son Morty makes the point seem a trifle moot. The cliché father-son football scene emphasizes the depths of knowledge throughout the comic: Zadok Allen in the original specifically called him Father Dagon. Another interesting possibility is the talk by the folks of Innsmouth of skinning the captured Summer and Morty. This is not textual from Lovecraft, but does appear as an important plot point in the 2001 Stewart Gordon film *Dagon,* which is—despite the name—an adaptation of "The Shadow over Innsmouth."

It is worth briefly discussing the two main creators of this work[3] to show how this interaction with pop culture reflects broader trends. The writer is Jim Zub and the illustrator is Troy Little, who previously collaborated on the Eisner Award–nominated *Rick and Morty vs. Dungeons and Dragons* (2021). Both have a long history with comics intersecting with pop culture. Little drew the graphic novel adaptation of Hunter S. Thompson's *Fear and Loathing in Los Vegas* (2015) and the 2013–14 *Powerpuff Girls* comic series, while Zub wrote such works as *Stranger Things and Dungeons & Dragons* (2021), *Samurai Jack* #1–20, and a number of Marvel superhero comics and direct *Dungeons & Dragons* comics in their Forgotten Realms setting. They are clearly immersed in a world wherein Lovecraft is a well-known figure. The art of the comic in particular is a well-balanced blending of the signature style of the *Rick and Morty* and the horrors and indescribable nature of Lovecraft's creations. It manages this while keeping core descriptions intact, offering a highly distinct portrayal of Rick as a Yithian and having at the conclusion a genuinely powerful take on Azathoth.

There are several curious additions, and omissions, in the comic. That the cats of the Dreamlands are the servants of Nyarlathotep "now that the Moon-Beasts have lost their way" may seem jarring to the Lovecraft purist and doesn't seem particularly in line with the independently minded felines and their own Temple of the Cats in Ulthar as portrayed in *The Dream-Quest of Unknown Kadath*. Equally to the opposite point, Nyarlathotep, as portrayed in his Egyptian guise, and the feline connection with that famously ailurophilic people do have a certain consistency. Notable by being largely absent is the *Necronomicon*. It is only referenced directly by name once, when Rick notes to Wilbur in the Miskatonic Library, "I heard a rumor

---

3. Obviously the colorists and letterers are important to comics—Leonardo Ito and Nick Filardi for the former and Christopher Crank and Troy Little for the latter—but such is not overly germane to our analysis.

you're looking for the *Necronomicon,* Satan's favorite black book of sorcery." This is of course exactly the reason Wilbur is there, and this closeness to canon seems at odds with the convectional mention of the nemesis of Christianity in Satan. This too is the only such direct mention in the work connected with traditional Western religion, and moreover is clearly just setting up the following line when Rick produces weapons and denies having a copy but offers, "You can track down an autographed copy when I send you to Hell!" There are a few other oblique references to the *Necronomicon* in the tome held by the Innsmouth cultists, titled the *Dagonomicon* and with the symbol of the defictionalized Simon *Necronomicon* emblazoned upon the cover; but given the oversaturation of Lovecraft's infamous tome in pop culture, its lack of centrality is a welcome change.

There are certain icons and symbols from the wider RPG universe in a number of panels, and the more Derlethian idea of antagonism between various forces in the Lovecraftian Universe in opposition to one another is certainly present in the conflict between Dagon and Nyarlathotep. There are also several interesting meta-commentaries in the comic. Rick states that the Yithans' search for knowledge "feels like hippy-dippy Roddenberry sci-fi s**t," referencing the famous creator of *Star Trek,* which itself has a number of Lovecraft connections. The commercialization of the Cthulhu Mythos is mentioned several times: Cthulhu's eyes are dollar signs in an early picture accompanying a rant by Rick about exactly such crass exploitation, although typically he later specifically notes the high value of the Cthulian Corpse Dust he collected, which is "Always in demand amongst a certain clientele of horror-wanks."

The mockery of the obsessive and nerdy fan—and there are many in connection with Lovecraft—is apparent with the playful title of chapter one given as "The Whisperer in the Dorkness." Other chapter titles are more intrinsically playful with less specificity as to the humor's target: "Shut Your Innsmouth," "Yith We Can," and "Nothing R'lyeh Matters," the last two riffing on a popular World War II slogan and lyric from a Queen song, respectively. The last also carries a nihilistic implication that subtly sets up the confrontation with Azathoth and its outcome.

There are also various homages to the history of comics themselves. The title page for chapter 3, showing Rick standing before the Yithian version of himself, has a caption stating "Horror as you like it!" and a large question mark asking "Is he man or . . . is he Yith." All this references the famous cover of *The Incredible Hulk* #1 from May 1962, which shows Bruce Banner standing before the Hulk and states, "Fantasy as you like it!" and asks in it the question "Is he man or monster or . . . is he both." The original Hulk comic too has a sub-headline that could easily be applied to Rick: "The Strangest Man of All Time!!" Finally, in the imminent confrontation with Wilbur the question is asked about the second target, "what are we up against—a vampire, a werewolf, a mummy?" Significantly, the asker of the question is Jerry, who is the buffoon of the show, and whom four pages earlier Rick had castigated for failing to get the terminology of his chosen weapon of the crossbow correct. He thus represents the staid conventionality of the occult and supernatural that Lovecraft decried, creating an entirely new paradigm in defiance of it.

It is highly illustrative that the most prominent aspect of the comic is an extremely negative one. Cthulhu et al. are not the villains of the tale; Lovecraft is. The entirety of the comic proper does not have a single positive thing to say about either the man or his writing. Instead, Rick, who is himself far beyond morally questionable and whose actions are almost invariably selfish and often outright malign, constantly belittles and outright hates Lovecraft and his writing. A full listing would again be tedious, but lines such as of Miskatonic University ("it's just a pompous s**thole full of cultists, bigots, and blowhards. Just like the wankmaster who thought it all up"), "The Shadow out of Time" ("it's Lovecraft's weirdest story and given the dude's super-f**ked up output, that's really saying something"), and Azathoth ("you're just a dumb racist's paranoia wanked out on a typewriter!"). Of course, it is important not to confuse the art and the artist. Rick is specifically a deliberately profane, egocentric jerk with no respect for anything or anyone, so this is perfectly in line with his character. Rick is also not above exploitation of racism and inflaming such. For example, in S2E3 Rick spray-paints graffiti on a ship he is looting to cast blame on the Korlocks, and in response to Summer's complaint that this is horrible he says, "I hear you man. Cops are racist." Yet the portrayal of Lovecraft seems more than this, and it is not open to the subjectivity of the reader. Writer Jim Zub opens his Eldritch Endpapers I with "H. P. Lovecraft was full of s**t," and after some highly complimentary words about his creation of cosmic horror he continues, "also, awful racist and paranoid s**t about his fellow human beings."

This brings us to a number of paradoxes about Lovecraft that are found in modern thoughts about him and adaptations of his work, which *Rick and Morty vs. Cthulhu* highlight. Perhaps the greatest inconsistency and illogicality is that, in spite of generations of praise from his fellow authors, untold millions of books sold to a public who never tires of his work, and a permanent place in both the literary and pop cultural canon, people constantly echo the refrain that Lovecraft is a bad writer. As with all authors, some of his work is better than others, but the idea that all the above has happened despite the writing being terrible is, *prima facie*, absurd: *res ipsa loquitur*. *Rick and Morty vs. Cthulhu* definitely falls into this trope. "The Shadow out of Time" is said by Rick as having "bored the ever-living s**t out of me, so I didn't finish reading it," and he goes on to castigate Lovecraft as using "a ridiculous amount of text to describe overwrought details" and then he'd "load up his well-worn thesaurus shotgun and haphazardly blast away what he thought was erudite language in obtuse, run-on sentences." The point of this discussion is not to defend Lovecraft against such attacks; readers are always free to have whatever perceptions they feel about the merits of a particular work. It is merely to highlight the incongruity of a surprisingly large number of people who have clearly spent enough time diving deeply into Lovecraft to have a solid knowledge of the lore about someone whom they maintain is a bad writer and thus, by implication, not worth reading.

Perhaps most egregious is Rick describing over two pages, some of which was cited above, the flaws in Lovecraft's writing ultimately being a result of "what happens when you pay these hacks by the word." This is of course a reference to Lovecraft's work having been initially published in the pulp magazines, most especially *Weird Tales,* which did in fact pay by the word. Many of Lovecraft's contemporaries, including numerous hugely popular and prolific writers in their day, created work with exactly that aspect of remuneration in mind. They are also, in the main, either completely forgotten or known only inside a specific fan base. Many of the works of Seabury Quinn, the most published author in *Weird Tales,* such as his Major Sturdevant and Prof. Harvey Forrester series in *Weird Tales'* sister magazine *Real Detective Tales*,[4] are today only known by title. Even a number of his stories in *Weird Tales* have never been republished, and those that have been often appear only in boutique collections. By contrast with this deliberate commercialism—which Lovecraft famously detested and for which he openly lamented "the literary ruin of brilliant figures" (*Letters to C. L. Moore* 183) such as Quinn for having succumbed to the dictates of the pulps— the most money Lovecraft ever made in sales was $350 for "The Whisperer in Darkness." Yet the published version is six pages shorter than the original draft. On the advice of his friend Bernard Dwyer Lovecraft enacted "considerable condensation throughout, & a great deal of subtilisation toward the end" (*Essential Solitude* 265), choosing to make a better story over a greater profit. The idea that Rick offers in the tale that Lovecraft was someone who would "just chew up pages and spit 'em out" is incorrect to the point of malfeasance.

Less defensible is the seemingly omnipresent issue of Lovecraft's racial beliefs. That Lovecraft was a racist is not in question. However, the shift in social attitudes toward racism means that this particular flaw—and it certainly is a blight on his character—holds a disproportionate weight. This is not to defend racism in general or Lovecraft's racism in particular. It is to

---

[4]. *Real Detective Tales and Mystery Magazine* as of January 1925.

point out that this sin is considered by many to be so heinous that anything else is not even examined. Racism is an evil that has caused an incalculable amount of suffering in the world. Lovecraft was a racist. Ergo, the thinking thus becomes Lovecraft is incalculably evil. He is then reduced to a great and influential writer but ineffably horrible because he was born in the nineteenth century and held to what were the common and social norms of his time and place. This is not to throw up a "of his time" defense to Lovecraft's racism, merely to remember that he lived in a radically different age, an era in which congressmen used the word "nigger" on the floor of the House of Representatives and marriage between people classed as black and white was illegal in most of the country—even the modern equality bastion of California enforced such laws until the 1940s, after Lovecraft's death.

But the larger issue of Lovecraft and his racism is one that we are not here to debate. Rather it is the perception of him as portrayed in the comic, and how they reflect the modern reconception of Lovecraft. This element of perception is important. Lovecraft's letters to Robert E. Howard show they are both in broad and often specific agreement with each other as concerns issues of race, and Howard's own approach is often blunter, more forceful, and more extreme than Lovecraft's. Lovecraft is frequently condemned for being in favor of lynching, but what is glossed over, ignored, or unknown is that he is merely agreeing with the proposal as put forth by Howard, whose Deep South views on the matter are not the merely theoretical ones of a man in urban Providence. Yet I have not read any work about Howard that begins by lambasting and abominating his moral character derived from his position of race: it is becoming horrible close to a default position on any discussion of Lovecraft. An exemplar[5] is another comic work contemporary with *Rick and Morty vs. Cthulhu*, Norm Konyu's whimsical *A Call to Cthulhu* (2023). His afterword, "Who was H. P. Lovecraft?" begins:

---

5. Anecdotally, but rather informing the broader point, this example was not sought out to be illustrative; rather, I chanced to buy this particular book as I was composing this essay.

"Simply put, H. P. Lovecraft was a writer with great horror concepts, questionable prose, and extremely bigoted views."

The previous popular construct of Lovecraft that prevailed over the twentieth century was of the misanthropic recluse. This is an equally flawed and false paradigm, and yet like the Cyclopean racist model has enough elements of truth to sustain it. This began to be torn down by the rise in a genuine scholarship of Lovecraft and his work, and with the publication of S. T. Joshi's extensive biography in *H. P. Lovecraft: A Life* (1996) and the Brobdignagianly exhaustive uncut version in *I Am Providence* (2010) to replace L. Sprague de Camp's poorly regarded *Lovecraft. A Biography* (1975). *Rick and Morty vs. Cthulhu* is clearly aware of this older and somewhat perennially undead view of Lovecraft, at one point having Morty call him "a f**ked-up paranoid shut-in." The printing of all Lovecraft's letters in full and by correspondent rather than in selection and heavily edited as previously is slowly consigning this old paradigm to the flames: it is hard to read hundreds of pages of travel narratives and still claim someone as a hermit.

Yet this publication of an unprecedented epistolary output also brought to light an abundance of proof of Lovecraft's own racism in a form that easily leads itself to excerpt, quotation, and condemnation. Perhaps the most commonly cited example is worth examining to show how this recrudescence of Lovecraft plays into the vitriol about him that pervades the comics. The poem "On the Creation of Niggers" is almost invariably mentioned in articles discussing Lovecraft and racism. It does, one has to admit, make a pretty damning piece of evidence. What is often forgotten is that Lovecraft wrote this piece of doggerel, a total of eight lines, before the First World War and it was cast aside, only discovered in his papers at Brown University in the 1970s. It neither reflects his work generally and is (unfortunately) in accord with the tenor of his times—the deliberately inflammatory poem "Niggers in the White House" was first published in newspapers in 1901 as a protest against Booker T. Washington being invited there by President Theodore Roosevelt. It was later read on the floor of the United States Senate in

June 1929 in a similar outcry against the invitation by Eleanor Roosevelt of African-American Jessie De Priest, wife of a congressman, to tea at the White House.

Lovecraft, who habitually denigrated his own writings, by his own admission stated that his poetry—"nature verse, satire, parody, political & patriotic verse, general light verse etc." of the era was at best "sadly mediocre" and the overwhelming remainder were "even worse than these." With an oddly specific aptness he offers "I'd pay blackmail to keep [these poems] out of sight today" (*Off the Ancient Track* 342). Yet this poem is frequently offered as if it represents Lovecraft's work generally, was held in esteem by him, and cited as if it were freely available.[6] The opening episode of the television series *Lovecraft Country* (2020)—where many people first even heard of the poem's existence—has a character discuss the poem, which would not have been procurable in the show's 1950s setting, as if it were common knowledge.[7]

This common knowledge aspect plays into *Rick and Morty vs. Cthulhu*. Reading Lovecraft's letters—or, more specifically, excepted portions of Lovecraft's letters—makes his racist views loom very large. Again this work is not an apologia, yet for clarity it is worth noting S. T. Joshi estimates the maximum total of Lovecraft's discussions on race matters make up, at maximum, some 5% of his correspondence, with the truer figure probably being about 2%. Furthermore, this is not to say that this percentage is all ranting and unpleasant language. Such discussion also includes a lot of anthropological matters such as the migrations of the Celts or the beauty of Japanese art, or is following the ideas of leading scientists of his day. Yet personal accounts of Lovecraft make it clear he was invariably a welcoming, friend-

---

6. Which today, because of the Internet, it is although its only appearance in print remains in *The Ancient Track*, being the complete poetical works of HPL. Kudos to editor S. T. Joshi for its inclusion despite its odiousness. It is a difficult thing to air one's idol's sins.
7. To be fair to Matt Ruff, author of the original novel, the appearance of the poem is therein presented in a decidedly more plausible manner, at least given a reasonable suspension of disbelief.

ly, and genial host and guest. The idea of him such as the comic depicts him as "a paranoid a**hole" is commonly promulgated but is in defiance of known facts. Many of his friends and contemporaries stated years later they came to know of his racial views only by reading the published accounts in Arkham House's *Selected Letters,* with his long-time gay and Jewish friend Samuel Loveman stating in 1949, "I have never known a human being to secrete less envy, malice, morbidity, and intolerance" (Joshi and Schultz, *Ave atque* Vale 90). But, and it feels here that perhaps I protest too much, this article is not part of a defense of Lovecraft's racism. It is to demonstrate that the idea that Lovecraft was an unlikable, hate-filled, frothing-at-the-mouth Klansman or Nazi—he repudiated the former and had many sharp words to say about the latter, especially as their true barbarity became more apparent—is a wildly false perception. Yet this portrayal, found in innumerable articles and in modern media depictions, is now seen by many as the foundational, and often only, aspect of his character, personality, and actions. Such a representation is reflected and encapsulated in Lovecraft's entirely off-screen depiction in *Rick and Morty vs. Cthulhu.*

This is all perfectly summarized in a scene in the second chapter. After being rescued by cats in the Dreamlands, Summer spies a cute black kitten and asks its name. He replies, "Awful," to which she queries, "Your name is 'Awful'?" and the kitten clarifies, "Yes. It's awful and racist and came from an awful, racist dickwad." The reference is of course to the infamously named cat in "The Rats in the Walls," Nigger-Man, whose name reflects that of a cat Lovecraft had owned in childhood. In the modern fashion this has become somewhat of a meme, and Google suggestions and auto-fill offers "Lovecraft cat name" as one of its top choices when typing in "Lovecraft." This highlights the ubiquity of the perception and importance of the narrative of Lovecraft the racist, which has become so all-encompassing that *Rick and Morty vs. Cthulhu,* deeply drawing from his fictional creations, has only this to say about him. It is a disappointingly shallow take from a work that otherwise makes excellent and interesting use of his ideas and published stories.

Works Cited

Joshi, S. T., and David E. Schultz, ed. *Ave atque Vale: Reminiscences of H. P. Lovecraft.* West Warwick, RI: Necronomicon Press, 2018.

Lovecraft, H. P. *Letters to C. L. Moore and Others.* Ed. David E. Schultz and S. T. Joshi. New York: Hippocampus Press, 2017.

———. *O Fortunate Floridian: H. P. Lovecraft's Letters to R. H. Barlow.* Ed. S. T. Joshi and David E. Schultz. Tampa, FL: University of Tampa Press, 2007.

———, and August Derleth. *Essential Solitude: The Letters of H. P. Lovecraft and August Derleth.* Ed. David E. Schultz and S. T. Joshi. New York: Hippocampus Press, 2008.

Briefly Noted

A French publisher, Editions des Saints Pères, has issued a facsimile of the handwritten manuscript of *At the Mountains of Madness.* It is an oversize volume (about 10″ × 13″), enclosed in a slipcase, the whole being a lovely shade of green (perhaps indicative of the green ichor-like blood of the Old Ones?). S. T. Joshi wrote the introduction to the book. In the US, the edition sells for $220, but copies are apparently selling at a brisk pace.

How To Read Lovecraft

A Column by Steven J. Mariconda

Part 7: An Interview with Peter Cannon

This installment of "How to Read Lovecraft" features an esteemed guest: author and Lovecraft scholar Peter Cannon. Peter is perhaps best known for *Pulptime* (1984), a mystery novella in which H. P. Lovecraft helps Sherlock Holmes retrieve stolen documents for an anonymous client in Prohibition-era New York City, and *Scream for Jeeves: A Parody* (1994), a collection of three stories combining Lovecraftian horror with Wodehousian humor, hailed as "a minor classic" by Pulitzer Prize–winning critic Michael Dirda. He is also the author of the excellent *H. P. Lovecraft* (Twayne's United States Authors Series No. 549, 1989), which remains one of the best general introductions to the Providence writer. Here he talks about what he's been up to lately.

Q: In 2023, you retired from *Publishers Weekly*, where you started as the mystery reviews editor in 2000. With more free time, have you resumed writing about things Lovecraftian?

A: Nothing major. Last year, after I left *PW*, I wrote two short pieces at the invitation of others. The first was a contribution to the Arthur Conan Doyle Society's "The Terror of Blue John Gap" digital project. Titled "The Beast in the Cave: A Lovecraftian Conan Doyle Tale," it amounts to an extended footnote to Doyle's horror story. The other was a toast to Irene Adler I delivered at a meeting of the Adventuresses of Sherlock Holmes, a Holmes scion society. I took the occasion to plug *Pulptime*. I don't see myself ever returning to writing essays like "H. P. Lovecraft in Hawthornian Perspective" as I once did.

Q: How about writing new fiction?

A: After publishing *The Lovecraft Chronicles*, my one full-length novel, in 2004, I lost interest in producing Lovecraft-inspired fiction, though a few years ago I came up with an idea for a time travel tale, provisionally titled "A Rhode Island Gentleman in Covid New York." I made a few notes and set it aside, in part because I feared I couldn't do the idea justice. My top priority now is researching and writing a family memoir for my three children.

Q: Anything of Lovecraftian interest in your memoir?

A: Since the focus is on my youth up to 1974, the year I got my master's degree in English from Brown, it will cover only my initial discovery of Lovecraft. There should be more in the planned sequel, which will cover the rest of my life, though I expect it will be a lot shorter. My adulthood doesn't interest me nearly as much as my childhood.

Q: Is there anything of interest you'd like to share about your family?

A: In 1896, Martha Hughes Cannon, my Mormon great-grandmother, was the first woman to be elected a state senator. Among the losing candidates for the Utah state senate that year was her husband, who had five other wives. This summer her statue will be placed in the Capitol rotunda to represent Utah. At the dedication ceremony, speakers will no doubt praise her legislative achievements, but I think it unlikely anyone will mention that her giving birth to a daughter in 1899 created a scandal that put an end to her political career.

Q: What do you mean by "scandal"?

A: After the Church of Jesus Christ of the Latter-Day Saints renounced the practice of polygamy in 1890, men like my great-grandfather weren't supposed to produce more children with their plural wives.

Q: What was the last Lovecraftian story you wrote?

A: "China Holiday," a novelette based on a trip my wife, Nan, and I took to China in 1999. I wrote it in the early 2000s for the British anthologist Steve Jones, but he rejected it, in part because he thought it was too slow, too long. It finally appeared in S. T. Joshi's third *Black Wings* anthology, in abridged form. I hope someday somebody will publish the full text.

Q: What was your last published book?

A: *Long Memories and Other Writings*, which Derrick Hussey's Hippocampus Press brought out in 2022. It contains essentially all the nonfiction and fiction I've produced about Frank Belknap Long, whom I got to know well in the 1980s. The only thing new is the general introduction. The centerpiece is my memoir of Frank, which was first published by the British Fantasy Society as a chapbook in 1997. This version includes corrections and minor revisions, notably some provided by my friend Ted Klein.

Q: Such as?

A: Adding a comment that Frank made to Ted about deliberately getting drunk at a dinner party my first wife and I hosted for Frank and his wife at our New York City apartment.

Q: Any sense as to what motivated Frank to do so? Was he socially anxious, or just attempting to numb himself to the antics of his rather eccentric wife?

A: Probably a combination of both.

Q: How was *Long Memories and Other Writings* received?

A: Michael Dirda gave it a nice notice in his *Washington Post* column, but the so-so *PW* review concluded it was only for a niche audience. The lack of any comments on Amazon suggests it wasn't much noticed, let alone greeted with enthusiasm. I avoid social media, so I can only blame myself for its not getting wider attention. I did do a reading at Manhattan's Mysterious Bookshop, however.

Q: You did a reading of a book devoted to Frank Long, known as a horror and science fiction author, at a mystery bookstore?

A: Well, as my friend Otto Penzler, proprietor of the Mysterious Bookshop, pointed out, Frank is also the author of a story collection entitled *John Carstairs: Space Detective,* so he kind of counts as a mystery author. I should say this isn't the only favor Otto has done for me. In 1983, in his then role as the U.S. representative of the Conan Doyle estate, he told me to go ahead and publish *Pulptime* without getting permission from the estate. But I had to remove a passage referring to a real-life séance involving Doyle and his friend Harry Houdini, an embarrassing reminder of Doyle's gullibility. I happily did so, as it was a digression that didn't affect the plot.

Q: How about later editions of *Pulptime?*

A: I restored the passage in *The Lovecraft Papers,* the Science Fiction Book Club edition that also reprinted *Scream for Jeeves,* and in the *Pulptime* text printed in *Long Memories and Other Writings.* I also have Otto to thank for accepting a non-Lovecraftian story of mine for a crime anthology of his, *Kwik Krimes,* and using one of my short Sherlock Holmes pastiches for another anthology, *The Big Book of Sherlock Holmes Stories.*

Q: Are you doing any freelance editorial work these days?

A: On occasion I'm a first reader for Otto's Mysterious Press. I help screen manuscript submissions for the editor-in-chief by drawing on the knowledge I gained assigning and editing mystery and thriller reviews for more than two decades.

Q: Did you write reviews for *Publishers Weekly?*

A: During my apprenticeship at the magazine, I reviewed a mystery a week. I probably wrote dozens of anonymous reviews over the years, along with the occasional so-called signature review. As an example of the latter, I grabbed the chance to review the late Paul La Farge's wonderful Lovecraftian novel, *The Night Ocean.* I also reviewed the Lovecraft collection put out by Oxford University Press in 2013. I didn't think much of it.

Q: Any possibility *PW* would allow you to collect and republish those reviews?

A: Since it would violate the magazine's policy to identify me as the author of the anonymous reviews I wrote, reprinting them isn't an option. For the record, I basically rewrote poorly written reviews from certain of my freelancers, rather as Lovecraft did with his weaker revision clients.

Q: Do you still read Lovecraft?

A: I try to remember to read a little something by him on his birthday and on his death day. It's been a long time, though, since I reread one of his works in full. The last might have been *At the Mountains of Madness,* which kept me occupied while waiting to be called for jury duty at a downtown Manhattan courthouse in 2011.

Q: What about Lovecraft's letters?

A: In the last decade or so, I've been trying to keep up with the many volumes of Lovecraft's correspondence issued by Hippocampus Press. Not all are scintillating, however. I confess I'm bogged down in the opening pages of the second volume of the letters between Lovecraft and Robert E. Howard, *A Means to Freedom.* I may never finish it.

Q: What's the last letters volume you did finish?

A: The two-volume *Letters to Family and Family Friends.* Many of the letters he wrote from New York, I discovered, had a personal resonance for me.

Q: How so?

A: In 2021, my family and I moved uptown to Washington Heights, near the Jumel-Morris mansion, which briefly served as George Washington's headquarters during the Revolution. Lovecraft and Long visited the mansion, then as now open to the public, on September 14, 1922. Lovecraft mentions signing a visitor's register as if he were an eighteenth-century gentleman. I approached a couple of staff members to see if they still had the register with that date in their archives. One said she'd check. Another said a display of the page with Lovecraft's signature would make a great Halloween exhibit. Alas, I never heard back from anyone at the mansion and can only assume that the century-old visitor's book is no longer extant.

Q: Any other New York connections with the letters?

A: In 2022, my family and I moved farther uptown, to the last address on Riverside Drive. We're a few blocks from Inwood's eighteenth-century Dyckman Farmhouse, which Lovecraft reports visiting with Long. I haven't made it there yet, but I did attempt to walk south on Riverside Drive, inspired by Lovecraft's comment in a letter about the architectural beauty of its upper stretch. Unfortunately, my walk ended abruptly at the Westside Highway, which many decades ago supplanted the section of Riverside Drive extolled by Lovecraft. Thank you, Robert Moses!

Q: Have you been to the Bronx to see the Poe Cottage, visited by Lovecraft and friends in 1922?

A: I'm ashamed to admit the Poe Cottage is still on my to-do list. It's an easy bus ride from Inwood to the Bronx, but the one time I tried to get there I mistakenly rode the bus well past the right stop and ended up aborting the mission. I'm determined to make it there one day.

Q: Will you be making it to this summer's NecronomiCon?

A: I've attended every Providence NecronomiCon since its inauguration in 2013, and I'm looking forward to this one, though in the past I've worried that I'm out of touch with current Lovecraft studies and the larger horror genre.

Q: Weren't you a guest of honor in 2019?

A: I was and felt duly honored, though I was disappointed on arrival that year to learn that a promised play adaptation of my first *Scream for Jeeves* story, "Cats, Rats, and Bertie Wooster," had fallen through. In addition, I felt I had little to contribute to the panels I was on. In 2022, I chose not to serve on any panels, though I did fill in last minute on one when the opportunity arose.

Q: What prompted you to do that?

A: As I recall, the panel's topic had something to do with nineteenth-century literature, and I saw it as a chance to talk about the link between Lovecraft and Melville. I was rereading *Moby-Dick* and noticed that certain passages in "The Whiteness of the Whale" chapter had a Lovecraftian ring. I read these passages aloud without identifying the source to test the audience. Immediately, a guy in the audience answered and said the prose was Melville's. Later, the question came up whether Melville's "The Piazza" influenced Lovecraft's "The Strange High House in the Mist."

Q: What did you say?

A: I said nothing, having not read either story in ages, but fortunately a young professor on the panel addressed the issue. At any rate, I like to think this discussion helped lead to the panel on Lovecraft and Melville set for this year's NecronomiCon. I just received confirmation that I'm on it. To prepare, I plan to reread "The Piazza" and "The Strange High House in the Mist."

Q: Are you on other NecronomiCon panels?

A: Yes, two others. As the author of *Long Memories*, I feel well qualified to be on the panel devoted to Frank Belknap Long, whose letters to and from Lovecraft will be out soon from Hippocampus. As a longtime Manhattan resident, I feel qualified enough to be on the one focused on Lovecraft's New York years, along with David Goodwin, author of a splendid biographical study, *Midnight Rambles: H. P. Lovecraft in Gotham*, which I added to my collection last year.

Q: Are you starting to think about disposing of your Lovecraft collection?

A: In recent years, on trips to Providence, I've been donating some of my lesser stuff to the Lovecraft Arts and Sciences shop. A couple of years ago, for example, I decided I no longer needed the three Arkham House volumes of Lovecraft's collected fiction I acquired in the early 1970s. These were used, non-first edition copies, yet to my astonishment I later learned that they each sold for hundreds of dollars. To me, such prices are a sign of how highly readers regard Lovecraft's work.

Q: As a young scholar, could you have imagined the popular and critical acclaim Lovecraft has achieved?

A: At the Centennial Conference held in Providence in 1990, I remember thinking that S. T. Joshi and my other colleagues and I were on to something, but, no, I could never have foreseen the heights to which Lovecraft and his reputation have risen in the years since. I'm amazed by the degree to which he and his fictional concepts have slipped into mainstream culture. I'm especially pleased whenever I run across a Lovecraftian reference in such august places as the *New York Times* opinion page or a work of literary fiction.

Q: Such as?

A: Andrew Sean Greer's 2017 Pulitzer Prize–winning novel, *Less*. A comic satire centered on a middle-aged gay writer named Less, it's about as far removed from Lovecraft and his world as you can imagine. But wait till you get to page 54 of the paperback edition. At a Mexico City market, a tour guide asks the group if anyone has allergies or things they will or cannot eat. In response, and I quote here: "Less wonders if he should mention make-believe foods like bugs and slimy Lovecraftian sea horrors . . ." No doubt Greer knew he could count on his readers to recognize the allusion—or enough of them anyway.

Q: Finally, is there a current book you're looking forward to reading?

A: I've requested a copy of Jonathan Lethem's *Brooklyn Crime Novel* from the New York Public Library. I hear it contains a Lovecraft reference or two.

Reviews

H. P. LOVECRAFT and FRANK BELKNAP LONG. *A Sense of Proportion: The Letters of H. P. Lovecraft and Frank Belknap Long.* New York: Hippocampus Press, forthcoming. 856 pp. $75.00 hc. Reviewed by Steven J. Mariconda.

Ladies and gentlemen! Back by popular demand, his twenty-first appearance! Presented by impresarios S. T. Joshi and David E. Schultz, exclusively for the Hippocampus circuit! Your literary song-and-dance man, Howard Phillips Lovecraft! Watch in amazement as he does a buck-and-wing on mechanistic materialism . . . croons the moon in June over Marblehead . . . does an alley-oop on New England history . . . hoofs it to the hilarious "is-it-or-isn't-it" routine . . . does a Brodie onto Friedrich Nietzsche . . . chews the scenery with his GOD SAVE THE KING! shtick . . . a soft-shoe on aesthetics . . . the dialect act . . . all your favorite baggy-pants characters: E'ch-Pi-El! Grandpa Theobald! Humphry Littlewit! Epicurus Lackbrain! Caelius Alhazred Moreton O'Casey! This all-singing, all-dancing extravaganza is about to begin!

After a period of more than twenty years, *A Sense of Proportion* is the twenty-first and perhaps final installment of Lovecraft's collected letters. In brief compass: this set of correspondence to Frank Belknap Long (which includes many missives from the latter as well) is among the most outstanding of the series. For those readers already engaged with the Lovecraft correspondence, this set is a must-have; and for those new to it, this is a good place to begin.

Since this set of books marks the end (at least temporarily) of the heroic effort to get all Lovecraft's extant letters into print, congratulations are due not only to the editors but also to the publisher. August Derleth and Donald Wandrei, of course, deserve praise for conceiving the idea that Lovecraft's correspondence should be preserved; they published five volumes over the period 1965–76. But Arkham House had only the surviving missives, and published mostly extracts. Marc Michaud and S. T. Joshi began tentative efforts to publish the entirety of Lovecraft's letters in 1990 with those to Henry Kuttner, followed a few years later with those to Richard F. Searight and to Robert Bloch; but Necronomicon Press experienced challenges and the series stalled. Undeterred, editors Joshi and David E. Schultz tapped Night Shade Books for the H. P. Lovecraft–Donald Wandrei correspondence (2002). Finally, Derrick Hussey, who had founded Hippocampus Press in 1999, stepped into the breach; the three colleagues have stayed the course for more than two decades. No editorial board, proofreading interns, production department, buyer consortia, third-party funding, Kickstarter, reader subscriptions; just several intrepid individuals, shoe leather, and keyboards. The tentative final tally for this series of volumes (caveat: my back-of-the-envelope estimate) is roughly 12,000 letters, consisting of approximately five million words. As a venture in small press publishing, the project is akin to putting a man on the moon.

Of the millions who read Lovecraft's tales, most may ask "Why bother reading the letters?" We only have around 100 pieces of fiction, depending on how one counts it; eventually we exhaust this body or work. But the unique *frission* we found in Lovecraft is addictive; some may look to Cthulhu Mythos pastiches or perhaps to role-playing games. But these have not the savor of the real Lovecraft. What we experience in the correspondence is the same compelling voice we have come to know in the stories. Given the word count of the letters and the average length of a typical tale, it is almost as if we have been given another 700 or so Lovecraft tales. One thing about him, we realize, is that he blurs the boundary of genre. Essays and tales bleed into one another (one thinks specifically of "The Whisperer in Darkness"); monographs read like fiction (e.g., "Supernatural Horror in Literature"); letters turn into flights of fantasy; prose turns into poetry (e.g., *Fungi from Yuggoth*). So fiction readers looking for a Lovecraft "fix" are advised to investigate the letters.

And what are we to make of this tremendous pool of "content"? What do we know now about Lovecraft that we didn't know in 2002?

Firstly, the totality of Lovecraft's racism is out in the open. This alone will put many off the correspondence completely; but it is part of the historical record that must be addressed. Lovecraft is not to be excused: while these attitudes were more widespread in American society at the time, they were wrong then and are wrong today. Is it naïve to hope that to acknowledge them, to understand the pathology behind them, and to renounce them may help prevent them from persisting? Indeed, how this flaw remained impervious to the keen analysis we see in so many other areas of Lovecraft's thought is a worthy puzzle in its own right. It originates, perhaps, in the shadow side of Lovecraft's psyche—a symptom of a complex borne of childhood trauma and of a dysfunctional family with a free-floating element of mental illness. Unfortunately, racialism was woven into the protective psychic carapace he created his 1908–13 period of isolation—the persona of the elderly eighteenth-century gentleman "outsider," last of his line.[1]

Secondly, the stereotype of the adult Lovecraft as a schizoid personality—aloof, apathetic, anhedonic, and generally miserable—is shown to be false. We have here not a sequestered individual, either literally or figuratively; not a semi-invalid in a stocking cap reading through pince-nez by a guttering candle. Instead, Lovecraft is cultivating friendships, doing, seeing, thinking. Intellectually, he is on fire; he investigates, consumes, reacts, and transforms, processing vast amounts of information.

Thirdly, Lovecraft was possessed of more cognitive firepower and encyclopedic knowledge than even his most vigorous advocates might have guessed. The range of subjects, along with his intellectual curiosity, verbal fluency, humor, powers of observation, and logical analysis, join with his exceptional imagination to produce innumerable fascinating passages. These letters are

---

1. The notion of an 18th-century persona literally taking over a 20th-century body is seen, in a different context of course, in *The Case of Charles Dexter Ward* (1927).

not of the quotidian "how's the weather?" variety found in the correspondence of other notable artists (Henry James springs to mind). The scope of his interests was immense. He had a specialist-level knowledge of New England history and material culture, and his travelogues on the region veritably sparkle.

Lastly, the correspondence is a kind of hothouse for Lovecraft's prose style. For fictional composition, he had explicitly identified several "distinct tones" (enumerated in his "List of Primary Ideas Motivating Possible Weird Tales"): "intense, clutching, delirious horror; delicate, dream-like fantasy; realistic, scientific horror; [and] very subtle adumbration" (CE 2.174). Similarly, in the letters he moves seamlessly among satire, patently theatrical rustic and ethnic patois, stream of consciousness, slang, eighteenth-century rhetoric, and plain-spoken, razor-sharp argumentation. What Lovecraft is really writing here is *dramatic nonfiction.*

In terms of subjects, we learn much about literature: poetry, narrative, rhetoric, aesthetics; movements such as Symbolism, Decadence, and Modernism; authors such as Poe, Lord Dunsany, and Arthur Machen; and influences such as Samuel Johnson. Lovecraft, too, had a high level of interest in contemporary science—anthropology, astronomy, cosmology, physics, psychology, economics. He exhibits in-depth knowledge of philosophy and philosophers (the Milesian school and other Presocratics, Epicurus, Schopenhauer, Nietzsche, Krutch, Santayana, Bertrand Russell). From all this Lovecraft formulated his own distinctive worldview, borrowing variously from determinism, Epicureanism, nihilism, pragmatism, and Stoicism. But the letters are by no means ponderous, for Lovecraft frames these subjects with wit and rhetorical pyrotechnics.

There are, of course, more mundane communiqués on workaday subjects—the amateur journalism and pulp magazine scenes, cinema, theatre, popular song, and current affairs. The latter discussions are often driven by the foment of the Great Depression: after 1930 there is much on the relative merits of capitalism, socialism, Marxism, communism, and even technological-based authoritarianism.

Turning specifically to this volume—it seems that Lovecraft

saw in Frank Belknap Long not merely a protégé, but also the very image of his youthful self. During a lengthy career, Long (1901–1994) wrote almost thirty novels, 150 or short stories, three poetry collections, and many magazine articles. He met Lovecraft though their shared membership in the United Amateur Press Association. Long was a resident of New York City and became one of Lovecraft's closest friends during the latter's stay in Brooklyn during 1924–26.

These missives see Lovecraft acting as a patient mentor, offering insights and counsel, sincerely attempting to help the younger man navigate the turbulent years of the 1920s and 1930s. Because Lovecraft saw Long as a kindred spirit, he felt free to espouse at length upon a wide variety of topics: cosmicism, amateur journalism, weird fiction, Colonial architecture, aesthetic sincerity, the decline of the West, Greek philosophy, Anglo-Protestantism.

Long is often articulate and sensible, but he has a challenge going toe to toe with the older man; his arguments are sometimes thin, and his tone occasionally callow. It is thus ironic when he censures Lovecraft for not being more selective in his pen friends: "I utterly fail to grasp why you enjoy corresponding with so many half-baked and grotesque and abysmally freakish persons!" A few of Long's critical judgment miss the mark. He places the very poor "The Horror at Red Hook" (1925; one of the few Lovecraft stories marred by racism) on par with "Dagon" (1917), "The Silver Key" (1926), and "The Shunned House" (1924). He dislikes Walter de la Mare's "The Recluse" and has no patience with Blackwood's *Incredible Adventures*.

To Long's credit, he does try to talk some sense into Lovecraft on several topics. The two men had joined in an informal revision service, and one of their clients was Zealia Brown-Reed Bishop (1897–1968), for whom Lovecraft ghostwrote "The Curse of Yig" (1928), "The Mound" (1929–30), and "Medusa's Coil" (1930). When Lovecraft advised Long to undertake original composition for Bishop instead of merely correcting her work for clarity and overall effectiveness, the protégé came back with guns blazing:

Have you gone suddenly quite mad? If you will look up the word "revision" in the *Oxford English Dictionary* you will discover that it is nowhere defined as creation—the creation of an original work of art. And do you imagine for a moment that I could possibly produce 60,000 words of original creative work in five or six weeks—at ⅓ cent a word? (8 July 1929)

Regrettably, this is exactly what Lovecraft did—creating "The Mound," a 30,000-word novella. Bishop's original plot-germ for the story (as recorded by R. H. Barlow on the surviving typescript) was merely: "There is an Indian mound near here, which is haunted by a headless ghost. Sometimes it is a woman."

This is one of the few correspondences where the topic of sex comes up, broached here of course by Long: "I like sex in a novel—I frankly enjoy pornography, for I hold that it is pornography which gives a degree of charm to all really great writing, writing in the great tradition, which it would otherwise lack" (30 January 1924). Perhaps to the eternal benefit of all, most of Lovecraft's rejoinders on this topic have been are lost.

The letters to Long have a vivacity not present in those to certain other correspondents (for example, those to the rather timid elderly poet Elizabeth Toldridge). Lovecraft bounces swiftly and assuredly from one topic to the next, lending an effect of almost cinematic montage. Even a simple request from anthology editor Edward J. O'Brien for a biographical squib (he had selected "The Colour out of Space" for *The Best Short Stories of 1928*) sends Lovecraft ricocheting around time and space:

In furnishing my Irish colleague with an account of my vivid & active career I did not think it necessary to mention trifles so tame as Satanism and neogonophagy [*sic*]—nay, nor my voyage up the Oxus, nor my visit to Samarcand, nor how and why I slew the yellow-veiled priest at Lhasa—that priest whose yellow silken veil stood out too far in front of where his face ought to be, & moved in a manner that I did not like. These nugae I have pass'd over altogether as unworthy of the career of a man of genius; but I did hint of certain travels through the aether in the dark of the moon, & give broad suggestions regarding certain queerly-dimensioned cities of windowless onyx towers on a planet circling about Antares, which the initiated cannot well read without forming their own conjectures about the first-handedness of my information. In relating my genealogy I omitted the Spanish ancestor, but was careful to include the Roman strain originating with Decimus Caelius Rufus, a tribunus militum under P. Ostorius Scapula, (who defeated the Welsh chief Caractacus 15 in A.D. 51) who settled near the camp of the Second Legion on the Isca, married the Welsh princess Galgaca, & became in time the progenitor of Owen Gwynedd, Prince of North Wales. Oh, yes—& the later Roman strain which came when Caelius' Romanised descendant Caius Caelius Galgacinus married Lollia Secunda, daughter of the praefectus M. Lollius Urbicus & his purely Roman wife Plautia Flavilla in the age of the Antonines. (mid-December 1927?)

This is positively carnivalesque.

The centerpiece of the Long correspondence, originally excerpted as "Letter 466" in *Selected Letters III* (290–342), is restored here; this single missive now comes in at around 29,000 words. (This exceeds Lovecraft's *annual* fictional output for thirteen years out of the seventeen years he wrote.) And there once was yet more—the editors note laconically, "The remainder of this letter has been lost." Joshi has elsewhere proposed that this particular missive "contains more philosophical substance and rhetorical flourishes than any [Lovecraft] story or essay . . . and ought to stand next to 'The Colour out of Space' and *At the Mountains of Madness* as one of his towering literary achievements."[2]

Another essential item is Lovecraft's 1927 "Roman Dream." This item is red meat for hungry Lovecraft carnivores. At 3,000 words, it is longer than many of his signed tales, including such things as "Dagon" (1917), "The White Ship" (1919), "The Outsider" (1921), "Hypnos" (1922), and "The Hound" (1922). The dream-narrative exists in multiple versions written to different correspondents (Long, Donald Wandrei, Bernard Austin Dwyer); one variant was published as "The Very Old Folk" in

---

2. S. T. Joshi, "A Look at Lovecraft's Letters," in *Lovecraft and a World in Transition: Collected Essays on H. P. Lovecraft* (New York: Hippocampus Press, 2004), 445.

the fanzine *Scienti-Snaps* (Summer 1940). The first-person narrator is L. Caelius Rufus, provincial questor in the late Republic. He is summoned to Pompelo in Roman Hispania because of strange doings in the hills above the town; he investigates with a cohort of soldiers and they meet with a nameless but distinctly Lovecraftian fate. The author gave Long permission to use the text of in *The Horror from the Hills* (*Weird Tales,* January and February–March 1931; Arkham House, 1963).

Some of the most fascinating passages come when Lovecraft attempts to argue Long out of converting to Catholicism (in the manner of other Moderns such as T. S. Eliot, Graham Greene, Evelyn Waugh, and Muriel Spark). Lovecraft goes into great depth, arguing that they are both intellectual heirs of the American Humanist position that Ralph Waldo Emerson and other New England thinkers had carved out:

> The Massachusetts Puritans—honest fools—were the first stage. The anti-Puritan revolt which founded Rhode Island, and which lies directly behind me, represents another stage. . . . The Unitarians are another stage[;] . . . the ethical humanists form another. They are all far more perfect traditionalists than your sniveling little neo-papists . . . [because] they are functioning absolutely in line with their original ancestral impetus. . . . The next stage of . . . thought-development after the Humanists is that of complete materialistic scepticism—the inevitable product of cosmos-confrontation by the honest, straightforward, and uncompromising mind. It is a Protestant, Puritan zeal—an Anglo-Saxon and early-American scorn for falsehood and evasion—which makes the modern American nihilist face openly the evident lack of purpose, values, goal, or central consciousness in the space-time continuum. . . . The next stage of racial thought-development after the [Puritans, anti-Puritans, and] Humanists is that of complete materialistic scepticism—the inevitable product of cosmos-confrontation by the honest, straightforward, and uncompromising mind. It is a Protestant, Puritan zeal—an Anglo-Saxon and early-American scorn for falsehood and evasion—which makes the modern American nihilist face openly the evident lack of purpose, values, goal, or central consciousness in the space-time continuum. We are *still*

Protestants though no longer Christians. [my emphasis]. It is the same old leaven at work—the feudal loyalty-instinct having been transferred from a non-existent deity to the one fundamental cosmic element of truth. (19 or 26 April 1931)

It is an astonishing and brilliant conceit. Somehow, Lovecraft anticipated by sixty years the same formulation as that of Harold Bloom in *The American Religion* (1992): "I argue in this book that the American Religion . . . masks itself as *Protestant Christianity, yet has ceased to be Christian.*"[3]

Lovecraft repeatedly advises Long to purge his arguments of sentiment and ideology, and to focus on empirical truth: "Our only watchword must be a resolve to seek nothing but the impartial probabilities in the matter of *what is* versus *what isn't*" (22 November 1930). Three months later, Long still does not get the concept, provoking a classic Lovecraftian screed:

Listen, young man. Forget all about your books & machine-made current associations. Kick the present dying parody on civilisation out the back door of consciousness. Shelve the popular second-hand dishings-up of Marxian economic determinism—a genuine force within certain limits, but without the widest ramifications ascribed to it by the fashionable New Republic & Nation clique. For once in your life, live up to your non-contemporary ideal & do some thinking without the 1930-31 publishers' sausage-grist at your elbow! Get back to the Ionian coast, shovel away some 2,500 years, & tell Grandpa who it is you find in a villa at Miletus studying the properties of loadstone & amber, predicting eclipses, explaining the moon's phases, & applying to physics & astronomy the principles of research he learned in Egypt. Thales—quite a boy in his day. Ever hear of him before? He wanted to *know* things. Odd taste, wasn't it? (February 1931)

Lovecraft's effort to cajole Long out of the pose of a sophisticated Latin decadent are somewhat hypocritical, in that Lovecraft himself assumed the pose of a sophisticated eighteenth-century

---

3. Harold Bloom, *The American Religion: The Emergence of the Post-Christian Nation* (New York: Simon & Schuster, 1992), 32 (my emphasis).

gentleman.[4] After one especially ham-handed foray, Lovecraft apparently realizes this inconsistently and makes a feeble attempt to excuse himself:

> As a final word on eccentrick conduct—one must of course make a distinction betwixt sheer unmotivated & ignominious exhibitionism, & that really spontaneous & occasional grotesqueness which has a genuine & adequate source; either in really relevant symbolism, or in truly pertinent irony as related to exaggerated & trivial conventions with disproportionate demands on detailed conformity. These instances of aesthetically justified grotesqueness are not difficult to distinguish from the cheap & squalid sort; since they invariably have a clear relationship to their personal & social background, & occur only in a light, sporadic, & appropriate way which shews that their perpetrators are not in truth insensible of the actual proportions of things. (February 1931)

Corollary to his advocacy of a modified American Protestant ethic, Lovecraft spills much ink promoting the writers' common English ancestry and its putative Saxon and Norman constituents. (He lets loose with "GOD SAVE THE KING!" no fewer than seventeen times.) He is also provoked into some monologues in which hilarity (intentional and unintentional) ensues:

> By Woden, were not our deeds & battles, our victories & empires, all parts of a poem more wonderful then aught which Homer cou'd strike from a Grecian lyre? Ho! Yaaah! We are men! We are big men! We are strong men, for we make men do what we want! Let no man balk us, for our gods are big gods, & our arms & our swords are tough! Hrrrr! The stones of towns fall down when we come, & crows love us for the feast of dead men we give them. The lands shake with the thump of our feet, & hills grow flat when we stride up & down them. The floods are dry when we have drunk them, & no beasts are left when

---

4. When James F. Morton teasingly called him on this, Lovecraft laughed and answered, "But isn't it an artistic pose?" "A Few Memories," in *Ave atque Vale: Reminiscences of H. P. Lovecraft*, ed. S. T. Joshi and David E. Schultz (West Warwick, RI: Necronomicon Press, 2019), 30.

we have killed & gorged. By day we kill & seize, at dusk we feast & drink, by night we snore & dream big dreams of strange seas we shall sail, old towns we shall burn, stout men we shall slay, wild beasts we shall hunt, deep cups we shall drain, fat boars we shall tear limb from limb with our hands, & gnaw with our sharp teeth. Great Thor, but this is life! We ask no more! We know the cool of deep woods, & the spell of their gloom & of the things void of name that lurk or may lurk in them. Bards sing them to us in the dark with great hoarse voices when the fire burns low & we have drunk of our mead. Bards sing them to us, & we hear. Great, gaunt bards with white beards & the old scars of good fights. And they sing things that none else have dreamed of; strange, dim, weird things that they learn in the woods, the deep woods, the thick woods. There are no woods like our woods, & no bards like our bards. (11 December 1923)[5]

More appealing to readers of the fiction are rich descriptions of multiple antiquarian trips Lovecraft made to Salem and Newburyport, places that served as the basis of his fictional towns such as Arkham and Innsmouth. In Salem, he patronized the shop of artist Sarah W. Symonds (1870–1965), still widely known for her bas-relief plaques of New England historic sites. Contrary to stereotype, Lovecraft engaged Ms. Symonds in a long conversation—obtaining introductions to local caretakers who could provide access to historic houses, and discussing their mutual admiration for Poe. Lovecraft recommend to Ms. Symonds the art of Clark Ashton Smith, and confessed to her that he himself was a writer of weird tales; she expressed interest and asked to

---

5. Speaking of mead (an alcoholic beverage made by fermenting honey, water, and various flavorings with yeast), it appears that Lovecraft was not a 100% teetotaler after all. He recounts a visit to the home of elderly amateur journalist Arthur Goodenough (1871-1936) in Brattleboro, Vermont: "Goodenough shewed us all over his ancient house, which has an enormous chimney whose brick foundations occupy half the cellar, & gave us a drink of an evil-tasting mead which I swallowed only because he assured me it was the traditional hayfield beverage of the colonial New England farmer" (24 August 1927). Lovecraftian humorists may wish to consider this minor revelation in conjunction with "A Good Anaesthetic" (1899?; repository.library.brown.edu/studio/item/bdr:425182), which sees the young chemist himself brewing up a batch of nitrous oxide.

see them. We have no record of any further contact with her, but he did come away with three highly prized works of regional art.

In the same letter is a passage showing how "The Festival" was inspired by Salem as well as Marblehead ("Kingsport"):

> Silently I descended past the leering houses with their centuried small-paned bleary windows, and as I did so my fancy brought vividly to my eyes a terrible procession going both up and down that hill beside me—a terrible procession of black-cowled things bearing bodies swathed in burlap. And so ample were the cowls, that I could not see the face of any of the things .... or whether they had any faces. (mid-February 1923)

Conversely, it seems that the fictional Innsmouth was inspired by Marblehead as well as Newburyport:

> It was that part of Colonial Marblehead call'd *Barnegat*, which the poorer Sort of Seamen inhabited, & in its Decay presented an Aspect of the greatest Picturesqueness. I stood for some Time transported, then proceeded to descend the Slope & walk bodily into that Picture whose Reality seem'd so incredible, & which I cou'd scarce imagine but as hanging upon my Wall, or peering at me from a Book of Engravings. There was one old House half sunken into the Ground, so that the Windows toward the south-west Corner sagg'd & slanted downward at an alarming Angle; & this was but a single Instance of that unearthly Charm which pervaded the entire Locality.... (24 July 1923)

Lovecraft also recounts several excursions to Newburyport, one with details that foreshadow Innsmouth's Gilman House hotel:

> There are only three restaurants [in Newburyport], two of which are Hellenick dumps [Greek diners?] frequented only by the peasantry, and the third of which is the cafe of the Adams House—an hostelry over a century old which keeps its original sign. This eating-house wou'd ... make any Cleveland Clark's Lunch look like the main dining-room of the Statler [Hotel] ... and yet it is Newburyport's only civilised place of refection! (May 1923)

Also compelling are passages concerning Harry Houdini; Lovecraft and his colleague C. M. Eddy had been retained by the magician for revision services. Writing to Long on 26 October 1926, Lovecraft relays:

> . . . our slippery friend Houdini, who was here early in the month . . . rushed me to hell preparing an anti-astrological article to be finished before his departure—a matter of five days; for which I received the not wholly despicable remuneration of seventy-five actual dollars. He says he has a devilish lot more for me to do, and has been trying to get me to meet him in Detroit at his own expense to talk things over—but I have maintained that I can do business best within sight of my native town's Georgian steeples.

This is Lovecraft at his arrogant worst. He continues:

> Just now I note in the [news]paper that Houdini has had a breakdown—which must have occurred just after the last letter he sent me—so I fancy there will be a lull in the negotiations. I'll send him a line of sympathy to jolly him along. Poor Eddy, who with my aid has been doing some revision for the nimble wizard, is quite worried about this unexpected intervention of the gods.

On Sunday, 24 October 1926, Houdini fell ill on a train from Montreal to Detroit. He performed there Sunday night, but collapsed and was rushed into surgery for a ruptured appendix. Wire services for 25 and 26 October indicated that Houdini's condition was "grave," and that he was fighting for his life; thus Lovecraft's casual brush-off is especially vexing. It was Eddy who proved correct: Houdini died of peritonitis in Detroit's Grace Hospital on 31 October. It is chilling to consider for a moment an alternate history in which Lovecraft had traveled to Detroit.

A little more than a year later, however, we see Lovecraft in a more favorable light. He offers a generous assessment of Houdini (the Jewish son of an Eastern European rabbi), and spins a finely turned paragraph on fraudulent spiritualism:

> Poor old Houdini—who actually had a tremendous amount of penetrative skill & workable erudition in this field despite his

general lack of culture, & who was incredibly honest in his researches despite the fact that publicity was his primary goal—had a long talk on this subject with Eddy & me less than a month before his death, & no one could fail to appreciate from his descriptions the way all great Hindoo fakir feats evaporate when one buckles down to get first-hand or photographic data. At the cost of much delving & evidential sifting Houdini arrived at the very reasonable conclusion that India's fakirs obtain their fame through a very shrewd mixture of publicity with a moderate amount of sleight-of-hand skill. Two classes of feats represent actual performances—(a) relatively simple feats, or feats due to abnormal physiological powers, performed in the open; (b) highly elaborate & ingenious miracles performed with apparatus under special conditions. . . . One of the greatest auxiliaries of the magic hierophant is the natural sympathy of the ordinary mind—the heir of thousands of years of myth & darkness as opposed to only a century or so of mechanical understanding of natural principles—with the indefinite & the marvellous; a sympathy subtly strengthened by the natural impatience of sensitive people against the prosaic limitations of the usual, & by the intellectual indolence which causes rebellion against the patient scientific subtleties whose difficulty of comprehension makes them seem far more improbable, despite their firm basis, than the flimsy hereditary myths which they have displaced, but which they may externally resemble. This sympathy enables the occultist to accomplish a highly sophistical shifting of the burden of proof; whereby he imputes to myth & folklore a weight of authority which no rational consideration could ever accord it, & brushes arbitrarily out of sight the carefully accumulated knowledge of natural law which enables the cautious investigator to say with a very close approach to finality that certain things are absolutely impossible. (30 November 1927)

By way of contrast, the best Long can come up with regarding the escape artists is this: "I wish I knew the secret of the late Houdini's telephone box tour de force (he could extract all the nickels from a telephone slot-machine in five minutes") (24 October 1928).

Lest I give the impression that Lovecraft was infallible: above and beyond the question of race, he was wrongheaded on many topics. It can be said relative to these lacunae, that he was intermittently aware of his own shortfalls. Writing at age forty, for example, he admits the "frightful state of bombastic and quasi-adolescent simplicity [of his thought] as late as only a few years ago") (19 or 26 April 1931).

The most tragic example of a Lovecraft blind spot comes in January 1929, when Long says he is depressed and has "a dread of the future—I am destitute financially, without a prospect of making money in the months and years to come." While Long had studied journalism at New York University and Columbia, he did not obtain a degree. Instead of advising Long either to return to journalism or to train for some other remunerative position, Lovecraft blithely rejoins with the following:

As for the problem of the moneyless aesthete in general—it is admittedly painful, yet I fear you give it a certain sentimental exaggeration. In particular, you couple it in some vague way with blame of somebody or something or other, when as a matter of fact it is merely an impersonal & unavoidable incident common to all social organisms & remediable in no way whatsoever. (17 October 1930).

Readers are referred to Peter Cannon's *Long Memories and Other Writings* (2022) to see just how poorly Long's situation played out.

It is difficult to articulate the totality of Lovecraft letters lacking some chronological distance from it. One thinks of the description of the Old Ones in "The Whisperer in Darkness" (1930): "prodigious surgical, biological, chemical, and mechanical skill." Or perhaps we may consider it a nonfictional *Comédie Humaine*—an observed world reflected in an alert and perspicacious mind, one in which a unique perspective engages with the seismic changes of the early twentieth century.[6] Call it Lovecraft's *Comédie Ludique*—a saga of all play and little work, the record of a peculiar if incredibly rich imaginative life. The twenty-one volumes of letters sit on the shelf; they await future generations of Lovecraft scholars to fully explicate and exploit.

---

6. But Balzac's magnum opus—around 91 finished works generally estimated at 3–4 million words—is smaller than this corpus.

JOHN L. STEADMAN. *Horror as Racism in H. P. Lovecraft: White Fragility in the Weird Tales*. New York, Bloomsbury Academic, 2024. 249 pp. $90.00 hc; $26.95 tpb. Reviewed by Dylan Henderson.

Though a relatively short book of 249 pages, *Horror as Racism in H. P. Lovecraft* consists of three parts subdivided into nineteen pithy chapters, not counting the introduction. There we find Steadman's thesis, which builds upon the theory of white fragility promoted by Robin DiAngelo. In short, he claims that the loss of 454 Angell Street shattered Lovecraft's white privilege, the trauma of this event intensifying his racist sentiments and reinforcing "a general pattern of loss and failure" that would handicap Lovecraft for the rest of his life. No matter how much readers might want to overlook or minimize the racist anger that this seminal event generated, Steadman argues that it cannot be separated from Lovecraft's fiction. Indeed, according to Steadman, Lovecraft deliberately infuses his fiction with racist conceptions in an attempt to "enhance the horror and repugnance" of his "hybrid, degenerative monsters" and to normalize slavery.

The first of the book's three parts, entitled simply "Beginnings," provides the context needed to understand Steadman's thesis. Its four chapters examine Lovecraft's life, the influences that shaped his racist beliefs (specifically, Houston Stewart Chamberlain's *The Foundations of the Nineteenth Century* and Oswald Spengler's *The Decline of the West*), and the presence of those beliefs in Lovecraft's poems, essays, and letters.

Part two analyzes five of Lovecraft's early short stories, specifically, "Herbert West—Reanimator," "The Lurking Fear," "The Rats in the Walls," "The Horror at Red Hook," and "Arthur Jermyn" (which is the title that Steadman prefers for that story). In these chapters Steadman discusses a recurring theme in Lovecraft's early fiction, the presence of the previously mentioned "hybrid, degenerative monsters." He believes that these monsters, no matter what outward form they may take, symbolize the products of racial miscegenation. Thus, the hybrid corpses that Herbert West assembles and reanimates (and which Lovecraft describes in that story as "human, semi-human, fractionally human, and not human at all—the horde [being] grotesquely heterogeneous") are symbolic of racial hybridity, even if they are composed entirely of Caucasian fragments. "Lovecraft uses these monsters," Steadman insists, "as he does all of the hybrids in the early tales to suggest half-black, half-white hybrids." As a result, the horror in these tales springs from the racist images and themes that Lovecraft embeds in them.

Part three turns to Lovecraft's later works, specifically, *The Case of Charles Dexter Ward*, "The Whisperer in Darkness," "The Shadow over Innsmouth," *At the Mountains of Madness*, and "The Shadow out of Time." With the exception of "The Shadow over Innsmouth," which returns to Lovecraft's earlier preoccupations with degeneration and hybridity, these stories all offer a subtle defense of slavery by suggesting that even superior intellects, such as the Great Old Ones, make use of the institution, Lovecraft's "argument being that if slavery is good enough for the highest, most advanced civilization in the cosmos, then it is certainly good enough for us on earth."

Because these chapters focus solely on primary sources, Steadman adds an additional chapter to parts two and three. These additional chapters discuss the scholarly debates surrounding the stories in their respective sections. The first of these responds to David Simmons and Jed Mayer, while the second critiques arguments by Graham Harman, W. Scott Poole, and Patricia MacCormack. Steadman also includes a separate essay, which appears in the appendix. In it he touches briefly on points of similarity between Lovecraft's work and Afrofuturism and criticizes Matt Ruff's *Lovecraft Country*, pointing out that, despite being "fast paced, well-crafted in terms of plot, and filled with personable, interesting characters," it "*is not Lovecraftian—not even a little bit.*"

Some Lovecraft scholars, I imagine, feel that this issue has been debated enough. Nothing more can be learned by reexamining the racist sentiments that appear in the life and works of H. P. Lovecraft. Others, however, may feel that a need exists for a comprehensive examination of the subject, one that follows this thread through every year, story, poem, and essay.

You may agree with the former view or the latter, but either way, I do not think you will find Steadman's monograph satisfactory.

The heart of this book consists of ten chapters, each of which analyzes a single story, but with few exceptions these chapters have little to offer the scholar, for Steadman bends each story until it fits the mold he wishes to apply. Some stories, of course, do fit—"The Horror at Red Hook" comes to mind—but others have to be stretched out of all proportion. Steadman argues, for instance, that miscegenation in Lovecraft's work takes two forms: by blood and by association. He then argues that the second of these appears in "Herbert West—Reanimator" and accounts for West's moral decline: "Indeed, it is not difficult to pick up on Lovecraft's equating of the West menagerie with the non-Anglo-Saxon races and Lovecraft's equally obvious implication that a close connection to Blacks or "mongrel" races can likewise turn an Anglo-Saxon into a monster."

It is worth pausing here to re-engineer Steadman's thinking: Lovecraft subtly but deliberately suggests that West's hybrid corpses represent non-white races and implies that, as a result of his association with these monsters, West declines morally and spiritually, his fall being a cautionary tale against racial miscegenation. Every link in this chain of reasoning strikes me as weak. Lovecraft descriptions of Buck Robinson, "The Harlem Smoke," are undoubtedly racist, but where does Lovecraft equate "the West menagerie with the non-Anglo-Saxon races"? In any case, West does not *associate* with his reanimated monsters. Some escape his control; others he destroys. He does not, however, fraternize with any of them.

Similar examples abound. Steadman reads "the degeneration of the Martense family" as "the usual, racist scenario," noting that its members marry into the local "'mongrel population.'" He insists that, in "The Rats in the Walls," Lovecraft again "deploys his miscegenation narrative, cautioning his readers about the threat that intermingling between different races or cultures can pose for white Anglo-Saxons," though Steadman admits that "there is no 'alien' or 'foreign' blood interjected into the de la Poer clan in the past." He even argues that Joseph Curwen, much like Herbert West, is "slowly degenerating" as a result of "miscegenation by association." For not only does Curwen purchase black slaves, but he also conjures up monsters that "are very much like the Blacks" whom Lovecraft derides in his early poetry. And so on. Henry Wentworth Akeley, the reclusive farmer, becomes "Lovecraft's privileged white Anglo-Saxon protagonist," and "The Whisperer in Darkness" becomes a story about slavery. Indeed, according to Steadman, "Lovecraft's slave master/slave narrative dominates 'The Whisperer in Darkness.'"

To make matters worse, Steadman's interpretations often flatten their respective stories, draining them of emotional and imaginative interest. "The Whisperer in Darkness," for instance, as I have argued in the past, derives part of its success from the ambivalence it engenders: though we know not to trust the fungi from Yuggoth, we cannot help but find their offer of a voyage beyond the stars tempting. In that light, Albert Wilmarth's flight from Akeley's farmhouse is both understandable and slightly disappointing—perhaps even small-minded. In Steadman's hands, however, every single tale collapses into either a simple warning about miscegenation or a bigoted attempt to bolster white supremacy. Lovecraft, it seems, had no other interests.

The problems do not end there. The chapters that will appeal to Lovecraft scholars the most, the ten devoted to individual stories, contain too much summary and too little analysis. Structurally, each chapter is divided into three parts: context, summary, and analysis, but bits of summary, and sometimes large chunks of it, keep resurfacing in the section devoted to analysis. Those interested in critical race theory and postcolonialism will find Steadman's lack of engagement with that literature no less frustrating, for he relies almost exclusively on DiAngelo and mentions only one or two other theorists.

Finally, admirers of Lovecraft will take issue with Steadman's portrayal of the author. Everyone, of course, has a right to an opinion, but Steadman's depiction of Lovecraft as a selfish, covetous, rage-filled bigot is contradicted by his good-natured correspondence and the many affectionate memoirs penned by his friends and acquaintances. To be clear, Steadman may dislike

Lovecraft as a person, or he may find Lovecraft's racist remarks so reprehensible that they overshadow his good qualities—both reactions are valid—but as a scholar Steadman has a professional obligation to present his subject accurately, and in this case he has stripped Lovecraft's character of all nuance and transformed him into a caricature, a one-dimensional villain without any good qualities whatsoever. He then proceeds to condemn virtually every aspect of Lovecraft's life and personality:

> Though all of these productions [Lovecraft's juvenile articles on science] were only minor, barely competent efforts and they plagiarized information from other technical and scientific publications of the day, nevertheless, they helped Lovecraft hone his developing writing skills [. . .]
>
> Similarly, he was so attached to Providence that he had no compunction about abandoning his wife in New York City and returning alone to his hometown, even given the fact that she was trying in a weakened, physical state to support them both—he even declares pompously: "I am Providence" when he got back home.
>
> Most fourteen-year-old boys would consider a part-time job, perhaps, especially if they had a parent who was struggling financially, as Susie Lovecraft was. But not Lovecraft. He remained withdrawn and immobile.
>
> But Sonia was of stronger stuff than Susie and got rid of Lovecraft when she reached the end of her resources.
>
> It seems incredible that Lovecraft was not able to make the connection between the nervous symptoms that his wife was experiencing in 1924 and the symptoms that his mother had experienced when she had been admitted to the Butler Hospital in 1919. Or even more incredible was that he didn't perceive that he himself was the common factor behind both sets of symptoms.

We might be tempted to dispute each of these passages—the claim that Sonia "got rid of Lovecraft" being especially misleading—but what I want to show here is a surprising lack of generosity. Steadman invariably views Lovecraft's beliefs and actions in the worst possible light and at one point even refers to him as "the man that we have come to know and dislike in this book." Such passages make me think of Lovecraft's response to Robert Bloch's first letter and the constant support he showed so many other young writers, but needless to say, Steadman almost never mentions anything positive or praiseworthy about Lovecraft.

I suspect that Steadman, having written a book-length analysis of Lovecraft's racist beliefs, found himself in an awkward position: in this context, any praise for Lovecraft might be misinterpreted as support for his racism. He might also have felt that praise would weaken his thesis, which argues that "Lovecraft's loss of privilege led to an increase and intensification of his racist beliefs [...] a common outcome when a white, Anglo-Saxon male's white fragility is challenged." If Lovecraft psychologically recovered from the "loss of privilege" that accompanied his grandfather's death and overcame the various other setbacks that he encountered in his life, becoming in the end a well-adjusted individual with many friends and interests, then Steadman's thesis starts to crumble. If Lovecraft, in other words, was *not* a miserable and bitter person who forever brooded over his lost privilege, then how can misery and bitterness be the source of his racist attitudes towards other groups, specifically, Africans and Aborigines? Steadman resolves this complication by ignoring it, and this results not just in a misleading analysis of Lovecraft, but also in a basic and rudimentary analysis of American racism.

Readers should know that the book, in addition to the major problems I have identified, has no shortage of minor ones. These often take the form of inaccurate or deceptive claims. Steadman insists, for instance, that "in 1917, Lovecraft decided to concentrate his writing efforts on commercial fiction." Elsewhere he states that, in *Winesburg, Ohio*, Sherwood Anderson "was making the claim (implicit though it was) that his grotesques may have come about due to Negro blood in their ancestry." I certainly do not remember that! Nor do I recall the following explanation appearing in "The Whisperer in Darkness": "The reason why the Mi-Go chose the earth to colonize in the first place was that it is ideally suited for their mining operations; the planet has minerals that can be used to grow the fungi that the

Mi-Go use as a food source. They eat the fungus by passing a metal capture containing it through their bodies." Steadman also misreads "The Lurking Fear." He claims that, when "the narrator finds himself facing down a swarming horde of the monsters," he "saves himself improbably by firing only a single shot, putting the rest of the cannibals to rout." That is not at all what happens: after the cannibals have emerged from their hole by the chimney, the narrator, "under cover of the thunder," shoots "the last of the monstrosities" so that he may inspect it. The others do not hear the shot and are not routed by it.

I would also argue that Steadman's comparison of "Herbert West—Reanimator" to *Frankenstein* closely resembles a passage in S. T. Joshi's *I Am Providence* and, as such, borders on plagiarism. Here is Steadman's analysis:

> Lovecraft scholars have seen parallels between the West series and Mary Shelley's *Frankenstein* (1818), a novel that Lovecraft knew and admired. It might do well to examine this particular issue up front before getting down to our analysis of the tale since, superficially at least, the two works appear to be similar [...] When we read the Shelley novel and "Herbert West—Reanimator" together, however, it quickly becomes clear that they are very different from each other in two significant ways. First, Victor Frankenstein creates a single entity from a collection of disparate body parts taken from charnel houses, dissecting rooms, and cemeteries and then infuses it with life. In contrast, West reanimates a succession of freshly buried dead bodies; he does not really create anything.

And here is Joshi's comparison of the two works:

> It has been taken for granted that the obvious influence upon the story is *Frankenstein*; but I wonder whether this is the case. The method of West's reanimation of the dead (whole bodies that have died only recently) is very different from that of Victor Frankenstein (the assembling of a huge composite body from disparate parts of bodies), and only the most general influence can perhaps be detected.

Obviously, the two passages differ significantly at the sentence level, but Steadman is, without any reference to Joshi, repeating a point that appears in a very prominent place: the most comprehensive and authoritative biography of H. P. Lovecraft. Curiously, Steadman never cites anything from *I Am Providence*, preferring to use *H. P. Lovecraft: A Life* instead.

Lovecraft scholars might or might not find Steadman's appraisals of specific stories of interest, for he rarely agrees with the consensus. Indeed, the stories that he favors are often those that other critics have scorned, and I suspect that, as a result, some critics will dismiss him as a contrarian. A few examples should suffice:

> There is little that could be considered formulaic about any of the installments [of "Herbert West—Reanimator"] and the series as a whole is well-conceived and well-written. In addition, the overall plot is strong [. . .]

> [. . .] Given the natural limitations of the serial format, "The Lurking Fear" is, on the whole, very effectively written and suspenseful and it builds to an impressive conclusion.

> "The Rats in the Walls" is among the best of Lovecraft's early tales—some critics argue, in fact, that it is *the* very best. I am not so sure that this claim is justifiable [. . .] The next tale that we will be considering, "The Horror at Red Hook," is a much greater literary work—much richer, fuller, and more coherently developed, both in terms of plot and characterization.

> Lovecraft, in the final section of the story, takes us swiftly to the conclusion. Lovecraft was very skilled in the writing of strong, action-oriented prose and he makes good use of this skill in his description of Dr. Willett's experiences in the catacombs.

For me, the flaws in Steadman's book raise important questions about the purpose of literary criticism. In his conclusion Steadman insists that Lovecraft is, despite his personal shortcomings, still worth reading. Steadman has, in his own words, attempted to "reexamine his works and discover anew how powerful Lovecraft's texts really are, thematically as well as stylistically." And yet, few readers, having finished Steadman's book, will agree. In his hands Lovecraft's fiction degenerates into a formulaic series of thinly disguised racist fantasies, which reflect the ugly bigotry of its detestable author. I doubt that any reader, having learned of Lovecraft through Steadman, would want to read any of his works.

As a graduate student I have often encountered the underlying mentality that, I believe, motivates Steadman. Academics increasingly view literature not as an art, but as a text, an object to be studied, much like a fragment of pottery found in a field. Literary critics do not have to enjoy or appreciate what they study, nor are they required to present it as enjoyable to their audience. If anything, appreciation poses a potential problem: it can cloud the lens, so to speak, and prevent a critic from viewing a work of literature objectively.

I see little value in such an approach to literary criticism. Literature exists to provide readers with pleasure—whether intellectual, emotional, aesthetic, or imaginative—and the experience of reading a specific work cannot be fully understood if it is approached from a neutral standpoint. Literary works are not, in other words, records that authors leave behind for historians to study. They are an attempt to entertain readers, to connect with them. There is something morally reprehensible about treating literature as if it were data generated by some sort of transmitter when it is, in truth, the innermost thoughts of individuals who are, for whatever reason, eager to share and communicate.

To me, the goal of the critic is not just to study literature, but to promote its appreciation. Literary critics are not detached bystanders watching from the sidelines as society rejects literature and reading in general; instead, we are committed partisans, struggling for the sake of an important cause. Our only weapon, literary analysis exists to reveal something insightful that has been overlooked in a work of literature and, by doing so, to amplify the enjoyment that the work being analyzed produces. In this case, literary criticism should strive to make Lovecraft's fiction more pleasurable—intellectually, emotionally, aesthetically, or imaginatively—not less. American audiences in the twenty-first century do not need another reason to not read.

Contributors

Isaac Aday received his Ph.D. in Literature from the University of Texas at Dallas in 2024. His scholarship on H. P. Lovecraft, seen also in the 2022 issue of the *Lovecraft Annual*, focuses on the formal, structural, and stylistic aspects of Lovecraft's prose. He currently works as a freelance writer and adjunct professor of composition at several colleges in the Dallas Fort–Worth area.

Holly Eva Allen is a graduate scholar and instructor in English with the University of Rhode Island. Holly's academic writing has been previously published in various peer-reviewed journals, including the *Journal of Popular Culture*, *Women's Studies*, and the *Journal of American Culture*. Her creative writing has appeared in a variety of magazines and collections, including *Foothill Journal*, *Obelus Journal*, and *Levee Magazine*.

Harley Carnell lives and writes in London. His fiction has appeared, or is forthcoming, in *Penumbra*, *Vastarien*, *Riptide Journal*, and *Confrontation*, among others. His critical work has appeared in *Gamut* and is forthcoming in *Aurealis* and *Roads Less Travelled*. He has an M.A. in Creative Writing from Royal Holloway, University of London.

At age seventy-six, **Ken Faig, Jr.** has been writing about Lovecraft for over fifty years. He recently concluded his Moshassuck Monograph series with an essay on Lovecraft's boyhood cat and has also been poking around about the Lovecrafts of Mount Vernon, New York. He and his wife Carol share a retirement apartment in Glenview, Illinois. They have two children, Walter, a statistician, and Edie Fake, the artist. A first grandchild arrived this summer.

James Goho is a researcher and writer with many publications on dark fiction. In 2014, Rowman & Littlefield published his

Journeys into Darkness: Critical Essays on Gothic Horror. McFarland published his *Caitlín R. Kiernan: A Critical Study of Her Dark Fiction* in 2020. His higher education research is found in academic journals, and his infrequent short stories appear in literary magazines. He lives in Winnipeg, Canada.

Edward Guimont earned his Ph.D. in history from the University of Connecticut and is currently chair of the history department at Bristol Community College in Fall River, Massachusetts. With Horace Smith, he is the co-author of *When the Stars Are Right: H. P. Lovecraft and Astronomy* (Hippocampus Press, 2023), and his next book is the upcoming *The Power of the Flat Earth Idea* (Palgrave Macmillan).

David Haden is a long-standing news-blogger and researcher on Lovecraft's life at *Tentaclii*. His recent books have examined the influence of North Staffordshire on *The Time Machine* by H. G. Wells, and on the poet of *Sir Gawain and The Green Knight*. He is also now becoming a Tolkien scholar, with the new 200,000-word book, *Tree & Star: Tolkien and the Quest for Earendel*, and his editorship of the *Tolkien Gleanings* online newsletter.

Dylan Lee Henderson is a doctoral candidate at Purdue University, where he is studying English literature. In addition to his degrees in English, he also has a bachelor's in history and a master's in library science and, for many years, worked in public libraries. His literary interests include H. P. Lovecraft, *Weird Tales* magazine, and weird fiction in general. He also dabbles in filmmaking and creative writing.

S. T. Joshi is the author of *I Am Providence: The Life and Times of H. P. Lovecraft* (2010) and the editor of Lovecraft's stories, essays, poems, and letters. His collected essays on Lovecraft were published as *Lovecraft and a World in Transition* (2014).

Steven J. Mariconda is the author of many essays on H. P. Lovecraft, some of which were collected in *H. P. Lovecraft: Art, Artifact, and Reality* (Hippocampus Press, 2013). He was co-editor (with S. T. Joshi) of *Dreams of Fear: Poetry of Terror and* *the Supernatural* (Hippocampus Press, 2013). His primary scholarly interests are in close reading and reader-response approaches to literature. Aside from Lovecraft, he has also contributed articles on T. E. D. Klein, Arthur Machen, Ramsey Campbell, Thomas Ligotti, M. R. James, and others. He was the Scholar Guest of Honor at NecronomiCon Providence 2017.

Duncan Norris lives in Brisbane, Australia, and spends his free time writing ridiculously long and abstruse books on Lovecraft and related topics than even S. T. Joshi says are too niche. Rumors that he is a scion of Atlantis are very strongly unfounded. He, naturally, owns a black cat.

Horace A. Smith is professor emeritus of Physics and Astronomy at Michigan State University. He and Edward Guimont recently authored the book *When the Stars Are Right: H. P. Lovecraft and Astronomy* (Hippocampus Press, 2023), and he has appeared twice before in the *Lovecraft Annual*.